The Michigan Historical Reprint Series

Reprints from the collection of the University of Michigan University Library

This volume is produced from digital images created through the University of Michigan University Library's preservation reformatting program. The Library seeks to preserve the intellectual content of items in a manner that facilitates and promotes a variety of uses. The digital reformatting process results in an electronic version of the text that can both be accessed online and used to create new print copies. This book and thousands of others can be found in the digital collections of the University of Michigan Library. The University Library also understands and values the utility of print, and makes reprints available through its Scholarly Publishing Office.

For access to the University of Michigan Library's digital collections, please see http://www.lib.umich.edu.

The Scholarly Publishing Office seeks to disseminate high-quality, cost-effective scholarly content through both print and electronic publishing. Information about the Scholarly Publishing Office can be found at http://spo.umdl.umich.edu.

The Scholarly Publishing Office
the University of Michigan
University Library

A FOREST TRAGEDY

AND OTHER TALES.

BY

GRACE GREENWOOD,

AUTHOR OF "HAPS AND MISHAPS OF A TOUR IN EUROPE," "GREENWOOD LEAVES," ETC. ETC.

BOSTON:
TICKNOR AND FIELDS,
M DCCC LVI.

STEREOTYPED BY
HOBART & ROBBINS,
New England Type and Stereotype Foundery,
BOSTON.

To

A DEAR FRIEND OVER THE SEA —

TO MARY HOWITT,

AS A PROOF THAT 'MANY WATERS CANNOT QUENCH LOVE,' — AS A TRIBUTE OF

ADMIRATION, ESTEEM, AND FAITHFUL REMEMBRANCE,

I Dedicate this Volume.

GRACE GREENWOOD.

CONTENTS.

A FOREST TRAGEDY.

A FOREST TRAGEDY;

OR,

THE ONEIDA SISTERS.

FOUNDED ON FACT.

CHAPTER I.

FORT STANWIX.

Majestical and calm through all they stride,
Wearing the blanket with a monarch's pride;
The gazers stare and shrug, but can't deny
Their noble forms and blameless symmetry.
If the Great Spirit their morale has slighted,
And wigwam smoke their mental culture blighted,
Yet the physique, at least, perfection reaches,
In wilds where neither Combe nor Spurzheim teaches —
Where whispering trees invite man to the chase,
And bounding deer allure him to the race.

MARGARET FULLER.

The garden rose may richly bloom
In cultured soil and genial air,
To cloud the light of Fashion's room,
Or droop in Beauty's midnight hair;
In lonelier grace, to sun and dew
The sweet-brier on the hill-side shows
Its single leaf and fainter hue,
Untrained and wildly free, yet still a sister rose!

WHITTIER.

AT the commencement of the American Revolution, no object was considered of greater importance by Congress than the obtaining pledges of neutrality from the powerful confederacy of the Six Nations. For this purpose a council was called at Albany in the year 1775. This was attended by a large number of the Oneidas, but by few of the Onondagas, Senecas, Cayugas, or Mohawks.

The Congressional Commissioners urged the justice of their cause in the conflict with the mother country, but demanded of their red brethren only simple neutrality.

Most of the chiefs and warriors gave their word to remain as mere lookers-on during the struggle ; but, with the exception of the Oneidas, all, sooner or later, proved false to their pledges.

In the summer of 1777 the British Commissioners called a grand council of the Six Nations at Oswego.

Here was a very large representation from all the tribes. The Iroquois were naturally royalists and aristocrats, and had an exaggerated estimate of the power and wealth of the king. On this occasion the commissioners spoke in a large style of boastful eloquence, peculiarly captivating to a savage audience, assuring them that the Colonies were poor and weak, and would easily and speedily be conquered; that King George was rich and powerful beyond all the monarchs of the earth, both in money and subjects; that his rum was as abundant as the waters of the great lakes, his warriors as numerous as the sands upon their shores. They also tempted them with a display of clothing, trinkets, and arms, bright stuffs, gay plumes, shining weapons in hand, and rivers of rum in prospective. It was too much for savage nature to withstand. All, with the one honorable exception of the Oneidas, pledged themselves to fight under the banners of the king, and do barbarous battle against the rebels.

At that time the young Mohawk warrior, Thayendenagea, or Joseph Brant, was appointed chief of the Six Nations.

It was in the summer of this year that the defences of Fort Stanwix were considerably strengthened in anticipation of an attack of the British and their new allies. This important frontier post, afterwards known as Fort Schuyler, was then commanded by Colonel Gansevoort, an able and experienced officer, assisted by Colonel Marius Willett, a gallant, daring, dashing soldier, whose bold exploits and 'hair-breadth 'scapes' had early and widely distinguished him in those peerless times of peril and adventure, and finally caused him to be regarded with a superstitious reverence by his savage foes, as one protected from bullet, tomahawk, and arrow, by some most potent charm.

One evening in July there arrived at Fort Stanwix a young French officer, attended by a small guard, and bearing despatches from the American commander-in-chief. He also brought a letter from the Marquis de Lafayette, commending him warmly to Colonel Gansevoort as a brave young soldier, who was ambitious of seeing some service on the frontier.

Lieutenant Maurice de Vaudreuil was one of that noble corps of young heroes who accompanied the chivalric and generous Lafayette to America, with almost unexampled enthusiasm and self-sacrifice forsaking the splendors and pleasures of rank and fortune, at a gay capital or magnificent court, for all the perils and privations of a doubtful and unequal warfare in a yet half-barbarous country.

Lieutenant de Vaudreuil, or 'Lieutenant Maurice,' as he was most often familiarly called, was under the especial guardianship of the noble marquis, into whose charge he had been reluctantly and solemnly committed by the Count de Vaudreuil, his father.

Though a younger son, the cadet Maurice was generally regarded as the prospective heir to the title and estates of the count his father, as the elder son had been an invalid, and nearly imbecile, from his childhood. A cold, stern, proud man, the old count looked forward without sorrow, and almost with impatience, to the time when death would remove the encumbrance and reproach of his house, and make place for an heir worthy of its ancient and honorable name.

Lieutenant Maurice was by no means unworthy of the friendship and brotherly care of General Lafayette. As a soldier he had already shown himself brave and able, though a little too impetuous and daring; as a man he was generous, chivalric, and loyal to the heart's core. At the time when he presented himself to Colonel Gansevoort he was a youth of barely nineteen, tall and slender, with but a faint prophecy of a beard shading his chin, and darkening into a slight moustache upon his upper lip. Yet the well-knit, athletic figure was far from effeminate, for all its litheness; and the face, though softly colored and delicately formed, was singularly expressive of the force and dignity of true manhood. The mouth was usually resolutely set, yet a peculiar curve of the lips and play of the thin nostrils bespoke, perhaps, more wilfulness than will, and more passion and bold self-confidence than real strength, decision, and enduring firmness of character. The eyes were dark, deep-set, and poetic — now smiling with pleasant fancies and genial feelings, now melting in woman-like softness, and now sending up from their clear depths flashes of pride and anger, revealing a spirit it would scarce be safe to trifle with.

The young stranger and his little band were heartily welcomed by the garrison, which then only consisted of five hundred and fifty men, ill supplied with arms, ammunition, and provisions; and this, with the immediate prospect of being besieged by a large body of British and Hessian troops, with their attendant hordes of infuriated savages.

A few days after the arrival of De Vaudreuil, there came to the fort a select deputation from the capital of the Oneidas, consisting of a somewhat celebrated old sachem, named Sadewana, with his two daughters, a young chief who bore the singular and Italian-sounding name of Garanguli,[1] and a small company of braves.

They came, they said, to assure Colonel Gansevoort and his friends of their sympathy in this time of peril; and, though they were not yet willing to take up the tomahawk and go on the war-path against their brothers of the Great Iroquois Confederacy, they would gladly renew their pledges of neutrality, and, for the purpose of rendering them more binding, had determined to offer themselves as hostages for their tribe.

After kindly and courteously thanking his faithful

Oneida brothers, the commandant assured them that he did not wish for their services in warfare, nor demand from them hostages, being quite willing to take their word alone for the honorable fulfilment of all their pledges. But the venerable sachem would not hear to this magnanimous rejection of his offer, little suspecting that the act was dictated as much by prudence as confidence, the limited store of provisions in the garrison forbidding any unnecessary addition to its inmates. He persisted that some guarantee should be given against their playing the false and recreant part of the Mohawks and Onondagas; he offered himself and his young friend Garanguli alone, — then his two daughters, Gahaneh and Onata. The commandant shook his head at each proposition, smiling slightly at the last, and proceeded to present a few gifts to his dusky friends, as a sign that the conference was at an end. But Sadewana, drawing himself up proudly, and folding his arms, said, 'If you no take hostage, me no take your tobacco and rum. I have spoken.'

Apparently the most interested listeners to this colloquy were the two daughters of the sachem. They were half-breeds, the children of a French Canadian captive, adopted by the Oneidas in her early girlhood.

Gahaneh, the eldest, was a woman of ripe, sumptuous beauty, tall, stately, and powerfully formed, like her father, and a thorough Indian in heart and habits. This savage princess regarded the mixed hue of her skin as a reproach to her, because of a peculiar hatred and contempt for the people of her mother, and pride in the free, warlike race of her father. That unfortunate mother had never been happy in her rude forest home, and had finally forsaken it and her family, and escaped to one of the Canadian settlements, with a treacherous French trader, leaving a helpless infant daughter to the care of Gahaneh, herself scarcely more than a child. And she was faithful to the charge thus cruelly laid upon her. With a courage and fidelity seldom equalled and never surpassed in civilized life, she cared and toiled for the poor abandoned little one, till from a pining, sickly babe, it grew and strengthened into health, vigor, and bloom. Not even when her charge — or 'child,' as she called her — had come up to beautiful womanhood, did she relax her motherly care. All the tenderness of her stern, proud nature was lavished on her sister — her sister, that feared rather than loved her in return. She turned coldly from the addresses of her savage admirers; she could not be tempted to forsake Onata and her father, to follow any brave, chief, or sachem, to his lodge.

But, with all her faithful affection and jealous care, she was disappointed in her sister, who, from her childhood, showed a strong partiality for her mother's race. Onata had few savage characteristics; she was gentle, affectionate, timid, and thoughtful, with a native love of luxury and ease. She gladly welcomed all white visitors to the Indian village at Oneida Castle, and courteously entertained them at the lodge of her father — himself a strong and constant friend of the white man. She sought, and, after some little hesitation on his part, and much opposition from her sister, obtained his permission to receive instruction in the English language and religion from a pious missionary, who, a year or two previous to the time when she is presented to my reader, took up his abode among the Oneidas. She also eagerly embraced every opportunity of visiting the forts and settlements of the whites, among whom her beauty, modesty, and intelligence, rendered her a great favorite. From an earnest, wistful way she had of searching the face of nearly every white woman she met, it was supposed that she cherished a vague hope of yet finding her lost mother.

Alas! that mother had long been dead, having sunk into the grave under the brutal treatment of her dissipated French lover, vainly longing in her last days to return to her simple savage home, — to the old chief, who had always treated her with kindness, and even with a most unsavage consideration and homage, and to those poor forsaken children — her proud, star-eyed eldest-born, who came to her in *summer*, and for that reason, and it may be with a mother's prophetic sense of the rich, deep bloom of her beauty, was called *Gahaneh;* and the fragile, sensitive babe, whom she had named *Onata*, because she was like a spring *leaf*, trembling in every wind.

It was evidently with very different feelings that the two Indian girls watched the negotiations now going on in the fort. Gahaneh looked alarmed and displeased; she listened to her father's last proposition with a frown, and seemed greatly relieved when Colonel Gansevoort so positively rejected it. Onata, on the contrary, at first regarded both speakers with eager, wistful interest; her rich crimson lips parted, her thin nostrils quivering, and her large, soft, hazel eyes dilated and sparkling, and, on hearing the decision of the commandant, seemed ready to weep with chagrin and disappointment. It was by no means an idle curiosity and love of change, nor an obsequious fawning on her superiors, which rendered her so intensely anxious to remain at the fort. Onata was among her friends. She had visited Fort Stanwix, and spent several weeks there, during the preceding season, as the guest of the young wife of one of the officers, who, while on a visit with her husband to the Oneida village to witness the great New Year Jubilee,[2] had taken a violent fancy to the graceful little daughter of Sadewana. This fair friend now stood by Onata's side, affectionately encircling her waist with a plump white arm, while her little boy, a pretty, flaxen-haired child, was clinging to one of the small brown hands of the Indian girl, looking roguishly up into her face, vainly striving to catch her eye.

As Colonel Gansevoort, somewhat struck aback by the injured tone and haughty air of the sachem, looked about him in perplexity, his glance fell upon this group, which happily suggested to him a compromise.

"Well, brother warrior," he said, "as you insist upon our receiving a hostage, suppose you leave us your daughter Onata. We all like her, and will take good care of her, and when the siege is over we will return her to you in safety. She knows us, and I think will be contented to stay with us until that time."

A speech of this length required interpretation; which being accomplished, the old sachem smiled a grim smile, and grunted out an acquiescent 'Good.' So it was settled.

The young chief Garanguli did indeed venture to remonstrate somewhat earnestly with his venerable friend, but by this time Sadewana was in the act of solemnly ratifying his little treaty by a glass of good Jamaica rum, and would hear of no reconsideration. The youth then hurried up to Onata, who stood smiling in a circle of old friends, and addressed a yet more eloquent, and, it seemed, a slightly indignant remonstrance to her. But she first laughed, then pouted, shrugged her shoulders, and began carelessly playing with a dainty little fan of wild turkey feathers. A court beauty at Madrid or Versailles could not have managed that little engine of coquetry with more art, nor shown herself more charmingly indifferent to a lover's woe, or more wilfully set upon having her own dear way. She effectually roused the spirit of her aboriginal admirer, at length, and he strode angrily away.

Gahaneh then approached, drew her sister aside, and addressed a few brief words to her in a low tone. They were evidently words of serious remonstrance and warning, if not of positive authority. Onata did not reply proudly or petulantly, but seemed to be pleading with her stately sister with all the passionate earnestness of a petted child. Gahaneh grew colder and stiffer every moment, and when at last the speaker pointed affectionately to her white friends, and the pretty child yet clinging to her hand, the proud sister-mother drew herself up haughtily, and turned away with a look of sullen sadness and bitter jealousy darkening yet more deeply her stern, handsome face.

Perhaps the most interested spectator of this scene was Lieutenant de Vaudreuil, to whom the sight of veritable savages was yet a novelty. He was struck by the more than princely presence of the old sachem, his head white with the snows of seventy winters, his brow and cheeks furrowed by barbaric passions and sorrows, yet his tall, powerful form unbent, and the young flash of his keen dark eye unquenched.

But the young chief Garanguli he viewed with an artist's surprised delight in beholding a living human form rivalling the old Greek ideals. In bold grace of attitude and pride of bearing, in the eagle-like clearness and steadiness of the eye, the scorn and fierce disdain which lay coiled, as it were, in the thin compressed lips, in the perfection of height and proportion, in arrowy straightness, in the suppleness and delicacy, yet firmness of the limbs, it was such a form as leaped forth from some ambush, as it were, in the memory of the painter West, when, on the first sight of the Apollo Belvidere, he exclaimed, 'My God, a young Mohawk warrior!'

Yet, notwithstanding the watchful pride and distrust which darkened the face of the young chief, it was by no means wanting in nobleness and gentleness of expression. When he smiled all was brightness, frankness, and cordiality; and his manner toward the whites, when kindly addressed, was courteous, if not conciliatory. With Sadewana, Shenandoah, Tiahogwando, and other prominent Oneida rulers and warriors, he was friendly to the cause of the revolutionists, not because of an especial liking for any of the people who were gradually dislodging his race from all their ancient possessions, but from a noble instinctive sympathy with the weaker party. For himself, he was but ill satisfied that the elders of the tribe had decided upon strict neutrality, and had more than once been tempted to take part in the great struggle. Had the question been merely of battle upon the American side against the British troops, he would have felt little hesitation; but he shrank from fighting against his brothers of the great Indian confederacy, mercenaries and pledge-breakers though they were.

Garanguli was by no means obstinately fixed in his savage habits and prejudices. He also had learned of the good missionary to speak and read English — even to write it a little. His dress was a curious though not an ungraceful mixture of the civilized and barbarous styles. He wore a handsome hunting-shirt of dark green cloth, rather gayly braided and fringed, a belt of rich wampum, and instead of moccasins, a pair of military top-boots drawn on over his embroidered leggings. His head-dress was a large crimson silk handkerchief, twisted into a sort of turban, and ornamented with eagle feathers; his hair was unshaven, and his face unpainted. He carried a knife, a rifle, and sometimes a long bow and arrows, or a slender lance, but never the tomahawk. He was still very young, yet had been more than once on the war-path. His fellow-warriors reported that he had fought bravely; but he brought home no indisputable proofs of his prowess, for, like many of his tribe, he scorned to take scalps.

Much of the interest he felt in the rebels may have

been owing to the influence of the gentle Onata, whose manners and dress were greatly softened and modified by ideas and tastes acquired in familiar intercourse with her friends at the forts and settlements.

She did not wear her hair floating and flying 'at its own sweet will,' or hanging down her back in long, ungraceful braids, according to the usual aboriginal modes, but neatly wound around her shapely head in massive glossy plaits, sometimes woven with flowers, and sometimes, as now, twined with strings of bright red berries, resembling coral. She wore ear-rings of chased gold, a memento of her lost mother, with bracelets and a necklace of amber-colored beads. Her slight, symmetrical figure was well set off by a jaunty little jacket of some kind of scarlet stuff, and a sash of gay wampum ; a short skirt of striped linen, red leggings, and embroidered moccasins, snugly fitting a pair of the daintiest of little feet, completed the costume. These last, the moccasins, were curiously trimmed with small shells and bits of shining metal, which gave out a low, bell-like tinkle when she walked. A dress barbaric and gaudy enough, surely, but far from unpleasing in effect to the most cultivated eye, and singularly suited to that round, elastic figure, with all its wild grace and unconscious freedom of action and attitude ; to that glowing complexion, with its quick crimson flushes and rich olive shades ; to that child-like, untutored being, careless and sorrowless as yet, with her sixteen summers' untaxed affluence of life and bloom, energy and passion ; with eyes that instinctively sought out beautiful forms, and revelled in gorgeous colors; and a heart that yearned for gentle pleasures and tender companionship — for a life brighter and larger than her rude forest home had ever yet afforded her.

Lieutenant Maurice studied the face of this strange and lovely creature with deep and absorbing interest. He saw at once, by the delicate features and coloring, that it was not purely Indian. He seemed to recognize the moulding spirit of a fair, gentle, sorrowful mother, in the soft, quivering lips, and tender, dreamy eyes.

Once, as he was gazing thus, wondering and speculating, he caught the eye of the elder sister fixed upon him. He started, almost as though he had been cherishing dishonorable and impure thoughts, from the fierce suspicion and dagger-like sharpness of her look; but recovered himself in a moment, and steadily returned the gaze.

There was far more of the Indian in Gahaneh's appearance than in that of her sister. She was darker by several shades, her cheek-bones were higher, her lips thinner and firmer, and her heavy raven hair of a coarser texture. Tall and large, she moved with the slow, majestic sweep of a true forest princess, and stood or sat in attitudes of stony dignity or grand repose. Her eyes were intensely black, and a slight habitual frown contracted her low, broad forehead. It was a face, for all its pride and defiance, stamped with deep suffering, — not in the sharp lines and strong shades in which the griefs and disappointments of a single life, however unfortunate, may trace themselves, but in the broad impress of a great, impersonal sorrow. In it one seemed to read the misfortunes and despair of a doomed and dying race.

Like her sister, Gahaneh was distinguished by an indescribable air of refinement and dignity; but, unlike the fanciful Onata, her dress was in strict conformity to the most severe and conservative fashion of the Oneida matrons. Yet in color and arrangement it harmonized well with her style. It consisted of a short gown of dark maroon-color, confined by a deer-skin belt, a skirt of black cloth, leggings and moccasins very slightly ornamented with beads. Her hair, of remarkable length and thickness, was braided in several massive plaits, two of which, falling in front of her shoulders, added to the fixed, sphinx-like character of her face. She was further distinguished from her companion by carrying a bow, and wearing a small quiver of arrows swung at her back.

The young French soldier was roused from his quiet study of the two nymphs of the wild by Colonel Gansevoort, who begged leave to present to him his savage guests. The lieutenant stepped courteously forward; but, to his surprise, the old sachem and Garanguli drew back with a frown at the sound of his name, and from the eyes of Gahaneh shot a sudden gleam of anger and aversion. The first, however, quickly recovered themselves, and amicably proffered their hands; but the latter turned haughtily away. She was faithful as well to the traditional wrongs and hatreds as to the traditional sorrows of her people. De Vaudreuil was an accursed name among them, for by one who bore it had their villages been destroyed, and a large portion of their tribe put to the sword — the De Vaudreuil who, in

1696, under Count de Frontenac, conducted a retaliatory and devastating expedition against the Oneidas.[3]

After a few moments of formal and restrained conversation, the old sachem, pointing to the declining sun, prepared to set out on his return with his party. In taking leave of his young daughter, he spoke to her earnestly and kindly, though with characteristic brevity, — doubtless giving her some excellent paternal advice, — then laid his hand on her head, and turned away. Garanguli was about to go with merely a stiff inclination of the head; but, Onata stepping frankly forward, and proffering her hand, he melted as readily as a fairer-skinned lover could have done, and parted from her in apparent good feeling.

Gahaneh came last. Grasping her sister's arm, and fixing her stern eyes upon her face, then glancing away to where stood the handsome young Frenchman, she whispered, hoarsely,

'Beware of the old enemies of our people, and *remember the League!*'

There was something in this last warning which produced a startling effect upon Onata; her wild eyes kindled with indignation, and she shook off her sister's hand with scorn, as though there had been insult and contamination in the touch. Yet it was only a flash; the next moment she was leaning her head on that sister's shoulder, murmuring gentle reproaches with earnest protestations and tears.

Gahaneh, for her sole caress, laid one hand on her forehead, and bent over her with something of the fierce tenderness of the brooding eagle or the suckling tigress; but her lips were firm, and her eyes dry. No one had ever seen them otherwise; she had never been convicted of the womanly weakness of weeping. She spoke with savage contempt of the pale-faced mother who had bestowed upon her sister, in so large a measure, the beggarly dowry of tears. Perhaps the bitter fountain may have existed, though unsuspected by herself, in her hard, strong nature, but lay so deep that no blow of misfortune or bereavement had ever yet cleft a way to it. With her the sense of wrong or grief found expression in anger, — as the rod of the patriarch may first have struck sparks of fire from the rock in the wilderness.

But Onata was comforted by even the stern show of kindness bestowed upon her, and smiled gayly through her April shower of tears; which Gahaneh seeing, put her not ungently away, and walked steadily out of the fort after her father and his companions, looking neither to the right nor the left.

Onata watched the party from the walls of the fort, until, striking a narrow forest path, they disappeared, as in a night of deep summer verdure, passing one by one from view, in stately 'Indian file.' When they were quite gone, her spirits rose. She played with the children, chatted with her friends, and seemed to feel at home and among her kindred. Lieutenant Maurice noticed that she spoke very intelligible English, and in a voice soft and sweet as the cooing of the wood-pigeon. He was yet more surprised when, a little later in the afternoon, he found her sitting on the breezy rampart, with her little playfellows about her, reading with them out of their story-books — not, it is true, without making frequent mistakes, at which her young listeners, with the magnanimity so characteristic of small critics, laughed uproariously, she very good-humoredly joining in their mirth.

CHAPTER II.

THE LEAGUE.

Ye say that they have passed away,
That noble race and brave;
That their light canoes have vanished
From off the crested wave;
That mid the forests where they roamed
There rings no hunter's shout;
But their name is on your waters —
Ye may not wash it out.
MRS. SIGOURNEY.

Give me your hands all over, one by one,
And let us sware our resolution.
SHAKSPEARE.

This shall make
Our purpose necessary, and not envious;
Which, so appearing to the common eyes,
We shall be called purgers, and not murderers.
IBID.

THE Oneidas were in many respects the noblest of the Six Nations. In warfare they often showed themselves remarkably humane and magnanimous; and in social relations honest, frank, generous, and hospitable. Vice of all kinds prevailed less with them than among their confederates, and they proved themselves possessed of a finer sense of justice, and more strength to resist the cunning flatteries and tempting promises of wealth and power, by the stand which they took in relation to the strife between the colonies and mother-country. There was much of real heroism in this simple neutrality, long and faithfully preserved, as it was, against the threats, allurements, and diplomatic influences, of the royalists. As a nation inactive, yet not uninterested, they showed too plainly their partiality for the American cause for their position to be altogether a safe one. Before the close of the war they had suffered very severely from repeated attacks of the allied British, Tories, and Indians. In the winter of 1779–80 their castle was destroyed and their houses and stores were utterly consumed, and they, or such of them as survived, were driven upon the white settlements for protection and support. Though no considerable body of the Oneidas were ever employed in the American army, single volunteers frequently pressed themselves into its service as warriors, guides, and scouts, and proved oftentimes efficient allies. In the course of the war, one of their most able and distinguished chiefs, *Louis Atayataroughta*, a devoted friend of the republicans, was commissioned a lieutenant-colonel by Congress.

But it is not with the Oneida braves, but with the Oneida women, that we have to do especially in this chapter of our story ; not with the great 'League of the Iroquois,' but with a compact no less important and solemn to those whom it concerned, though having nothing to do with great national interests.

The Oneidas took kindly to the civilizing influences of education, and, in some degree, of religion. A short time previous to the breaking out of the Revolution, there had been established at Oneida Castle, the capital of their territory, a small church and school, conducted by the good missionary before mentioned, the Rev. Mr. Kirkland, a true and devoted minister of God to his wild and wandering children. A few of the old natives found the peace and comfort for which their troubled and benighted souls had long been secretly but vaguely yearning, in the wondrous tidings of love and redemption which he preached to them; and more of the younger, ambitious for knowledge, or by curiosity attracted toward 'some new thing,' attended his school, preferring rather to grapple with the difficulties of the spelling and writing book, than with the divine mysteries of the Gospel.

The old sachem Sadewana was one of the first who attached himself to the church, and was accepted as a believer, though his orthodoxy may have been a matter somewhat doubtful, and was a point on which the prudent minister did not question him too strictly. His daughter Onata was among the most studious and promising pupils in the school, and a very punctual attendant upon the Sunday meetings; but Gahaneh sternly and scornfully refused to have anything to do with either. She was not only obstinately fixed in her Indian customs, but fanatically assured in her heathen faith. Those customs and that faith, she said, had been good enough for their great forefathers, and should they now, in the days of their weakness and poverty, not only basely cringe before and imitate their enemies, but seek to creep after them, like tame dogs, into their psalm-singing heaven? As for her, she would rather wander forever in the solitude and darkness of an Indian hell, within sound of the war-song and the chase in the 'happy hunting grounds' of her people. As far as she had seen, book-learning only made the white man more insatiable in avarice, and more subtle in wicked craft; she would have none of it! She was satisfied with the sermons which the Great Spirit preached to her in winds, and waters, and thunder. She needed no schoolmaster to teach her to read His great book, opened above her in the heavens, pictured with the sun and moon, rainbows and clouds, and lettered with the eternal stars.

So great was her influence with, and, indeed, power over the women of her tribe, that not one among them ventured upon entering the meeting-house or school without long hesitation, and 'a fearful looking for of *contempt* and fiery indignation' from her; but, as I have said before, the love of novelty among them was sometimes too strong even for her to contend successfully against.

The Oneida women were industrious, orderly, and in general remarkably modest and virtuous. So high-toned were their notions of female chastity and constancy, that when a woman was proved unfaithful to the brave or chief who had taken her publicly to his lodge, — thus, after the Indian custom, making her his wife, — her crime was punished by a severe public whipping. Unmarried women, convicted or suspected of unchaste lives, received a punishment scarcely less to be dreaded, in the general scorn and avoidance of the virtuous maids and exemplary matrons of the tribe.

Thus sternly discountenancing this vice among

themselves, there were no bounds to their disgust and indignation when the guilty parties were an Indian woman and a white man. They knew enough of the customs of civilization to be aware that marriage is a sacred, honorable, and lasting compact between *equals*, and that any connection of the sexes without its sanction was unblessed and unrespected — in all cases an especial indignity and disgrace to the woman.

If one of their number so erred and was forsaken by her seducer, or failed to escape with him, hard indeed was her lot, for small mercy was shown the frail sister by the irreproachable women of her tribe. If married, the lash was laid on unsparingly, and with peculiar gusto; if unmarried, she was shunned, despised, taunted incessantly with her shame, and in some instances driven out of their villages.

At the commencement of the war, the Oneidas were more than usually favored by white visitors; agents, officers, and commissioners, of both parties, seeking in every way and by every means to secure the interest and coöperation of the chiefs and warriors in their undertaking.

It happened that some of these ambassadors and negotiators did not choose to confine their eloquence to the weighty political matters in question, nor to exhaust their powers of persuasion upon the 'potent, grave, and reverend signiors' who sat in solemn conclave around the council-fire, for meditation and sententious discussions,

"*With interludes of pipe-smoke and strong water,*"

but were unprincipled enough to pay dishonorable

court to some of the most attractive young squaws at the castle; who, for their part, were weak and ignorant enough to listen with pleased ears to the treacherous flatteries of the pale-faced strangers, who wore such fine regimentals, and made such gaudy presents. Alas, poor aboriginal Ariadnes! more unfortunate than she of old; for, to these, after the shame and sorrow of the sure desertion, came the pain and exposure of the whipping; or the sorer lashing of taunting tongues, from the 'unco guid,' the stern and strong-minded, and the ugly, untempted, and envious, of their sex.

It was after the conviction and punishment of several of the frail offenders, that a singular council of the principal women of the tribe was called to discuss the melancholy prevalence of such crimes and scandals, and to devise means to arrest them, by forming yet stricter regulations for the conduct of the young and thoughtless, and fixing upon harsher penalties for the transgressions of the vicious and hardened. It was a movement for defence, intimidation, and vengeance.

This novel council met on a still, warm afternoon, in the latter part of May, when the air yet breathed the sweet spring softness, and the green of the grass and the foliage was delicate and fresh; when the streams were yet full and impetuous, like veins of the new year, leaping with the lusty strength of its youth, and the fair but hardy spring-blossoms had not yet been supplanted by the warmer and more luxuriant summer bloom.

The place of meeting was in a beautiful lonely glen; a small forest-opening, in the shape of an amphitheatre, nearly surrounded by thickly-wooded knolls, and enclosing a spring of clear, sparkling water, which, gushing from under a mossy rock in full volume, and with almost the force of a fountain, and running with frolicsome tumbles, and mad little eddies, and low gurgles of elfin laughter, down a small rocky descent, as though revelling in new-found light and freedom; and then, gliding, with a slow, contented sweep, over smooth, white pebbles, and silver sand, and under long, bending grass, swaying young willow-trees, and the blue, fragrant flowers of the wild Iris, stole away into the dark, dank, impenetrable wood.

The trunk of a tree felled near the spring, and several large stones placed around it, showed that this was not an unfrequented spot. In fact, it had long been the council-chamber of the Oneida women, where they were in the habit of meeting to discuss and decide upon all such questions as concerned them solely, or especially. In short, they occasionally held here a kind of savage 'Women's Rights Convention,' but something more exclusive in its character than the great convocations of their white sisters of our day, inasmuch as no male was ever allowed to be present as spectator or reporter — much less invited to take part in the proceedings of the meeting. Their deliberations were strictly private, and they bound themselves to secrecy, in all matters under action, or discussion, by oaths of barbarous solemnity. Whatever may be the truth with regard to the fair members of civilized societies, they certainly demonstrated the fact that squaws could 'keep a secret.'

One by one the dusky confederates now arrived at the little glen, coming through different forest-paths, as they had stolen off singly from their respective wigwams. Gravely saluting one another, they walked about, two by two, or stood in little groups, conversing upon domestic and social matters; and, not having the fear of their lords before their eyes, even venturing to touch upon political subjects, and in some sort to discuss the question of the great quarrel between the king and the colonists.

When their number was complete, they came together, and seated themselves about the spring, — some upon the fallen tree, some upon the stone seats, some upon the ground, — and fell into silence.

They were a singularly stern, harsh, and hopeless-looking set of women; most of them past middle age, and worn and haggard with the toils, hardships, and privations, of savage life; but there were about nearly all a Roman-like dignity and pride of bearing, seldom seen in their race at this age of its more utter degeneracy.

Gahaneh, the daughter of the sachem Sadewana, was the youngest woman present. But she was older than her years in her more than maternal cares and labors, her profound, unimparted sorrows, and 'the intuitive experiences of genius.'

By the subtle influence of this genius, and the force of a masculine intellect, by great courage and eloquence, and the entraining fascination of fanaticism, she had caused herself to be regarded by her tribe, at least by the female part, with peculiar respect; almost reverenced as a priestess of nature, and a prophetess of Manitou.

But a prophetess 'hath honor save among her own kin.' The old sachem Sadewana had small reverence, and less affection, for his stern and high-spirited daughter. To him she was only a violent-tempered and somewhat strong-minded member of the inferior sex; and, if there was anything he especially and sturdily set his face against, it was strong-mindedness in squaws. An obstinate favorer and an almost obsequious admirer of the whites, he had little sympathy with her peculiar pride of race — her uncompromising nativism. He also discountenanced her unfeminine habits and Amazonian propensities; though not to the extent of refusing to partake of the good game with which she always returned from the chase, and the fine fish she brought from the lake and forest-streams. He often deigned to 'hold forth' to her, very much in the style of some of the venerable fogies and pious prosers of our day, defining a squaw's proper sphere; telling her that it did not extend, at the farthest, beyond the corn-field and the melon-patch, and that her fittest, noblest, holiest 'mission' was to minister, like the submissive slave the Great Spirit meant her to be, to the wants, the vanity, and pride of her grim master — veiled away from the world's gaze by the curtaining skins and smoke of the wigwam.

Gahaneh, never contended with her father, whose theories and arguments, all savage as she was, she had intellect, shrewdness, and logic enough to despise; but kept resolutely on the course dictated by her own bold, independent spirit. —

'Child of the forest! strong and free,
Slight-robed, with loosely-flowing hair,
She swam the lake, or climbed the tree,
Or struck the flying bird in air.
O'er the heaped drifts of winter's moon
Her snow-shoes tracked the hunter's way;
And dazzling in the summer noon
The blade of her light oar threw off its shower of spray!'

Onata was her father's favorite. He had really loved, as far as it was in his savage heart and untutored intellect to love, his beautiful French wife; and he was proud to see her beauty and grace, and that refinement of manner and character which he had felt and admired, without comprehending, all relive in his child. So far was he from having been embittered, by her mother's desertion, toward her race, that, from the first, he favored Onata's natural partiality for it, and thus created the only subject of violent dissension between himself and Gahaneh; who, however, in this matter, was always obliged to yield to his superior authority and persistent will.

But we must return to the forest-council.

For several minutes all sat in utter silence; so still that the lowest gurgle of the spring, the lightest shiver of the aspen, the swaying of the wild grape-vines, the rustle of the young oak-leaves in the sweet south wind, and the soft sigh of the melancholy pines, could be distinctly heard. Then the birds, which had been frightened away by the intruders, returned to the tree-tops near by, and indulged themselves in a wonderful variety of trills and gushes, merry revelries, and mad ecstasies of song. If this was a combination to call a faint listening smile to some of those hard, solemn faces, that seemed to have set themselves to awe down the indecorous gladness of nature, the result was a total and mortifying failure. The poor, silly creatures might have sung till they burst their little hearts, before they would have won any slightest token of pleased attention from that grave, meditative group.

The eyes of many were fixed expectantly upon Gahaneh; but she sat most silent and motionless of all, on the rock of the spring, her feet buried in the moss and ferns. With the long bow at her side, the quiver at her back, her hound crouched at her feet, her eyes fixed on the water, her hands clenched across her knees, and her brow contracted with its habitual frown of haughty disdain, she looked like a bronze statue of Diana, meditating vengeance against some intruder upon her haunts, or contemner of her sylvan divinity.

At length, an elderly squaw arose, and made a long speech, in solemn tones and sententious language, but with such skilful circumlocutions of the subject in question, as to leave her auditors in complete doubt as to her opinions, or even whether she had any at all. Others followed; some advocating measures of more severity, and some recommending more mercy, toward their offending sisters. The latter class of speakers were among the half-Christianized Sunday listeners of the white teacher, and now made use of some small texts of Scripture to give unwonted authority to their mild suggestions. Whenever they came out with these — mostly oddly-garbled and misapplied—Gahaneh's eyes would send a sudden flash of scorn from under their dusky lids, and from her quivering nostrils would come a fierce snort of mingled anger and contempt.

One high-spirited young squaw, with strong reformatory sentiments, not only advocated the adoption of more severe laws for the intimidation and punishment of native offenders, but a different mode of action, defensive and offensive, toward all white visitors to their villages. They should be coldly and haughtily received; their fine speeches should be met with sullen silence, or contemptuous laughter; their seductive gifts should be flung in their faces! Indian women should refuse to cook the venison, or concoct the succotash, for them to eat; to spread the mat and the skins for them to sleep upon; and, if all milder means failed, they should smoke them out of their wigwams!

This brave speech was very well received on the whole, though not a few of the hearers shrugged their shoulders, and winced involuntarily, at the thought of the sound beating which such an independent and inhospitable proceeding would inevitably bring upon them from their liege lords. It suggested, in a new form, the old dilemma as to who should 'bell the cat.'

The ultra reformer was followed by a staunch conservative, decidedly of the 'old school' in sentiments, though in years not yet past the warm, fast season of youth. This was a handsome half-breed; a stout, indolent, sensual-looking woman, of considerable shrewdness and ability.

She made a very smooth and plausible speech against the adoption of any more severe measures; against any legislation whatever upon this delicate subject, except to formally and finally do away with all present pains and penalties.

She affirmed that these 'notions' about female dignity and virtue were of very recent date, and had been inculcated by the very pale-faced enemies against whom honorable members were inveighing. In the good old times, when the Iroquois were most great and powerful, and white traders and settlers came as courtiers and suppliants to their castles, they were received with courtesy, and entertained with honor ; and *then* it was not thought that all the duties of a generous hospitality had been performed, unless their guests had been offered their choice of a servant and companion from among the handsomest young squaws of the tribe, made cleanly and dressed in their best for the occasion. Then such a temporary connection was considered no disgrace, but rather an honor ; then their wisest sachems and most pious prophets had countenanced such customs ; and, in her opinion, it was wicked presumption for a parcel of ignorant young squaws, in these degenerate times, to set up their fanatical, sentimental ideas against the wisdom and piety of the past ; and in some instances — here she glanced at Gahaneh — even casting reproaches upon their own fathers and mothers. For her part, she was not ashamed, but rather proud, of the English blood in her veins. Her father was a brave who wore a coat of the color of the ashberries in the autumn, with buttons that outshone the sun, and carried a long-knife that dazzled the eye, and struck down his enemies like lightning. Her mother had never felt shame or sorrow for having been the white warrior's slave for a little while. He treated her kindly, and, when he went away, gave her a wonderful, embroidered blanket, such as only the king's daughters wore in his own country; gay ribbons, and head-dresses of feathers, and a string of beads, bright and varied as the rainbow, and — so long! — widely extending her hands in airy measurement of the marvellous bauble.

Her mother, she continued, had been happy in the stranger's wigwam, because he was good to her, and did not make her work hard; and happy when he went away, because he left her so many fine things. She very soon made a good marriage with a chief's nephew, and there was no harm done, nor any trouble made for anybody. One time, the white brave came on another visit to the village, and she went again to the lodge which the chiefs had provided for him, and served him while he stayed, and got other presents; while her husband sat at home, and smoked his pipe in peace. When she came back, he took the tobacco and drank the rum which she brought, and asked no questions. And again there was no trouble for anybody; for this was before the cruel and shameful whipping-law was established.

As the speaker concluded, among some rather ill-defined murmurs of applause, and sat down with a self-satisfied smile on her fat, good-humored, yet cunning face, Gahaneh leaped to her feet; her eyes ablaze, her thin lips and nostrils quivering with indignation and scorn. In height towering above the tallest woman of her tribe, and powerfully formed, her appearance was at all times imposing. But, when, animated by any strong emotion, her great, gloomy eyes flashed their keen fires upon them, and the bold, imperious tones of her voice broke upon their ears, she subjugated, awed, swayed, and led them, according to her own sovereign will.

Gahaneh began by indignantly denying that female dignity, chastity, and constancy, were modern 'notions,' derived from white visitors or teachers. They were eternal principles, indestructible instincts, implanted in every woman's heart by the Great Spirit himself. There was an age, she said, beyond the time referred to by the last speaker, — a noble, golden age, far back toward the beautiful morning of the world, — when Indian men and women lived in purity, honor, and equality, together; when the squaws were brave like the warriors, and the warriors counted it no shame to be gentle and soft-toned like the squaws; when they went together to the chase and on the war-path, together planted the corn and gathered the harvest, and together sat in the great council, around the sacred *Oneöta*;[4] when each brave took one mate to his wigwam, and went not after other squaws; when the wigwams were large and warm, and filled with skins, and corn, and fruit, and happy children; when fish, and deer, and wild fowl, were abundant, and the harvest never failed; when Manitou himself often came down in the shadowy twilight, and talked with his red children of the forest.

When He gave such strength to the arms, fleetness to the feet, and unerring sight to the eyes of the young braves, that death ever followed swift and sure on the twang of their bows and the whistle of their arrows — that the wild deer stood still, tame with despair, the bear and the panther howled with terror at their approach, and their bravest foes, when they found the print of their moccasins and their trail in the forest, fled in fear, crying, *'It is the track of the Oneida!'*

When the old men were wise and worthy of reverence; for *then* their heads were whitened with the snows of many noble winters, not with the untimely frosts of disease and dishonor; for then their faces were furrowed with deep thoughts and mighty cares for their people, not scarred and scratched with vile passions and petty malignity; then their eyes were dazzled and made dim by the near brightness of the happy land of Manitou rising before them like a great sun, not darkened by films of stupidity and slavish fear, or burned out with fire-water!

Then came a time when the Indian grew proud and insolent — when he thought that he could do without the help and counsel of Manitou, neglected sacrifices to him, and began to sacrifice to the Spirit of Evil. Soon he learned of *him* to despise and ill-treat woman. He drove her away from the council-fire; he sent her back from the chase; he confined her to the wigwam and the corn-field; he made her a slave, a dog!

Still he went further and further from the Good Spirit, who gave him no more wise fatherly talks in the pleasant twilight of summer woods, nor bestowed upon him good gifts of fruit and abundant harvests, but spoke only in thunder and tempests, and sent blight, and famine, and disease, to scourge and destroy him. But the Evil Spirit drew nearer and nearer, till he wound about him like a great serpent, hissed his bad counsels into his ear, and stung every noble virtue in his heart till it died! So he grew weaker and viler, till at last one brave would take two or three *slaves* to his wigwam, and one squaw would have two or three masters. Then the white man came, and joined his wickedness and treachery and accursed cunning to the Indian's weakness and vice ; and thenceforth the Evil Spirit had reigned supreme, and the Good Spirit had utterly withdrawn himself into the far brightness of his heaven, and dropped a great cloud between him and his red children, that he might be vexed with them no more.

At this point the speaker paused, and stood for a few moments perfectly silent, in an attitude of utter dejection and despair, her hands falling at her side, her head drooping, and the flash of her stormy eyes sheathed under the tawny lids. Then suddenly rousing herself, and taking the craft and aggressions of the white man and the wrongs of the Indian for her text, she burst forth again into an overwhelming torrent of impassioned eloquence, scathing denunciation, and bitter invective.

So far was she, she said, from being *proud* of the pale blood that had thievishly crept into her veins, that she regarded it with loathing and shame. Willingly would she drain out every drop of it, if it were possible so to do! But her *heart* was dark — *that* was all Indian, in spite of her faded face ; here she struck her forehead indignantly. She was in soul a true child of the noon-day sun and the deep forest shade, and would not yield to the purest-blooded Oneida of them all in strong, uncompromising, unslumbering hatred of the stranger who had wronged and contaminated their race!

It was true the Indian had received the white man hospitably — all too hospitably; it had made him even more insolent and grasping than he was by nature, and he had proceeded to rob his host of his stores of grain and skins, of his hunting and fishing grounds, of his honor, and, finally, through the devilish agency of the fire-water, of his wits. He had left him nothing but revenge; and even that last dear right the Indian too often shamefully abandoned.

The pale-faces might smile, and flatter, and use big words at the council-fire, but *in their hearts* they despised the Indian, and made merry over his wrongs and decay. He was a poor brute, a dog, *a sick hound*, in their sight!

When a white man saw a white woman that he liked, he made her his wife for always. He treated her with kindness and respect; took her with him when he journeyed, and to all the great pow-wows of his people; labored for her support, and nursed her, and called the medicine-man when she was sick. But, if an Indian woman struck his fancy, he made her his paramour and his slave; she toiled for him, served him, and when he was tired of her he kicked her out of his wigwam, and when she was sick he let her die!

Who ever heard of a white man taking an Indian woman for his lawful wife? No! the meanest interloper among them all would feel himself degraded by such a permanent connection with the daughter of a great sachem — a native princess!

Must these things be? she continued; was there no pride of sex and race among the Indian women, that cried out against this baseness, this shame, this outrage? The Great Spirit was discouraged with his sons, and called now to his daughters, through her, to whom he deigned yet to whisper in the awful stillness of midnight, telling them to lift their heads, so long bowed low, heavy with degradation and bondage — to make themselves a new name, and shame their chiefs and braves back into manhood and freedom! Would they heed this command, or would they still help to sink their race deeper into the blackness and mire of infamy and vice? — for the sake of a few false smiles and falser words, and miserable toys, brave the eternal anger of the Good Spirit, to become the playthings, slaves, despised *paramours*, of their treacherous and tyrannous enemies?

'No! no! no!' was almost yelled out by several voices among the audience, wrought up to a terrible pitch of excitement by the wonderful power and electric passion of the speaker.

The ghost of a smile of gratified pride and conscious power flitted across Gahaneh's face at these cries, which were so many tributes to her eloquence; and, proceeding to strike while the heavy metal of the dull intellects around her was at white heat, she briefly and hardily proposed that they should make a law which no Oneida woman, however bold and reckless, would dare to disobey, knowing that from its terrible penalty no one could escape.

Let them resolve that any Oneida woman who should hereafter consent to a dishonorable connection with any white man should suffer death at the hands of her sisters of the tribe!

As these fatal words fell from the stony lips of the

prophetess with the dread weight of doom, the ultra reformer who had spoken in the early part of the discussion sprang up and proposed a sort of an amendment; that the white seducers and adulterers should be taken off by assassination or open attack, whenever it should be safe and practicable.

Gahaneh received the suggestion with a grim smile and an ejaculation of 'Good!' and then proceeded to propose further, that the squaws present who should approve of these measures should form themselves into a solemn league for the apprehension, trial, and punishment, of native offenders.

Some were too faint-hearted or felt too conscious of frailty to join; and a few had avowed Christian principles, and were opposed to the shedding of blood, especially on a question of morality, which seemed to them a little doubtful at the best, seeing that one of the parties to the temporary connection, so hastily condemned, might be a good Christian, and prove the means of the hopeful conversion of his benighted paramour. On such as these Gahaneh contemptuously turned her back, and made another brief, passionate appeal to the fearful and the undecided. So powerfully and authoritatively did she speak, that thirty out of the fifty squaws present came forward and solemnly pledged themselves to abide by and faithfully carry out the new law, in defiance of resistance and regardless of consequences, even though their nearest and dearest should be among the culprits and victims.

This was '*the League*' of which, later, Gahaneh so meaningly reminded her sister in parting from her at Fort Stanwix.

The oath was administered — a brief, barbaric form, which sent a chill of horror through the hearts of the least courageous, but which Gahaneh uttered with the stern solemnity of a Fate, and some of her haggish followers repeated with the fierce gusto with which she-panthers might lap blood.

The council then broke up and dispersed, the members of the league remaining a little while after the others, and then setting out for home together, striding along the narrow forest-path in single file, slowly and silently, their stern, fixed faces growing sterner and harder in the deepening twilight.

CHAPTER III.

THE SIEGE AND THE HOSTAGE.

Sad was the year, by proud oppression driven,
  When transatlantic Liberty arose,
Not in the sunshine and the smile of Heaven,
  But wrapped in whirlwinds and begirt with woes,
  Amidst the strife of fratricidal foes;
Her birth-star was the light of burning plains,
  Her baptism was the blood that flows
From kindred hearts.

CAMPBELL.

The floating clouds their state shall lend
To her; for her the willow bend;
  Nor shall she fail to see
Even in the motions of the storm
Grace that shall mould the maiden's form,
  By silent sympathy.

The stars of midnight shall be dear
To her; and she shall lean her ear
  In many a secret place
Where rivulets dance their wayward round,
And beauty born of murmuring sound
  Shall pass into her face.

WORDSWORTH.

WE must now return to Fort Stanwix and its inmates.

There was, as yet, no appearance of the expected besiegers, though rumors of their coming were constantly reaching the garrison, through scouts and friendly Indians. Small parties of Mohawks and

Cayugas were occasionally seen lurking in the woods about the fort, and precautions were taken to prevent any of the garrison from falling into their hands. The men were strictly forbidden to go out of sight of the fort for the purposes of fishing, hunting, or reconnoitring, except in large authorized parties. Yet, in spite of these regulations, one of the officers, Captain Gregg, and two of his men, enthusiastic sportsmen, once ventured several miles beyond the prescribed limits, while pigeon-shooting, and were all three shot and scalped by Indians in ambush.

There was one circumstance of this painful incident which, as an ardent dog-lover, I cannot deny myself the pleasure of relating.

Captain Gregg was not killed, though left for dead by the savages. With great difficulty he dragged himself to the body of one of his companions, and laid his bleeding head on the dead breast, thinking that he might thus find some little relief from his intolerable sufferings.

It happened that he had been accompanied by his dog, a faithful and intelligent animal, who, having fled from or been overlooked by the savages, had escaped unharmed, and now came and stood by his master, with an almost human sympathy and sorrow in his eyes.

Captain Gregg looked at him earnestly, and said, 'If you really feel sorry for me, don't stand there watching to see me die, but go and bring somebody to help me!'

By some wonderful instinct the dog understood his meaning, and set out on the run through the forest.

About a mile away he found two men fishing, and by the most extraordinary demonstrations — by running back and forth, barking violently, fawning on them, whining piteously, and pulling at their coats — he prevailed on them to accompany him to the spot where he had left his wounded master.

Once they became alarmed at being led so far into the woods, and turned to go back; but the dog first sprang before them, fiercely contested their way, then crouched at their feet with a mute agony of entreaty which they could not withstand. They went on a little further, found Captain Gregg, and conveyed him to the fort.

That officer, after a tedious illness, recovered from his terrible wounds; but, for all his sufferings and scars, he never was regarded as the hero of his own adventure, all the admiration, wonder, and praise, being heaped upon his dog-deliverer, who bore his honors with exemplary meekness, walking about the fort, or, sentinel-like, making the rounds of the walls in grave unconsciousness of his own distinction.

Another tragical incident occurred about this time, to prove to the garrison that they were environed by barbarous and blood-thirsty foes. Several little girls ventured out one morning to gather wild berries, and, though only a few rods from the fort, were fired on by skulking savages, and two of their number killed.

Still no bold and open attacks were made upon the fortress, and for many days nothing save these cowardly murders occurred to break the monotony of garrison life, or disturb the deep, midsummer quiet of the surrounding forest wilds.

The weather was warm and sultry; a peculiar, expectant stillness seemed brooding upon the air. Nature herself seemed waiting in breathless awe and silence for the opening scene of some fearful tragedy.

Our hero, Lieutenant Maurice de Vaudreuil, to whom it is fully time to return, sought to relieve the *ennui* of inactivity and waiting by making the acquaintance of all in the garrison. So frank and engaging were the manners of the young Frenchman, and so amiable and cordial was his disposition, that the humblest and rudest among them felt no lasting jealousy of his wealth, rank, and elegant breeding. Pride, shyness, national prejudice, and rampant young republicanism, all speedily yielded before the pleasant, confident warmth of his smile, and the easy *bonhommie* of his talk, which to them lost none of its charm by the unconscious *naïveté* of its broken English.

With the children of the garrison, Lieutenant Maurice, almost as careless, gay, and restless as they, soon became an especial favorite; and among the children he was after a time most likely to be found, for here he always met Onata.

The singular beauty of the young Indian girl, — a type so rare and unlooked-for among her race, — with its exquisite blending of sweetness and dignity, had charmed him at first, but he soon became more deeply interested in contemplating 'the inner visage of the mind.' He saw that her simplicity was more that of childhood than of barbarism; that her instincts were noble, delicate, and true. To him she was simply the primitive woman, fresh from God's hands, and revelling in all the joy and freedom of nature, yet innocent, tender, and full of unconscious poetry. Poet and idle dreamer as he had ever been, till the spirit of Freedom seized upon his unoccupied heart and drew him into her western crusade, he would at any time have been interested in a study so pleasing and novel; but, coming as he did from the most artificial, corrupt, and heartless society in the world, there was to him an inexpressible charm in the freshness and purity of this untutored child of nature — this delicate flower of the wild, coming up at God's call, hearing his voice in the wind, taking his baptism in the dew and his smile in the sunlight, and slowly and quietly blossoming into a beauty and sweetness unmatched by the stateliest hot-house blooms of the world.

From the first, the young soldier had been struck by the softness and melody of Onata's voice. It seemed to have been attuned by nature's gentlest and sweetest woodland sounds, such as the pleasant laughter of rivulets, the low rippling of indolent summer waves gliding up a pebbly beach, the sighing of the winds among the pines, the dryad murmurs, the mysterious, inarticulate talk of fluttering leaves, and the varied warbling of birds.

Having been thus impressed by merely her speaking tones, the lieutenant was hardly surprised at finding the Indian girl, one evening, delighting a group of children by a series of wonderful and delicate imitations of bird-songs. She paused suddenly on seeing De Vaudreuil approach, dropping from a wild, joyous carol, into a merry little embarrassed laugh, scarcely less musical. But at his earnest solicitation, joined to the clamorous entreaties of the children, she recommenced, though with much shyness and a consequent unsteadiness of voice; or, as might be said of a modern *cantatrice*, on the occasion of a slight stage-fright, 'a little want of precision in the notes of the upper register.' As she went on, however, taking part after part in Nature's winged choir, she gained confidence, and sung as she had never sung before, even in the deepest solitudes of her native woods, to a twittering audience of her jealous and astonished rivals. The blue-bird, the black-bird, the wood-pigeon, the robin, the bobolink, the oriole, the lark — one after another chirped and whistled, cooed, warbled, and trilled, through her rich flexible voice!

As she stood in the mellow sunset light, her dark dreamy eyes flashing with childlike pleasure and a little womanly vanity, her slender throat swelling, and her crimson lips quivering with the fountain-like gush of sylvan melody, she seemed to De Vaudreuil the beautiful incarnated spirit of music — the music of nature and of heaven.

The interest which the young officer took in Onata was not unresponded to by her. She seemed to feel toward him a peculiar, childlike sympathy and trust, almost from the first, perhaps because he was of the nation of her mother — her unknown, unfaithful, lost, but still beloved mother.

One day, with her usual impulsiveness and simplicity, she asked her new friend to teach her a few words of his beautiful language. He consented with a kindly smile, and, seating himself by her side in a shady angle of the wall, prepared to play the grave and to him most novel part of tutor.

She first asked, with a peculiar, serious eagerness of tone and manner, for the words meaning the *Great Spirit* and *Mother*. When they were given her, she cast up her eyes and repeated them reverently, her face glowing with inexpressible tenderness and devotion — '*Dieu! Mère!*' crossing herself meekly at the same time.

'Onata, my child, who taught you *that?*' asked De Vaudreuil, with great surprise.

'Nobody teach me,' she replied. 'I have French mother long ago; she do so before she sleep, all the nights. She very pretty woman, white like the snow; she despise the Indian — his wigwam too small and cold for her; she not love her dark babies — their wild eyes make her sad, and she go away!

'Sometimes, when I little child, I cry for her in my sleep, my heart grow so hungry for her; and then I hear her say, "Onata!" and she come and make a little light in the dark wigwam, and I very happy, and sleep with her till morning, and Gahaneh not know anything about it. Now she never come any more. I dream, but I never hear her voice in the beautiful sleep-land. I cry, but she does not pity me. She forget Onata, or she *dead!* But *Dieu* not dead; *He* never despise the dark children born in his great shadow. Onata love *Him*.'

The simple pathos, unconscious poetry, and pure religious feeling, of these words, impressed the romantic Maurice; and he entered upon his task of teaching with a deeper respect for his pupil than he had ever before felt. Yet, after all he had seen of her peculiar gifts, he was astonished by her quick apprehension and retentive memory, and delighted by the exquisite purity and nicety of her pronunciation. She caught the words from his lips eagerly, yet accurately; in some instances even appearing to anticipate sounds, if not meanings. In fact, she seemed more like one recalling than actually learning a language; and it is possible that many words, breathed into her infant ear by the captive mother, may have slumbered unsuspected or uncomprehended in her brain through all these years.

But this pleasant occupation, and all other amusements, came to an end with the coming of the besieging army, which arrived before the fort on the 2d and 3d of August.

The principal force was of Indians, led by Thayendenagea, and consisted of troops of warriors from the several tribes of the Six Nations, the Oneidas alone excepted. St. Leger's army was a motley collection of British regulars, Hessians, Canadians, and Tories. The whole force of the besiegers amounted to seventeen hundred men, thoroughly armed and equipped.

The garrison numbered only some seven hundred and fifty fighting men. They had provisions for six weeks, and a sufficient supply of ammunition for small arms to last, with prudent use, for that length of time; but for their cannon they had barely four hundred rounds. They were even without a flag up to the day of the investment of the fort. But the patriotism and ingenuity of the soldiers' wives soon supplied this deficiency. From a blue military cloak, strips of white linen and red flannel, they manufactured a homely national standard, and hoisted it above the ramparts, where it was regarded with as much patriotic pride and chivalric devotion as though it had been of the costliest silk and the most gorgeous embroidery that ever rustled in the wind or flashed in the sun.

The history of the siege and gallant defence of this frontier post has always seemed to me so full of interest, and so worthy of admiration, that I trust I shall be excused for giving it here, somewhat in detail. It was but a small, remote point on the vast battle-ground of the Revolution; yet here was displayed a spirit of calm determination, unflinching courage, and heroic endurance, not surpassed anywhere, through all that long and desperate struggle.

Immediately on his arrival, General St. Leger despatched a manifesto to the garrison, graciously offering the rebels honorable employment in the king's army in case of a prompt and humble surrender, and threatening them with the extremest horrors of savage vengeance should they persist in holding out a vain resistance against him and his barbarous allies. Colonel Gansevoort, his gallant officers, and brave men, received both threats and bribes with indignant scorn, and the next morning the siege commenced. A few shells were fired into the fort, but did no material injury; and during that day and the following, the Indians, skulking behind trees and bushes, fired upon the workmen engaged in raising a parapet. But a few skilful sharp-shooters, well posted, finally put an end to this sport.

Indians are by no means patient besiegers, and when the second day drew to a close without any signs of the garrison surrendering, great was their indignation and disgust. They even began to entertain a distrust and contempt for the 'big guns' of their allies, and felt disposed to take matters more decidedly into their own hands. They first resolved upon intimidation, and formed a monstrous plan for horrifying the incorrigible rebels into submission. Distributing themselves through the forest, and totally surrounding the fort, they commenced the most terrific and unearthly uproar conceivable, — yelling, shrieking, howling, and whooping, — a vocal pandemonium, a demoniacal concert, which was prolonged through the entire night. Upon the hardy pioneers and iron-nerved fighters of the fort the plan failed to produce the desired effect; though, it is true, it deprived them of their usual amount of sound sleep; and dire was the cursing among some of the heartiest Indian-haters. The women and children, however, were duly horrified and alarmed at an uproar so ferocious, and so appallingly prophetic of horrible massacres, scalpings, and burnings. Even Onata shuddered and trembled at the yells of rage, the howlings of hate, the fiendish laughter of anticipated triumph and revenge, bursting from a thousand throats, and 'making night hideous' for miles around.

In the woods there was a frightened flutter, chirping, and flying to and fro among tree-tops, and a precipitate rush of alarmed beasts, tearing and crashing through entangled branches and dried underbrush. The owl hooted, the hawk screamed, the wild-cat yelled, the wolf whined, the panther wailed; the lazy bear stirred uneasily in his slumber, and growled out a surly defiance; while his more watchful mate glared fiercely from the thick darkness of her den into the clamorous night without, clutching her scared cubs, and setting up a mighty maternal howl. And this was all. As the savage serenaders returned to their camp, all hoarse and exhausted with their tremendous vocal exertions, to their amazement, rage,.and aggravation, they were saluted by a saucy morning-gun from that contumacious fort, and saw that home-made rebel flag waving coolly in the winds of dawn.

In the course of that day the besieged garrison were gladdened by the arrival of an express to Colonel Gansevoort, informing him that General Herkimer was marching to his relief with a force of one thousand men.

General Herkimer was to halt at Oriskany until he should hear signal-guns from the fort, announcing the arrival of his messenger. Then he was to come up promptly, and cut his way through the besieging army; and he requested that he might be aided by a simultaneous sortie from the fort.

Unfortunately the courier was delayed several hours, and the force of General Herkimer, both officers and men, became impatient, and demanded to be led on immediately toward the fort. The general, who was prudent as he was brave, refused to advance before hearing the signals, or receiving reinforcements; but, at last, stung beyond endurance, by the sneers, taunts, and reproaches, of his officers, he gave the fatal order.

The troops were chiefly composed of militia, half-mad with untried military ardor, and a blind hate of their enemies; undisciplined at the best, and now in a state of utter insubordination, almost amounting to actual mutiny, moving with reckless irregularity, eagerness, and foolish bravado.

Thus they marched, if such a helter-skelter, straggling progress could be called a march, through the ominous gloom and stifling stillness of a cloudy and sultry August morning, in apparent safety for about two hours ; when, on entering a deep, marshy ravine, they fell into a complete ambuscade of Indians and tories, arranged by Brant, at whose signal the circle closed around the entire patriot force, the war-whoop was sounded, and a furious onslaught was made.

From behind every tree whistled a rifle-ball, every clump of underbrush blazed with musketry, tomahawks and spears and deadly arrows were hurled and stormed upon them from every direction. Some of those who had been loudest in bravado, and most insolent in their charges of cowardice against General Herkimer, took flight at once ; but, pursued by the savages, reaped no advantage from their treachery and poltroonery. Most of the officers and men, however, bravely bore their part, manfully striving to atone for the error of their rashness and inexperience, and fought not only with noble courage, but wonderful skill, one of the hottest and most unequal battles of the Revolution.

General Herkimer was severely, and, as it afterwards proved, mortally wounded, in the early part of the action ; yet he did not give up the conduct of the battle, but, reclining against the trunk of a tree, continued to give his orders with the utmost coolness and intrepidity. It is even related that he took out his tinder-box, lit his pipe, and smoked, with true Dutch philosophy and phlegm.

The conflict continued for nearly six hours; the latter portion of that time becoming fearfully fierce and desperate — a hand-to-hand struggle. At length a brisk firing was heard in the direction of the fort, and soon after both Indians and tories yielded, and fled in the utmost confusion. The provincials found themselves masters of the field, but with such a terrible loss of officers and men that they hardly dared to claim a victory. They were, of course, obliged to relinquish their purpose of going to the relief of Fort Stanwix, and were only too happy to be able to retreat in safety from the battle-ground, bearing their wounded.

Meanwhile the sortie from Fort Stanwix, advised by General Herkimer, had been most successfully accomplished by the gallant Colonel Willett, who, with a detachment of only two hundred men, fired by his own magnetic, Murat-like spirit, made a sudden and furious attack on that portion of the enemy's camp occupied by Sir John Johnson and his troops, 'the Royal Greens.' From this part a large number of men had been drawn away to intercept the force of General Herkimer; the remainder now made a slight but ineffectual resistance, became panic-stricken, and fled across the river to the camp of St. Leger. The patriots then attacked the Indian encampment with like success; driving the astonished savages into the depths of the forest, whither they very wisely concluded not to follow them.

They then returned to the fort in triumph, carrying with them no less than twenty-one wagon-loads of camp-equipage and stores, the baggage of Sir John Johnson, and other officers, containing papers and despatches of importance, and especial interest to the garrison; and, last, but in the scale of glory not least, five British standards!

Incredible as it may seem, and almost impossible of belief as they themselves felt it to be, the patriots had not lost a man, though several of their number were severely wounded. Among them was the noble young French volunteer De Vaudreuil, who had received a bayonet-thrust through his sword-arm. But, in the excitement of the engagement, he scarcely felt it, pausing only to bind it up hastily with his silken sash, whose crimson hue concealed, if it did not stanch, the copious bleeding; then, plunging again into the fight, he performed some wonderful exploits by left-hand cuts and thrusts, and returned with his companions to the fort, bearing one of the standards, as the prize of his valor, and followed by a fierce, black-bearded, foreign-looking prisoner, who, however, proved to be nothing more formidable than a Hessian chaplain, who, while on a visit or embassy to the camp of Sir John Johnson, had found himself, by accident, involved in the affray, and, happening to possess, in spite of his holy orders, more of that unsanctified quality called 'pluck' than the professional fighters in the camp, sturdily stood his ground, and scorned to fly.

Onata had watched the sortie from the extremest tenable point of the southern bastion, and strained her eyes to follow, through the smoke and tumult of the fight, the slender and graceful figure of the young French soldier. Once she shrieked out, and almost staggered from the perilous point where she stood when she saw him wounded; but the next moment she gave a cry of joyful triumph, as she saw his enemy disarmed, and bowing submissively before him. When the victors reëntered the fort, forgetting her usual shyness and instinctive modesty, she sprang forward with childlike eagerness, and flung her slight brown arms about her friend, weeping and smiling in a passion of mingled grief and gladness. It may be that the embrace hurt his wounded arm, or that the lieutenant was too deeply absorbed in graver matters to be gratified by it, or even that his sense of delicacy was somewhat shocked by the freedom of the half-savage child; certain it is that he hastily shook himself free from her fond arms, and more sternly than gently reproved his wild pet, telling her to be quiet, and go back among the other women. Poor Onata shrank away, wounded and humiliated, and watched with a half-sad, half-sullen expression, the exulting victors as they proceeded to run up the captured British colors on the flag-staff, underneath the homely standard of the fort.

The entire force of the garrison then mounted upon the parapets, and gave three cheers of triumph and defiance, which rung over the forest, and, reaching to the furthest point of the enemy's camp, caused the baffled besiegers, civilized and savage, to curse and howl with ineffectual rage.

In the midst of the cheering, Captain Gregg's famous dog gave vent to his feelings on this proud and hilarious occasion, by a joyful barking.

'Well done, old fellow!' said a rough soldier, patting him on the head, 'yell away — bow-wow to your heart's content! If "a cat may look at a king," it's a pity if sech a brave, human-like dog as you be can't bark at King George's cussed old colors!'

As Onata stealthily watched Lieutenant Maurice, as he stood waving his hat upon the parapet, she noticed that the thick scarf which bound his arm was beginning to drip with blood; she saw that he was deathly pale — that he staggered, and seemed to have been struck with sudden blindness. The next instant she had leaped to his side, had caught him in her arms as he sank upon the wall, and, with almost superhuman strength, had drawn him from the outer edge, toward which he was falling. Now he did not send her away, he did not reprove her by look or word, for he was in a deep swoon. As she bent over him and held his head upon her heaving breast, and saw that it was a swoon and not death, and felt that no one, not even he, could dispute her right to hold him thus for a little while, the light of a fierce and stormy joy flashed over her face, dispelling the unusual shadows of humiliation and anger.

Those shadows, that light, were the first ominous clouds, the first lightning-gleam of womanly passion, which had ever visited the quiet sky of her happy young life. Thenceforth she was a child no more.

When the men came to lift her friend down from the wall and bear him to his quarters, she arose quietly and followed him, and from that hour installed herself as his nurse and faithful attendant.

The wound of Lieutenant Maurice was by no means dangerous, but, as he had lost much blood, and suffered a good deal from nervous excitement, he was for several days succeeding the sortie quite prostrated, and confined to his couch. Colonel Gansevoort, Colonel Willett, and the other officers, visited him frequently, and, as far as their sterner duties and more absorbing responsibilities would allow, ministered to his wants; but, strangely enough, his chief dependence, for watchful, womanly care, was upon the Indian girl he had so short a time before looked upon as, at the best, but a charming mystery of barbarism, a beautiful savage, slightly softened and humanized, but still wild, restless, and untractable. As a nurse, she proved so gentle and devoted, and seemed so happy in her office, that he had no heart, no wish, to send her away. It relieved the *ennui* of his sick room merely to observe her dainty, graceful ways and movements; he loved to lie with half-closed eyes, watching her slight figure as it flitted here and there with the quickness and stillness of a bird, and his heart sometimes confessed to a little thrill of vanity — very natural and pardonable in a handsome young man, and a Frenchman at that — to think how soon this wild young creature had been tamed to his hand, had stayed her wandering flights, had sunk her brave, capricious carol of freedom, half glad, half defiant, into the gentlest household strains of tenderness and pity.

Onata had considerable skill in the Indian modes of treating wounds and fevers, and the surgeon of the fortress making no objection to the use of her simple remedies and medicaments, Lieutenant Maurice quietly submitted himself to her care, smiling now and then at her grave professional airs of authority, responsibility, and science.

As her patient became convalescent, Onata took it upon herself to amuse him by relating romantic tales and traditions of her people. Though they were all more or less strange, tragic, fanciful, and sometimes grotesque and horrible, they had all one strong, real element of life and nature, one vital passion — love. Through the most monstrous and improbable beings of tradition, through the most mystical and impalpable creatures of her imagination, throbbed at least this one warm purple pulse of humanity.

Unconsciously the maiden seemed to choose and invent such touching tales and marvellous legends on the one tender and inexhaustible theme, at all times gifting with the strength and warmth of her own mixed organism the savage lovers of her wild romance ; thus, in most cases, doing no little violence to nature — the pure Indian being in all the gentler passions singularly cold and apathetic.

During these talks, the lieutenant often sought to draw Onata to speak of herself and of her sister, whose peculiar pride of bearing and Amazonian style of beauty had impressed him deeply, though not altogether pleasantly. But the maiden seemed strangely shy of the latter topic, and, though she manifested always a sort of distant deferential pride in her stern, undemonstrative protectress, it was evident that she felt for her little sympathy or spontaneous affection. It was not in her impulsive, yielding, and trustful nature to comprehend Gahaneh's impassable reserve, isolation, and self-sustainment, nor in her unreflective youth to appreciate that which was noblest and rarest in a character so widely different from her own. A visible shadow of fear or awe came over her at the mere mention of Gahaneh's name, and her voice in reply took strange low tones, as though she were speaking of some half-dreaded, half-worshipped being — an incarnated mystery and power. She would say:

'Gahaneh very kind — very good to me. I poor sick baby, not worth to live; she take care of me all the nights; she hunt, and fish, and gather the wood-berries for me all the summer days; make me good clothes, and keep me warm in the winter, till I grow so strong and well that I call the fleet young deer my brothers, and kiss the red wild-roses for my sisters. She wise — wiser than old sachems; so wise the Good Spirit have long talks with her, and she tell him many things. And she brave — so brave she have no fear of the Bad Spirit, him you call Devil. Ah! too good, too wise, too brave! I afraid to look in her eyes sometimes, when she look through the great cloud at Manitou, and its darkness is on her face; then they burn me down *so small!* Onata poor foolish child, not good for anything — afraid of Great Spirit and Devil both; a little squirrel,' she added, with a merry laugh, 'can make Onata run.'

During one of these conversations, Onata confided to her new friend the history of the singular 'League' of the Oneida women, of which her sister was the forming and ruling spirit. As De Vaudreuil listened to the strange account, related in an awe-struck, hesitating voice, a visible shudder passed over him, a blush rose to his cheek, and he turned his face away from Onata. If the wild grace, beauty, and evident loving devotion, of the Indian maiden, had ever brought vague, passionate temptations to the susceptible heart of the young soldier,— a heart by nature noble and honorable, but illy fortified by strict principles of morality, — if ever his idle imagination had pleased itself with romantic pictures of love in the wilderness, free from the restraints of religious and legal forms, or the obligation of perpetuity, — the fine instincts of purity, delicacy, and womanly pride, unconsciously revealed by Onata in her narration, and the knowledge of the fearful penalty which might be visited even upon *her* head, should she defy not only the newly-aroused moral sense of her savage sisters, but their more terrible 'League,' — dispelled all such temptations, and banished such pictures forever. He resolved henceforth to regard her as a sister — an innocent child-sister; under that tender and sacred character alone to care for her when present, and remember her when absent. He would steel himself against her winning, dependent ways, which he had already begun to feel upon his heart, though like the half-playful, half-caressing touches of an infant hand. He would disentangle his fancy of her artless fascinations; he would think that he had seen a wonderful revelation of purity walking unconsciously in the light of nature, of beauty unsunned by the admiration of the world, or that a peerless wild-rose had blossomed out upon him from the depths of the wilderness, to glad his eye for a moment; that was all.

During this time Lieutenant de Vaudreuil had not forgotten his prisoner, the Hessian chaplain, who, priest though he was, had given his captor the troublesome wound in his arm, having caught a bayonet from a fallen soldier to defend himself with, at the moment when all the royalists about him were making choice of the 'better part' of valor, and flying before the impetuous charge of the rebels. Yet this fiery representative of the church militant proved himself to be a very agreeable and well-informed person. He was not alone learned in church lore, but a man of general intelligence; and, though by 'poor carnal nature' more of a soldier than a priest, not wanting in refined religious feeling. De Vaudreuil, who, unlike most young Frenchmen of that period, had failed to imbibe atheistical principles, — who, if he did not feel, through his wild, passionate youth, the seal of the baptismal consecration on his brow, felt always the more sanctifying blessing his 'mother left there when she died,' and was, in his way, a devout Catholic, — fraternized with the priest on many points, and found him by no means an uninteresting companion.

But Onata was jealous of the black-coated stranger, whom she evidently considered as more of a conjurer than a true 'prophet,' and suspected, from his dark looks, and quiet, insinuating ways, of having more to do with the Evil than the Good Spirit.

Whenever he paid a visit to the quarters of the lieutenant, to see how his wound was getting on, and to repeat, as he never failed to do, his polite regrets that *he* should have been the cause of so much pain and weariness, Onata, after giving him a cold recognition, proudly withdrew; but at such times it is doubtful whether her little friends of the garrison found her a very lively playmate.

On the evening of the first day of the lieutenant's

leaving his room, he was sitting on the western wall of the fort — a rather perilous situation, which he loved for its coolness, and the wide view it gave him over the white tents of the encamped besiegers, and on the midsummer greenness of wood and field. Near him stood Onata, silent and quiet, idly playing with the fringe of her wampum belt. She was in a thoughtful, not to say sullen mood, this evening, because of the marked change in the manner of her friend toward her, since her last conversation with him. He was now constrained to coldness, or he treated her with the condescending kindness which one gives to a petted child. She felt wronged alike in her single-hearted devotion and womanly dignity; so she did what too many of the most highly-civilized of her sex would have done — put on an injured look, stood apart, and sulked. The lieutenant did not notice her at first; he was occupied in observing the Hessian priest, who had stationed himself on the bastion opposite, and was intently gazing toward the camp of St. Leger. Turning to his companion, he said,

'See that poor captive; how he looks away to his comrades! Are you not sorry for him?'

Now, Onata had her suspicions that the poor Hessian had in some way brought about that mysterious change in De Vaudreuil's manner, and, with a look and tone of dislike and resentment, as nearly approaching to hate and spite as she could give, she exclaimed,

'No! I hate him! He make long talks that I not understand; he steal your good thoughts away from me; he make you despise your poor Indian friend, and treat her like little child. I know him bad; — black clothes, black heart! Why you not send him back? Why you not *kill* him?'

As she hissed through her gleaming teeth the last, for her, most unnaturally cruel suggestion, a strange thrill of pleasure shot through the heart of Maurice at an evidence of such passionate womanly jealousy on the part of one whom he had vainly been schooling himself for the last twenty-four hours to consider a mere child, a wild elf of the woods. But the next moment he remembered his virtuous resolution, and, assuming a displeased and shocked expression, he called her a 'wicked, vindictive little savage,' and sternly desired her never again to speak to him in that manner.

Onata did not attempt anything like conciliation, but stepped further off from him, and stood for some moments silent and immovable, with folded arms, proudly looking away over the forest, in the direction of her Indian home.

She longed, with a wild, bitter longing, to escape — to bury herself in the depths of the dark wilderness, and die. No! she would go back to Gahaneh, and let her make her hard and stern like herself; and when Garanguli solicited her again, she would go with him to his wigwam, and be savage with the rest. When her brave should go upon the war-path, she would tell him to kill every false Frenchman he met. No — to spare *one* always, and to tell him that Onata commanded mercy to be shown to one who had been very cruel to her. Then *he* would be sorry he had rebuked her so harshly, and called her hard names.

As though her wild thoughts had evoked him from

the earth or air, Onata suddenly saw, down before her, a little way beyond the wall, peering through a thick clump of bushes, the dark, fierce face of her Indian lover! His eyes were fixed with savage eagerness upon the young French officer, now standing and regarding with curious interest his beautiful *protegée*, over whose face lowered and lightened a sudden storm of wild passions before unknown to her gentle heart. Thus absorbed, Maurice saw not the ominous object that had arrested her wandering eyes; he was unprepared for the shriek which rung suddenly from her lips, for the quick leap to his side, and terrified flinging of her arms about him. But the next instant a sharp whistling through the air, and the quivering of an arrow in that delicate shoulder, told him all. She had flung herself upon him as a shield! she had saved him from death!

She had indeed saved him, but not, as he at first feared, at the sacrifice of her own life; for the Indian, though he had seen her purpose, too late to spare her wholly, had so relaxed his bow-string that the arrow sped with comparatively little force. It was easily extracted, and as it proved not to have been poisoned, no more serious consequences followed than a copious bleeding, and some slight inflammation and lameness, for which the sufferer was pitied and petted by the ladies of the fort to a degree that was more embarrassing than pleasing to the modest, simple-hearted girl. As for the 'heroism' for which she was praised by all the garrison, she shrank from having so lofty a name applied to an act so natural and involuntary. De Vaudreuil's first alarm and grief for her, and his few after words of loving thanks, spoken in a voice tremulous with emotion, were reward enough, and more than enough, for her. She wished that no one else would ever speak of it; she almost resented any further mention of it, even from him.

But, as may be supposed, the event made a deep impression upon the heart of the romantic and chivalrous Maurice. He saw in the impulsive, self-forgetful act of the simple Indian maiden, the purest and most heroic womanly devotion which poetry could chronicle, or love immortalize.

'With education, and judicious religious culture, what a glorious creature she would become!' he exclaimed, to himself. 'She is God's child now — God's cherished and blessed child — beautiful, and pure, and noble. Who dare despise her from the height of an accidental and corrupt civilization?'

In this state of feeling the impulsive young enthusiast was not long in coming to a decision. There seemed to him but one just and honorable course to pursue.

'The poor child loves me,' he said; 'and, by the joy that comes to my heart with that conviction, do I know that I love her. God has given into my care this tender flower of the forest. For some wise purpose, he has made her so infinitely dear to my heart. I must be her protector, her guide, her teacher — almost her Providence.'

In short, he resolved to make Onata his lawful wife — but by a secret marriage, for fear of the disapprobation of his friend and guardian, the Marquis de Lafayette, and the more serious displeasure of his stern father, who, he felt little doubt, would haughtily disown him, on being made abruptly acquainted with such a singular *mésalliance.* His plan was to carefully conceal the connection until the close of the war; then to take Onata with him to France, in as private a manner as possible, and there place her in a convent, for the completion of her education. Then, when mentally and socially prepared for so great a change of condition, he would reveal her existence to his father and family, and, by arguments and entreaties, prevail upon them to receive her as his wife.

It is true, stern reason and homely common sense whispered that this was a rash, boyish plan, full of difficulties, if not perils, and likely to bring him into absurd dilemmas and serious embarrassments; but the prudent suggestions of these honest monitors were silenced by the louder and more eager prompting of manly generosity, romance, and passion. It is true, something of dismay came over him as he mentally contrasted that untamed, unsophisticated child of nature with the fair and stately 'dames of high degree' whom he had seen on his presentation at court. But, when his imagination painted Onata in the maturity of her rich, peculiar beauty, with all the added graces of a refined civilization, arrayed in gorgeous brocade and costly jewels, his proud heart assured him that she would outshine and out-queen them all.

The mere *mésalliance* had no terrors for him. A dependent younger son, simple and poetical in his tastes, and in general indolent in his habits, he had been, even at home, very little of an aristocrat, or man of the world; and, on his hearty espousal of the cause of American independence, had speedily become imbued with the liberal and democratic principles, towards which he was by nature so strongly inclined.

And yet, when, on the morning succeeding his escape from the fate intended for him by his jealous rival, he asked Onata to be his wife, he was scarcely satisfied by the flush and light of maidenly joy which his words brought to her face, and with her simple, undeprecating consent. She expressed neither wonder nor gratitude; she evidently had no sense of sacrifice or condescension on the part of her lover. He, however, soon reconciled himself to her quiet manner of receiving his proposals, by remembering her small knowledge of the social distinctions of civilization, and her own sense of dignity, as the daughter of a native prince.

She seemed troubled, at first, by the proposal of a secret marriage, asking if it would not be 'doing a lie.' But De Vaudreuil by a few words of explanation having convinced her that any other course might do him harm, love and trust soon got the victory over her truthful and delicate instincts, and she consented, solemnly pledging herself to secrecy, till such time as he, in his better judgment, should see fit to reveal their relationship to the world.

We must now return to the siege of the fort, which, during this time, had been steadily but most ineffectually carried on. The besiegers had prevented any true account of the battle of Oriskany from reaching the garrison, but had boasted to them of the total destruction of the rebel force engaged in that action. They continued to send their white flags to Colonel Gansevoort, with threatening messages, and insolent recommendations to surrender at discretion. But all these pompous proposals and solemn warnings had only the effect to fix more firmly than ever the resolve of the stout-hearted patriots to defend their fortress to the last.

The cannon of the enemy had no effect upon the solid sod-work of the fort. But at length they formed a project of sapping and mining, and commenced operations somewhat alarming to even the bravest soldiers in the garrison.

The situation of the besiged was daily becoming more critical. Should reinforcements arrive to the enemy, the siege would doubtless be prosecuted with irresistible vigor; or, should it continue as now, their own ammunition and provisions would soon be exhausted, and they reduced to the necessity of an unconditional surrender — without the poor choice of starvation, or a reasonable hope of escaping a revengeful massacre. In this extremity, it was resolved that a message should be sent to Fort Dayton, imploring immediate aid. The duty of conveying this message was one of absolutely appalling danger; yet two young officers, Colonel Willett and Lieutenant Stockwell, with more than Roman devotion, volunteered to execute it. They stole out of the fort on the night of the tenth of August, in the midst of a violent thunder-storm, crept on their hands and knees to the river, which they crossed on a log, and made their way past the Indian camp, through entangled forests and treacherous morasses, and down the beds of dark streams, hiding by day, and travelling by night, until the evening of the twelfth, when they reached Fort Dayton in safety.

They there heard that General Schuyler was already in communication with General Arnold, in devising means for the relief of the besieged. The latter officer did not arrive at Fort Dayton, with the troops under his command, until the twentieth. He had intended to await at this point the arrival of the Massachusetts brigade, under General Larned, as his own force was too inconsiderable to warrant an engagement with the army of St. Leger, Johnson, and Brant. But, on learning the extremely critical situation of the garrison, he concocted a very clever and remarkable stratagem, which proved successful beyond his highest hopes.

Among the tory prisoners lately taken with the notorious Walter Butler was a very singular personage, half knave, half idiot, named Hon-Yost Schuyler. He was condemned to death: but, at the almost frenzied entreaties of his mother,—a strange, powerful, gypsy-like woman,—General Arnold consented to spare his life, on condition that he should go to the camp of St. Leger, and so alarm him and his allies, by stories of the strong force of the Americans coming against them, as to cause them to raise the siege, and retreat from Fort Stanwix.

It seemed a hard task to set such a poor, witless fellow; but, with that fearless confidence full as often belonging to folly as to genius, he cheerfully undertook it. He left his brother in his place, General Arnold having refused the eager offer of his mother to remain in confinement as a hostage for her 'uncanny' son. Then, after having several bullets fired through his clothes, as proofs of the story he was about to tell, he set out for Fort Stanwix with a friendly Oneida, who promised to assist him.

As they neared the camp, they separated. Hon-Yost entered first, and, running breathless and trembling into the midst of the Indians, to many of whom he was known as a sturdy tory, he told them that he had made a marvellous escape from the rebels, who were fast approaching the camp, in number like the leaves on the trees. He said that, as he was flying before them to warn his friends, he was repeatedly shot at; and he pointed, with a horrified look, to the unmistakable bullet-holes in his dilapidated garments as 'dumb witnesses' to the truth of his story.

The Indians had been for some time sullen and dissatisfied. Their great loss at the battle of Oriskany, and their long waiting before the fort, had disheartened and disgusted them. At the moment of Hon-Yost's appearance, they happened to be holding a solemn pow-wow, for the purpose of consulting Manitou as to the course which they should pursue. They received, or pretended to receive, the alarming tidings which he brought as an answer to their prayers and incantations, and resolved upon immediate flight. When they announced their sudden determination to St. Leger, he sent for Hon-Yost, and gave him a severe cross-examination; but the rogue stuck to his story with cunning pertinacity, assuring the general that Arnold would shortly be upon him, with an army of full three thousand men.

In the mean time, the friendly Oneida, with two or three Indians of his tribe, whom he had encountered on his way, appeared in opposite directions, and gave similar and even more alarming accounts. A perfect panic spread through the entire Indian camp. It was in vain that St. Leger threatened, and stormed, and promised. They shrugged their shoulders and laughed at his anger; they scorned his bribes; they even sternly waved away his proffered 'fire-water;' fly they would, and fly they did.

This panic was speedily communicated to the remainder of the royalist army, who also took flight, with the utmost precipitancy and confusion, leaving behind them their tents, artillery, camp-equipage, colors, baggage, and in many instances flinging away their knapsacks and arms, that they might run the better from their imaginary foes.

A most unlooked-for and unaccountable sight to the garrison was this sudden and panic-stricken breaking up of the besieging host, which happened just as some of the bravest among them were falling into despair, and the heroic Colonel Gansevoort was forming the desperate resolution to sally forth at night, and cut his way through the enemy's camp.

The dispersion of the besiegers occurred on the twenty-third, but not until the twenty-fifth did Arnold arrive at the fort. Both he and Colonel Gansevoort had already sent detachments after the enemy, and taken some prisoners and considerable spoil; but fear has more speed, if less 'bottom,' than duty, and by far the greater number of the fugitives were beyond the reach of pursuit, on their way toward Canada.

A few days later, De Vaudreuil's prisoner, the Hessian chaplain, was placed under the care of a faithful Indian guard, and sent after his friends; but not until he had united in marriage his generous captor and 'the little demi-savage,' as he called Onata, in a manner so strictly private that not a soul in the garrison suspected the occurrence, save the one witness to the ceremony, an honest old soldier, who had taken a great fancy to both the young Frenchman and the handsome Indian girl, and in his simplicity could see no possible objection to their union.

After all that Lieutenant Maurice had seen of Onata, he was agreeably surprised by the beautiful propriety and dignity with which she bore herself throughout this ceremony. He had been half afraid that she would disgrace herself before the accomplished and cynical chaplain, by some savage awkwardness or childish freak. He trembled when placing on her finger a jewelled ring which he was obliged to use for want of a plainer one, with a foolish fear that she would betray the natural delight of an Indian woman at the sight of a pretty bauble. But she went through with her part with a chastened pride and a half-*naïve*, half-solemn earnestness, more likely to impress the beholder to tears than provoke him to smiles. She scarcely glanced at the ring, at first; but De Vaudreuil afterwards found that she received it not only as a sacred symbol, but in all its poetic significance. When, an hour or two later, after taking leave of the Hessian priest, he sought his bride, he found her sitting quietly alone, attentively regarding her ring. Smiling, and speaking very softly, as though unconsciously thinking aloud, she said, touching the sparkling stones:

'Pretty little stars! how they light my heart with *love-shine!'*

Then, turning the ring on her finger, she added,

'It have no end — no end! It like God's life!

More than satisfied,—joyful, loving, proud,—Maurice bent over her, and murmured for the first time into her ear the name alike grateful to the princess and the peasant — ever sweet and sacred to the woman who loves — the new name, '*Wife.*'

CHAPTER IV.

SEPARATION.

Why art thou so far away from me?
I have whispered it unto the southern wind,
And charged it with my love : why should it not
Carry that love to thee, as air bears light?

My thoughts are happier oft than I,
For they are ever, love, with thee ;
And thine, I know, as frequent fly,
O'er all that severs us, to me ;
Like rays of stars that meet in space,
And mingle in a bright embrace.

FESTUS.

A SHORT time after the sudden and unprecedented termination of the siege, recorded in the last chapter of our story, the Oneida sachem Sadewana and his haughty elder daughter appeared at the fort to reclaim their hostage.

Now always meek and trustful in the full assurance of her happy love, Onata was easily persuaded by her husband to return quietly to her father's lodge, and there to remain, faithfully guarding their secret, until the close of the war, which his sanguine spirit told him would be at no distant period; or till some fortunate change in his own circumstances should give him the power to claim her, and remove her from her wild home and rude natural guardians. This seemed the only prudent and practicable course to be pursued. As we have seen, he dared not as yet acknowledge her as his wife; and to take her about with him in a less honorable character would, he knew, besides being a great wrong to her, create a scandal unendurable in the respectable and somewhat puritanical American army, and be certain to bring upon his head the serious displeasure of his beloved friend and noble commander, Lafayette.

In parting from Onata, the young soldier hung about her neck an enamelled gold cross, not alone as a pretty love-token, nor even as a secret *gage* to take the place of the wedding-ring, which she would be obliged to conceal during their separation, but as a sacred symbol of the religious faith which, since the hour of their friendly intimacy, he had been zealously and not vainly seeking to impart to her.

To take away the appearance of any particular meaning in bestowing this gift, Maurice also presented his savage father-in-law with a handsome rifle and a generous supply of ammunition, and courteously proffered to Gahaneh a necklace of red and white coral and gold beads, saying that he had brought it from his own country as a fitting offering for some noble native princess, such as now stood before him. It was an ornament which many a fair dame would have been well pleased to wear; yet Gahaneh, deigning but one glance upon it, waved it away with a look and gesture of more than queenly scorn — the contempt of a stern, strong, *manly* woman for all mere feminine gauds and trinkets. But, on seeing the expression of disappointment and confusion that overspread the fine frank face of the young soldier, her innate sense of courtesy was touched, and with a slightly softened voice, and a cold smile flickering for an instant about her firm lips, she said, half-haughtily, half-deprecatingly,

'Me no like such things — me no *girl*. Me rather have the little knife in your belt.'

The 'little knife' was an antique dagger, with a curious, jewelled hilt, and a veritable Damascus blade, and valued as a family relic far more than for its intrinsic worth. De Vaudreuil inwardly winced at the demand, and anathematized the unfeminine fancy of the Amazon; but both gallantry and policy forbade him to hesitate, and he made the little sacrifice with the best grace and the best face possible.

Gahaneh drew the blade from its sheath, and eyed its sharp point and keen edge with much apparent satisfaction. She did not appear to notice the elaborate chasing of the gold handle, but seemed struck by a large diamond set in the end. Pointing to this, she said to the lieutenant, with a grim smile, more terrible on her face than the blackest frown,

'It make much light, so me see to strike straight in the dark.'

After having returned the dagger to its sheath and thrust it into her girdle, she condescended to thank the giver with a half-propitiated graciousness of manner, and a momentary unknitting of her haughty brows.

It is scarcely necessary to say that the *real* parting of De Vaudreuil and his young wife did not take place on this occasion. On the preceding day they had been apprised by an Indian runner of the coming of Sadewana, and knew that the dreaded separation was at hand. Late that night they had taken a solemn and tender leave of one another, pledging themselves to be constant in love and patient in waiting till the happy day of their reünion.

They parted now without the evidence of anything more than friendly feeling — De Vaudreuil's fear of the discovery of his secret overmastering all softer emotions, while Onata, meekly taking her tone from him, and bringing into exercise somĕthing of the stoicism of her Indian training, betrayed nothing of the keen sorrow and desolate sinking of her heart, even to the jealous eyes of her sister.

The garrison were all sorry to lose their playful and graceful pet, their 'little brownie,' their 'young fawn,' their 'wild singing-bird,' as they called the beautiful Oneida. The officers' wives embraced her, and the children crowded around her to the last, protesting that she 'should not go back into the great gloomy woods, among the cruel wild Indians, and bears, and *painters!* She was,' they said, 'only the least bit in the world of a savage herself; she was most like white folks; if she would stay with them and be made a Christian of, maybe she would bleach out by and by, and God would let her into heaven for a white girl when she died.'

Onata only shook her head sadly in reply to these entreaties, and pointed to her father and sister, who were waiting impatiently for her near the sally-port of the fortress. From one pertinacious little pet, the fair-haired child who had most joyfully welcomed her on her coming to the fort a few weeks previous, she now had a slight struggle to disengage herself. As she strove to unclasp his little arms from her neck, her calmness suddenly forsook her, and, laying her face against the bosom of the boy, she burst into tears. The child was surprised and touched, and began in his simple way to comfort her, little suspecting for whom those tears were really shed. Then *he* stepped forward and addressed a few words to her in an earnest under-tone, and in an instant she stood up strong and bright again, smiling around upon all her friends a silent last adieu, but most kindly upon *him*. She even bent to give a gentle word and a farewell pat to Captain Gregg's gallant dog, who was always to be found wherever there was anything going on, a grave but not unsympathizing spectator.

Lieutenant de Vaudreuil stood on the south-western bastion watching the Indian party on their homeward trail, while they crossed the partly-cleared plain that intervened between the fort and the primitive forest. Just as they reached the borders of the wood, Onata, who walked last in the 'Indian file,' turned for the first time, and waved her hand toward the fort, toward *him*, with a gesture at once mournful and tender. In another moment the fluttering sprays of flowering shrubbery and the long waving branches of leafy trees seemed to have reached forth and caught her eagerly from his sight.

The forest had reclaimed her child.

A short time after this parting, Lieutenant de Vaudreuil left Fort Stanwix, rejoined Lafayette, and entered upon active service, in the duties and excitements of which he soon ceased to feel his first sense of deprivation and loneliness, and forgot his sorrow, if not his sylvan bride. He never failed, however, whenever a faithful messenger could be obtained, to send gifts and assurances of remembrance to Onata, and he sometimes received a kind word and some token of thoughtful affection from her.

Once, on the arrival of *Nihorontagowa*, or 'Great Tree,' a friendly Seneca chief, at the American camp, on a visit to General Washington, he was very pompously presented with 'a letter from the daughter of the Oneida sachem, Sadewana.'

The 'letter' proved to be composed simply of a few of the French words Maurice had taught his wife, linked together according to the loving and poetic instinct of her heart, rather than rules of sense or construction, and faintly scrawled with a pencil on a fly-leaf of a prayer-book which he had given her; but they breathed the soul of her artless faith and childlike affection. They ran thus:

'*Mon cher ami. Mon bon soldat. Aimez-moi toujours. Comment-vous portez-vous? Je suis triste. L'amour. La Sainte Vierge. Dieu!*

'ONATA.'

'Great-Tree' had stopped on his way at Oneida Castle, and been entertained at the lodge of Sadewana, and to him, as a chief of known honor, Onata had ventured privately to intrust her curious *billet-doux*.

Never was the most dainty and elaborate love-missive, coming rose-tinted from the fair fingers of a noble dame to the eager hands of a gallant knight, and brought by Cupid's own postman, the carrier-dove, more joyfully welcomed, or more sacredly treasured, than was this same hesitating, almost illegible scrawl, by that rash, ardent, loyal heart. Though not without real passion, and even depth,

De Vaudreuil's love was essentially romantic and fanciful. He suffered little from the peculiar position in which he was placed in regard to Onata; — he rather liked the singularity, the mystery, even the concealment, of his marriage. He pleased himself with idly speculating upon obstacles and embarrassments which would have roused a profounder nature, and painfully worn upon more delicate sensibilities, than his. Even his forced separation from his young wife scarcely troubled him, — except that it *was* forced. He loved to think of Onata as safely cloistered away from the world, faithfully nurturing in holy solitude the germs of knowledge and religious truth which he had planted in her rich nature, and hiving up for him the first summer sweetness of her pure virginal heart.

There were times when he shrank, with a strange misgiving, almost a sense of wrong-doing, from the thought of removing her from her native wilds. Would she not, like a forest-flower, coming up with so glad and brave a beauty in its sheltered woodland haunts, shrink, and pale, and die, in the cold, hard, stranger soil of form and fashion? Would not her happy young life, which hitherto had run its quiet, shadowed course, like a forest stream weaving a thread of silver through the dark greenness of deepest shade, cheering with sweet laughter the loneliest glens, — would it not lose its pleasant murmur in the noise of the world, and waste away under the full glare of its pitiless sky?

Onata was just one of those beings who must have given to the poet and artist the idea of

'A Nymph, a Naiad, or a Grace.'

Her freedom, her naturalness, her bloom, and delicate vigor, were such as only could be found in those hidden primeval solitudes wherein seem to linger still the first dewy freshness, and the clear, untainted air, of the world's morning. Or she seemed a vestal, — a gentle priestess of nature, and the great forest, with its grand arches and dark majestic columns, the temple in which she should serve. Although, as we have seen, her heart yearned mysteriously toward the customs, the beliefs, and hopes, of her mother's people, her vitality, her form, the spirit of her physical life, seemed essentially derived from and peculiarly in harmony with the wild and primitive scenes in which she was born. Her complexion had the rich summer glow of the sunlight in open glades, and the soft shadows of autumnal leaves; her motion was like the undulating wave of grain and long grass in the wind, and the graceful yielding and elastic rebound of lithe branches; her modesty was the shyness of hidden violets, and her smile like the silent laughter of a bank of wild daisies, moved to mirth by a frolicsome breeze. Flowers, birds, trees, clouds, waves, waterfalls, sunbeams, stars, snow-flakes, showers, were infinitely more to her than to the most poetic or learned of her civilized sisters; they were companions, friends, monitors, thought-inspirers, life-givers and ministers of exquisite delight. Every day she participated in the 'dawn-joy' of the world, revelled in its sunset splendors, and was subdued to reverential quiet by its solemn midnight show. Her eyes had a sweet, brimming light, as unlike that of the bright, wandering eyes that have looked upon and been looked into by the world, as the clear, concentrated beaming of rare stars, peering through the thick interlaced foliage of pathless woods, seems to the restless twinkle of indistinguishable orbs, which swim in wastes of light over crowded towns. There was in them not only an affluence of brightness, but an unstirred depth of soul, which it hardly seemed possible could belong to them with other than their native surroundings.

Yet, though there might be something unnatural and perilous in translating a being like this into a life so utterly strange and foreign, the rash lover could not hesitate as to his final course, knowing that she must become *inured* to civilization, or that he must descend at least to a condition of semi-barbarism; for, linked indissolubly together for good or evil fortune, in soul as well as in name, he felt that they two were — felt it all the more deeply and solemnly for this separation, in spite of his fanciful and philosophical speculations, and soldierly *insouciance.*

Lieutenant de Vaudreuil accompanied the army of Washington to the winter encampment at Valley Forge, and manfully bore his part in the perils and hardships which there awaited the devoted patriots and their generous allies. This severe winter was the darkest period of the Revolution. Even to the bravest and most sanguine spirits it was cheered by few successes and illumined by few lights of hope, while it shut down upon the fearful and disheartened like a long, drear Arctic night of tempest, gloom, and despair.

But the weary months wore on with the young soldier until midwinter, when he was made happy by being selected by Lafayette to accompany him on an expedition against Canada, to the command of which the marquis had been appointed by Congress, under the title of 'General of the Northern Army.'

Early in February, 1778, the noble marquis set out for Albany, where it was promised he should find a force of twenty-five hundred men, well armed and equipped, awaiting his orders. He was accompanied by twenty French officers; for he was resolved that the conquest of 'New France' should be owing, in great part, to French valor and enthusiasm.

They made their way through storm and snow, through pathless forests, and over frozen floods, to Albany, to have their brave hearts, which tempests could not subdue, nor the utmost rigors of winter dismay, baffled by a mean breach of faith, and chilled by a bitter disappointment. To his grief and mortification, the ambitious and high-spirited marquis found that he had been most dishonorably dealt with by Congress, who, in giving him this important commission, had, as he then little suspected, been influenced by jealousy of General Washington, to whom a slight was intended; the success of the undertaking, and the wishes and fame of the young French commander, being matters of much less moment in their eyes.

Instead of the respectable and efficient force promised him, Lafayette found at the *rendezvous* barely twelve hundred men, and they, for the most part, 'too naked for even a summer campaign.' In short, the chivalric young soldier, panting for action and distinction, was compelled utterly to abandon an undertaking which promised so much of both. All his disappointments, all his privations, all his unprecedented sacrifices, were as nothing compared to this forced surrender of his great heroic hope. He felt, in the bitterness of his first chagrin, that a cloud of unmerited disgrace hung over him ; and not only over him, but that it would reach to his old-world home, there to sadden loving hearts, and darken his name forever. Yet his generous devotion to the cause of American freedom seems not to have been shaken by this occurrence. He seems rather to have labored on afterwards with a subdued ambition and greater singleness of purpose, in a more endearing and disciple-like companionship with Washington.

During this visit of Lafayette to the north, Congress, resolving to make one more effort at conciliating the Six Nations, invited them all to a grand council, which was held at Johnstown, on the ninth of March. At the invitation of General Schuyler the marquis attended, and took part in the negotiations.

There were present at this council, which was meant to be a general gathering, but about eight hundred Indians, including women and children. This number was composed of Onondagas, Oneidas, Tuscaroras, a few Mohawks, and only three or four Cayugas. No Senecas deigned to appear ; they would not bury the tomahawk long enough. On the contrary, they sent a bold and angry message, saying that 'they were surprised that, while the tomahawks of the whites were yet sticking in their heads, their wounds were still bleeding, and their eyes streaming with tears for the loss of their friends at the battle of Oriskany, the commissioners should dare to invite them to a treaty.' It was evident that they meditated the terrible vengeance which a little later they wreaked upon all the settlements of the frontier, when valley after valley rung with their war-whoops and the shrieks of their victims, and the midnight sky again and again reflected the hell of their insatiable ferocity, in fires at the stake, and the blaze of burning homes.

An old Onondaga chief spoke in behalf of the tribes who had broken faith. He exculpated the venerable leading men, and laid all the blame on the hot-headed, rebellious young warriors, who despised alike their authority and their counsels, and were tempted into bad faith and bloody deeds by the flattery and bribery of the royalists. Young men, he said, were not what they used to be; in these degenerate times, the wisdom and experience of old age availed little against red-coats and fire-water.

The Oneida sachem Sadewana spoke very eloquently for his own nation and the Tuscaroras; promising that they would, through all things, hold fast to the covenant-chain which bound them to their white brothers; enjoy with them the fruits of victory and peace, or be buried with them in the same grave.

Here a cynical young Mohawk chief cried out, with a bitter laugh,

'They no let you lie there, you poor Indian dogs! — *they kick you out!*'

Lafayette distributed among the savages, friendly and disaffected, some gay stuffs and trinkets, and a few *louis-d'ors* in the form of medals; but these and the presents of the commissioners, though received with a decent degree of graciousness, produced little effect, after the more gaudy and bounteous gifts of the English. However, a treaty of strict neutrality was again entered into, and the conference broke up with the utmost apparent good feeling and good faith.

Our hero, De Vaudreuil, had looked forward to this council with peculiar interest, hoping to meet there Onata, with her father and sister; and he was not disappointed. On his first entering the council-chamber, and anxiously glancing over the dusky crowd, *her* soft, startled, beaming eyes struck upon him, from out of a multitude of fierce, sombre, or vacant orbs, fixed in sullen defiance, or rolling in stupid wonder; *her* sweet face met his gaze, flushed with the glow of a joyful surprise, and the sudden overflow of feeling so long imprisoned in her heart—more marvellously beautiful, noble, and ingenuous, than ever, among all those stolid and embruted faces, those cunning counterfeits, those stony masks of humanity.

The venerable sachem was accompanied not only by his daughters, but by his friend and *protegé* the young chief Garanguli. The presence of the latter, who stood scowling at him with the bitterest enmity, and jealously watching his every movement, did not, it is true, add materially to the young officer's comfort; but, with *her* tender, appealing eyes stealing frequent glances at him, and her somewhat wan and faded cheek flushing under every look of his, nothing could trouble or alarm him seriously; nothing could vex or depress his heart, steeped anew in the joy of love's perfect assurance, exalted with new ardors of romance and passion.

In spite of the difficulties, and even perils, that surrounded them, these lovers found opportunities for meeting, to renew their vows of love and fidelity, and strive to form some plan for their future union. That some change must be made in Onata's condition, De Vaudreuil was convinced by the troubled and hesitating account given by her of the pertinacious solicitations to which she was subjected by her Indian lover, Garanguli. The suit of this young brave was favored by the old sachem, who had long looked upon him as his future son-in-law; and by Gahaneh, who was passionately desirous that her sister should marry a chief of pure Indian blood, though she felt some contempt for the predilections toward civilization and the 'Christian notions' which this youth held in common with her degenerate father. She saw that she had already gained considerable power over him, by her alliance, and the natural force of her stern, masculine character; and she was not without her hopes of strengthening that power by more familiar intercourse — of drawing him back into the brave old barbaric ways, and hardening him into a good heathen at last.

Onata confessed that she had been greatly annoyed and troubled by the young chief's persistent suit; as he and her sister gave her no respite from their solicitations and arguments, and even her indulgent father had turned a deaf ear to her objections and entreaties, and sternly warned her that at the next harvest-feast he should give her to the husband to whom she had so long been promised; that she must then go with him to his lodge, to grind his corn and cook his venison for the remainder of her days.

As Onata concluded this account of the domestic persecutions she had been called upon to endure, De Vaudreuil drew her closely to him, with a quick, jealous embrace, and sat for some moments in deep and silent thought. At last his face brightened out of its cloud of vexation and perplexity, and assumed an expression of relief and decided resolve. He had formed a plan, somewhat wild and desperate even in his eyes, but scarcely the less attractive on that account to his adventurous, boyish spirit. It happened that he had met his friend Colonel Willett at the council, and been cordially invited by him to return to Fort Stanwix, and spend a few weeks or months at that fortress, where he was most kindly and pleasantly remembered. He had little doubt of obtaining his general's consent to his leaving, should he express to him a wish to accept this invitation, as the marquis had about him more young French officers than he could find honorable employment for in those days of difficulties and discouragements. That consent gained, the lieutenant's plan was to return to the fort with his friend, and when there endeavor to obtain possession of one of the small farm-houses in the vicinity, long since abandoned by the terrified or disaffected owners. To this he would secretly bring his young wife, provide her with all the home-comforts it might be in his power to obtain, and place over her a guard of Oneidas, whose fidelity he would insure by kindness, confidence, gifts, and generous pay.

In the then quiet condition of the country about

Fort Stanwix, there seemed little danger to be apprehended to either of the lovers in this plan for providing the persecuted bride with a temporary sanctuary; while to both it promised too much of happiness in the opportunities it would afford for reünion, or, rather, frequent meetings, for its difficulties and perils to be very seriously regarded. With love-blind rashness, that would give no thought to the future, Maurice proposed it; and with the simplicity of trust and inexperience Onata joyfully consented, promising the utmost courage and prudence in making her escape from the Oneida village to join her husband, whenever he should come or send for her.

The next morning the council broke up, and the Indians and commissioners went their several ways; many parting to meet but once again, and then in deadly conflict, in desperate hand-to-hand encounters, in massacres and burnings.

Before the departure of Sadewana with his party, De Vaudreuil sought a private interview with him, and it may be supposed, from the old sachem's subsequent indifference to, if not connivance at, the young officer's relations with his daughter, confided to him, under promise of secrecy, the fact of his clandestine marriage with Onata, and gave him satisfactory assurances of honorable intentions for the future. Certain it is that they parted with the appearance of perfect kindliness and good understanding — a happy state of feeling, with which the transfer of a well-filled purse from the pocket of the lieutenant to the pouch of the sachem may have had something to do. It were scarcely a reflection upon the aboriginal character were we to suppose that it had *all* to do with the obtaining of his favor, and that the young Frenchman's secret was still hidden in his own breast. I have seen Indians far more advanced in civilization than Sadewana,—many an one who has been induced by the 'talk of the good teachers' to abjure the 'old Adam' of barbarism, renounce his grand savage patronymic for some mean-sounding but sanctified name,

'Get him a coat and breeches,
And look like a Christian man.'—

I have seen some become cleanly, orderly, industrious, and temperate; I have even heard of one who, under an especial gift of grace, was known to carry his wife's pappoose for her when she was ill, and to give over beating her when she was well; but I have never yet known an Indian arrive at such a sublime point of virtue as to look with righteous contempt on the 'filthy lucre' of this world. All our preaching, and, strange to say, all our example, have failed to bring him up to this.

As Maurice had anticipated, his good friend the marquis made no decided objection to his plan of paying a second visit to the lonely frontier fort, though he expressed some surprise at the singular wish. He consented with a smile, and an expressive shrug, saying:

'*Chacun à son gout; mais je n'aime ni les forets, ni les sauvages, moi.*'

De Vaudreuil blushed at this chance shot, but, turning to Colonel Willett, and laying a hand on his sturdy shoulders, he replied, in his somewhat imperfect English,

'Ah, my dear general forget; I shall have de best

of society, de bravest of men, de most *patriotique* and *heroique* of women, and, if it please to God, some good fighting at the fort.'

Lafayette laughed, took a pinch of snuff, shook hands with his eccentric young countryman and the brave American officer, sprang into his sleigh, and set out on his return to Albany.

CHAPTER V.

THE SANCTUARY.—THE RIVALS.

They were alone once more: for them to be
  Thus, was another Eden; they were never
Weary, unless when separate; the tree
  Cut from its forest root of years, the river
Dammed from its fountain, the child from the knee
  And breast maternal weaned forever,
Would wither less than these two torn apart;
Alas! there is no instinct like the heart! BYRON.

'Men of all countries,' says Sir James Mackintosh, 'appear to be more alike in their best qualities than the pride of civilization would be willing to allow.'

MORE than two months had gone by since the great council at Johnstown; and, though there were rumors of preparations being made by Brant, the Butlers, and the governor of Canada, for an extensive and destructive campaign against the frontier forts and settlements, all was peace and tranquillity around Fort Stanwix, along Wood Creek and the Mohawk river, the scenes of some of the most important movements of the preceding year. No sound now broke the forest echoes, that had so often given back the roll of musketry, the thunder of ordnance, and the menacing yells of infuriated savages, save the occasional shout and rifle-shot of peaceful hunters, and the morning and evening gun of the fort.

The only savages that now presented themselves

before the walls were Oneidas, and they not as besiegers, but as friends, and sometimes as secret or open allies.

The children climbed and played about the parapets and bastions, and the women strolled or sat upon the ramparts in pleasant evenings, indulging in comfortable, home-like gossip, 'with none to molest or make afraid.'

But both officers and men wearied of the monotony and inactivity of this life, and were almost ready to welcome a second army of besiegers. De Vaudreuil was the only one among the younger officers who expressed a quiet, philosophic spirit of patience and satisfaction. Yet even he, of late, was not content to remain constantly immured in the fort, but every day went out sporting, hunting, or fishing, in the neighboring forest, alone, or accompanied solely by a lank Indian hound, a stray cur who had obstinately attached himself to him on his first arrival at the fort, and had finally, for his very forlornness and persistency, been taken into favor.

These strange and rash proceedings of the lieutenant excited much surprise, and called forth some remonstrances from his friends, at first; but the reserve and dignity of his bearing soon silenced even the most familiar and privileged among them, till finally no one presumed to question or comment upon his out-goings or in-comings, and his secret — for it was surmised that he had one — was courteously respected. The men, however, would occasionally laugh among themselves at the worse than indifferent success which attended his expeditions, when, after days ostensibly spent with his fowling-piece or rod, he would return with perhaps a squirrel and a pheasant or two, from woods alive with game, — or a little string of very 'small fry,' from streams well stocked with the most respectable trout.

De Vaudreuil usually took a southern, eastern, or western direction from the fort; but, could his dog have been questioned in the canine dialect, he might have testified, had he chosen to inform, that his master invariably changed his course after reaching the woods, and marched rapidly northward, making a wide circuit of the fort to avoid observation.

We will take the liberty of following his steps on one of these solitary and eccentric excursions.

It was a delicious morning in the latter part of May, a month this year so unseasonably warm that it almost seemed that June had stolen into her sister's place, and was coaxing out verdure and bloom before their time. The river reflected the bluest of skies, and sparkled with sun-kissed ripples; the young grass of the glades and the foliage of shrub and tree waved in a light west wind, and their delicate green glistened through the tears of an early shower.

The woods were not yet dense and dim with the lush luxuriance of summer; the frolic sunbeams strayed, danced, and glinted, in every direction, wooing the flowers and drawing sweet responses from their inmost hearts, sliding on wet leaves, sleeping on mossy banks, sounding pebbly brooks, welcoming the up gush of springs and crowning cascades with rainbows. Everywhere murmured and fluttered the happy insect-life; the audible joy of birds overflowed the wood, and on the soft, still air could be perceived by a delicate sense, not only the fragrance of a thousand wild-flowers, but the subtler perfume of unfolding leaves. It was one of those mornings, all life and beauty, which almost cheat one into the belief that he can measure by his senses the growth and perfecting of things about him from moment to moment; when he takes all low, vague noises for the sounds of Nature's mysterious labors; when he watches the brightening of the wild-rose under her invisible pencil, and half fancies he has detected the cunning secret of her alchemy in turning the pale-green buds of the dandelion into coin-like shapes of shining gold, which gleam up from the grass as though a prince had passed by and scattered largess with a bounteous hand.

But, I am sorry to say, my hero made little pause amid all this loveliness, beguiled by choice bits of forest scenery, or beset by poetic fancies. It was evident that he had ears that heard not and eyes that saw not the woodland sounds and scenes around him. He sprang over singing brooks, broke through tender shrubbery, trampled on moss and flowers, and only felt the *spirit* of that beautiful morning pervading his happy thoughts, and steeping his heart in the balm of perfect peace.

As usual, after reaching the forest, he had turned and taken a circuitous way toward the north, refraining from giving any intimation of his course by the discharge of his fowling-piece, but suffering several tempting birds to flit by him unharmed, much to the disgust of his dog *Owena*, or the 'The Wind.' At length he reached a little opening in the forest — a secluded yet sunny spot, where, in the midst of a neglected garden, stood a solitary cabin, overhung by a single tree, around whose trunk twined a luxuriant wild grape-vine, its long branches now in bloom, swinging in the wind, and dropping in fragrant festoons above the humble little roof.

Pausing at the entrance of the garden, — or rather the small plot of ground which was once a garden, but where now a rank growth of weeds and brambles were insolently triumphing over a few stunted fruit-trees, struggling shrubs, and medicinal herbs, — De Vaudreuil announced his approach by a shrill, peculiar whistle. After a few moments the door of the cabin was cautiously opened by an old Indian, who stood, rifle in hand, awaiting the visitor, while a somewhat younger Indian looked over his shoulder. With three or four eager bounds, Maurice cleared the tangled shrubbery of the garden, and, passing the grim warders with a hasty salute, entered the little cabin. This contained, in reality, but one room, but a pair of large Indian blankets, depending from the ceiling, divided it into compartments. Lifting this rude curtain, the lieutenant stood face to face, and in another instant heart to heart, with his wife Onata, who was impatiently awaiting him, but had modestly refrained from hastening to meet him.

And this had been the secret attraction which day after day had lured him to the woods; and here was the sylvan temple in which was enshrined the unknown divinity of his heart!

Onata had now been in this lonely, unsuspected retreat several weeks. Soon after his arrival at the fort, De Vaudreuil had discovered the deserted cabin on one of his excursions, and, thinking that it would admirably answer his purpose, he had, after making some necessary preparations, sent for his wife by two friendly Oneidas, upon whose fidelity and discretion he was convinced he could rely. He managed to absent himself long enough from the fort to meet the party about half-way from the Indian village, and to escort Onata to the temporary home he had provided for her. She had been so fortunate as to effect her escape in perfect safety and secrecy, during a somewhat prolonged absence of her sister. She had even brought with her all her simple wardrobe, and a female attendant, who was no other than the handsome half-breed *Ahwao* (or Rose), who had pleaded so ably, at the wild woman's convention, for the largest liberty in all affairs of the heart. Ahwao, though a merry, good-humored girl, was not an especial favorite with Onata; who, however, on receiving her husband's injunction to provide herself with a female companion, thought it best to make choice of one who would be likely to entertain no scruples of delicacy or morality against the relations in which it would be supposed that she stood toward the rich and noble young Frenchman.

The three accomplices in the elopement of Onata were retained as her guards and attendants by De Vaudreuil, who did his best, by handsome presents and generous promises, to secure from them the utmost secrecy and faithful service.

Maurice had long had a fancy to see his wild little wife dressed in the costume of the English and American ladies of that time; though he often doubted if anything would become her so well as her own semi-savage dress, modified and embellished as it was in a thousand little coquettish ways by her exquisite native taste. But, finally, he had it in his power to test this important question to his entire satisfaction. He had, by a good deal of trouble and expense, been able to procure, through an Albany trader, the larger portion of a very handsome wardrobe, which, by a happy chance, fitted Onata tolerably ; though no completely civilized form, stiffened by whalebone, and corseted into slenderness, could approach hers in straightness, delicate symmetry, and absolute perfection of proportion.

This morning, she was arrayed, for the first time, in her best new garb for her husband's eye, and had stood for nearly an hour, not daring to sit down on anything so grand as her rich, rustling gown, half eagerly, half timidly awaiting his company; her heart now swelling with the hope of his smiling approbation, now fluttering with doubts and misgivings ; her cheeks burning, and her limbs seeming to stiffen with a painful sense of awkwardness ; a feeling utterly new to her, in the simple, natural life she had hitherto led.

But the dress, though so strange and oppressively magnificent to her, was, in reality, more marked by simplicity than splendor. It was a brocade of crimson and black, little, if any, the worse for wear. Heavy point lace edged the low, square neck, and close sleeves, hanging in deep ruffles at elbow. Strangely enough, stockings and shoes had been forgotten, and Onata's little moccasined feet peeped from beneath the ample folds of the brocade skirt. She still wore her beautiful dark-brown hair plaited about her head ; but, instead of strings of red berries, or wild-flowers, it was confined by knots of crimson ribbon. The only ornaments which she wore were the cross and chain given by her husband at their first parting; her wedding-ring, restored to its place immediately on her making her escape from the Indian village, and a small, round clasp of gold filigree, which fastened her girdle.

After the first tender embrace, and a few words of kindly greeting and inquiry, De Vaudreuil held his wife at arm's length, and surveyed her attentively, even critically, but with an expression of growing satisfaction; she smiling, blushing, and looking anywhere but into his eyes. He found some fault with the fit of the dress, and laughed at the incongruity of the moccasins; but finally pronounced his opinion that she would do very well, and, after a little practice in lady-like habiliments, be able to pass anywhere as one fairly entitled to wear them, and ended by saluting her, with playful formality, as '*Madame de Vaudreuil.*' This was the first time that he had addressed her by her new name, which still had a grand, strange sound to her. She replied at first with a smile of grateful pride; then a shade of sadness flitted over her face, and, with a wistful look into his eyes, she asked,

'You no like *Onata?* You no speak it any more? Must poor wild-woods' "*leaf*" grow pale, fall down, and the wind blow it away?'

'No, no,' he replied, with a frank, reässuring smile; 'Onata is a pretty name — I called you by it first — I shall always call you by it. The wild-woods' "leaf" shall always be kept green, and I will wear it as a proud love-favor, in my casque, against the world.'

The full significance of the last gallant assurance was scarcely perceived by the simple Indian girl; but it had an imposing sound to her ear, and flattered her heart quite as much, perhaps, as though she had been better versed in the light lore of chivalric romance.

The humble apartment in which the lovers stood was very scantily and primitively furnished, yet displayed many nameless little tokens of taste, tender care, and an appreciation of home-comfort, far more attractive than the cold, elaborate luxuries of state-chambers and fashionable drawing-rooms.

Onata's couch, which was simply a pile of the soft, elastic boughs of the hemlock, and fine dry grass, covered with Indian blankets, was gracefully draped with a bright Scotch shawl, and canopied with garlands of evergreens and flowers. The rude plank floor was almost completely carpeted with the neat mats, woven by Indian women, of wild grass, rushes, or the dried husks of maize; and beautiful spotted fawn-skins covered the rough log-seats that stood along the wall in the place of chairs.

To one of these seats, below the little four-paned window, De Vaudreuil now led his wife, who seated herself submissively, but with an awful sense of the liberty she was taking with the stiff folds of her dress.

'*Eh bien, chère amie,*' began the lieutenant, 'how do you get on with your studies?'

'O, me do very bad, and learn slow — so slow! Me poor savage child still, who grow ignorant every day. Me, know nothing — nothing only to love, and to pray a little. Yes, me learn to pray fast to *le bon Dieu* and *la Sainte Mère* for *you*.'

Maurice smiled at this naïve confession, and replied:

'That is well. But how often do you pray, Onata? — Will you tell me — only, *chère enfante*, please try to say *I* sometimes, instead of "*me*." *C'est mieux*.'

'O, I pray all the nights, before I go asleep, and all the mornings, when the sunshine open my eyes — and many more times. When I think of you, and feel so happy as I can be, I pray. In gone-by days, when I feel happy, I sing, like the birds — now I pray. Then, it a little bird-joy — I sing, and I feel better; now, it a great soul-happiness — it burst my heart till I tell it to *le bon Dieu*.'

'*Bien!*' said De Vaudreuil, with a smile and an embrace; 'now we must attend to our lesson.'

Onata took her little French prayer-book from the window-sill, and handed it to her husband, who proceeded to read a short prayer, and then translated it into English. Though an accomplished scholar in our language might have suggested some improvements in his style and the choice of words, to Onata it was all very beautiful and marvellous. With the admiring faith and docility of a child, she hung upon every word, eagerly watched the play of his lips, and repeated with wonderful exactitude the slightest intonations of his voice.

It was scarcely a marvel that the romantic young soldier should forget for a while the schemes of ambition, the love of glory, and become insensible to the wild fascinations of adventure, in watching the development of that quick, poetic intellect, and that pure, receptive nature, which drank in knowledge and affection as thirsting flowers drink in dew and sunshine; breathing out rarer thought, growing in strength, and blossoming into more exquisite beauty, day by day.

So deeply interesting, indeed, was his novel employment, that hour after hour went on unheeded, and he was scarcely ready to pause when the simple noonday meal was prepared and served by Ahwao, in the next apartment.

For a short time in the afternoon De Vaudreuil resumed his duties as tutor; not over a book, however, but by familiar oral instruction. Onata now sat in her favorite place, — the place to which every loving woman sinks, as by the natural gravitation of the heart, — at the feet of her husband, on a little foot-stool, — a rather fanciful affair, and the work of his ingenious hands; being a small block of wood, cushioned with soft grass, and covered with a white rabbit-skin.

Onata rested her small brown hands, and her round, dimpled chin, upon her husband's knee, while her rich, changeful face was raised towards his; the red, parted lips quivering with interest and wonder, the great, deep eyes, now shadowed by a momentary perplexity, now radiant with intelligence, faithfully reflecting the love and the thought in his, as still summer lakes give back heaven and the stars.

It was of his home beyond the sea, and the life that awaited them there, that he spoke, at first. Onata was never tired of hearing of these wonderful things, though she secretly shrank from the thought of looking for herself upon such strange scenes — of encountering such strange people, and adopting habits to her simple sense so unnatural and absurd. Still, she would try to accustom herself to them, in imagination, at least, that she might not be altogether overwhelmed by the awful reality. In thinking of the people she must prepare herself to meet, she, woman-like, only feared her own sex. She felt that she could behold, without terror, the great white chiefs, sitting in the grave national councils; or look on the law-men in their solemn courts, wrapt in their black blankets, and wearing their mighty wigs; or on holy priests, in all the splendor of sacerdotal robes, performing their mysterious rites, and praising God in great prayer-houses, with great music that was like imprisoned thunder; or on brave warriors, going forth to battle, shaking the earth with their heavy tramp and the roll of their big guns, beating back the winds with the flap of the great silk wings of their standards, and making the sun ashamed with the shine of their swords. She even thought that she could look on the face of the king, and live; but she could not think without mortal fear on those fair and haughty court-dames, in the unapproachable grandeur of their hooped skirts and high-heeled shoes; with their lofty powdered head-dresses, like the cones of pine-trees, crowned with snow; with great jewels flashing on their brows like stars, girdling their waists like fire, and flowing about their necks in little rivulets of light. How she could ever find courage in her simple little heart to face these gorgons of rank and fashion, she could not tell. Had she been classical, as well as poetical, she might have wished for the aid of Minerva, and an invisible helmet; as it was, she put up timid little prayers to the Virgin Mary, and relied upon her husband's greatness to protect and overshadow her, in the contemplation of all such fearful future ordeals.

The conversation of the lovers gradually came round to religion, and Maurice, to the best of his ability, gave Onata instruction in the simplest doctrines of his church; endeavoring to answer satisfactorily her eager and sometimes profound inquiries.

The worship of the Virgin Mary had not only a peculiar poetic charm for her, but took strong hold on her affections. Her heart had always yearned sadly and unceasingly for a mother's love and care, and something of that lost joy and peace seemed restored to her in this sweet and comforting faith; she no longer felt utterly motherless. She explained the feeling to her husband somewhat in this way: When her soul would ascend to the great God, she sometimes found the way cloudy and stormy, and, O, so long! She would grow very tired, and be ready to sink all the way back; then she would seem to feel the hand of the kind Mary-mother take hers, and draw her up; and she would rest in her lap, like a little child, and ask her to speak to the good God for the poor, ignorant Indian girl.

De Vaudreuil was struck by this naïve confession of faith, and, for some moments after Onata had ceased speaking, sat in deep, abstracted thought, reflecting upon what seemed to him the profound and universal truths involved in her faltering, childlike words. To this simple faith in the peerless intercessory influence and divine grace of the Virgin Mary, taught by the church, he ascribed its deepest power over the hearts of men, rather than to its outward pomp and greatness, its autocratic papal rule, its magnificent machinery, its mystery, its omnipresent and omniscient intelligence. To him it seemed not a dogma that flattered alone the poetic fancy, or justified itself by the highest reason, but a natural faith, that took hold on the strongest and most indestructible instincts of the human heart. To how many debased and despairing souls, that would be smitten with hopeless awe at the thought of approaching Deity itself, did that sweet, motherly help seem to stretch forth tender arms of mercy and succor, to draw them to her knee, to gather up their broken murmurs of penitence and prayer, and breathe them anew into the ear of the Father! Less dear to the weak and sinful the grander faith in the Christ, though his dual nature made him thoughtful of our infirmities, and 'he was tempted like as we are.' The saint who has triumphantly 'finished his course,' the martyr from the midst of flames, might confidently call upon the Crucified; but the mother, bending over her dying child, murmured the name of one who has tasted her 'bitter cup;' the brigand upon the scaffold, though with the crucifix at his lips, clutched at the robes of the merciful Mary.

De Vaudreuil had at one time been somewhat shocked by hearing Onata call the Virgin '*the woman-God.*' But, after a moment's reflection, he felt that he could scarcely reprove her, conscious as he was of the natural need of the heart to recognize something in tenderness like to the feminine and maternal element in Deity; something to inspire the most loyal devotion of manhood; something for fearful childhood to cling to; something for despairing guilt to appeal to.

Next to the faith in the Virgin Mother in its hold upon the heart of the devout Catholic, he thought, is the worship of the saints — those half-human, half-angelic intercessors; those heavenly helps; those ushers into the Divine presence. There was no reproach, no despair, in their holiness, born 'through much tribulation' from their conquered humanity; they stood on no far, unattainable height, but on every steep of the heavenly ascent, and reached downward helpful, fraternal hands; their names were rounds in the ladder of prayer, by which clomb upward souls not gifted with strong faith to 'mount as on wings of eagles.'

Let us add to these beliefs the doctrine of an intermediate state and the possible restoration of the lost, the eternal hope and the temporal beauty thrown about religion, and we have the chief secrets of the spiritual supremacy of the church; and, until the hard, stern, face-to-face-with-God theology of the severest form of Protestantism, with its doctrines of utter, innate depravity, implacable wrath, eternal, irremediable wretchedness, — the awful fatalism of the Genevan school, — can be modified and liberalized by some merciful, hopeful, and human-hearted beliefs, answering to, if not identical with these; until the church of Christ is really preached and accepted, in all his 'divine sufficiencies,' as intercessor, help, and refuge, — as the lover and savior of the world, not as a God of judgments, vengeance, and 'fiery indignation,'—will not Roman Catholicism, with all its errors, abuses, and tyrannies, continue to rule the world, her temples stand like its 'eternal hills,' and the smoke of her incense ascend as uninterruptedly as its morning exhalations? The natural cry of humanity to God is not a shriek of fear, or a wail of despair, but the child's trustful and loving appeal, '*Abba, Father.*'

But to return to our story.

Late in the afternoon, recalling with his well-known signal the Indian guardians, who usually took advantage of his visits to make excursions into the forest, the young soldier departed, with an oft-repeated promise to come again the next day.

Onata watched through the little window till the last glimpse of his tall, slender form had disappeared down the winding forest path; then, summoning Ahwao, she hastily disrobed herself of her strange, grand habiliments, and, resuming her picturesque, half-savage costume, declared, with a childlike laugh and skip, that she felt natural and breathed easily, for the first time that day.

De Vaudreuil walked slowly and thoughtfully homeward, not alone reflecting, lover-like, upon the singular beauty and wild graces of the mistress of his heart, nor conning over her pretty, suggestive sayings, but speculating upon the still existent difficulties of his position, and studying more earnestly than ever to lay out some plan for providing for his wife a more safe and permanent asylum. He could not count upon being permitted to linger much longer at his present post; he felt that he could not with honor remain in safety and inactivity away from the army which he had joined scarcely a year before in all the fiery ardor of a young soldier of liberty, smiling at hardships, difficulties, and dangers, hungering and thirsting after a noble renown.

In the deepening abstraction and perplexity of his thought, his step grew slower and slower, till he paused altogether, and stood quite still for several moments — an almost unprecedented length of time for him to give to profound reflection. When he walked on, it was with a quick, firm stride. He had formed an important, though by no means a new resolution; he had determined to lose no time in confiding his secret to the marquis, and acquainting him with all the painful awkwardness of his position. But soon he paused again, in redoubled doubt and perplexity. Would not his aristocratic superior be shocked inexpressibly by such an unheard of *mésalliance,* and would he not feel in honor bound to reveal the whole matter to his father? Of the old count's reception of such tidings there could, unfortunately, be no doubt. Wounded in his pride of family, and defied in his paternal authority, his anger would be fierce and unrelenting, and his first act might be to disown and beggar the degenerate rebel in a strange land.

Formerly, in his brave philosophic dreams of independence and equality, poverty had worn a rather attractive and debonnair aspect to the young enthusiast; but now, when brought face to face with her, even in imagination, he found her full of repulsiveness and terror. Now, to be deprived of the means with which his father had hitherto generously supplied him — now to be reduced to his good name and good sword — would be more than a double misfortune, involving, as it did, separation from or destitution with his beloved Onata, and the abandonment of all his beautiful plans for her happiness and improvement.

He was at last roused from his troubled revery by the fierce growls and defiant attitude of his dog, who apparently scented something more formidable than game on their path. The young soldier glanced around him somewhat anxiously — not in fear of his life, but of the discovery of his secret by some prowling spy. After looking and listening for a moment, he was about to proceed upon his way, when there leaped out before him, from behind a huge chestnut, the graceful and well-remembered form of the handsome Oneida, Garanguli. The young chief stood within a few paces of his rival, and called out in English, which, like Sadewana's family, he spoke quite intelligibly:

'Defend yourself, Frenchman! I go to kill you!'

Suiting the action to the word, he bent his bow, and drew a long iron-barbed arrow to the head. His eyes were ablaze, his lips and nostrils quivering with rage and exultation, and so exactly had he taken the attitude of the Belvidere Apollo, that for a moment De Vaudreuil was paralyzed by his unconscious majesty and grace. But the instinct of self-preservation quick returning, he levelled his good rifle against the more classical weapon of his dusky foe, and the sharp crack of the one and the twang of the other were simultaneous. The hand that aimed the shaft had seldom erred before, but now it must have trembled slightly with the eager thrill of anticipated vengeance, for it hit upon the barrel of the rifle and glanced off; but the ball grazed the Indian's skull, and carried away his brave head-dress. The wound was not serious, but it stunned the young chief for a moment, so that he dropped his bow and staggered back against the chestnut behind which he had waited for his rival. The next instant the sword of De Vaudreuil was at his breast, and he was completely in his adversary's power. As his brain steadied, and the mist of partial unconsciousness cleared from his eyes, the Oneida still stood thus, looking calmly and proudly into the lieutenant's face, awaiting his next act with a sort of defiant submission. At length, in a cool, haughty tone, and with a look of as much surprise as an Indian will ever deign to express, he asked,

'Why you no kill me?'

'Because,' replied the young officer, 'I do not want your life. And why,' he continued, in a gentle, conciliating tone, 'have you twice attempted to take mine? What wrong have I done you, that you should hate and pursue me thus?'

The Indian's eyes flashed with renewed anger as he answered,

'I hate you because you steal Onata! She mine. Sadewana promise her for me, many summers ago — you thief! You make her your slave; you make her a shame to her father and her tribe, you damn villain! *Now* kill me!'

'No,' said De Vaudreuil, dropping his sword and letting his enemy free, 'I will not kill you. I am your friend; I am no thief, no villain. Sadewana has given me his daughter, and'—here there was a pause of prudent hesitation, but generosity and the sense of honor triumphed—'she is not my slave, nor my mistress; *she is my wife!*'

'*Wife!*' repeated Garanguli, in bewildered surprise.

'Yes, my true and lawful wife—married to me by a priest of my own religion, almost a year ago.'

'But,' said the Oneida, shaking his head, incredulously, 'you rich, proud Frenchman; you soon grow tired and 'shamed of Indian girl. You go away and leave her to sit alone in her wigwam and cry. I only poor savage, but I make my lodge warm and dry for her. I hunt for her, fish for her, be kind to her, and never go away from her.'

'No, no!' replied De Vaudreuil, with a frank smile; 'I will not grow tired of Onata; I will not leave her; I will not bring her to any shame or sorrow, if I can help it. Listen to me. You wanted the daughter of Sadewana for your wife; but you were like a brother to Onata. She never was willing to go with you to your lodge, and be your squaw. She never loved you; she loves me. Listen: Onata is not like other Indian women; she is more like her mother's people. She is not strong and brave; she is tender and timid. The life of the savage is too hard for her; she would have grown sad, she would have drooped and died, in your lodge. She likes the customs and ways of the pale-faces; she is hungry for their book-wisdom, and her heart sighs after her mother's God. I will take tender care of her—I will teach her many things; and when the war is over, I will take her across the sea to my own country, and there she will be a great, rich lady, and never be troubled or tasked any more.'

De Vaudreuil had designedly spoken somewhat in the Indian's own simple, laconic style, thinking that his talk would thus be more intelligible and convincing to his auditor. The style, as will be seen, we have preserved, but not in all cases the exact words, the young Frenchman not yet being complete master of the language.

Garanguli remained for a few moments silent, with his eyes cast down, his hands clenched, and his slender black eyebrows knit together. It was evident that a fierce, mighty struggle was rending the passionate yet generous heart of the young chief. But at last the higher instincts of love and manliness conquered, and through them the unlettered young savage won a victory over himself infinitely more glorious than many of those vaunted conquests of chivalry, for which the heroes of old received the honors of knighthood and the crownings of tournaments. With a look of perfect sincerity and a brave attempt at a smile, he extended his hand to De Vaudreuil, saying:

'You have well spoke; it is all true. You have well done; it is all right. Garanguli very much satisfied. Garanguli your friend. He has buried the tomahawk.'

Maurice grasped cordially the hand so frankly proffered, and gladly pledged himself to a faithful friendship with his transformed rival and foe. In proof of his confidence, he acquainted the generous Oneida, while walking slowly toward the fort, with the peculiar reasons that existed for the present concealment of his marriage with Onata, and slightly touched upon the vague and varying plans for the future, which he had been discussing with himself more and more earnestly for several weeks past.

Garanguli voluntarily pledged himself to secrecy, but did not venture to give his new friend any advice, except that the utmost care should be taken lest Onata's present retreat should be discovered by her sister. He said that the elopement had produced great excitement and inquiry at the castle; that Sadewana had maintained a stern silence, which by some was pronounced a sage indifference, and by others a patient brooding over some deep plan of revenge; but that Gahaneh had been at first like a she-panther deprived of her cub — had broken out of her usual moody calm, and raved with almost insane passion. Yet she also had become quiet, in obedience, it was said, to her father's angry commands, and was never known to speak upon the subject of her sister's flight or abduction, or to take counsel of any one.

The young chief seemed to think that this quiet was little to be trusted; and that, notwithstanding some grand elements in her character, Gahaneh was as capable as any of her race of

> 'The patient search and vigil long
> Of one who treasures up a wrong.'

Garanguli had supposed from the first that Onata was within the fort, and of late he had watched about it to catch a glimpse of her, and, if possible, obtain an interview, to prevail upon her to return with him to her father's lodge, or to cover her with the reproaches of his honest, outraged heart. Failing in this, he had lain in wait for De Vaudreuil, resolved upon a last, mortal struggle with his rival.

When the two new-made friends came in sight of Fort Stanwix, they paused, and De Vaudreuil, after vainly pressing the noble Indian to enter and spend the night at the garrison, gave a yet greater proof of his faith and kindly feeling by inviting his companion to accompany him on his next visit to Onata. Garanguli at first haughtily refused, but, seeing that the young officer looked hurt, relented, and consented.

So they parted, Maurice watching with strange interest the young Oneida, till he disappeared in the deep twilight shadows of the wood. He took his way toward a dark cedar swamp to the southward, not by any path, but plunging at once into the densest part of the forest, seeming to find a fierce pleasure in wrestling with the sturdy undergrowth, battling back branch and brier, and trampling down entangling vines. De Vaudreuil felt that it was well for that wounded and passion-shaken spirit to be alone with Nature for a time; that she who had nurtured her wild child into such manly strength and beauty, and gifted him with instincts of generosity and honor which might shame the highest nobility of the great world, could best administer to him in her own voiceless, mysterious ways counsel and consolation; that on her gentle maternal breast could he pour out the full bitterness of his heart; only from the calm breathings of her deep life receive strength to endure in the proud silence which best became one of his stern, impassive race.

Late on the following morning, Onata was unspeakably surprised by seeing her husband enter their little cabin with the formidable Indian rival who had once, to her knowledge, attempted his life, and the fear of whose revengeful pursuit had haunted her continually since the escape from her father's lodge. Yet she did not for a moment lose her quiet presence of mind and gentle dignity of manner, and a few words of explanation sufficed to banish from her soft, antelope eyes the half-startled, half-distrustful look with which she first met the unexpected guest. She extended her hand to him, saying,

'I very glad; I shall not be afraid any more; Garanguli never tell lies!'

Onata was dressed, as on the preceding day, in the strange, rich costume which became her so well, and it was almost with the stately grace of a dame of the *ancien regime* that she received her husband and his friend, and did the honors of her humble home.

Garanguli saw at that moment, more vividly and sadly than ever before, how immeasurably she was above the associations of her birth, the friends of her savage childhood, her kindred, even him; and as he, with innate courtesy, bent over the hand which she extended to him half unconsciously, with the graciousness of a superior, he breathed above it not alone the lover's sigh of eternal renunciation, but the proud brother's inarticulate blessing. Not even in his heart did the generous aspiration take the form of eloquent or sacred words. It was the blind, voiceless wish of a soul scarce half redeemed from heathenism; but it may have found its way to God, nevertheless.

Yet, with all his strength and generosity, the conquest of that passion, which had so long been the most vital and refining element of his life, was too recent for him to feel quite at ease and free from gloomy regrets in the society of the happy lovers; and soon, resisting all their kind entreaties, he took his leave, strode rapidly across the wild garden-plot, and plunged into the forest.

De Vaudreuil stayed later than usual, yielding to the solicitations of Onata, who seemed strangely loth to have him leave her. The poor child was, in truth, unusually troubled and fretful that day, yet dared not name to her husband the cause of her uneasiness, lest he should think her weak and cowardly; and, as a soldier's wife, she felt that it behooved her more than ever to be strong and courageous. All the night preceding she had been visited by unhappy and ominous dreams; in which, again and again, her stern sister's dark presence had fallen like the shadow of death on her heart, and her sister's fiery eyes burned into her soul. Once she had risen and looked out of her little window for the morning; but she had started back in affright, believing that she had seen the tall and stately form of Gahaneh gliding along on the edge of the wood.

Afterwards her suspicions were somewhat aroused by finding that Ahwao was not, as usual, lying on the bear-skins which formed her bed, near the couch of her mistress. After calling her name repeatedly, and receiving no answer, she questioned the Indian guard, and was told that the girl had passed them and gone out, more than an hour before.

As we have said, Onata was several times on the point of confessing her vague fears and doubts to her husband; but, to the last, the apprehension of being thought by him childish and superstitious sealed her lips. Something of the secret anxiety of her heart, however, must have been unconsciously revealed in her face, and troubled the usually quiet depths of her eyes; for, after parting with her,— even after having passed the threshold of the cottage, —Lieutenant Maurice returned to fold his trembling little forest nymph in his arms once more, to assure her of his constant love, and bid her hope for happier days — days of peace, security, and perfect union. Onata watched his disappearing form that night with a strange, heavy foreboding at her heart, which she could neither banish nor comprehend. And when he was utterly gone, she still sat at her window, watching, with the same fixed, comfortless expression darkening her bright face, like some chill, unearthly shadow the glowing and paling of the sunset splendors:

'Those large black, prophet eyes seemed to dilate
And follow far the disappearing sun,
As if their last day of a happy date
With his broad, bright, and drooping orb, were gone.'

That night, with a look and tone of unusual authority, she forbade Ahwao to leave her side, reproving her at the same time for her wanderings in the woods on the night preceding. The dusky abigail received the command in sullen silence, but gave a slight start of surprise and alarm at the reproof, which revealed to her that her proceedings had been observed; yet a moment's searching gaze into the face of her mistress convinced her that but very vague suspicions had been excited.

In truth, Onata little divined the extent of the falsehood and treachery of her attendant. When that gay and pleasure-loving Indian girl joined the daughter of Sadewana in her flight with a gallant young French officer, she looked forward to a merry, adventurous life in garrisons, or following the camp. She had never conceived of anything like the quiet, studious, and romantic seclusion of the lonely retreat in which these strange lovers chose to bury themselves. Not having been taken wholly into their confidence, she knew nothing of their true relations to one another, and the life they led was incomprehensible and intolerably wearisome to her. Proud and selfish, she rebelled against being degraded from the position of friend and confidant, to which she had aspired, to that of a mere attendant, and was enraged at missing the peculiar rewards and pleasures upon which she had counted.

So, dissatisfied and disappointed, irritated and ennuied, she did not scruple to betray the lovers on the first opportunity, and to discover their hiding-place to the spies of Gahaneh and Garanguli. This last, on learning the truth, that Onata had indeed suffered no dishonor at the hands of his rival, hastened to withdraw his emissaries, and set out at once for the Indian village, determined to use his influence with Gahaneh in persuading her to resign her revengeful plots and purposes against Onata and her lover, and to leave them in peace.

On reaching the castle, he went at once to the lodge of Sadewana, and inquired of him for his elder daughter, who was, as usual, absent from the domestic sphere; and was informed that she was away to the lake, fishing, with several of her masculine-minded followers. The old sachem added, with a short, contemptuous laugh, that it was a great pity such brave and enterprising squaws had not been created of the privileged sex in the beginning, and that he feared they would never forgive the Great Spirit for the blunder he had made in their particular cases. Such excursions were, of course, too common to excite the suspicions of the young chief, who, like all of the ineligible sex, was in utter ignorance of the existence of the formidable League; and he concluded it would be best to quietly await the return of his haughty friend before entering upon his new office of mediator and peace-maker.

CHAPTER VI.

THE SACRIFICE.

Je tremble,
Quoi ! je vais donc mourir ; —
Mourir avant seize ans, c'est affreux ! Je ne puis.
O, Dieu ! sentir le fer entrer dans ma poitrine !
Ah, — j'offre ma vie en sacrifice.
VICTOR HUGO — *Le Roy S'amuse.*

How now, ye secret, black, and midnight hags !
What is 't ye do ? SHAKSPEARE.

ON the day succeeding the visit to Onata with Garanguli, De Vaudreuil was prevented from joining her at the usual hour, by the arrival at the fort of a countryman in the suite of the Marquis de Lafayette, bringing despatches to the garrison, and private letters to himself. The latter were of unusual interest and importance. The Count de Vaudreuil wrote to recall his favorite son to take the place of his elder brother, the half-imbecile heir to the family title and estates, who was no more. There was also a letter from the marquis, advising him, in a tone which was equivalent to a command, to leave his present post of inactivity, and rejoin his general at his head-quarters.

One thing the young lieutenant now saw clear and indisputable, through all his doubts and perplexities ;

he could no longer remain at the fort; and the hidden happiness of his carefully-concealed love, the romantic adventures of his stolen interviews, the poetic pleasures and occupations of his unsuspected 'forest sanctuary,' must be abandoned. In spite of his philosophy and boyish love of change, there was a pang at his heart as he confessed all this to himself. On the other hand, he saw that the change which had taken place in his fortunes and position involved the long-desired security for his love, and the removal of all imperative obligations of secrecy. His aristocratic father might, and doubtless would, be seriously offended by his imprudent marriage, but would no longer have the power to make his anger felt in disownment and destitution, as the bulk of his property went with the title, and was inalienable.

After a little anxious reflection, the lieutenant came to the resolution to confide his singular story to his friends at the garrison, bring Onata to the fort, acknowledge her as his wife before them all, and leave her under their protection, while he should rejoin his general, and make arrangements for a return to France.

His disclosure was received with some surprise, but with more sympathy than disapprobation, by the female portion of his friends at least, who were womanly enough to be captivated by its poetry and romance, even amid the hard realities, the rigors, and rude fortunes, of border life. Onata was personally beloved by them all, and they were generous enough to rejoice in the marvellous good fortune which had come to rescue her from the uncongenial, barbarous condition to which she had been so unhappily, and, it seemed to them, so unfittingly born.

They readily promised her husband to treat her not only with the respect due to her new position, but with sisterly care and kindness, and at once set about preparing a comfortable apartment for her reception.

So long had De Vaudreuil hesitated in making his confession, from a very natural embarrassment and *mauvaise-honte*, that it was some time in the afternoon before he set out, with two or three soldiers, to bring Onata to the fort. He pursued the familiar woodland path in almost utter silence, his thoughts busy in anticipating the surprise of his wife at the tidings he should bring, and in speculating as to whether the announcement of the change awaiting her would be received with womanly pride and joy, or childlike apprehension and regret.

As he came in sight of the lonely little cabin, he missed her waiting, welcoming face at the window, and quickened his steps with a vague feeling of alarm. He found the door, usually so carefully barred and faithfully guarded, ajar, and, pushing it open, he saw his two Indian sentinels lying on the floor, disarmed, bound, and in a complete state of intoxication. Each had been left sufficient use of one hand to reach a large jug of rum, which stood between the two, and they seemed to have availed themselves of this privilege to the utmost.

De Vaudreuil, half beside himself with terror, rushed into Onata's apartment, shouting her name. She was not there! No glad voice answered his wild cry; no smiling face met his quick, searching gaze! The primitive little boudoir had been rudely disarranged; the flower-wreathed canopy above the couch had been torn down; Onata's books and some articles of apparel were scattered on the floor, and a little oratory which he had constructed for her in a corner near the window was overthrown. The desolation and desecration of the place, and the terrible fear they aroused, so smote upon the heart of Maurice that he turned away from his companions, covered his face with his hands, and groaned aloud, — the first outcry of that young heart under the sharp discipline of sorrow. It was not only grief and deadly fear which assailed him, but the more bitter and hopeless pang of remorse, for the rashness and selfish weakness which had put in peril that innocent and devoted life. But this was no time to give way to regrets and self-accusations; the next moment he was kneeling beside one of the drunken Indians, and besieging his dull ear with questions.

In the midst of his heavy stupor, an expression of sullen rage, disgust, and shame, passed over the face of the savage, as he answered:

'Squaws, squaws, — all squaws! Ugh! Ahwao let 'em in — Ahwao wet our powder — steal our knives — Ahwao give us fire-water, so squaws too much for us. Ugh!'

'Good God!' exclaimed De Vaudreuil, across whose brain flashed Onata's story of 'The League,' 'she is in the hands of that fiend Gahaneh, and all the she-devils of the tribe!'

On this, he recommenced questioning the savage with more vehemence and authority than before, but could gain no more information from him or his companion. A stupor more deadly than that of drunkenness seemed to be weighing more and more heavily upon their senses; a condition which was soon accounted for, by an examination of the little rum yet remaining in the jug beside them. It was drugged. All that could be done was to pour this out upon the ground, cut the thongs that bound their benumbed limbs, and leave them to sleep themselves sober as best they could; for De Vaudreuil was in a frenzy of impatience to set out in pursuit of his stolen wife.

Fortunately one of the soldiers in his service knew the way from the fort to the village of the Oneidas (whither it was conjectured she had been carried) by the Indian trail, and offered to conduct the young officer. Maurice cordially grasped his hand, and promised him fifty louis-d'ors if through his means the lost bride should be recovered.

Pausing only long enough at the fort to obtain a small stock of provisions and torches for a night-march, the lieutenant and his two hardy friends set out just at sunset, encouraged by the good wishes and cheerful prophecies of the garrison.

We will leave them on their toilsome and somewhat perilous march, while we return to Onata.

Throughout that morning she had watched and waited for her husband with unusual impatience and anxiety. Two or three times she had been on the point of leaving the cottage and its little enclosure, and taking the direction of the fort, to anticipate somewhat his tardy coming; but always the remembrance of his repeated and earnest injunctions against exposing herself to danger or observation deterred her.

She had at length become seriously alarmed by the restlessness and sullen insolence of her attendant. The loyalty and honesty of her own nature would have made her slow to suspect falsehood and crime in others, but that, from the singular purity and fineness of her mental organization, her instincts were marvellously quick and unerring. She perceived a taint of treason in the very air about her; a strange, stifling element, foreboding to her inner senses the near approach of some great peril.

So it was that with a vague, undefinable, but ever-increasing terror at her heart, she waited all through the long, cloudy morning, and the still, hazy noon, for the coming of him before whose brave, smiling presence all forebodings, all sad imaginings, were wont to disappear like cold mists, and dim, spectral shadows, before the genial power of the sunlight; — thus she waited — but in vain!

It was nearly noon when she first became alarmed by loud talking and confusion in the next apartment, and, lifting the heavy screen, saw that her hitherto sober and faithful guardians were resigning themselves to a drunken carousal. She reprimanded them as sternly as she was able, reproaching them for their unfaithfulness to their kind employer; and, with much apparent shame and regret, they promised to desist at once from drinking. But their good resolutions soon evaporated before the fiery breath of the tempter; they recommenced their carousal, quietly at first, but finally becoming more noisy and reckless than before. Onata again came out, not to remonstrate, but resolved to deprive them, if possible, of the means of further intoxication. This time they withstood her; but she firmly insisted, and was just about to lay her hand on the jug of 'fire-water,' in spite of their sullen defiance of her authority, when a low, peculiar call was heard outside the door. Ahwao glided behind the group, hastily undid the fastenings, and the next moment a score of squaws, headed by the tall and powerful form of Gahaneh, poured into the room! The guards were still sufficiently sober to stand on the defensive and level their muskets against the dusky Amazons; but Ahwao, as they afterwards told De Vaudreuil, had dampened the powder; she had even cunningly contrived to abstract knife and tomahawk from their belts during their last dispute with their mistress; so they were speedily overpowered, laid prostrate, and bound.

Onata, at the first sight of the ominous face of her sister and her fierce followers, had uttered an involuntary shriek of terror, then clasped her slender hands, and raised her startled eyes in one brief, mute, piteous appeal for mercy. Through that shriek her timid heart had cried out with a wild, passionate plaint; through that eager upward gaze all its childish love of life — all its dread of the dark and terrible things of death — had looked, and longed, and implored. But the face above her, for all its familiar kindred lineaments, was pitiless stone — the eyes that met hers were avenging fire; and, without a murmur of complaint, or a gesture of remonstrance, she resigned herself to the fate which she saw awaited her, exhibiting far more of the quiet submission of the Christian martyr, than the lofty pride and defiant dignity of her father's race.

Onata was dressed in the European costume already described. This struck Gahaneh's eye at once. She grasped her sister's arm and turned her round, calling the attention of the squaws to her strange appearance, with sarcasms and bitter laughter. Suddenly her mood seemed to change to one of fierce anger and scathing contempt; she burst upon poor Onata with a torrent of reproaches for having sold her honor and the honor of her family for flaunting silks and miserable gewgaws. She tore the rich lace from her sleeves, the ribbons from her hair, the girdle from her waist, and trampled them under foot. Onata bore all submissively, until the cross and chain, so doubly sacred, were menaced; then, with something of

'The tender fierceness of the dove
Pecking the hand that hovers o'er its mate,'

she struck off the desecrating grasp of her sister, and commanded her to stand back, with a strange power of authority speaking in her usually gentle tones, and a sudden splendor of womanly pride kindling in her soft eyes and breaking over her childlike face, which awed as much as surprised her captors. Gahaneh's great heart was touched as tears and entreaties would never have touched it, and the captive's treasure of treasures was not again molested.

Gahaneh questioned Ahwao concerning De Vaudreuil, whom it seemed she had hoped to encounter at the cottage, and frowned savagely when told that the hour of his visit was long past, and he would probably not come that day. Her heart must 'starve on' a while longer, she said, but it should taste vengeance at last. She then gave the order to march immediately, and with her grim followers, between two of whom was placed Onata, took her homeward way.

Ahwao lingered behind for a few moments to gather up such articles of ornament and dress as tempted her taste or cupidity, regarding them as her rightful perquisites. No one contended with her for the possession of these, as the other confederates of Gahaneh were, or affected to be, stern, warlike women, bent on redeeming a solemn vow, and executing a dread penalty upon a guilty culprit, whose hitherto high position would only make the example more complete. The distinction given to Onata by her beauty and refinement, and the friendship of the pale-faces, had anything but endeared her to her least favored sisters on the shadowy side; and such were now too much absorbed by the fierce pleasure of gratified envy and malice in her capture and humiliation, to be moved by curiosity or the love of plunder. Some were doubtless genuine Amazons (in all save backing war-horses, which were as scarce as unicorns in that Indian country), and, after the style of the singular woman who led and ruled them, had acquired a lofty contempt for all the little feminine adornments commonly so attractive to Indian women; and those of poor Onata they now professed doubly to despise, for the shameful price at which they supposed they had been bought. The only exception was made by Gahaneh herself, who was observed to take the gay Scotch shawl which had draped Onata's couch from Ahwao, without as much as a 'by your leave;' but it was with the old habit of motherly care, to wrap it around the shoulders of her poor child-sister, the only blanketless one of the party, who was seized with a half-nervous shivering on reaching the deep, sunless forest.

Their way until they struck the trail was difficult and obscure, obstructed by tangled undergrowth, and disputed by formidable briers. But before Gahaneh's strong arm and resolute step they parted as by magic — seemed almost to recoil in terror. She walked always in front, never looking back but to see that her immediate followers and their charge got safely over some difficult spot, then striding on, relentless and unswerving as a Fate, resistless and untiring, like some great embodied force of nature. Yet once, soon after the night came on, she was startled from her stony calm by the near cry of a panther, — sharp, piteous, prolonged, — and, obedient to the old instinct of protection, she leaped to the side of Onata, flung her arms about her with a sort of ferocious tenderness, and glared into the dark, herself like a tigress at bay. The next moment, by her command, a light was struck, and soon a large pine torch flashed its ægis of flame about the party, now gathered into a compact group. At once there was a bound and a rush through the thick undergrowth, the rustle of leaves and the snapping of twigs, and soon from the far depths of the forest came back that wild, despairing, fearfully human cry.

Gahaneh then released her trembling sister from the close embrace in which she had half-unconsciously held her, and, thrusting her back almost rudely into the hands of her grim guards, again strode on alone.

It was deep night when the party drew near to the castle, and Onata felt that her darkest forebodings were about to be realized, when she saw that her sister turned from the direction to her father's lodge, and led the way toward the little glen of the spring — the spot where the solemn councils of 'the daughters of the Oneöta' were held — where the fatal League had been formed.

When the party reached the glen, they found that a fire had been kindled in the midst of the little opening in the forest. The fuel was green, or moist with the perpetual dampness of the place, and burned low and fitfully, seeming to carry on but a faint and doubtful contest with the dewy air and thronging shadows of night. Over this fire crouched two weird-looking hags, who growled out a sullen greeting to the belated party, and glowered at Onata with the fiendish satisfaction of sinful and loveless old age, ugliness, and deformity, exulting in the misfortunes of youth and beauty.

The members of the League seated themselves around this council-fire, and fell into profound silence, broken after a while by brief whispered consultations, — the flickering flames, and the moon plunging in and out of dark billowy clouds, now vividly lighting up their hard, dread faces, now leaving them in dim spectral shadow, more gloomy and awful than utter darkness.

Onata, immediately on reaching the glen, had flung herself prone upon the ground, her strength and courage wholly exhausted. Some refreshment was offered her by one of the most humanely disposed; but she waved it away, and, hiding her face in the long, dewy grass, wept and prayed in secret and silence.

Gahaneh walked apart, and strode up and down the little open space, restless and impatient, but still terribly stern, unyielding, and defiant, like a captured lioness. Onata now and then lifted her sorrowful eyes and stole a look at her face, and in the fitful gleam of the fire-light, or away back in the sombre shade of the pines, or under the full light of the moon, at every view and every moment, its deathly fixedness grew more appalling. She read in it only despair and doom — doom so sure, so speedy, that she was scarcely startled when she heard the sound of spades breaking the turf under a tree by the brook, and saw two of the squaws digging there what she knew must be her grave. The first sound seemed to strike on the steeled heart of Gahaneh like a heavy blow, and to shiver through her frame. She staggered, and bowed her forehead on her clenched hands for a moment; then raised her head, threw up her cold face in the moonlight, and walked as firmly as before.

Onata had not marked this involuntary show of emotion; she still looked and listened quietly, almost like an unconcerned spectator. Physical weariness, and the very greatness of her extremity, had mercifully benumbed her sensibilities, and even somewhat bewildered her brain. The present scene seemed to her like some fearful vision of the night; the forms, the lights, and shadows, about her, were unreal, unearthly; even the murmur and shiver of the woods, and the low gurgle of the brook, so familiar to her from childhood, sounded strange and dreamlike — the ghosts of sounds. Her thoughts wandered from subject to subject, with the mournful vagrancy of sudden, half-comprehended, and overwhelming sorrow; she could not even fix them upon her husband, though he was never wholly absent from her heart, which now flattered itself with the thought of his bitter grief and long remembrance, now chided itself for its selfish weakness, and strove to pray that he might grieve lightly and forget speedily.

But that gentle, forgiving heart was by no means benumbed or void; it seemed steeped in the divine sweetness of charity, and overflowing with tenderness for all souls and all things in God's beautiful world. She looked around upon her judges, and repeated to herself, with inexpressible satisfaction, the words of the Crucified — 'They know not what they do.' She remarked the place where they were making her grave; she remembered it well, and thought it kind of them to have chosen so lovely a spot. She even remembered the violets and windflowers that grew there, and she pitied those which must be uprooted to make room for her.

She was at length roused from her dreamy abstraction by the command to stand up and answer to the formal charges to be brought against her. She stood forth meekly, but not without a certain dignity, which was felt by the coarsest nature and the most callous heart present. Her sister confronted her as her accuser, and the other members of the League ranged themselves in a close circle around her.

Gahaneh repeated the gross charges which she had made a few hours before, but in a calmer, colder, more utterly merciless tone and manner. She again accused Onata of basely betraying the honor of her family and her people, by selling herself to one of a hated race and a most accursed name — to a vile descendant of the arch enemy and destroyer of the Oneidas, De Vaudreuil, the miserable tool of Frontenac. The daughter of a great sachem, the descendant of chiefs and warriors, she had forgotten both the ancient greatness and the unavenged wrongs of her race; she had despised their customs and their faith; she had looked with scorn and disgust upon her red brothers; she had defied the solemn League of her sisters, and degraded herself to a life of vile service and shame as the slave and the paramour of the white man!

Under this terrible arraignment and denunciation, the cheek of the poor girl flushed and blanched, her lips quivered, and her slender hands were clenched convulsively together, but she 'answered not a word.' Child as she was in all but her great love, she was not for an instant tempted to deny the shameful charges which burned like fire into her heart, or to save her life by announcing the fact of her lawful marriage with Lieutenant de Vaudreuil. She had solemnly promised him never to reveal it until he should give her leave. Her word had ever been sacred: it was doubly so when pledged to *him*; and her simple, loyal heart took refuge in no sophistries or suppositions in this fearful extremity. She could die, but she could not betray the honor and integrity of her soul, and the faith of love. So it was that she was 'dumb before her accusers,' though they granted her leave to speak, and Gahaneh even adjured her to defend herself.

The circle then withdrew to a little distance, not to consult upon the penalty, — that was fixed unalterably by the terrible League; nor upon the time of execution, — all knew it must be that very night, if at all; — but to decide upon the mode of death, and to select an executioner from among their number. All, savages as they were, shrank from the cruel office. There was something in that still shadowy place, — in the time, near 'the witching hour of night;' in the youth, and beauty, and dumb resignation, of the victim, — which awed even them. At last they concluded to cast lots, and it fell upon Gahaneh! She started back in horror, and all consented to make another trial, when, by a strange fatality, the lot again fell to her!

'The Great Spirit wills it!' she said, gloomily, and, advancing to her sister, announced her fate, and proclaimed herself as the executioner.

Onata gave a low cry of irrepressible grief and terror, but almost instantly calmed herself, and replied:

'It is well, — *you* will not be cruel with me. I am ready.'

At this moment Ahwao, who had thus far silently watched the proceedings, rushed forward and flung herself at the feet of her mistress, entreating her forgiveness. She had not, she averred, contemplated such tragical consequences from her treachery; she had not believed that the League would dare to put to death the daughter of Sadewana, and the sister of Gahaneh.

All falsehood and treason were so abhorrent to Onata's sincere and loyal nature, that at first she shrank from the wretched creature with involuntary horror and disgust. Yet the next moment she turned, and not only 'looked upon' her betrayer, but lifted her in her arms, and bade her go in peace.

Again the circle formed; not, as before, to glower upon their victim, in awful waiting silence, immovable and stern, but to move around her slowly, chanting a low, solemn strain, which gradually rose higher and higher on the winds of night, and took a more fearful and menacing character, till the still woods rung with the ominous, unearthly sounds. Onata knew that this was her death-song; yet she was not affrighted from the martyr-like submission and determination which had taken possession of her soul. She grasped her little cross, the divine emblem of her new faith, but, perhaps, more precious to her, even then, for love's dear sake, pressed it to her lips, and, looking upward, strove to lift her soul up the infinite heights, to God and the merciful saints, to Him who was unjustly condemned and sacrificed, and to the sorrowful Virgin Mother. As she stood thus, the moonlight fell like a sign of peace upon her brow, but flecked with shadows from passing clouds and waving branches above her, types of the shadows of doubt and fear falling dark and chill upon her soul; for the human love was yet strong at her heart, and the human death-agony broke over her meek, childish face, not in 'bloody sweat,' but in the fast-continued flowing of bitter tears.

In the pauses of that wild song she yet heard the sough of the wind among the pines, and it now seemed to come to her in low murmurs of pity and horror and dismay, and fearful boding whispers. As clouds swept over the face of heaven, she had a strange fancy that the gentle stars were not willing to look upon her death, but were hiding themselves. Even the brook, with which she had so often played in her childhood, had to her ear no longer a sound of musical laughter, but of alarm; and seemed speeding away from that dread scene, to rouse the dreaming woods with the tragic and piteous story.

Still higher and wilder swelled the death-song, and faster whirled the savage circle, in a maniac dance of murderous fury, around their victim, when, suddenly, up the winding path leading from the Indian village came the sound of voices, and the tramp of hurrying feet. Instantly ceased chant and dance; Onata gave a start and a cry of joy, which was answered by a well-known voice shouting her name. The circle broke up, and shrank back in dismay; all but Gahaneh, who sprang forward, her great eyes blazing with the frenzy of fanaticism and hate; and, snatching a dagger from her belt, the same weapon which De Vaudreuil had given her the year before, plunged it into the bosom of her sister! Onata sank to the ground, with a single agonized cry, at the very instant that her husband leaped into the glade, followed by his men and the young chief Garanguli, whom he had found at the castle, and who had guided him to this spot as the likeliest place in which to find Gahaneh and her confederates.

'Onata, Onata! Where are you?' he cried, looking eagerly about him.

'*There,*' replied Gahaneh, quietly, pointing down to her sister, not dead, but mortally wounded, and dying fast.

'My God! who has done this?' exclaimed Maurice, horror-struck and bewildered.

'*I,*' answered Gahaneh, standing calm and defiant before him. 'I killed her with your pretty knife,' she added, holding up the dripping blade, and smiling in demoniac triumph.

Maddened with grief, indignation, and horror, De Vaudreuil drew his sword, and was about to strike her to the earth, when he felt a soft, restraining clasp around his knees, and, looking down, saw Onata's pleading face upraised to his, and her blanched lips striving to speak his name. He instantly dropped his sword, and, sinking to his knees, clasped her to his bosom, kissed her already chilled face, and cried, in a passion of grief and despair,

'Onata! my child! my love! my wife! — speak to me! Live for me! O, God! I cannot let you die!'

Then, placing his hand on her side, he exclaimed, joyfully:

'Thank Heaven! The fiend struck more lightly than she thought! See; there is but little blood! Let me bind my scarf about you, and you will be better soon, *chère enfant!*'

Onata could not speak, but she shook her head, and signified, by an expressive gesture, that her wound was bleeding inwardly. Then she lifted her failing arms, wound them about the neck of her husband, and rested her head upon his breast, with a smile of ineffable content, the peace of perfect love overmastering the death-agony.

It was then that Gahaneh, seeming to have recovered from a momentary stupor, sprang forward, and standing over them, fiercely grasping the arm of De Vaudreuil, exclaimed, with stern solemnity, yet passionate eagerness :

'You lie to her, Frenchman! She no your wife! You steal the daughter of Sadewana for your paramour!'

'No,' replied Maurice, awed and strangely touched by her tone of mingled anger, doubt, and grief; 'I did her no dishonor; she is my true and lawful wife. We were married by a priest of my holy religion many months ago. See her wedding-ring!'

Saying this, he lifted the left hand of Onata, but the ring was gone from its place. Thoughtful as faithful, she had feared that the sacred emblem might be understood by her sister, and had removed even this silent witness to her innocence soon after she had been taken captive, and had hidden it in her bosom. She now, with a last effort, brought it forth, and signified to her husband that she wished him to replace it on her finger. As he did so she smiled, with something of the old brightness in the tender dark eyes. Suddenly all the wondrous loyalty and heroism of the simple-hearted girl flashed upon De Vaudreuil.

'Holy Mother, can it be possible!' he cried. 'Onata, my poor child, you chose rather to *die* than to reveal our secret!'

Again she smiled, but more faintly than before, and more dimly shone the love-light in the tender, dark eyes.

During this time Gahaneh had stood silent and immovable as a statue; but now she turned, and, fixing her terrible eyes upon Garanguli, cried, in a voice rendered hoarse and unnatural by contending passions,

'Lies! lies! They mock me with lies! Proud French soldier never make wife of poor Indian girl!'

'No,' answered the young chief, sternly, 'he speaks truth — all truth. He husband — she wife; you murderer!'

At this moment a wild cry from De Vaudreuil announced that Onata had breathed her last. Garanguli sprang to her side, all his savage stoicism melting in a burst of uncontrollable, almost boyish sorrow; but, with a mad shriek, whose immeasurable woe, remorse, and despair, drew the eyes of the two mourners even from the dead to her, Gahaneh again clenched the dagger on whose blade the blood of her sister was scarcely yet cold, and drove it into her own heart! [5]

She fell where she stood, but toward Onata, about whose feet she writhed her arms, and held them in a close death-clutch, half tender, half savage, and, hiding against them the dark agony of her face, expired without a cry.

Most of the Indian women had fled on the appearance of De Vaudreuil and his party, but a few had lingered under the shadow of the trees at a little distance, and had witnessed the tragic scenes that followed. They now came timidly forward, and offered to take charge of the dead. De Vaudreuil waved them sternly away from Onata, but allowed them to remove Gahaneh. He even assisted to unclasp her arms from the feet of her victim, gently, almost reverently, so softened was he by that last act of humiliation and penitence, so awed by the terrible vengeance she had wreaked upon herself.

The squaws then constructed a rude litter of boughs, on which they laid the body of their proud chieftainess, and, taking it on their shoulders, bore it slowly and silently homeward.

The night grew more chill and gloomy as it advanced, and the two soldiers from the fort piled fresh fuel upon the fire, and fell asleep by its genial warmth. But De Vaudreuil and Garanguli still sat apart, watching over their dead, speechless and motionless, scarcely conscious of each other's presence, yet feeling a strange kindred and companionship in grief.

The moon went down, the stars waned, and the first dim, uncertain light of dawn crept over the sky, more the premonition than the presence of morning; yet still they sat thus over their dead.

There was a peculiar, watchful, wistful look in the eyes of Maurice; for all his dumb quietude, it was with secret impatience and insane hope that he awaited the coming of the dawn. 'Surely,' said his fond fancy, 'she will awake with the nature of whom she was a part. My Onata, like the other forest leaves, will stir and flash in the breath and brightness of morning! The first sunbeams will kiss open her heavy eyelids, and set her chilled pulses in play!

The song of the earliest bird will reach her dulled ear, and thrill her with the ecstasy of life!'

Alas, poor boy! — for he was indeed little more than a boy, — his sudden bereavement had not only bewildered his reason, but the subtler instinct of the heart, or that would have told him that no smile or glow of nature could unseal those lids that had lain still and cold under the pressure of his lips and the hot rain of his tears; that no voice of living creature, no sound of earth, could pierce the ear deaf to his tender words and desolate sighs.

Yes, the birds only sung to make her death-stillness more profound; the sun shone only to reveal with more fearful distinctness the death-shadows fixed forever on the beloved face before him, and to flash and burn upon his brain the dread certainty of his loss. At length, wholly resigning the wild hope which had tortured even more than sustained him for the last few hours, he laid Onata's head off his breast, stretched her slender form upon the turf, crossed her hands upon her bosom, and smoothed down her shining, abundant hair, with reverent kisses, and soft, lingering touches. Then, hiding his face in his hands, he sat beside her for some minutes, communing silently with God and his own soul.

When he looked up, he saw standing opposite him, with drooping head and folded arms, the old sachem Sadewana, gazing on the dead face of his child with the imperturbable calmness befitting his age, dignity, and race. Yet there was in his dark, hard face an expression of profound though jealously-repressed sorrow, far more touching than that abandonment of grief audible and visible to all, in stormy gusts of sobs and tears. After a moment he bent and laid his hand in a half-caressing, half-benignant way upon the brow of the dead; then turning to one of the soldiers who stood near, he said:

'She pretty girl;' and then added, with a quiver of the lips, 'she good child, always.'

Soon after, he asked permission of De Vaudreuil to have the body of Onata taken to the Indian village for the funeral rites. But the young officer clasped it again with jealous fondness to his heart, and declared that he would only lay it out of his arms into the grave, and that the burial should be there, in that lonely forest dell, where she had perished.

On looking for a spot near by in which to make a grave, the soldiers came upon the one already prepared. It was shallow, and roughly dug, but they deepened it somewhat, and shaped it as best they could with the rude wooden spades which they found beside it, and Garanguli went away and gathered fresh green leaves, and tender sprays, and wild-flowers, and flung them down in such abundance that the dark, damp earth was quite concealed. He then went to De Vaudreuil, who still sat gazing more and more tenderly upon the dead face of his child-wife, and told him that all was ready.

Maurice started, and murmured,

'So soon!'

Then gently removing from Onata's neck the sacred chain and cross, he hid them in his bosom with a long lock of dark hair which some time before he had severed from her head, resolving that there they should be reverently treasured till *his* heart also should be cold in death. Then he kissed those little brown hands, — now almost fair, — her delicate lips, her round, childish brow, for the last time, lifted her in his arms, bore her to the grave alone, and laid her down among the flowers, wrapped only in the soft plaid shawl beneath which she had slept so often the light, dream-haunted slumbers of her happy married life.

All stood beside the little grave in utter silence for some moments, looking their farewells. No tears were shed by those most desolated by her 'untimely taking off,' but the two hardy soldiers repeatedly drew their rough hands across their eyes, touched by the pitiful and beautiful sight.

At length, De Vaudreuil, taking a missal from his pocket, strove to read some suitable prayer for the acceptance and repose of the soul departed; but his voice soon faltered, then failed him utterly.

'*Je ne peux pas!*' he exclaimed, sadly; then added, in English, 'God will take her as she is; poor innocent child, she does not need our prayers!'

He rejected the offer of the old sachem's embroidered blanket to be flung into the grave, and, with Garanguli, began to drop more leaves upon the body, saying that they made the most fitting pall for her fresh young beauty, which had seemed born of the woods — informed with its free, graceful life, in motion and repose. The death-blight had struck her early; it was meet that sister leaves and flowers, plucked ere 'their time to fall,' should perish with her, and pass into darkness and 'cold obstruction.'

Gradually, limb after limb, and lineament after lineament, disappeared from sight. Under crimson wild-roses, and pale-red columbines, her bosom, stained with the deeper red of its cruel wound, and her small, clasped hands, sunk away; but upon her face they flung only the sweet spring violets, which grew in such profusion along the brook-side,—so that it vanished like a pale star, fading slowly behind an azure cloud.

Over the flowers they laid thick boughs of evergreen and oak, and then the soldiers stepped forward and began to fling in the earth. At this, the saddest sound which can ever strike on mortal ear, softened though it was now by the earth falling on leaves and flowers, instead of the resounding coffin-lid, De Vaudreuil shuddered; he could not stand under it alone, but, stretching out his hand, grasped that of Garanguli. When all was finished, and the violeted turf replaced, the two friends constructed a rude cross of the trunk and limbs of a young pine-tree, and, wreathing it with evergreen, placed it at the head of the grave. Then Maurice, after looking down upon the little mound for a moment, again turned to his companion, and said, in a kindly, earnest tone,

'We both loved her, Garanguli. She is gone. We cannot be rivals any more. Let us be friends, more than friends—brothers.'

The young chief, with a look and tone of equal cordiality and frankness, replied:

'If you want poor Indian friend, he give himself to you,—his heart, his life, all. He stands alone in the world now—he very sad, very ignorant; but he can hold his head high, for he has always spoken truth. He forgive you for Onata; but he love you because you, too, speak truth, and have no small thoughts in your heart.'

He then went on to say that De Vaudreuil was of a favored race, that had grown wise, strong, and fair, in the perpetual smile of the Great Spirit, as grain grows heavy-headed, fruits ripen, and flowers brighten, in the sunshine; while he came of a people less beloved by the Master of life,—who had hidden away from Him in the great forest, till they had grown weak, and darkened, physically and mentally, in the shadow of his forgetfulness. 'Yet,' he added, 'you have said the words—we are brothers.'

Thus these two—one a representative of the highest civilization, the other an untutored child of the forest—were drawn together by a holy, mysterious sympathy over the grave of one beloved of both. O, Love is truly the natural religion of the heart, and Sorrow is its divinely-appointed apostle.

When, at length, the two friends turned to leave the spot, henceforth to be to each heart a haunted shrine of gentle and mournful memories, they found that the old sachem Sadewana had already disappeared.

CHAPTER VII.

THE FRIENDS.—FRANCE.

Dost thou hear?
Since my dear soul was mistress of her choice,
And could of men distinguish her election,
She hath sealed thee for herself; —
——— Give me that man
That is not passion's slave, and I will wear him
In my heart's core, ay, in my heart of hearts,
As I do thee. SHAKSPEARE.

Thy storms have awakened their sleep,
They groan from the place of their rest,
And wrathfully murmur and sullenly weep —
BYRON'S ODE TO 'THE LAND OF GAUL.'

I HARDLY know how I can continue this history, now that the fiery spirit which inspired my thought, and that gentle heart of love which seemed almost to beat against my own, are both gone to the long rest. Gahaneh's stern and powerful nature has still a hold upon my imagination, strong as her own death-clutch; and poor Onata's tender eyes, they haunt me yet. My heart *will* linger beside that lonely forest-grave, where she is lying, under her flowery pall, mingling her dust with that of the perished violets, whose kindred still make beautiful the place of her repose.

But, for the sake of him whose love and faith inspired her with more than Roman courage and constancy, for whom she stilled the cry of her young heart for life, and meekly 'consented to death,' and for that other yet profounder and rarer nature, redeemed from the thraldom of wild passions, lifted out of barbarism itself, by love for her, a love which despair and death but deepened and sanctified — for their sakes I will go on.

Lieutenant de Vaudreuil rejoined Lafayette in time to share with him in the glory, and in what to his then despondent heart had greater attractions, the peril, of the hard-fought battle of Monmouth.

In this engagement it was observed that the young French officer, who fought with almost the recklessness of a madman, was constantly accompanied by a tall stranger, in the uniform of a French private, but whose grave, bronze-like face, and fine, athletic figure, proclaimed him of Indian blood. He was like the shadow of De Vaudreuil, pressing with him, shoulder to shoulder, into the thickest of the fight; now thrusting himself forward to arrest an impending sword-fall, strike up a threatening musket, or anticipate a bayonet-thrust; more than once saving the life of the melancholy mad-brain by his quick eye and powerful arm, and by a skilful use of the lance, a favorite weapon of his savage life, to which he still clung.

It was thus that the young Oneida chief, Garanguli, first took part in the great revolutionary struggle — not as a partisan, but as an accidental ally, inspired not by patriotism, but by a passionate friendship.

Throughout this battle the two friends fought together, scarcely at any time more than a foot apart; and while the one fiercely courted and the other calmly defied death, seeming to share a charmed life. Many a musket was levelled at the one and the other, with apparently a deadly aim — many a shot fired; but, when the smoke cleared away, there were the pale, fixed face, and its dark shadow, still pressing on, reckless and relentless.

On the night succeeding the battle, Lafayette summoned De Vaudreuil to his tent, and, after gently reproving him for the recklessness which even he, careless for his own safety as he usually was, had observed with alarm, proceeded to congratulate him on the true bravery he had displayed, and the distinction it would doubtless bring him.

'It is a pity,' he continued, 'that you cannot stay to add to your laurels; yet I hold that there is no duty so sacred at this time as that you owe to your father, and I owe it to him to speed you homeward. But you will go off with *éclat* — that is well. You will make your exit from our stormy stage like a true dramatic hero, covered with glory and gunpowder. Ah, tell me,' he added, after a moment's pause, 'who was that aboriginal recruit who fought with you, more effectively than scientifically, it struck me? *Morbleu!* he did good service with that strange, Tartar-like weapon of his — actually impaling men with it, and then tossing them off, as lightly, it seemed, as a harvester flings off grain-sheaves from his fork; and when that finally failed him, I noticed that he was no mean hand at the musket and bayonet.'

'Yes, *Monsieur le Marquis*,' replied De Vaudreuil,

'he fought gallantly, but only in my defence. He had little heart in the fight, except as his heart was with me. He is my friend, my adopted brother, and sets an infinitely higher value upon my poor life than I myself do; indeed, had it not been for his jealous guardianship over it this day, I very much doubt whether I should now have the honor of addressing you.'

'*Mon Dieu!*' exclaimed the gay marquis, politely suppressing a yawn of weariness. 'I would guard such a friend—he is a gift of the gods, a native-born Pylades, a primitive Pythias! In truth, such a loyal heart is better than a breast-plate of steel!'

'You are right, *mon Général,*' responded Maurice. 'I will guard and prize this noble Oneida as long as he will honor me with his friendship. Strange as it may seem to you, our lives, our fortunes, are already inseparable. Garanguli's is a high, honorable nature, with which I am only too proud to claim kindred. All that is wanting to a complete sympathy is education; which, fortunately, he has the intellect to receive, and I have the means to bestow.'

'And so the Indian accompanies you to France?'

'I have obtained his promise that he will do so.'

Lieutenant Maurice and his friend reached France in safety, though the little craft on which they took passage was more than once threatened with capture or destruction by formidable British vessels of war, and escaped only by fast sailing, or some nautical Yankee trick, so unlooked-for, and executed with such daring and cleverness, as to leave the enemy rather amazed and amused than vexed at his loss.

The Count de Vaudreuil welcomed his heir with proper paternal affection, tempered, indeed, by the pride and stateliness of his character, yet marked by unusual warmth and *empressment.* Garanguli he received with the high-bred and somewhat cold courtesy of the old nobility of his time; indicating by not so much as an inflexion of the voice, or the uplift of an eyebrow, his natural surprise at his son's singular choice of a friend and companion in arms.

As soon as the *fête* given to the peasantry of the estate of the De Vaudreuils, in honor of the arrival of the new heir, was over, and a few visits of ceremony had been exchanged with the neighboring nobility, all became quiet at the old chateau, and Maurice was at liberty to begin the great work of educating his Indian friend. He entered upon this work with the utmost zeal and earnestness; not, as in the case of Onata, taking the entire tutorship upon himself, but merely the general direction of the studies to be pursued. He appointed experienced masters, who were obliged to commence at the very rudiments of knowledge, as the Oneida's modest acquirements in English of course availed him little in the French. But the duties of his masters, though unfamiliar, and requiring the exercise of no little patience and tact, were far from uninteresting and thankless. Garanguli displayed a wonderful aptness for learning, and an insatiable thirst for knowledge. He was earnest, docile, faithful, and tireless, in his new pursuits. The influence of civilization rested upon him like some mysterious but most potent spell of magic; one after another he abandoned his savage habits and propensities, and adopted those of the society around him, with a marvellous, an almost unconscious ease. Maurice had feared that his friend's intellect, quick and powerful as it seemed in the native lore of savage life, and the unwritten wisdom of nature, would give but slow and slight returns to the belated culture of literature and science, the labors of learned tutors, and the wisdom of schools and systems. But, to his happy surprise, it soon appeared that the mind of the youth, naturally a generous, receptive soil, had only lain fallow through all these years to become enriched, and strengthened, and ready for cultivation. Thoughts were there, a lusty, luxuriant growth; some springing up stately and fair, like harmonious responses to the call of the 'Master of Life;' some distorted by errors and superstitions, and nearly all needing the pruning-knife, and the restraining or guiding hand. Primitive philosophies of life, and crude, extravagant theories, grew there spontaneously, entangling themselves together, and wandering at their own wild will, but which caught eagerly at the supports of knowledge, and followed with a glad, instinctive obedience the direction of art. There were also sweet, shy fancies, the unconscious poetry of a generous youth, flowering in stillness and shadow, and needing only kindly culture to call forth from them a richer bloom, and to imprison their subtle sweetness in words.

Happily, this wild intellectual domain had no waste, arid places, no obstinate growth of noxious vices, no defiant steeps of rock-seated prejudice; but, kept fresh and fair by its native intuitions of purity, justice, and freedom, and by inspirations of eternal truth, welling up like perpetual springs, it seemed to smile unconsciously toward the heaven whose care had been over it, even in its utmost apparent abandonment.

It is true that, though Garanguli conformed to the customs of civilization and the wise regulations of society with wonderful adaptiveness, there were times when the habits of his savage life struggled mightily to regain their ascendency; times when they possessed him with a wild unrest, or weighed upon him like a mortal sickness. There were times when he became half-frenzied by the restraints of that strange, new life, sorely wearied and bewildered with the rush of new thoughts, and tossed his arms with a childlike despair, and cried aloud with a wild, irrepressible longing for the freedom, the space, the balm-breathing quiet, of his great forest-home. But these paroxysms of his dying barbarism grew less and less frequent and violent, till they ceased altogether, and Garanguli was apparently and essentially 'a new man,'

Yet, though he devoted himself to study with hearty enthusiasm and a steady purpose, and in general conformed with cheerful readiness to the wishes and customs of his new friends, he shrank with proud shyness from society, and the observation of the curious. It was seldom that he could be prevailed upon to meet any of the guests at the chateau; and though but a few leagues from Paris and Versailles, it was many months before he would consent to visit either. It is true, De Vaudreuil did not at first very urgently insist upon his *protegé's* leaving the retirement of the old chateau, to see the world, at capital, or court, being himself so oppressed with a melancholy indolence, a weight of regrets, and sad recollections, as to have little heart for the office of *cicerone*. But through the elasticity of youth, rather than the teachings of his philosophy, he finally got the better of this unnatural depression, and his restless, exacting spirit, robbed alike of the soldier's 'occupation' and the lover's secret joy, imperiously demanded change and distraction. He owed it to the purifying and subduing influences of love and sorrow, that he did not at this time plunge into any of the wild dissipations and vicious excesses of the young *noblesse*, did not seek to drown memories and regrets in the wine-cup, or the wilder intoxication of gaming, and to sun his chilled heart in the smiles of courtesans. As it was, he did not seek refuge from, but a new direction to thought; not oblivion, but inspiration, in the society of the wits and philosophers of the capitol — the bold, strong thinkers, and splendid theorists, born to be the martyrs or the scourgers of their time.

In the summer of 1779 the Marquis de Lafayette returned to France, principally to solicit aid from his government for the struggling American colonies. He was received with the utmost enthusiasm by the people, and with much kindness and distinction by the king, who, from the first, had been disposed to favor the transatlantic rebels, — partly, doubtless, out of a hereditary hostility to England, and partly from a generous and most unkingly sympathy with the oppressed.

It was on the occasion of his formal reception by

their majesties that De Vaudreuil prevailed upon his friend Garanguli to join with him the suite of the illustrious marquis, in order to witness the grand spectacle of the most magnificent court in the world.

It was in the gorgeous throne-room of the palace of Versailles that the young Indian first looked upon the ill-starred monarch of France, surrounded by all the imposing accessories, symbols, and pomps, of kingliness, and seated by the side of the young and lovely Austrian princess, whose proud presence alone would have thrown around him the splendor of royalty. It was, in all, a sight to have struck with loyal awe hardened courtiers, 'to the manner born;' and yet, the half-savage alien kept his head clear, and, with his discerning, divining eye, was able to pierce through the trappings and wrappings of royalty, to the *man* within, and to judge him and weigh him by the impartial standard of nature.

'What think you of our king?' asked De Vaudreuil, during the presentation of his general, remarking the earnest gaze of Garanguli, and the 'speculation' in his eye.

During his twelve months' student-life the young Oneida had devoted himself especially to the acquirement of the language of his adopted country, and now spoke it with considerable fluency, though there still clung to him many of the peculiarities of his native speech. He enunciated slowly and gravely, and made use of a figurative, indirect style, picturesque and poetic, yet far from wanting in strength and point. Now, shaking his head, and smiling, half-lightly, half-sadly, he replied to his friend:

'A great king should be like a great rock, shadowing the land with its dark grandeur, or standing firm against the waves of the sea, and lifting its head above the storm. Your king is a gilded tower, or what you call a pleasure-temple, made to shine in summer days, and look a little way over quiet palace-gardens; a strong wind would shake it to pieces, a winter flood would sweep it away. See, his face is weak, like a woman's; it can look nothing strongly. Smiles and frowns drift over it like clouds, and leave no mark behind them. He is merciful and good, I have heard; he looks as though he could harm no man. But the Iroquois would not follow such a chief; their enemies would take courage at the sight of him, and confusion would come upon the great councils of the nations.'

'That,' replied Maurice, smiling, 'is because you poor, ignorant savages know nothing of the ministerial system of government. Our kings are seldom more than the imposing representatives of the true royalty — the sacred symbols of the state. The real power is behind the throne. There,' pointing to M. de Maurepas, 'is the present ruler of the French.'

'Ugh!' said Garanguli, with a shrug of the shoulders, which said, plainer than words, 'worse and worse.' '*He* is weaker than the other, because he believes that he is strong and wise. He will fill the king's ear with sounding wind, instead of the counsels of wisdom, and feed a hungry people with the chaff of parades and promises. He is too old to stand so high; he cannot hear the first low growlings of the storm; he cannot see the little clouds which run before the great tempests.'

Nearly a century later, a great English historian and satirist confirmed the judgment of our bold wild-woods' critic, by repeatedly referring to this minister of Louis XVI. as the 'poor old Maurepas,' 'blind old Maurepas,' etc.

'I cannot say that you are far wrong in your last judgment of character,' replied Maurice; 'and now tell me how you are impressed with her majesty the queen, — not alone of *La Belle France*, but of love and beauty, *n'est ce pas?*'

'She is beautiful and noble,' answered the young Oneida, fervently, almost solemnly, 'but she is too proud, too tender. She is ice — yet she is fire. When trouble comes, the ice must be shattered, or melt away in tears, and the fire may eat into her heart. Her head is lifted high, and seems to have gathered the stars about it; but it cannot awe down the sullen murmurs of your nation's discontent, or dazzle back the clouds of its own misfortune.'

'Heaven save us alike from your criticisms and your prophecies!' replied De Vaudreuil, laughing, and glancing at the queen, his heart throbbing with a double loyalty for the sovereign and the beautiful woman, as she sat radiant with gracious smiles, and the half-tender, half-triumphant consciousness of her own loveliness; in the words of Burke, 'glittering like the morning star, full of life, and splendor, and joy.' He added, with enthusiasm,

'Can any harm out of heaven, or earth, come to so adorable a creature? She is good and merciful, so the saints will defend her. We Frenchmen worship beauty and grace. Remove from her the splendor and sanctity of royalty, and we would still bow before her sovereign charms, and shield her with our hearts against the world. Princess of a regal line, the daughter of the kingliest woman that ever filled a throne, called to be the consort of the mightiest king and the queen of the grandest nation of the world — let her be proud! it is her right; it is the signet of her royalty, the crowning of nature. She once said of herself: "If I were not a queen, people would say that I have an insolent look." But she *is* a queen, — young, fair, with a thousand exquisite womanly charms,— and insolence is impossible to her. See, with what a noble grace, with what refinement of condescension, she receives the homage of the American minister, in his homely republican costume! Ah, think you that those firm-set, philosophic lips confess to no delightful thrill, as they touch that dazzling hand? And mark the look she casts on M. de Maurepas! 'tis that of an angered Juno — proud, calm, contemptuous, scorching with its very coldness! *Mon Dieu!* I would not be in his place, at this moment, for all its honors, emoluments, and the king's spasmodic favor thrice told.'

Hearing no reply to his somewhat prolonged burst of admiring loyalty, Maurice followed, with some curiosity, the gaze of his friend, and found that it was fixed no longer upon the queen, but upon a lady who stood behind her royal chair, in whispered conversation with the good and high-hearted sister of the king. This lady was distinguished from the other dames of the court by wearing her hair, which was peculiarly beautiful and abundant, and of a rare auburn hue, unpowdered, and arranged in a style of simple elegance, with no ornament save a slender circlet of diamonds. She was more regularly and delicately beautiful even than the queen; her form was more artistically perfect, her face had more womanly sweetness, and at the same time a more heroic character. Her smile, which was not frequent, was rather sad than gay; it was not alluring, but subduing; it did not dazzle and flatter those about her, but melted and searched into all hearts. Her complexion, which owed nothing to art, was exquisitely fair, truly reminding the beholder, by its whiteness and delicate texture, of the leaves of lilies, camelias, and faint blush-roses. Her full, soft lips had the tremulousness of feeling and tender sentiment, and her large blue eyes looked strangely deep and dark, with a profound though prophetic sadness; an instinctive out-looking of the soul for the tempest whose blackness should overspread a life as yet clouded only by the incense of love and homage; whose bolts should fall upon a path as yet strewn thick with the flowers of a happy fortune; whose fury should desolate, and desecrate, and destroy beauty in its radiant prime, the pride of high degree, and the majesty of stainless womanhood.

Garanguli, at length rousing himself, and turning to his friend with a sigh of inexpressible admiration, simply asked,

'Who is that woman?'

'That,' replied Manrice, 'is the new court beauty, Louise of Savoy, Princess de Lamballe.'

The friends did not pursue their conversation further, as at this moment they were summoned to the foot of the throne, to be presented to their majesties, by the Marquis de Lafayette. They were both very gracefully received; Garanguli, especially, exciting the interest of the queen, and the curious court ladies in attendance. Not supposing it possible one so lately rescued from American barbarism could understand the language of the most refined court of Europe, her majesty indulged in some rather free remarks upon the copper-colored stranger, and complimented De Vaudreuil upon the beauty and dignity of his savage *protegé*; but, quickly perceiving her mistake, by the confusion of the young Indian, she first laughed, with the gay, childlike abandon peculiar to her in her happiest season, and then apologized, with the grace and benevolence which never left her, even in her darkest days.

Garanguli was peculiarly impressed by the refined gallantry, the graceful deference, almost reverence, displayed by the courtiers, heroes, and philosophers, present on this occasion—not alone for the lovely queen, but for all the ladies of the court; and, on his return to the chateau, he remarked to his friend, with unusual enthusiasm,

'The true secret of your greatness, the security of your power, and the highest result of your civilization, lie in your respect for woman, as well as in your fidelity to your holy religion; for I have noticed that Frenchmen yield their homage, not alone to Deity, the Blessed Virgin, and the saints, but to the purest and brightest of earthly beings, the living Madonnas around them.'

Maurice smiled half bitterly, half pityingly, in answer to his unsophisticated companion, but said nothing at the time to enlighten his blissful, poetic ignorance.

Shortly after, however, he took his friend, loth and reluctant, as though from a prophetic sense of the shock of disenchantment before him, to a gay gaming party, from which ladies were excluded, and where met together many of the gallant young courtiers and members of the highest noblesse; and from thence conducted him to a secret convocation of philosophers — some wild dreamers and harmless theorists, but mostly men in whose bold brains and dark, unscrupulous hearts were already surging and seething the dangerous elements which a few years later convulsed the empire, and horrified the world.

At the first gay gathering the young Oneida heard the same noble courtiers and brave soldiers whom he had seen bowing in loyal homage before the majesty and loveliness of womanhood, as though penetrated by the ineffable light of beauty, purity, and gracious sweetness rayed upon them, now speaking with irreverent lightness and freedom, or foppish boastfulness, of the fairest and highest ladies of the court. No name was too lofty to be reached by the shining shafts of their wit and satire; no fame too pure to be slimed over by the serpent tongues of slander. Not even the queen's majesty was spared, and the peerless Lamballe received her share of insolent innuendo.

When Garanguli heard spoken with flippant familiarity the name of one whom, from the first moment of beholding, he had enshrined as the secret divinity of his soul, its transcendent ideal of womanly purity and loveliness, he turned away, angry and sick at heart, with an indignant imprecation upon his lips.

At the club of philosophers and reformers he heard not only kingly rights and hereditary privileges questioned, but infidelity openly avowed, the church reviled, and the holy saints derided.

The veil had, perhaps, been too suddenly torn from the eyes of the young Indian. He should have suffered a more gradual disenchantment; have been allowed to fall by easy, unconscious gradations into the cool, unexacting, unbelieving, *blazé* condition of the world around him. As it was, he mourned too bitterly the generous faith and the fair illusions of which he had been robbed.

'Your civilization is rotten!' he cried to De Vaudreuil; 'its manliness and its sanctity are dead. You mock woman with a false homage; you betray her with honeyed lies; and you have no God. Better, a thousand times, our honest barbarism; for, though we have degraded our women, we have not dragged down the Great Spirit from heaven. He still looks forth in the sunshine, and moves in the dark of the storm; and we, poor, powerless, and ignorant as we are, still lie at his feet, and dare to call him "Father." We know that we are not the best beloved of his children; we know that he has long frowned upon and scourged us; — but we hold that it is better to live in the shadow of his anger, than in the light of a great lie.'

When the Marquis de Lafayette was about to return to America, Lieutenant de Vaudreuil, by much earnest and persistent solicitation, obtained the permission of his father, the count, to accompany him. Never since his return to France had the young soldier been entirely free from regret, and a secret sense of shame, for having suffered himself, while in America, to become so absorbed in his *affaires de cœur* as to forget for a time the larger interests of freedom, and the generous purposes for which he crossed the sea, and thus to miss the honorable distinction which he might have won. Though in the yet sorrowful depths of his stricken heart he read his own best justification, and felt that it was much to possess the sweet and ennobling memory of such love and devotion as had been his, he yet burned to redeem himself before the world, and especially in the eyes of his general, from the reproach of indolence and inconstancy which he felt rested on his name. So, having received a colonel's commission in one of the new regiments about to be sent to the aid of the colonists, he took leave of his family and friends, leaving his father to the monotonous routine of duties and the sombre amusements of an elderly country nobleman of that day; and Garanguli, sorrowful but submissive, to his books and masters; — and, with the devoted Lafayette, set out for America in the summer of 1780.

They went the harbingers of hope and the messengers of sympathy and fraternal alliance, confidently trusting soon to return to their generous native land with the tidings of victory and a glorious peace. But nearly four years of struggle, hardship, and incalculable sacrifices, wore on, with alternations of success and defeat — of sun-bursts of hope and prosperity, and thick darkness of discouragement and misfortune — before their blood-bought liberties were secured to an oppressed but indomitable people.

We cannot follow our chivalric hero through all the events and experiences of his second crusade in the New World, — a crusade not undertaken to recover an empty sepulchre, but to 'save alive' the hope of humanity, Freedom, the political redeemer of the world.

Through all that unequal conflict he worthily bore his part, and was unsurpassed by any of his heroic and disinterested countrymen in brave deeds upon the field, and in the better bravery of patient endurance. He was present with Lafayette at the siege of Yorktown; at the head of his gallant regiment he stormed one of the redoubts, and with his own hand planted above it the banner of the republic.

Though the surrender of the Earl of Cornwallis and his army was in reality the great concluding act in the long drama of the Revolution, yet the defeated actors lingered tediously upon the scene, obstinately refusing to take 'the cue,' which was simply *exeunt*; and a weary, profitless time went by before the royal prompter rang down the drop-curtain, in the shape of a treaty of peace.

A short time previous to their return to France, the Marquis de Lafayette and his friend Colonel de Vaudreuil were present at a treaty of the United States with the Six Nations, which was held at Fort Stanwix.

On this occasion, Indians, commissioners, and spectators, were electrified by a powerful burst of eloquence from a fiery young chief, who passionately opposed the burying of the tomahawk, and the acceptance of the pacific and generous overtures of the federal government. Now that they were basely forsaken by their woman-hearted British allies, he said, let them resolve to carry on a war against the United States, single-handed and alone. Let them not consent to wear away their lives in shameful vassalage and fear, and at last creep forth in the dark, cowed and noiseless, from the world! Let them rather perish, if perish they must, in a great tumult of fighting, in blood and flame, shouting out their souls in a defiant war-cry, amid heaps of slaughtered enemies, and be borne in triumph to the spirit-land, as on a whirlwind of their affrighted ghosts!

Unwise and desperate to madness as were his arguments, with such force, passion, and splendor of diction, were they delivered, that for the moment they fired the humbled and discouraged hearts of the Indians with new ferocity and defiance, and even drew from his white auditors an involuntary tribute of applause.

'Pray, who is this savage Demosthenes?' demanded Lafayette of one of the commissioners.

'*Sagoyewatha*, or Red-Jacket, a famous young chief of the Senecas,' was the reply; 'and much I fear he will make trouble for us with his "blood and thunder" eloquence. His words are bigger than his heart, for they say that he decidedly lacks courage in battle.'

'That may be,' rejoined the marquis; 'but his words are arrows of flame, maddening the heart; his voice is one to drive others into the mouth of hell itself! *Dieu!* such a spirit would work mischief among our half-savage lower classes in Paris!'

Alas! when the time was ripe, the *sans culottes* had their own orators, who were actors also in the dread scenes they conjured up, — harder, subtler, more daring and desperate, than their dark brothers over the sea, — more brutal in cruelty, more demoniac in revenge.

During the brief stay at Fort Stanwix, Colonel de Vaudreuil mysteriously disappeared from the circle of his friends, and was absent for several hours. When he returned, his face wore an expression of profound sadness, almost of recent bereavement. It was a look that awed back all idle curiosity; his companions forbore to question him concerning his temporary absence, and to them it was never explained.

He had visited the lonely grave of his forest bride, and alone, with his face against the flowery turf of the little mound above her breast, had tasted again the divine sweetness of his first love, and the mortal bitterness of his first sorrow.

Maurice, like his illustrious superior, returned to France burdened with the thanks and blessings of a grateful people, and bearing, as his highest honor, — the dearest, most sacred meed of fame, — the commendation and friendship of Washington.

The Count de Vaudreuil, softened by age, and somewhat broken by infirmities, welcomed his son with more than the old paternal warmth. He embraced him long and tenderly, alternately clasping him to his breast, and pushing him back the better to examine his now unfamiliar face, bronzed by exposure, and hardened, at last, into soldierly manliness.

Garanguli met his friend with a quiet, manly joy, not affluent in words, but eloquent in look and gesture, and in tones that seemed to rise tremulous and humid from the heart.

The Oneida was also greatly changed. He had lost much of that physical beauty which had first struck the classic eye of Maurice. He was now slender almost to emaciation; the arrowy straightness of his figure had given place to a slight, student-like stoop, and its pard-like grace and suppleness of action to a quiet, almost languid movement. He was pale, and habitually serious; his eyes were usually cast down, or wore an absorbed, introverted expression, while his brow, once borne high in the instinctive supremacy of his savage beauty and strength, inclined forward, as though heavy with thought.

Yet, when affectionately questioned by his friend, he said that he was happy, deeply happy, and content in this laborious student life, and the yet higher and profounder spiritual life, upon which he had only truly entered during the last year. He had begun the study of religion very much as a science, but he had finally embraced it as the richest birthright of humanity, the grandest guerdon of immortality. In referring to the apparent wasting away of his physical energies, he said, with a smile of inexpressible sweetness and pathos, 'It is the mental treading down the sensual; it is the soul burning its way toward the infinite goodness and wisdom.'

Not long did the returned French heroes enjoy in tranquillity their well-won honors. The 'many waters' which rolled between the two countries could not quench the fire of republicanism. It stretched across the deep, and caught beyond the sea, appearing at first as a cheering, purifying warmth and light, breathing alike upon the heart of peasant and noble, but soon turning into a lurid, devouring flame, menacing the most sacred institutions of religion, the most venerable structures of society, the supremacy, authority, and glory, of royalty. Princes and heroes were eager to stand forth, at first, before an amazed world, transfigured in its treacherous radiance; and the king himself, in generous madness, fanned the flame. Now, princes and heroes were beginning to feel the too near approach of its fiery tongues, and to shrink back aghast; and the king and his countless contradictory advisers were making wild, ineffectual efforts to stay its course. But it was winged with the hate of an infuriated and half-brutalized populace, fed by the heaped-up wrongs of centuries, and no human power could arrest its work of vengeance and destruction.

It was the night of the 5th of August, 1788 — the night when an armed mob, furious and half-famished, besieged Louis XVI. in his palace at Versailles. General Lafayette had arrived from Paris at the head of the National Militia, commanded to bring the king to the capital, but resolved reverently to protect the person and dignity of his sovereign, and to defend the law. Unfortunately the guard of the palace was not intrusted to him; but he had charge of the outposts, which were not even attacked during that stormy night.

The king and queen, tranquillized by the presence and loyal assurances of the brave marquis, who was known to have an almost unrivalled influence with the people, retired to rest; and Lafayette, overcome with fatigue, and trusting that all was well, flung himself upon his couch for a little repose.

Lafayette had again under his command his friend and late companion in arms, Colonel de Vaudreuil; and that officer was once more accompanied by his adopted Indian brother, who, for friendship's sake, had been induced to leave his peaceful retirement and beloved pursuits for the tumult and peril of military life in 'troublous times.' In their fraternal compact, strange to say, Garanguli was the Jonathan — gentle, loving, self-sacrificing; and Maurice the David — generous and ardent, but restless and belligerent; — one of those 'quick spirits' to whom 'quiet is a hell.'

These two did not sleep, but watched with intense interest, hour after hour, the novel and fearful scenes around them.

The night was chill and rainy, but large groups of half-intoxicated and thoroughly brutalized men and women were seated around watch-fires, singing revolutionary songs, full of gross ribaldry, threatenings, and blasphemy. Now and then they formed into circles, and danced about the flames with frantic gestures, fiendish laughter, and howls of rage and hate.

Once, as their maniacal shouts and yells rose loudest and most appalling on the night, De Vaudreuil turned with a shudder to his friend Garanguli, saying:

'It reminds me of the night when Brant's savages surrounded Fort Stanwix, and besieged us with an infernal concert of whoops, yells, and howlings.'

'These voices have more *blood* in them,' replied the Oneida.

Mingled in with the mob, and foremost in ribaldry, obscenity, and all brutal excesses, were hordes of abandoned women, — some monsters of ugliness and crime, veteran hags rallied from the lowest haunts of infamy and vice, and some yet young and unwasted by want and debauchery, in the prime of a bold, baneful beauty, transcendent in sensuality and wickedness.

The leader of these was a tall, handsome woman, with a dark, powerful face, large, flaming eyes, and a ringing, electrical voice. Eloquent, passionate, and fearless, with an intellect of no ordinary stamp, though with a tendency toward insanity, and with a certain personal grandeur of bearing to which not even the most degraded are ever quite insensible, Theroigne de Mericourt exercised over the women of her class an undisputed ascendency, while by intrigue and the basest means of corruption, joined to a fanatic revolutionary zeal, she acquired no inconsiderable power in the army, and influence among the leaders of the popular party. She went from province to province, the missionary of insurrection and massacre; she was the chief of the revolutionary furies — the Roland of courtesans and *sans culottes* — a demoniac Joan d'Arc.

This night she was in all the glory of successful

intrigue, — insolent and drunken with popularity and power. Here and there she passed among the mob of ruffians and desperadoes, stirring them up to a higher pitch of fury by her eloquence, her sarcasms, her bitter denunciations, and Cassandra-like ravings. Among the disaffected soldiery she moved more cunningly and seductively, followed by her most attractive confederates, appealing successively to cupidity, jealousy, revenge, and yet viler passions — the fell, incarnate spirit of disloyalty, anarchy, and rapine.

Once, as she stood haranguing a ruffianly crowd, as she afterwards harangued the republican clubs and assemblies of Paris, standing under the glare of a torch, her strong, stern face now glowing with unholy enthusiasm, and the fierce, prophetic joy of vengeance, — now black with fiendish hate, and a fury which could not spend itself even in the stream of scathing curses which seemed to blaze from her lips with every bold assertion, bitter invective, or powerful dramatic gesture, calling yells of frantic applause from her audience, — Garanguli, turning to De Vaudreuil, said:

'There is a *civilized* Gahaneh! Is she less barbarous, less degraded and dangerous, than the savage?'

'No, by Heaven!' replied Maurice; 'there is no barbarism so fearful, so inhuman, as that created by the profligacy and tyranny of a corrupt civilization. Society breeds its own scourges and destroyers; savage beasts, nurtured in the dens and jungles of neglect and crime, who every now and then pour forth to flesh their fangs in its very heart, and satiate in blood the long hunger of hate; monsters born in the slime of its secret vices, rising at last from unimagined depths to poison the world with the pestiferous breath of a ripened corruption.'

At length, partly by treachery, the besieging mob effected an entrance into the palace, and made their way to the apartments of the queen, the principal object of their hatred. Her majesty was only alarmed in time to escape in her night-dress, through a private passage, to the chamber of the king; while the brigands, foiled in their murderous purpose, vented their fury upon the royal bed, by thrusting it through and through with their bayonets.

Two of the faithful life-guards were killed in the defence of their royal master and mistress, and their heads were shortly after seen borne upon pikes, ghastly, bleeding trophies, tossed hither and thither by the surging crowd.

The heads of royalty might have been subjected to a like indignity, — a fate attended by less regicidal 'pomp and circumstance,' but in reality more merciful, than the one they met a few years later, — had it not been for the timely arrival of Lafayette, who, followed by his gallant grenadiers, rushed to the rescue of the life-guards, and the defence of the king.

It was on this night that the unfortunate Louis was compelled to make his first concession to the people, by appearing upon the balcony of the palace, and promising to proceed to Paris in obedience to their insolent commands. It was on this night that Marie Antoinette was first made bitterly aware that the people who had received her with the enthusiasm of admiring loyalty, when she came to reign over them in the pride and joy of her beautiful youth, were now maddened against her by jealousy and slander, and athirst for her blood. When she first appeared before them, beside her husband, and accompanied by her terrified young children, such a tempest of yells, threats, and imprecations, came roaring up from the hell of human ferocity beneath her, that she was driven back, tearful and appalled. But the mob having been somewhat conciliated by the king's act of unkingly submission, Lafayette led forth the queen. She was again received with some threats and derisive cries; but the noble marquis, with fine tact and understanding of the French character, stooped and respectfully kissed her hand.

It was an exhibition of courtly gallantry, — a little dramatic scene, — which was sure to strike the fickle mob. In an instant they burst forth with shouts of '*Vive Lafayette!*' '*Vive la Reine!*'

This was the first time that the Oneida, Garanguli, had beheld Marie Antoinette since the memorable occasion of his presentation at court. Sad indeed was the change. She was now pale and agitated; her white dress was in disorder, her head uncovered, and her beautiful fair hair dishevelled. Yet, as she stood thus facing the motley multitude of her enemies, motionless and silent, looking, to use the words of another spectator, 'like a victim upon the scaffold,' there was about her a mournful majesty more impressive than the gay and haughty queenliness of prouder and happier days. It was the dignity of a noble womanhood, wronged but not humiliated, — the heroism of love and maternity.

Early on the following day, the king and royal family set out for Paris, escorted by the main body of the militia and the deputies of the assembly, preceded and followed by the mob of *sans culottes*, hags, and courtesans, more than ever insolent with success, and, like hungry beasts of prey, maddened with a taste of blood.

Theroigne de Mericourt and her shameless corps marched in front of the king's carriage, but seized every opportunity of falling back to rail at the royal inmates. They sung songs of the coarsest character, containing insulting allusions to the queen, and more than once shouting exultingly to passers by:

'Courage, friends! we shall now have plenty of bread; for we have got possession of the baker, the baker's wife, and the baker's boy.'

De Mericourt was on horseback, her beauty rendered more conspicuous by a blood-colored riding habit, a plumed hat, a sabre at her side, and pistols in her belt.

At one time, taking her chance when Lafayette and his aids had ridden forward to make some arrangements for the march, she approached near to the royal carriage, and addressed the queen, less coarsely than one of her illiterate and vulgar companions would have spoken, but in a manner of cool, quiet insolence scarcely less offensive.

'Which of us, Austrian,' she said, 'is the true queen, thou or I? Where is now thy lofty state? where are now thy palace slaves, with their silken speech and their perfumed homage? What power hast thou, poor alien? If we flout thee, darest thou resent it? If we harm thee, canst thou revenge thyself? But behold *my* courtiers, — *my* dames of honor! True, these are somewhat brazen-faced, haggard, and bedraggled, and understand better how to bestride a cannon, and sing merry songs in honor of thy little frailties, than to dance a minuet, — but they are brave girls for all that! True, those are most of them rough, hard-handed, uncombed, and somewhat tipsy; but drunkenness is a courtly vice, *grâce à Dieu!* They are also ragged, dirty, and hungry, — *les pauvres diables!* — but they are all honest, loyal fellows! I have but to wave my hand, and scores of them would leap forward to do my will, even were it to take thy royal life, *ma chère!* I am not sure,' she added, with a taunting laugh, 'that they would find *that* altogether a painful duty!'

'Yes, yes! she is a brave queen — the Mericourt!' shouted the ferocious Jourdan; 'we will acknowledge no queen but *La Belle Liégoise!* — let us crown her, friends!' and, riding forward, he removed her hat and placed upon her head the plumed casque of one of the murdered guardsmen, amid shouts of '*Vive la Reine!*'

The insolent cyprian laughed, and, thrusting her hand through the window of the carriage, said, with an air of mock condescension,

'We will suffer thee to kiss our royal hand, thou poor deposed one!'

Marie Antoinette shrank back in disgust and horror, for the hand was stained with blood. Theroigne de Mericourt had been the bearer of one of the pikes on which were perched the dripping heads of the guardsmen.

Fortunately, at this moment Lafayette returned with his aids, drove back the vile crowd, and reproved the sullen or cowardly National Guards for having suffered them to approach His Majesty's carriage.

He succeeded in preserving his royal charge from further insult, and lodging them that night at the palace of the Tuileries in safety, but exhausted with fatigue, worn with the cruel anxieties and harrowing emotions of that night of terror and that journey of humiliation and horrors.

CHAPTER VIII.

REVOLUTION.—LOVE.—REST.

At length I perceive that, in revolutions, the supreme power ultimately rests with the most abandoned. DANTON.

I know
That love makes all things equal: I have heard
By mine own heart this joyous truth averred;
——— in her beauty's glow
I stood, and felt the dawn of my long night
Was penetrating me with living light;
I knew it was the vision veiled from me
So many years — that it was Emily. SHELLEY.

Come, obscure Death,
And wind me in thine all-embracing arms!
Like a fond mother, hide me in thy bosom,
And rock me to the sleep from which none wake.
IBID.

It is not our task to follow, step by step, the blood-tracks of the French Revolution, through all its fearful excesses, terrors, and retributions, nor to chronicle the humiliations and sufferings of its royal victims. From that memorable night at Versailles, the tempest of misfortune deepened and darkened about them, till the end came.

There was a brief, deceptive sunburst of peace and joyful assurance at the great fête of the federation, when the monarch and the people met together like brothers, and swore solemn oaths of mutual friendship and fidelity; when in the *Champ de Mars*, king and queen heard once more the loyal shouts of an enthusiastic populace, with no dark, prophetic spirit picturing to their dismayed souls the crowd which should gather around them in the *Place de la Révolution*, with no thought that the gorgeous throne on which they sat was but a scaffold in disguise.

There was, for a while, a little gray light of hope — not of triumph, but of escape; but that was soon whelmed in utter gloom, and the dark drama swept swiftly on to its close.

Our hero, Colonel de Vaudreuil, had been from the first more deeply tinged with republicanism than the Marquis de Lafayette; but he was for moderate and as far as possible pacific measures; and believed that reform, to elevate without intoxicating the people, must be gradual, if not partial.

The virtues of the amiable king, and the rare womanly charms of the queen, had endeared them to him by a stronger sentiment than loyalty, and he was firmly resolved never to consent to the immolation of victims so innocent, even upon the altar of liberty.

At his own request, he was appointed by Lafayette to the immediate service of the king; a post which made him obnoxious to the populace, already blind with the fury of disloyalty, and an object of suspicion to the Assembly. Yet he continued faithfully to discharge its duties till the autumn of 1792, when Louis XVI., after having been formally 'suspended from royalty,' was imprisoned with his family in the temple. De Vaudreuil, deprived under some pretext of his command of the royal guard, was on the point of setting out to rejoin Lafayette, who was then at the head of the army of the centre, when a more sacred and imperative duty compelled him to take another course.

The work of revolt and revolution was no longer confined to Paris, and the larger towns; insurrections and massacres were occurring here and there throughout the kingdom, and especially in the vicinity of the capital. The chateau of the Count de Vaudreuil was attacked, at last, as 'the den of an aristocrat,' by a furious mob, sacked, and nearly destroyed. It fortunately happened that the attack was made during one of the brief and unfrequent visits of Maurice and Garanguli; but, though they made at first a gallant and effective resistance, at the head of the faithful servitors of the chateau, they were unable long to contend against the crowd of their maddened assailants, and were forced to fly. They made their escape through a private passage, — Maurice, like another Æneas, bearing his aged father in his arms, — and found a temporary asylum in the cottage of an attached tenant. Here the count, who had long been vainly urging his son to avoid further participation in the crimes and perils of the Revolution, by emigration, laid upon him a solemn command to form some plan of escape to England, and to accompany him thither.

Maurice yielded, but with the secret resolve to return at once to France, after seeing his father in safety, and to stand by the forlorn hope of French freedom, — to oppose cruelty, injustice, and anarchy, to the last.

With considerable difficulty he obtained the necessary passports during the following day, and at night set forth, with the count, for the coast; both so completely disguised as to defy the scrutiny of the most zealous and jealous officials along their route, and at length to effect in safety their landing on British ground.

At his own earnest request, Garanguli was suffered to remain behind, for the purpose of rescuing, if possible, some important papers and valuables from the half-ruined chateau, and of obtaining funds from the steward of the estate, sufficient, at least, to establish the elder De Vaudreuil respectably and comfortably in London.

In truth, the Oneida incurred little or no danger in remaining to execute this important duty. He had taken no prominent part in the revolutionary struggle, and was only known to the popular party and its leaders as the friend and personal attendant of Colonel de Vaudreuil, an officer of undisputable republican sentiments, whose only failings were too great moderation, and a weak tender-heartedness toward the vacillating king and haughty queen.

With the mob the best guarantee of Garanguli's safety lay in the recognition of his Indian blood. They respected his supposed barbarism, and, as he boasted no title, not even that of 'citizen,' were instinctively disposed to extend to him the red right hand of fellowship, with the privileges and protection of their horrible order.

It was in vain that the Oneida searched throughout the undestroyed portion of the chateau for the papers and treasures of his friends. The work of plunder had been complete; cabinets had been demolished, secret drawers and panels had been discovered and forced, and every portable valuable carried off. Nor was this the end of misfortune and disappointment; the steward for whom he sought was nowhere to be found, or heard from. It was supposed that he had been murdered, or captured by the mob; or, what was more probable, had absconded, with all the funds in his possession.

Deeply grieved at the unsuccessful result of his generous effort, Garanguli returned to Paris, for the purpose of obtaining a passport, promised him by the influential official who had favored his friends, as his desire was to rejoin them in England as speedily as possible.

He arrived in Paris during the memorable massacres of September, when the fiends of the nethermost pit seemed to have broken loose, to revel and rage throughout that unhappy city, in a prolonged debauch of butchery and rapine. Hordes of half-naked men, howling out revolutionary songs and watchwords, and reeling with blood-drunkenness, marched from church to church, and from prison to prison, murdering priests and prisoners — the weak, the unprotected, the innocent — by scores and hundreds.

Again Theroigne de Mericourt, in her blood-red riding-habit and black plumes, flamed across the scene, at the head of her army of furies, brandishing her '*sabre d'homme,*' and urging them on to yet more demoniac deeds, and more awful heights of crime. It was then that her betrayed heart tasted the draught of vengeance for which it had so long madly thirsted; when she met her seducer, and doomed him with one glance of the eyes into which he once looked with treacherous tenderness — waved him to death with the hand he had so often clasped with false protestations.

On the morning of the third day of the massacre, Garanguli accidentally found himself near the prison of La Force. Seeing a crowd gathered at the entrance, and remarking that they seemed comparatively quiet, and for the moment unoccupied by any work of slaughter, he was impelled by a natural curiosity to approach, and make his way through the circle, which evidently surrounded some object of interest.

A moment after, his horror-struck eyes fell upon a face all pale, lifeless, and ghastly with the recent death-agony; yet a face which through all the long years since he first beheld it, in the glory of its matchless loveliness, had shone in his secret soul, enhaloed with an adoring admiration and homage.

Before him lay the murdered Princess de Lamballe. Her beautiful auburn locks were clotted with blood, from a cruel wound upon her forehead, and her fair body was pierced by many spear-thrusts; her fiendish murderers had stripped it, and one of their number had stationed himself beside it, with a napkin in his hand, with which he wiped away the blood as fast as it oozed from the wounds, calling upon the crowd, meanwhile, to admire the exquisite symmetry of the limbs, and commenting with licentious gusto on the whiteness and smoothness of the skin.

Barbarian-born as he was, Garanguli grew sick, blind, staggered, and fainted, at the fearful spectacle. He fell among the crowd, who at first trod upon him with jeers and laughter, menaced him with their spears, yet dripping with the blood of the hapless princess, and would have murdered him upon the spot, had it not been that one of the leading '*ouvriers*,' Charlot himself, on looking more narrowly into the stranger's face, cried out,

'Hold! he is an American Indian, — a brother-savage, a blood-drinker like ourselves, and no aristocrat. He must have fainted from hunger or sickness. Bring him wine; see to him, *citoyennes!*'

And it was actually through the kindly ministrations of one of the unsexed sanguinary creatures to whom the '*ouvrier*' appealed, that Garanguli was restored to consciousness from his death-like swoon. He was assisted to rise, and allowed to proceed unmolested to his lodgings, which he reached in time to escape a second sight of that face, beautiful even with the haggard look of pain and horror into which it had hardened, borne aloft upon a pike toward the Temple, there to be thrust against the windows of the royal prisoners, and smite their souls with dismay and despair.

Garanguli was obliged to wait until the popular tumult had in some degree subsided, before he could obtain permission or an opportunity to leave Paris; but, during the remainder of his stay, he kept himself as much as possible confined to his apartments, to avoid witnessing the excesses and atrocities of the frenzied mob.

When at length he was able to depart, he did so with joy inexpressible, shaking the dust of that city of abominations from his feet, exclaiming, as he looked back upon its palaces and towers for the last time:

'Farewell! thou "whited sepulchre" of cities, full of corruption and "dead men's bones," thou splendid asylum of barbarisms at which barbarians shudder, nursery of monsters, paradise of fiends! The savage-born flies from thee with horror, and abjures thee with curses!'

Colonel de Vaudreuil was bitterly disappointed at the result of his friend's mission to the chateau. The sum of money with which he and his father had provided themselves at the time of their flight was inconsiderable, and had been nearly all expended, in the confident expectation of a larger supply.

There was but one course open to him now. He must resign his cherished project of returning to France, and seek out some honorable employment, by which to secure shelter and daily bread for his father, himself, and his adopted brother. Garanguli he had been so long accustomed to protect and provide for, that it never occurred to him at this time that his *protegé* had extraordinary energies and attainments of his own, which might be put to use. He smiled with surprise and incredulity when the Oneida expressed his modest conviction that he could make his own way in the great, strange world of London, and that henceforth it devolved upon him not only to provide for his own wants, but to share in the filial obligations of his brother.

However, the two friends set out together on that long, disheartening search for employment, which thousands, both before and since their time, have pursued over the same crowded but dreary ways.

Garanguli, after some weeks of patient effort, obtained a few pupils, there being an attractive novelty, to young ladies especially, in the idea of taking lessons in French and Italian from an American Indian. But Maurice was not so fortunate; London was already swarming with needy French exiles and *emigrés*, all pressing into the same over-filled ranks, and month after month went by ere he found employment, during which time he and his father were actually dependent upon the humble earnings of Garanguli for a respectable subsistence. Thus was returned to them the bread cast long ago upon the waters.

But the young teacher's income, carefully and economically expended though it was, proved barely sufficient for the most pressing daily wants of the little household. The old count was deprived of those luxuries which, by the habits of a long life, had grown to be simple necessities to him, and his health and spirits visibly failed. The wardrobes of the three began to suffer, and to exhibit the first pitiful, disheartening stages of shabbiness.

In this extremity, it fortunately, or, rather, *providentially*, happened that Maurice encountered, in one of his now almost aimless and hopeless morning walks, an English officer whose life he had generously saved, at the peril of his own, in one of the hard-fought battles of the American Revolution.

Colonel Leslie seemed rejoiced at meeting his magnanimous foe, and kindly questioned him concerning the fortune which had led him to London at a time like this. With the bravest simplicity, and the philosophic *insouciance* of his nature, Maurice told him all, briefly, yet faithfully, adding nothing and sparing nothing. He related, without a blush or a twinge of shame, his adventures since his arrival in London, in his fruitless daily search for bread; he freely confessed his dependence upon his Indian *protegé* — he smiled lightly as he glanced down upon his dress, which unmistakably proclaimed the gentleman in distress; but, when he spoke of the privations and humiliations to which his poor, proud old father had been subjected, his voice trembled, tears rose to his eyes, and he turned his face away.

Colonel Leslie, deeply moved, and feeling far more delicate confusion than his friend had exhibited, yet replied with a cheery English bluntness of speech and manner, dashing at the matter in hand without any needless preamble.

'I' faith, my dear De Vaudreuil,' he exclaimed, ''twas a lucky chance for *me* that I took this way through Hyde Park this morning. You see, I have a son, — one only son, now at Eton, — a clever, bravely-disposed lad enough, but sickly. Poor boy, I have been fearful that he has inherited his mother's malady; she died of consumption while I was in America. Well, Clarence writes, and his masters write, that he cannot keep up with his classes, he loses so much time from absolute illness, and I have bethought me that we must fix upon some other plan for his education, — say a private tutorship. In short, my dear friend, if you will accept of such a situation, until something better offers, I will bring Clarence home at once and place him under your care, knowing that, though he be not crammed with Greek and Latin, like a collegian, he will acquire of you what better befits the son of a soldier — pure, manly tastes, and sentiments of generosity and honor.'

It is hardly necessary to say that Maurice gladly accepted this offer, bowing, with all the gracious politeness of a true French cavalier, to the compliment with which it closed. He soon entered upon his new duties, at the town-house of his friend; not, however, wholly separating himself from his father and Garanguli. The generous salary which he now received, joined to the earnings of his adopted brother, enabled them to remove to more comfortable lodgings, and there to surround the old count with many of the luxuries of which he had been temporarily deprived.

The pupil of Colonel de Vaudreuil was an intelligent, amiable lad, whose ill-health, and a naturally shy, sensitive disposition, gave him an appearance of almost girlish delicacy and gentleness. He was, at first, fascinated by the grace, gayety, and elegant accomplishments, of his noble instructor, and soon became ardently attached to him for his many generous and lovable qualities, — for that soul of honor, that brave and cheerful heart, which no misfortune could embitter, and no humiliation subdue.

In the life of quiet and comparative ease which our little household of *emigrés* now led, they might have been happy, could they have cut their hearts free from all anxieties for their unhappy country and countrymen. But across the narrow channel which divided their asylum from France came, with little delay or merciful intermission, appalling tidings of executions and massacres, — of the ever-deepening and blackening enormities of a nation mad with sensuality and crime, — of the prolonged orgies of a prostituted freedom.

The execution of the king, at which the eloquent Abbé Edgeworth immortalized himself, while commending his meek master to immortality, not as a monarch, but as a martyr, in the inspired words, 'Louis, son of Saint Louis, ascend to Heaven!' the murder of the queen, her fair face prematurely furrowed and wasted by sorrow, and her beautiful hair whitened by untimely frosts; the martyrdom of Roland; the glorious self-immolation of Corday; the heroic death of the Girondists, — dread national events though they were, of mighty political import, and destined to take their dark place in the history of the world, they fell upon those poor, exiled hearts like shock after shock of personal misfortune and bereavement.

But the full catalogue of those crimes, committed in the name of Liberty, was not destined to vex the loyal soul of the aged count. He had been deeply grieved and appalled by the execution of his king; but he never could be brought to believe that the lovely queen, toward whom he had cherished the half-religious devotion of a chivalrous courtier of the *ancien regime,* would be called to mount the same scaffold, and submit to the same ignominious fate; and when, at last, intelligence reached him of that consummation of injustice and dastardly cruelty, her execution, he bent his head despairingly upon his breast, murmuring,

'My God, thou hast, then, utterly abandoned France!'

These were the last words he ever uttered; the next moment he fell forward upon his face, and when his son raised him and laid him upon his couch, he was dead.

The count had been threatened with apoplexy, and his physician decided that he had fallen under a sudden stroke of that disease; but Maurice and Garanguli secretly believed that he had died of a more mysterious malady, one whose existence has been often denied by science, but which poetry, by its deeper truth, substantiates, — a broken heart.

It was shortly after this event that the decline in the health of young Leslie took a more rapid and alarming form. He lost his little stock of health, and wasted visibly, under repeated and violent hemorrhages; and the duties of De Vaudreuil, who was sincerely attached to his pupil, gradually became more those of sick-room companion than instructor. He watched over and ministered to the dying boy with all the tenderness and devotion of a brother, and felt upon his own heart, like a cold, creeping shadow, the slow, darkening approaches of the angel of death.

Yet in that sick room there first dawned for him a new, sweet light of hope and joy, an infinite consolation; in the beginning, tremulous and faint, but, at last, deepening and glowing into more than the spring warmth and brightness of early romance, — the quiet, golden summer radiance of the heart.

By the bedside of his young friend he first met the only daughter of Colonel Leslie; a gentle, fair-haired, poetic being, whose lovely presence in the chamber of the dying would alone have brought visions of heavenly peace and purity, and whose low, sweet tones seemed to prelude angel-voices.

Since the death of her mother, Emily Leslie had resided with a maternal aunt, a lady of rank and fortune, whose heiress she was acknowledged to be; but, upon the first intelligence of her brother's alarming illness, she had returned to her home, and, with loving and anxious devotion, lingered beside the sufferer till the night when, leaning on his father's breast, and holding a hand of De Vaudreuil and her own, he gently breathed out his brief, innocent life, and had

'Another morn than ours.'

Again the *emigré* found his 'occupation gone;' but he was no longer utterly friendless and unknown in a strange land. Colonel Leslie had influential connections, through whose interest he procured for the noble Frenchman a small civil appointment under government, the pay of which, though modest, was sufficient for the simple wants of a soldier refugee.

The two friends, drawn together by closer sympathies and more intimate association in the mournful and monotonous life of exile than in the career of excitement and change which they had led in France, remained quietly in London, patiently following their humble avocations, with no heart to mingle again in the stormy scenes of a revolution which had passed from a noble national struggle for long-withheld liberties and rights, into a frightful political pandemonium, a moral convulsion and chaos.

De Vaudreuil seldom trusted himself to speak of the utter annihilation of his early hopes, those radiant visions of French freedom cheering and lighting the nations of the earth, which he had beheld narrowing and darkening down to the prison and the scaffold; of the transformation of Liberty herself from the beneficent genius which was to redeem humanity, to a fury, a she-fiend, rioting in unimaginable crimes, crowned with the red cap of carnage, and throned upon the guillotine.

On his part, Garanguli seldom referred to the revolutionary incidents to which he had been a witness, — especially to those last sanguinary scenes in Paris, — feeling the utter powerlessness of words to express the horror, the indignation, and loathing, of his soul, at deeds so inhuman and passions so diabolical.

The Oneida had grown more and more silent, reserved, and melancholy; a man with but one earthly affection and no earthly hope, feeling more deeply and desolately day by day that he had no place, no purpose, in the world, — a stray child in God's great universe. Yet, out of this lonely and joyless life, over broken strength and spirit, sprang a gracious growth of Christian virtues, — humility, resignation, and faith, ardent, yet patient, looking forward to 'a better country,' and a life of infinite compensations.

The friends had few acquaintances in London, out of the circle of French *emigrés* and the family of Colonel Leslie. Whenever this officer, now a member of parliament, was in town, they were cordially invited to his house, where they frequently met his lovely daughter — happy happenings, gratefully chronicled in the secret heart of De Vaudreuil.

Emily Leslie was now, by the death of her aunt,

wholly under the guardianship of her father, and soon to become the legal mistress of her fortune.

Since our hero first met her beside her brother's death-bed, she had expanded from timid girlhood into a noble womanhood, rich in rare intellectual culture, and the highest graces and accomplishments of refined life. Yet in heart she was still singularly unchanged and childlike, — ardent, impulsive, tender, simple, fresh, and pure, — the dew of her youth unwasted by the thirst of social ambition, or the sunglare of worldly admiration. Her young life had never been dwarfed or stiffly trained in the hot-house of fashion, but had grown straight, and fair, and free, in the open air of nature, and the genial nurture of affection and truth. She was proud without arrogance, soft without weakness, pure without coldness, beautiful without vanity. She was like some of Shakspeare's women: like Imogen, whose brave modesty rebukes both presumption and prudery; like Perdita, whose gentle spirit steals upon and abides in the memory like the delicate perfume of such flowers as she took delight in; like Viola, whose love breathes through the heart like one of her own tender melodies; like Miranda, free as the waves around her lonely island, and pure as the foam-wreaths that crowned them — to the weary and tempest-tossed, help and cheer, recompense and delight.

On the occasion of Miss Leslie's attaining her majority, Colonel de Vaudreuil and his friend were invited to spend a few weeks at the country-seat of her late relative, now one of her own possessions, when a series of rural fêtes and other entertainments were to be given.

Garanguli gently but firmly declined, and Maurice accepted with mingled feelings of pleasure and apprehension.

Emily Leslie moved among her gay and titled guests like the peerless 'Lady Geraldine' of Elizabeth Browning, the envied and stately yet thoughtful and gracious mistress of sumptuous halls, noble grounds, and 'lovely woods;' while Maurice, not unlike the poet 'Bertram,' wandered restless, moody, and jealous, feeling wretchedly *de trop* and out of place, yet utterly unable to break the spell which bound him there. True he had not that poet-lover's sense of social inferiority, for, though he had never laid claim to his father's aristocratic title, it was universally accorded to him; but he was poor, proud, and passionately in love, and, whatever 'flattering unction' he may have laid to his soul during his former familiar acquaintance with Miss Leslie, in the little home circle of her father's modest household, *here* he felt no faintest hope that his love was perceived and returned. She appeared deeply absorbed in the occupations, cares, and courtesies, of her new position, and to him seemed to smile on all her guests alike.

At length he wound himself up to a desperate determination, not to declare and press his love, but to tear himself from its object, and leave the wild, hopeless passion forever unconfessed.

He first sought Colonel Leslie to take leave of him, which he did with a rather confused announcement of his having found it necessary to shorten his visit somewhat, and return at once to town. The honest soldier set himself earnestly against his departure, and pressingly demanded the reason for so unexpected a step. After a moment of proud hesitation, De Vaudreuil came bravely out with the truth.

'The reason is, my dear friend,' he said, '*that I love your daughter*; that I am bitterly aware that there is a great gulf of national and political prejudices set between us; that she is young, happy, fortunate, and that I am but a poor, friendless *emigré*, saddened and aged before my time; that I cannot, dare not build any hope upon the kindly thoughts and gentle words which her good and noble heart prompts her to shower upon all around her, like God's impartial gifts of dew and sunlight; that, in short, I feel there is but one course which I can pursue in honor and self-respect. That, my dear colonel, which in the soldier is cowardice, in the lover is sometimes the highest heroism — *a timely flight*. This is all that is left me now — this, and a mighty, manly effort at forgetfulness.'

'You are frank, Count de Vaudreuil,' replied Colonel Leslie; 'honest, brave, and soldier-like; and, in return, I will be equally frank with you. I will even confess that my daughter is far from indifferent toward you. Nay, don't look so incredulous, and don't question me. I *know it* — it matters not how. True, she is young, light-hearted, and they say beautiful; but, pardon me, you are not old, except in your own conceit, nor are you greatly battered and broken by wars and misfortunes; and even were it otherwise, like Desdemona, she might love you "for the dangers you have passed." True, she has wealth; but you are noble, and even by the miserable standard of the world rank is a fair equivalent for gold. It is true I have prejudices — the strong national prejudices of a loyal English soldier against a French revolutionist and an ally of American rebels; yet I have also a soul to appreciate honor and generosity even in a natural foe, and gratitude to remember services such as yours. My prejudices are, after all, not so hard and deep-seated that my daughter must break her heart against them. I know you to be a brave soldier, heroic, and, I truly believe, patriotic in your way. I owe my life to you, though "that 's not much," — and — and — *my boy loved you!'*

After a moment's pause, he continued, grasping the hand of his friend,

'So, in short, my dear fellow, I offer my free and full consent, and wish you God speed in your wooing.'

The wooing was not, like Bertram's, a storm of despairing passion, ending in a blinding burst of sunshine, — bliss almost cruel in its suddenness, love almost overwhelming in its completeness. It was but a step from flattering hope to full assurance, — but the earnest utterance of a few tender words, of a response timidly yet joyfully murmured, and 'the great gulf' was passed!

Henceforth the 'fair English rose,' as Maurice often called Emily Leslie, filled with its rich bloom and sweetness a heart in which the hapless forest 'leaf' fluttered out its little summer of joy, and perished long ago.

For some days after his return to London, De Vaudreuil kept the blissful secret of his accepted love imprisoned in his heart, hoping for some affectionate inquiry from his friend, to open the way for a confidence.

But, though Garanguli soon perceived, from the cheerfulness and tenderness of his manner, and the unconscious irradiation of his face, that a happy 'change had come o'er the spirit of his dream,' he forbore to question him, partly from feelings of delicacy, and partly because of a natural shrinking from the knowledge that a new and strange inmate had taken possession of even the vacant chambers of the only human heart in which he cared to have a lodgment.

At length, one evening when the two friends had been sitting together alone and unoccupied, in one of those long silences which are the proof and the luxury of a perfect friendship, — when the mere mutual presence is speech, communion, sympathy, — Maurice, shading his face from the firelight with his hand, confided all to Garanguli, and threw somewhat of its precious weight of joy and hope off his heart on to that of his friend.

As he concluded the story of his wooing and betrothal, he added,

'She is beautiful, brilliant, and an heiress; she has many rich, powerful, and titled suitors, and she has chosen *me*, a poor, obscure, dispirited *emigré*. Is she not a noble creature, Garanguli?'

'She is worthy to fill Onata's place,' was the sole reply; and Maurice, to whose heart his fair love stood transfigured in the new light of a passionate adoration, yet felt that no higher praise could be bestowed upon her than that contained in those simple, eloquent words.

A year later, when he had been some months married, it happened that his wife observed that he wore around his neck a little cross of gold, with a locket containing a tress of dark brown hair, and two or three wild violets, withered, and almost colorless, — and that she ventured to question him concerning those mementos. Then he told her the strange sad story of his first love, — the secret marriage, the stolen happiness and romantic seclusion of his brief union, and the scene of darkness and death with which all closed.

He told her that not even one of her golden ringlets, sunned by happy summers, could replace that dark, shining tress, though to his eye a fearful midnight tragedy lay, as it were, coiled within it; nor could the fair living loveliness over which he bent, the smiling light of azure eyes, the fresh rose-tint of delicate cheeks and lips, ever banish from his heart the sweet darkness of *her* remembered face.

'For you see, dearest,' he said, 'the poor child died rather than break faith with me; in truth, died for love of me.'

'Then let her live immortally in your love, and in *mine*,' replied his wife, with generous emotion. 'And, dear Maurice, never for a moment fear that I can be jealous of that noble, buried heart, or the sad mementos that rest upon yours — of the faithful thoughts which still visit her grave, or the dead flowers which once grew upon it. I will not be jealous of *her*, who was able to prove and seal her love by such a sacrifice. I will trust that you will believe me capable of all faith, all devotion, though no such dark extremity comes to test me.'

During the Consulate, Colonel de Vaudreuil returned to France, and served for a time under Napoleon, whom he had formerly known.

At the capital he again met the Marquis de Lafayette, but lately released from captivity, and a few more of his old political friends and companions-in-arms. But, alas! the sword and the axe had been busy cutting down a noble growth of manliness and virtue, with the tares of a slothful aristocracy and the poisonous weeds of vice and crime. To some the scaffold had been but a step toward the immortal heights; to others, a dark elevation, from which they were goaded to take the final plunge down

'Abysmal depths of endless night.'

There were deaths that seemed to kindle about the guillotine a great glory of devotion and heroism, like the fires of sacrifice and of martyrdom; and deaths where defiant infidelity and crime seemed to wrap it in such darkness and lurid flames as might accompany the disappearance of demons. Roland, Corday, Lucile Desmoulins, the noblest of the Girondists, when surged about by the 'vile rabble,' may have beheld with prophetic vision the great multitude of pitying and admiring spirits beyond, and, with sublime faith, trusted to the last in the truth for which they died. But what vision, what faith, comforted their remorseless destroyers, when the day of their reckoning came; when the yells and curses of the crowd around them but preluded the exulting shouts of an outraged humanity, and the execrations of a world, — an apotheosis of infamy, an immortality of hate!

But to return to our story.

On the assumption of imperial state and power by Napoleon, the Count de Vaudreuil, who had not, for all his instinctive admiration of the great soldier, renounced his republican predilections, requested, and with some difficulty obtained, permission to retire to private life.

He returned to his estates, rebuilt the old chateau, and there, in the midst of his family and attached tenantry, in study and the pursuits of literature and science, he lived through all the political changes that followed an uneventful, unillustrious, but useful and happy life. Heaven blessed his house with health, peace, and prosperity, and crowned the generous love of his heart with constancy, sympathy, and parental joy. Noble sons were born to him, and fair daughters, in whom the dissimilar but not inharmonious qualities of the Gallic father and the Saxon mother seemed to intertwine and blossom together.

And Garanguli — where was he? He had no longer a place in his friend's household; his friend's children had never looked upon his face; his name was seldom uttered now in the old chateau. He was gone.

A short time previous to the marriage of De Vaudreuil, the Oneida announced to him a resolution to return to his native country and people. It was in vain that Maurice argued and plead with him; no remonstrance, no entreaty, could change his purpose, or reconcile him to a future return to France.

'I have flung my years of strength and hope into the great life of your race,' he said. 'I have wasted away under your civilization. I would give my last days to my poor wild brothers. I would die in the lap of my mother-Nature.'

And so he went.

For a while he seemed to revive in his native air and among the scenes of his early youth, changed though they were, and lonely and estranged as he found himself. From the first, he dwelt among his people, adopting to some degree their habits and customs, and affectionately devoting himself to their help and instruction.

'I am in love with barbarism once more,' he wrote to De Vaudreuil. 'It is degraded, but it is honest. It is cruel and revengeful, in obedience to the precepts of a false religion, not in defiance of the spirit of a *true*,—after the traditions of its heroes and wise men, not in despite of the teachings and example of the great and good of many centuries. It is hard, stern, and remorseless; but it is without hypocrisy and miserable pretension. It does its savage deeds in the shadow of superstition and ignorance, not in the blaze of morality and knowledge.'

At another time he wrote:

'I find inexpressible relief and repose in the freedom, simplicity, and tranquillity, of this life. The failing springs of energy and hope seem to have taken a freshened flow; yet, in truth, they run but feebly as it is.

'O, the solemn stillness, the noble spaces, the

sweet, sheltering shadow, of these primitive woodlands! O, the grand companionship of these wild waters, — the deep, delicious repose of these lonely shores!

'Yet there are times when I seem strangely pursued and beset by the world from which I have fled; when the mighty noise of crowded cities seems to roar in winds and waves, and a great rush of people to invade these forest solitudes. There are times when my mind seems shaken again with the convulsions of your fearful revolution, and to groan under the nightmare oppression of its terrible memories; when my imagination swarms with monstrous forms and fiendish faces, and my thoughts run dark and sluggish with the blood I saw flow in the human shambles of Paris.

'Still, Nature is gradually soothing and comforting me with her beneficent ministrations, and I doubt not I shall fall asleep in perfect peace at last.'

Yet later he wrote:

'I hear voices in the winds of these wild autumnal nights, — solemn, but not unwelcome voices, — calling me hence; and the drooping flowers beckon, and falling leaves lead the way to the repose so grateful to a weary heart like mine.

'Dear brother! generous friend! I have one last kindness to ask of you; grant it, and I am happy. Let them make my grave where my heart long ago laid itself, — at the feet of your Onata.'

In reply to this letter, Maurice, after cheerfully rallying his friend on what he hoped were utterly groundless apprehensions, continued:

'In answer to your touching request, dear Garanguli, when they make your grave, — many years hence, I trust, — let it be *by the side*, not at the feet, of my wife Onata.

'She should have loved you, — so much worthier than I. It would have been happier for her; but God willed it otherwise. Had she lived, she surely would have grown to regard you as a brother. As *mine*, you have a right to repose by her side.'

There came no answer to this letter, but several months after there arrived from America a missive addressed to the Count de Vaudreuil in a strange, formal hand. Over this letter Maurice, too truly a man to be ashamed to weep, bowed his head with a burst of passionate emotion, murmuring broken words of endearment and sorrow.

Garanguli was dead.

Many years had gone by, and Maurice de Vaudreuil was again in America. Again he accompanied his illustrious friend the Marquis de Lafayette, — not, as before, to aid a struggling people, but to behold the glory and prosperity of a great nation.

Our hero was an old man now; but his heart was still warm with the noble ardor of freedom and heroism, — still capable of the great sympathies, the generous exultations, of friendship. Thus he gloried and rejoiced in the triumphal progress of his beloved general, in the hero-worship of a grateful nation.

Again, however, he left his companions for a time, to make a lonely pilgrimage to a spot still sadly dear to his heart, — the grave of his Indian bride.

The face of the country had undergone so marvellous a change that it was with difficulty he found the little woodland dell so distinctly pictured in his memory. The thick forest no longer encompassed it, and the peculiar greenness and freshness of the place were gone. But a little plot under a willow had been piously enclosed by a railing, and carefully kept, first by Garanguli, and afterwards by his pupils and converts and their children, — Indian youths and maidens, who had been taught to love and reverence his memory. The little rustic cross at the head of Onata's grave had long ago mouldered away and been replaced by one of stone, which was even now freshly wreathed with evergreens. Rude wreaths and bunches of wild-flowers lay also on her grave; and not on hers alone, but on a mound near by, — for Garanguli slept where he wished to be laid, *at the feet of Onata.*

Maurice de Vaudreuil, forgetting the changes around and within him — the long, eventful years — and tenderly murmuring the names of his friend and his forest bride, idly plucked up violets, so like those that blossomed there many floral generations gone by; then, laying his blanched head upon the turf, the present, the real, glided from him, while he dreamed again the sweet dream of his youth.

It was during this great ovation of Lafayette that the celebrated Seneca chief Red-Jacket was presented to him. In the course of the conversation which followed, the Indian remarked that he remembered having seen the noble marquis, many years before, on the occasion of a treaty at Fort Stanwix.

With a vivid recollection of the scene alluded to,

but without recognizing the changed form and face before him, Lafayette exclaimed, eagerly,

'Ah! I remember a young Indian orator who was then present, and spoke against the burying of the tomahawk in a strain of matchless eloquence. Pray, can you tell me anything of him?'

A gleam of proud pleasure flashed from the deep, dark eyes of the old chief as he replied:

'He has the honor to stand before you!'

NOTES TO 'A FOREST TRAGEDY.'

1 This young chief (Garanguli) must not be confounded with the great Onondaga of that name, who founded the celebrated 'League of the Iroquois.' The custom of giving distinguished names to their children prevailed almost as extensively among the Indians as it does among civilized people.

2 The 'New Year's Jubilee' was a singular and interesting festival of the Oneidas, held about the first of February, or at the time of the old moon in January. It was both religious and social in its character. Several days before the time appointed for its actual celebration, the people assembled for the confession of their sins. Seven days were kept. The first four were devoted to dancing, feasting, and the playing of various games ; on the fifth took place the great ceremony of burning the white dog, which, however, was always killed on the first day. A pure white dog, without blemish or imperfection of any kind, was selected, and strangled, without the shedding of blood or breaking of bones. He was painted ornamentally, and decked with ribbons and wampum — voluntary offerings, for which each giver expected a special blessing. It was then hung up and watched constantly till the fifth day, when it was burned, with numerous and imposing rites. The Onondagas and others of the Six Nations had similar ceremonies, which, however much they seemed to resemble the ancient Jewish sacrifices, are said not to have been distinctly expiatory in character.

[3] The Count de Frontenac, Governor of Canada, was one of the most powerful, persevering, and remorseless enemies that ever did battle against the Iroquois. He rivalled the most savage of their warriors in cruelty, revenge, terrible energy, and lust of carnage. In 1696 he headed an expedition against the Onondagas, and destroyed all before him with fire and sword. It is related that in 1696, when a very old man, he attacked a Mohawk fort, and, on gaining possession of it, found it deserted by all except an aged and infirm sachem, who sat quietly smoking, but with the air of an ancient Roman in the capitol. He saluted the white hairs of his foe with dignified courtesy, but the count, choking with rage at having his fierce blood-thirst mocked by a prey so miserable, commanded his men to hack the old heathen to pieces with their swords. As the ferocious soldiers set upon him, fifty to one, the aged Mohawk raised his voice — not in remonstrance, but in defiance and derision — calling upon them to put him to death by burning and torture, that he might teach the French how to suffer and die like men.

[4] The Oneota was the 'sacred stone' of the Oneidas, often referred to in the history of the Iroquois. It formerly stood on a high hill in the midst of their territory, overlooking several lakes and rivers, and vast stretches of hunting-grounds. Around it the sachems sat in the great councils of the nation, and the warriors marched before going on the war-path. The tribe took its name from it, and it was the distinguishing symbol of the Oneidas, though there were individuals among them of the clans of the Turtle, the Bear, and the Wolf.

What wonderful changes time has wrought! That sacred and memorable stone now occupies a conspicuous place in the beautiful new cemetery at Utica, New York; a portion of the consecrated ground having been appropriated by the proprietress to the remnant of the Oneida nation, yet remaining in that county, haunting, more like troubled ghosts than like living men and women, the ancient hunting-grounds of their fathers.

On a late visit to Utica, I saw, surmounting a smooth, green knoll, surrounded by peaceful shades and pure monuments of the dead who 'sleep in Jesus,' 'the great stone,' once the proud symbol of a powerful heathen people, and around which countless portentous councils have sat, and wild war-dances have whirled. It is a rude, common-looking stone enough ; but to the true Oneida — if such a being now exists — it is a relic more proudly and mournfully significant than is Plymouth rock to the New Englander. For him it is mossed over with sacred memories of a nobler past ; or on its rough face are written glorious records, invisible to other eyes.

At the consecration of the cemetery, some two years since, the Oneidas were invited by the proprietors to attend and inaugurate their 'great stone' in its new place. The Oneidas thought it incumbent upon them to extend the invitation to their brothers the Onondagas ; and both tribes came, a full representation, to the no small embarrassment of the committee of arrangements. 'It seemed,' said my informant, 'that not a squaw or a pappoose had been left behind.' However, by engaging the whole of a large hotel, they were finally accommodated. After witnessing the ceremonies at the cemetery, and partaking of a sumptuous dinner at the hotel, they proposed to devote the night to a grand pow-wow. But, their white friends having represented to them the great impropriety of such a proceeding, they were, with much difficulty, persuaded to depart by special train ; the squaws, to the amusement of their hosts, packing up and taking with them every scrap of food remaining of the dinner provided for them !

Such, with, I fear, but few exceptions, are the Christianized (?) Oneidas and Onondagas of our day.

[5] Thinking it possible that the character of Gahaneh may be objected to as seeming too high-toned and heroic, and withal too fiercely independent, and defiant of Indian regulations and discipline, to be strictly historical, I subjoin, in my support, a highly interesting incident in the life of James Dean, from the appendix to Stone's 'Life of Brant,' to which, and numerous other works, I have been much indebted in the writing of this story.

Mr. Dean was a true patriot and a good man. At the solicitation of a connection of his father's family, his parents devoted him to the service of religion, in the trying character of a missionary to the Indians. In order that he might obtain a knowledge of the Indian tongue, he was sent, at the early age of eleven years, to a branch of the Oneidas, at a settlement on the Susquehanna, called

Onaquaga. He was adopted by these, and lived among them until he reached a suitable age to enter Dartmouth College, which institution had then just received its charter. He graduated in 1773, and immediately entered upon the study of theology. He received his license, but, owing to the near approach of the great national crisis, he was never ordained. He was employed by the Continental Congress in various capacities, and was ultimately appointed Indian agent. During the whole of the Revolution he acted in that capacity, and resided in the neighborhood of the Oneidas At the close of the war that nation granted him a tract of land on Wood Creek, near Rome, N. Y. But, after residing on it two years, he effected an exchange with the nation for a tract in Westmoreland, known as Dean's Patent, to which he removed in 1786. The state afterwards confirmed the grant to him by patent, under which a portion of the land is held by his family at the present day. Two or three years after Mr. Dean's removal to the latter place, the following incident occurred:

'An institution existed among the Indians for the punishment of a murderer, answering, in some respects, to the Jewish code. It became the duty of the nearest relative of the deceased to pursue him, and avenge his brother's death. In case the murder was perpetrated by a member of a different tribe, the offence demanded that the tribe of the murdered man should require the blood of some member of the offending tribe. This was regarded as a necessary atonement, and as absolutely requisite to the happiness of the deceased in the world of spirits, and a religious duty, and not as a mere matter of vengeful gratification. At the period to which I have referred, an Indian had been murdered by some unknown white man, who had escaped. The chiefs, thereupon, held a consultation at Oneida, to determine what was to be done. Their deliberations were held in secret, but through the friendship of one of the number Mr. Dean was advised of what was going on. From the office that he had held, and the high standing he maintained among the white men, it was urged in the council that he was the proper person to sacrifice in atonement for the offence committed. The question was, however, a very difficult one to dispose of. He had been adopted into the tribe, and was held to be a son ; and it was argued by many of the chiefs that he could now be no more responsible for the offence than one of the natives of the tribe, and that his sacrifice would not furnish the proper atonement. For several days the matter was debated, and no decision was arrived at. While it was undetermined he continued to hope for the best, and his friendly informant kept him constantly advised of all that was arrived at. At first he reflected upon the propriety of his leaving the country, and escaping from the danger. But his circumstances, together with the hope of a favorable issue of the question in the council, induced him to remain. He had erected a small house, which he was occupying with his wife and two children, one an infant ; and it was idle to think of removing them without exciting observation, and perhaps causing a sacrifice of all. As the council continued its session for several days, his hopes of a favorable decision brightened. He, however, kept the whole matter to himself, not even mentioning it to his wife, and prepared himself for any emergency which might befall him. One night, after he had retired to bed, he was awoke by the sound of the death-whoop at a short distance from his house. He then, for the first time, communicated to his wife his fears that a party were approaching to take his life. He enjoined it upon her to remain quiet with her children in the room where they slept, while he would receive the council in an adjoining one, and endeavor to avert their determination, trusting to Providence for the result. He met the Indians at the door, and seated them in the outer room. There were eighteen, and all chiefs or head-men of the nation. The senior chief informed him that they had come to sacrifice him for the murder of their brother, and that he must now prepare to die. He replied to them at length, claiming that he was an adopted son of the Oneidas ; that it was unjust to require his blood for the wrong committed by a wicked white man ; that he was not ready to die, and that he could not leave his wife and children unprovided for. The council listened to him with profound gravity and attention, and when he sat down one of the chiefs replied to him. He rejoined, and used every argument his ingenuity could devise in order to reverse their sentence. The debate continued a long time, and the hope of escape grew fainter and fainter as it proceeded. At length he had nearly abandoned himself to the doom they had resolved upon, when he heard the pattering of a footstep without the door. All eyes were fixed upon the door. It opened, and a squaw entered. She was the wife of the senior chief, and at the time of Mr. Dean's adoption into the tribe, in his boyhood, she had taken him as her son. The entrance of a woman into a solemn council was, by Indian etiquette, at war with all propriety. She, however, took her place near the door, and all looked on in silence. A moment after, another footstep was heard, and another Indian woman entered the council. This was a sister of the former, and she too was the wife of a chief then present. Another pause ensued, and a third entered. Each of the three stood wrapped closely in her blanket, but said nothing. At length, the presiding chief addressed them, telling them to begone and leave the chiefs to go on with their business. The wife replied that the council must change their determination, and let the good white man, their friend, her own adopted son, alone. The command to begone was repeated, when each of the Indian women threw off her blanket, and showed a knife in her extended hand, and declared that if one hair of the white man's head was touched they would each bury their knives in their own hearts' blood. The strangeness of the whole scene overwhelmed with amazement each member of the council; and, regarding the unheard-of resolution of the women to interfere in the matter as a sort of manifestation of the will of the Great Spirit that the white man's life should not be taken, their previous decree was reversed on the spot, and the life of their victim preserved.'

THE MINISTER'S CHOICE.

14

THE MINISTER'S CHOICE.

CHAPTER I.

Yes, that is the way with you all, you young men. You see a sweet face, or a something, you know not what, and flickering reason says, Good-night! amen to common sense! The imagination invests the beloved object with a thousand superlative charms; adorns her with all the purple and fine linen, all the rich apparel and furniture, of human nature. — LONGFELLOW — *Hyperion.*

THROUGHOUT a brilliant season at Newport, some nine or ten years ago, the honors of supreme bellehood were accorded, by almost universal acclamation, to a beautiful French Creole, from New Orleans.

Undeniably, M'lle Estelle Le Grange was a very charming creature. With little pure intellect, and no solid culture, she had much ready, available talent, many showy accomplishments and native graces, with art, tact, and finesse, inexhaustible. Before fair English girls of her age had discarded short frocks and Kenwigsian braids, she had opened her first campaign of fashion, and closed it with brilliant success, parading, like a warlike Roman empress, a goodly host of captives in her train. From this time, an unquenchable thirst of conquest burned in her heart, and the pure draughts of intellectual pleasure and the sweet waters of affection alike palled upon her lips. In short, by nature and choice, through art, and by want of principle, she was a coquette, — and a coquette of the most dangerous type, making successful attacks upon the best-guarded hearts, through subtle, unsuspected ways, — veiling her cruel intent with a sort of innocent *naïveté*, which, like the long lashes that softened the keen flashing of her dark southern eyes, only added to her circean fascinations.

An only child, a beauty and an heiress, spoiled alike at home and abroad, much was pardoned in her of wilfulness and waywardness and whimsical caprice, by all men, and most women. She was 'so young,' 'so sweetly pretty,' 'so delightfully *naïve*,' 'so childish and playful.' Nobody, except it might be a rival belle, or a beauty *passée*, thought of calling her to account for her words and ways; while, as for opinions, she was too exquisitely feminine to have anything of the sort.

At the time of her advent at Newport, she was just gliding out of the rosy teens into the golden twenties, and entering upon the prime of that early-matured southern beauty with which she was so bounteously endowed. Again she came forth 'conquering and to conquer.' Past seasons in her native city, at Saratoga, Cape May, and various southern watering-places, were quite thrown into the shade by the triumphs of this. All felt, confessed, and bowed to her sway. Such as were not dazzled by her wit, her grace, and piquancy, were flattered into admiration by her appealing softness of speech and manner, or melted into love by the brooding passion in her eyes, and the languid sweetness of her smile. She preferred, whenever it was possible, to converse in her own language, which she spoke charmingly; with our grave mother-tongue she gracefully trifled, twisting and wreathing it into a thousand quaint little Frenchified expressions, trilling out the familiar, homely words with a sweet, bewildering foreign accent; so that it was said, 'her delicious broken English' had broken scores of hearts, and her sins against grammatical construction captivated poets and scholars.

I have said that *all* acknowledged the supremacy and the charm of her beauty. But no; there was one handsome young Mordecai who coolly refused his homage, till the heart of the belle was disquieted within her. This audacious incorrigible was a young clergyman, from Virginia, remarkable alike for the beauty of his person and the refined elegance of his manner, with the reputation of possessing a brilliant intellect, enriched by careful culture.

The Rev. Charles Ellsworth — for such, dear reader, was the name and title of my hero — mingled very little in the fashionable society of the sea-side; but, reserved to haughtiness, poetic or melancholy, coldly stood aloof from all its artificial pleasures and pleasure-seekers. Much too handsome to be made the object of pertinacious attentions from his own sex, and apparently insensible to the admiration and timid advances of the other, he went his proud and solitary way, — bathing, strolling, and lounging on the rocks, — the most stolid or the most sentimental of men. Many a moss-hunting beauty laid little plans, and executed skilful little manœuvres, to meet him frequently face to face on the sands; many a gay dancer left the ball-room, to promenade on the piazza of the Ocean House, where he gracefully reclined in an easy-chair, or stood leaning against a pillar, his pale, classical face looking 'so interesting and poetic in the moonlight.'

It never came out by what masterly manœuvre M'lle Le Grange made the acquaintance of Mr. Ellsworth; but she did make it, and a decided impression at the same time; which, however, she, with her usual art, declined to follow up, leaving everything in the hands of that gentleman himself, counting securely, in her exulting heart, on the result.

It was gradually and reluctantly that the young clergyman resigned himself to the spells of the sorceress, and listened to 'the voice of the charmer.' It was not that he feared for his success, should he really enter the lists as a suitor; for his holy profession had not, I am sorry to say, wholly subdued, or greatly chastened, a goodly share of natural vanity, for which weakness there was, indeed, a very fair excuse. But Mr. Ellsworth was a gentleman of refined, even fastidious tastes, and manners peculiarly reserved and circumspect; and the first thought of wooing and wedding a fashionable belle, with a sad reputation for flirtations and coquetries, and some rather unfeminine eccentricities of character and life, quite revolted him. Nor was he wanting in acute perception of the peculiar proprieties belonging to his position; and his sober judgment told him at once that such a woman as Estelle Le Grange were a most wofully unsuitable wife for him, with his sacred engrossing duties, his quiet, studious habits, and modest means. No; actual love and marriage were altogether out of the question; but M'lle Le Grange, *malgré* her grave faults, was a very charming woman with whom to while away an idle hour occasionally. She treated him with such a delicate yet childlike deference, she received both his coldness and his satire with such a delicious unconsciousness of manner, that he was struck, interested, and secretly enchanted.

The beautiful Creole had been, from the first, piqued out of her proud languor and quiet insolence of power by Ellsworth's polished indifference, into an interest keener and more ardent than she had ever before felt; and in her wicked little heart she vowed a wicked little vow to use every wile and art which nature, practice, and experience, had given her, to bring the audacious rebel to her feet, and then to *spurn him*. She was clever enough to see that Ellsworth's heart was not one to be dared or dazzled into love, but to be gradually and softly approached, and insidiously won upon. So it was that she modestly deferred to him in countless little ways, and seemed to be ruled and satisfied by his decisions. So it was that she subdued her own wild, passionate spirit, till her waywardness, her freaks of humor, and bursts of petulance, gradually assumed a mythical character in his mind. To humor his own serious moods, she had a way of pausing in her wild flights of merriment at his approach, and sinking at once into the most feminine quietude, like a poor tamed bird that had been tossed into the air by cruel jesters, sorely against its will, and now dropped wearily to his hand, and cooed its gentle content into his ear.

Slowly, but steadily, she went on, conquering or corrupting guard after guard of his well-defended heart, till the citadel was won.

Yes, the fastidious and dignified divine was overcome at last, — pride, proprieties, prejudices, judgment, and all. Slowly and imperceptibly the subtle intoxication stole over his senses, till every vein thrilled with the strange rapture, and his brain swam in the pleasant delirium of a first passion.

The infatuated lover was not wholly without warning of the doleful fate which awaited him. Several pitying hands clutched at his clerical robes as he was about to take the cold plunge of a hopeless declaration. One kind friend, in especial, took occasion to caution him, in a delicate way, as they two sat at breakfast one morning in Ellsworth's room, by relating his own sorrowful experience. But, as Ellsworth looked from the diminutive form and commonplace features of his companion — a fashionable youth, with a very sparse growth of pale yellow beard and moustache — to the reflection of his own symmetrical figure and handsome face in the glass opposite, he proudly tossed the rich curls from his forehead, and said to himself, with a confident smile, 'The cases are hardly parallel, my poor fellow.'

At last he took the fatal, irrevocable leap; not, as he thought, in the dark, but in the full, jubilant torch-light of hope. Love and joy, fair enticing shapes, beckoned him from below, and held up their inviting arms; but, as he leaped, sprang treacherously aside, and, when he was down, turned upon him, and, like malicious elves, laughed at his fall; — something such a reception as, it is said, the wily sea-maidens give the simple landsmen whom, with singing and smiling, and the reaching upward of fond arms, white as the sea-foam and wreathed about with ocean-gems, they allure to plunge from beetling rocks into the sparkling deep, where they mock them, and flout them, and lash them to death with their tails.

In short, the Reverend Charles Ellsworth was rejected, as many respectable but unfortunate laymen had been before him.

Yet not at once did he receive the word of doom. The fair Estelle took twenty-four hours — an unprecedented thing for her — for the consideration of his proposal, which was made through a very carefully and eloquently worded letter. With his profound respect, not to say admiration, for himself, and with, as he believed, his perfect understanding of the state of his mistress' affections, it must be confessed that he preferred his suit with few misgivings. Yet did he condescend to plead where he felt assured he might virtually command, and feigned the modest doubts and palpitating fears so becoming to a lover.

This conquest had cost the lovely Creole no little thought, care, and management. It was a triumph of art and feminine tact; — she was proud of it, and, now that her work was crowned with complete success, she found how much her heart had been in it. She had never before suspected herself of possessing so much of that romantic quality denominated *heart;* it never had troubled her till then. It was really unpleasant; she should grow thin and lose her bloom next, and the pale and interesting was not by any means her style.

She read Ellsworth's letter several times, with a half-triumphant, half-petulant expression on her pretty piquant face. She was almost as much vexed as gratified at her own conquest, and was really reluctant to resign the lover, though she could not bring herself to accept the husband. And the love itself, which had cost her such unusual pains, so much humbling of her haughty spirit, such patient taming of her wild fancies,—to resign it just as it was becoming so pleasant to her! She even wept over the cruel necessity;—but she had done as much, the winter before, when a careless servant spilled a cup of chocolate over a piece of exquisite embroidery which had employed her dainty thoughts and delicate little fingers for several months.

Scarcely for a moment did she entertain the idea of accepting the proposal of her new lover. She admired his beauty and faultless elegance, and she honored his character more than that of any man she had ever met; she even thought that she had some love for him, as far as she understood that mysterious sentiment; but the idea of becoming the wife of a clergyman was absolutely insupportable to her. A dull, prosy life of church-going, of charitable and parochial visitations, of dinner-giving to bishops, of long, doleful evenings of serious conversation, without cards or dancing, no balls, no plays, no private theatricals—bah! the picture was excessively *ennuyant.*

While her father lived M'lle Le Grange was the mistress of but a small fortune, not sufficient to make any material change in the position and circumstances of Mr. Ellsworth, who was confessedly poor, depending entirely on his profession for support. *And then her vow!*

So, when the twenty-four hours had elapsed, she despatched her missive. It was gently worded, but mortally decisive, — a dainty, lady-like note, on pale, rose-tinted paper, perfumed with the essence of the flower whose language speaks most hope to the heart of the lover. All was *coûleur de rose* without, — all humiliation and despair within.

Ellsworth was stunned and stupefied at first; then swept over him a strong, bitter torrent of mortification and anger. He crushed the billet in his hand, tore it, and flung it fiercely upon the floor. While giving way to this boyish and undignified fit of passion, he caught a view of his face in the mirror opposite, — the very glass whose flattering reflection of his handsome face had, but a few days before, so smilingly assured him that *he* could not bow in vain at the shrine of any woman whose heart looked through her eyes. Now, in his sudden humiliation, he could not even face himself, but sullenly turned his back to the mirror, and, dropping his head upon his hand, sat hour after hour cooling down and schooling his proud heart in the hard lesson of his first great disappointment. At length he rose, carefully collected the fragments of the letter which he had flung upon the floor, and burned them, longing to destroy at the same moment the remembrance with the evidence of his folly.

The next morning he left Newport for the south.

It was not till the first bitterness of his mortification was past that Mr. Ellsworth truly realized how deeply and ardently he had loved the beautiful Creole;

how, aside from the flattering unction he had laid to his soul, of complete ascendency over her,—how, underneath all his self-complacency and gratulation, had been kindled a strong, eager, unreasoning passion, whose generous glow had touched his cold heart with new fervors, and whose light transfigured life before his languid eyes.

As the wounds of his pride healed, he strove to salve those of his heart by the thought that perhaps it was well to have had the experience, painful though it had been, and murmured to himself axioms like this:

'"T is better to have loved and lost,
Than never to have loved at all.'

So it was, that, ere many months had passed, he grew to think of the heartless Estelle with more of tender regret than harsh condemnation, though yet manfully resolved to forswear her, and drive her from his heart forever. To this end, he could think of no better course than to set up some nobler divinity in the niche she was unwilling and unworthy to occupy,—to kindle a pure living flame over the smouldering embers of his unhappy passion. In short, to seek and woo another and a more complying love;—shorter and plainer yet, *to take a wife.*

CHAPTER II.

Your lineage I revere —
Honor your virtue, in your truth believe,
Do homage to your intellect, and bow
Before your peerless beauty.
BROWNING.

But love is such a mystery,
I cannot find it out;
For when I think I'm best resolved,
Then am I most in doubt.
SIR JOHN SUCKLING.

IN a quaint old Virginian mansion near the city of R——, in a chamber through whose vine-hung eastern windows struggled the full morning tide of the light and warmth of a sunny day in the early southern spring, there sat, half buried in a luxurious easy-chair, a young lady apparently about twenty years of age, earnestly intent on reading a note which she had just received.

This lady, Miss Elinor Campbell, was not precisely beautiful in the common acceptation of the word, but she was certainly a very noble-looking woman. She was tall and rather grandiose in all her proportions, but with a gracefully-rounded form, and she moved with a lightness and energy unusual in a southron. She was fair, but her hair was of a dark, lustrous brown, and her large blue eyes were so deeply set and so heavily shaded by dark lashes as to seem almost black. The predominant expression of her face, and perhaps the ruling element of her character, was *pride*, — softened, usually, toward those whom she loved by much womanly tenderness, but toward those whom she disliked or despised most openly and mercilessly manifest. Though in common gentle and yielding in look and manner, there was at rare times an expression of marble-like firmness about her mouth, a cold, steel-like gleam of relentless will in her eye, and in her manner a profound calm of passionless dignity, as imposing as it was peculiar.

Our heroine had seen very little of the world; she was singularly unsophisticated, though far from wanting in the best culture and the truest grace. Born to wealth, and belonging to one of those old and highly respectable families which are the proverbial boast of Virginia, she knew that an honorable position awaited her in aristocratic society, and was content with that knowledge. Since her return from school at the north, she had been satisfied with the hospitable home-life of her father's house, of which, by the death of a beloved mother, she had become the mistress. Loving nature intensely, almost devoutly, she had found a poet's pleasure in the mountain scenery surrounding their estate, and, with a passion for out-door sports and exercises, she had felt all an Amazon's joy in the fulness of a healthful and active physical life. But as she grew into womanhood her calm was troubled with aspirations and needs which her quiet home-life, happy though it was, could not wholly satisfy. It was not alone that vague, sweet want planted in the child's nature, stirring with uncomprehended yearning the heart of the girl, and feeling its dim way upward toward the light of the dawn of love; but the consciousness of untried mental power, of unused moral energies and sympathies, — a generous longing for a life of more beneficent actions and of deepened experiences, both of the world and of the spirit.

It was in this state of mental unrest, and of eager but undirected aspiration, that Elinor accepted the earnest invitation of a newly-married friend, and went to spend a winter at R——.

Here she first mingled in the society of a gay city. She was amused at first, then charmed, then absorbed. Her brain caught the dizzy whirl of fashionable life; her heart began to beat time to the senseless music of that round of folly, as though its strong womanly pulsations were touched into life by the hand of the Creator for no nobler purpose. Then all those true aspirations stood off, mournful and silent, and the angel of great purposes, with which her soul had blindly struggled, glided from her relaxed grasp, and passed swiftly away. And then came one whose calm eye sobered her, whose grave voice stayed her steps in that intoxicating round, whose hand seemed about to swing wide before her the gate of that *new life* about which those aspirations now clustered, eagerly waiting.

But we must not anticipate.

As I said long ago, Elinor sat in her chamber reading a note. A light, merry little rap-tap came at the door. She hastily crumpled up the note, and thrust it into one of the dainty little pockets of her apron, and then answered, in a slightly unsteady voice,

'Come in!'

It was her friend Mrs. Morris.

'Ah, Fanny, this *is* an honor, — the very first time, I think, that you have ever paid me so early a visit; you are such a wonderful little housekeeper, that one seldom catches more than a flying glimpse of you before dinner. Pray, what 's on the tapis now?'

'That 's just what I came to ask you,' replied the pretty young housekeeper, sitting down by her friend, and looking her searchingly in the face. 'I have come to confess you, Mistress Nelly, and I am not to be sent away no wiser than I came. So make a clean breast of it at once, for I *will* know.'

'Will know *what?*' asked Elinor, coloring slightly, in spite of herself.

'All about you and Mr. Ellsworth,' replied Mrs. Morris. 'Tell me, does he love you?'

'No, — I mean I don't know. He never has told me that he actually loves me.'

'Now, Nelly, this won't do,' pursued the relentless inquisitor. 'Here has been this reverend gentleman, — a proud, fastidious, reserved man, — paying you the most devoted attentions for the last two months. At first they were very delicate, and offered shyly; but now all the world sees them, and understands them. Calls in the morning, in the evening strolls in the garden, *tête-à-têtes* in the library, while notes and books come so often that it is evident that poor little Ethiopian Mercury of his, Tony, finds his office no sinecure. Ah, Nelly! you are a sly puss; but *me* you cannot deceive.'

'Nor do I wish to, my dear lynx! But you know that Mr. Ellsworth visited here quite frequently before I came; you know, also, that those notes have always accompanied books, and that the books have always been of the most serious and unromantic kind. Even those which Mr. Ellsworth has read to me in the library have usually been moral essays or theological disquisitions.'

'O yes, I know; I found him reading *Childe Harold* to you, the other morning. I have never yet counted Byron among serious writers; I should not say that theology was exactly in his line.'

Elinor bit her lip, half in merriment, half in vexation, as she answered,

'I assure you he was only reading those glorious stanzas descriptive of a thunder-storm in the Alps, which, on my word, were suggested by a passage in Isaiah.'

'Well, never mind that. What innocent theological work did he send this morning by the fleet-footed Tony, — "*Edwards on the Affections*"?'

'What nonsense!' said Elinor, laughing. 'He did not send any book; he sent a little bouquet, this morning.'

'Aha! we are on the *scent* now. Pray, where is the bouquet? Ah, I see it, smothered down under your handkerchief. Fie upon you, to treat the sweetest and delicatest of love's offerings so lightly! Give it me, and let me place it in your vase. Quite orientally arranged, I declare! Impatient little rosebuds, with their red lips pouting to reveal the love-secret glowing in their hearts; tender violets and mignonette, and tell-tale forget-me-not; — Elinor, this man certainly loves you!'

'I think so,' said Elinor, in a low tone, blushing deeply.

'Well, now, that is frankly spoken; but it is not enough; I must know more, — all. Do you love him?'

'I — do — not — know,' said Elinor, very slowly, with an expression of painful perplexity shadowing her fine face. 'I only know,' she continued, 'that he exercises a strange new power over me. He is the most intellectual man I have ever known, and I believe him to possess, under all his languid calm and proud reserve of manner, a good deal of latent enthusiasm and generous passion. I believe him to be entirely pure and honorable, and, in spite of a little tinge of worldliness, faithful to his high calling. I admire him — have faith in him; my only distrust *is of myself.*'

'How so? do you doubt your own worthiness?' asked Mrs. Morris.

'*No!*' said Elinor, very decidedly, with a slight curl of the lip; 'I am not so humble as that. A proof, it may be, that I do not love, for they say that such pride never goes hand in hand with genuine love. No, — what troubles me is this: when Mr. Ellsworth is present, I am charmed, absorbed, and content, though conscious of a kind of thraldom. But when he is absent, he is so *utterly* absent that I cannot comprehend his power over me; I rebel against it, and have back the old sense of freedom. I seem to but vaguely realize his existence, and then as having no vital relations with my own. I think the quiet elegance of his manner, the melody of his voice, and the mere beauty of his person, affect me more powerfully than they should.'

'Yes, he *is* handsome,' replied Mrs. Morris, musingly, 'undeniably, very handsome; but that is neither here nor there. Of what account is beauty in a husband?'

Elinor smiled a little archly at this, for Frank Morris, Fanny's *caro sposo*, though universally pronounced 'one of the best fellows in the world,' was by no means distinguished for his outward personal attractions.

'But tell me,' continued Fanny, after a pause, 'tell me truly, — are you quite sure that you do not love another than Mr. Ellsworth?'

'Why, yes,' answered Elinor, quickly, but blushing to her temples; 'how could I? Before coming to R——, I knew very few men out of our immediate neighborhood and circle of relatives — mostly father's and brother Fred's companions — a careless, jovial, hospitable set, given to fox-hunting and high living, large-hearted and free-handed; yet would I rather run the risk of leading immortal apes in the place you wot of, than choose a husband from among them.'

'But what of the young elected cousin you used to tell me about in our school-days, — the youth to whom you were so romantically affianced in your childhood?' asked Mrs. Morris.

'O, you mean Malcolm Bruce,' replied Elinor, striving to steady her voice, which trembled in spite of her. 'It is all over between us, — if there ever was anything more than childish folly, — over and forgotten. I will tell you all about it, Fanny, if you will not look at me so searchingly. I *did* like Malcolm Bruce very much; indeed, I loved him dearly when I was a little girl, especially after our fond, novel-reading mammas betrothed us. Then, when my own dear mother died, and soon after Malcolm's, I think we both grew to regard that half-playful engagement as something solemn and sacred, for their sakes. I continued to love Malcolm better than anybody else in the world, except, *perhaps*, papa, brother Fred, and my little sister Julia, till the time when I left school and he returned from college.

'Then, you know, I was a woman of full eighteen, and felt that a vast distance lay between me and my old self, and the old times. As soon as I met Malcolm, I felt that he presumed too much on our old betrothal. I was not to be won without a wooing; so I received his familiar and matter-of-course tenderness, and his rather premature petting, with pride and growing coldness, for I was really very much vexed, and I finally quarrelled with him out and out because he would insist on calling me his "wife." I don't remember just how this was made up, but after a while we were reconciled, and went on for some months very well, and then quarrelled again, though I must confess that I both opened and closed the battle, as he quickly left the field. So matters went on, — abrupt break-offs and slow reconciliations, pride, jealousy, misunderstandings, and change, — nothing, nothing like the old peaceful, careless, merry times. I fear I grew very petulant and passionate, and perhaps poor Malcolm was afraid to woo me in earnest. Certain it is that he never spoke to me of love or marriage, except in that old familiar, half-playful, half-confident tone, which always vexed me beyond endurance.

'Last spring it was rumored that Malcolm was about to go abroad for two or three years, to travel and complete his medical studies, for he was to be a physician. I could not believe it. I was sure he would have told me of his intention *first,* and I was only less astonished than grieved and offended, when I heard him calmly announce, before a whole dinner-party, that the time of his departure was fixed: he was to sail by the next steamer for Havre, — which left him but two days longer at home and in our neighborhood. I was indignant at this want of kindly frankness, and, while all around were expressing surprise and regret, I said, carelessly,

'"Ah, indeed! then Friday will be doubly unlucky for us, as we shall lose both an old friend and a very welcome guest, for Mr. Robinson returns to R—— on that day."

'I referred, in this remark, to a classmate of brother Fred's, a rattle-headed, rollicking, coxcombical fellow, Tom Robinson, — everybody's Tom, and everybody's butt. I cared nothing for him, and I knew that he was thoroughly detested by Malcolm. *He* felt the cut keenly, and I acknowledge it was the most heartless thing I ever did. But I felt myself slighted and wronged, and all that evening I kept aloof from him, for fear that the memory of old days, and something in his voice harder to bear, might break down my pride. I was gay, — O, very gay! I sang, because my voice seemed to lift the strange weight a moment from my heart; I danced, because the music and motion distracted my vexed and wounded spirit.

'After the evening was passed, just as I had finished "one last song" for the pertinacious Robinson, who vowed, and perhaps truly, that I had never sung so well, Malcolm came up to take leave of me.

'"Good-night," I said, quietly; "we shall, of course, see you again before you sail?"

'"Yes — no; upon second thoughts I fear not," he replied; "I have very little time, many friends to take leave of, and countless last things to attend to."

'"Then," said I, by a strong effort crushing my heart down, "I must say *adieu* and *bon voyage.*"

'I extended my hand, — it was warmly grasped; I heard a low "God bless you," and I stood alone, — for Mr. Robinson, with wonderful consideration for him, had moved away when Malcolm came up. I was disappointed, bewildered, and utterly unsatisfied by this parting; but I felt almost sure that I should see him again. I had put on but one glove since playing, and when, as soon as my stupefaction went off, I looked for the other on the piano where I had laid it, it was gone. I have always believed that Malcolm took that glove.'

'Maybe it was Tom Robinson,' put in the provoking and matter-of-fact Fanny.

'Well,' continued Elinor, 'I saw no more of the play-husband of my childhood, though for the next two days I watched and waited from morning 'till midnight, and was even foolish enough to feel that I would unsay every hard thing I had ever uttered, if he would only come back to say "good-by" in a kind and Christian way. But he never came, though he had time to join a shooting party, which passed our very door, — the cold-hearted, ungenerous fellow! No doubt it was his conscience that troubled him, and would not let him sleep that last night; for his sister said that he did not go to bed at all, but walked his chamber hour after hour, and only took a little doze in his easy-chair toward morning. Neither did I sleep. I shed my last tears for him that night.'

'Elinor Campbell,' said Mrs. Morris, in as solemn a tone as that merry little woman could possibly make use of, 'I am really afraid that you love that Malcolm Bruce in your secret heart.'

'O, don't say that *now*, if you love me! never say it again!' exclaimed Elinor, in a tone earnest to sternness, rising and walking hurriedly up and down the room. 'It was ungenerous and unkind in him, in the first place, to treat me so like a child, — a plaything that belonged to him of right, — and then, when I proved myself a proud, sensitive woman, to oppose my mere coldness of manner — a thin, transparent ice, which a few words of loving deference would at once have melted into warm tears — with a pride of manhood, hard and cold as adamant. No, Fanny, the day he went away without one word more of affectionate, of even friendly farewell, I thrust him resolutely from my heart. I have kept him out ever since, and, with God's help, I will keep him out forever!'

'*Bravissima!* that is the true spirit. But suppose we return to your present, *real* lover,' said Mrs. Morris.

A shadow passed over Elinor's face, but she answered, very quietly, 'Well, if Mr. Ellsworth asks me to become his wife, I shall probably consent; not—Heaven forbid!—to escape from the unhappy "old love," for *love* that bit of romance should surely not be called, but a childish dream, that has dissolved in the light of womanly reason. No—I shall marry Mr. Ellsworth because I honor and can love him, and because I have been long yearning intensely for a wider field of action—a nobler heart-life and thought-life than I have ever yet known. Now that sister Julia is old enough to take my place at home, I feel that I can do more good elsewhere; and I think that I long more to *do good* than to be happy. With the fortune that I possess, I think I could aid Mr. Ellsworth very greatly; and, with my ready heart and active energies, I am sure that I should be no clog upon him in any way. With God's blessing, I think we might be very happy ourselves, and make others happy.'

As Elinor concluded this sentence, she stood beside her friend, with her hand resting lightly on the back of the chair in which she sat. A beautiful glow of earnest feeling deepened in her cheek, and the light of a pure, unselfish purpose gave an intense brightness to her eyes.

Just then there came a knock at the door, and to Mrs. Morris, who opened it, a servant gave a message from Mr. Ellsworth for Miss Campbell. He awaited her in the library. An instant change came over Elinor; she turned pale, and grasped tightly the back of the chair by which she stood.

'Fanny, dear, go down with me!' she exclaimed;

'I think, from the note I received this morning, that this will be a decisive visit, — and — and I fear I am not quite ready for it. So come down with me, and we will take it as an ordinary call. Come, dear!'

'Dear me no dears,' replied Fanny, 'for I shall do no such thing, but stay where I am, and you must meet the shock of doom alone. But *do* brighten up a little! Just loop back those curls — don't let them droop in such a forlorn, weeping-willowy way. Now *don't* put on that resigned expression! Why, you look like Mary Queen of Scots on her way to execution, though she went to lose her head, while you go to gain a heart and a hand. There, that is a little better, — now go! I do hope it is for the best, but certainly this was not the way with me when I went down into that very library to receive my Frank's declaration. To be sure, I had got used to expecting it. I really began to think it never would come; and, as it was, I had to help it along.'

Elinor laughed, and with a brightened face and calm step descended the stairs. She put her hand on the library-door and partly turned the handle, then paused and looked round, as though contemplating a retreat. But Fanny, leaning over the balustrade of the stairway, shook her head reprovingly. Then the door before her was opened from within, and Mr. Ellsworth took her hand, drew her gently forward, closed the door, and shut out all the world.

Somewhat more than an hour after this, Mrs. Morris heard Mr. Ellsworth come out of the library and leave the house, walking, she fancied, with a lighter and prouder step than usual. She restrained her womanly curiosity for a few minutes longer, then softly entered, and found Elinor sitting apparently just as her lover had left her, in the embrasure of a heavily-curtained window. Her head was drooped, and her eyes, slightly suffused with tears, were fixed on a ring of gold, simply set with pearls, — the ring of betrothal, — which she was turning and turning round her finger, in a dreamy, abstracted way. Fanny sat down beside her, put her arms about her waist, kissed her cheek, and whispered,

'God bless you dear!'

'Thank you,' said Elinor, softly, and then became silent as before. After a while she spoke — still very softly, but in a fervent, assured tone — 'He loves me, Fanny, nobly and very dearly, I think; *solely*, I am sure, for, though I have not questioned him, I know him to be too honorable and true to woo me, if his heart held any dearer or deeper love; and he says that I can do much for him — be all the world to him. His is not the love I used to dream of, over poetry and romances; it is calmer, more assured, less impassioned and demonstrative; but I believe it to be very pure and constant, and I see that it may open for me a useful, and so a *beautiful* life, if God will only help me to be strong and good.'

CHAPTER III.

Give me more love, or more disdain :
  The torrid or the frozen zone
Brings equal ease unto my pain,
  The temperate affords me none ;
Either extreme of love or hate
Is sweeter than a calm estate.   THOMAS CAREW.

A FEW weeks after her betrothal, Elinor returned to her home, bearing a letter from Mr. Ellsworth, respectfully soliciting the paternal sanction to their engagement. Elinor was not sorry to be thus spared the necessity of making an oral announcement of the matter to her father. Not that Major Campbell was at all in the line of those terrible, ogre-ish papas whom novel-writers usually delight to depict,—monsters of paternal tyranny, who take a fiendish pleasure in troubling, turning, and damming (be careful, Mr. Compositor, not to insinuate an *n* into that word) 'the course of true love,' that it may never, under any circumstances, 'run smooth.' Though a man of strong prejudices, and a proud, quick spirit, he was by no means rigorous, harsh, or obstinate. There was a soldierly sternness about him at some times, and a brusque, country-squirish hilarity at others, which alike did injustice to a heart of almost womanly tenderness, and the finest gentlemanly instincts. Elinor did not fear any unreasonable opposition to her choice, but she knew that her father loved her with a proud, peculiar affection, and she could not expect him to part with her, without regret and some misgivings, to a stranger, whose name he had scarcely heard. She so shrank from paining his loving heart, that she delayed for several days to give him Mr. Ellsworth's letter; but at length, her conscience troubling her for her concealment, she put it into his hand as she gave him her good-night kiss on retiring, begging him, in a whisper, not to open it until he should be quite alone.

She soon heard him enter his chamber, which adjoined her own; she listened at a closed door which was between them to his every step and movement. She heard him seat himself at his writing-table, and hastily open the letter. She heard the nervous rustle of the paper as he read; she even heard the deep sigh with which he finished the reading, and the heavy sinking of his head upon the table before him. Then all was silent for several minutes, and Elinor knew that her father, a man at times irreverent in his wit and profane in his passion, was now praying for her and for himself; and her own knee instinctively bent, and her own lips moved in fervent supplication for the Divine blessing and guidance.

For more than an hour Elinor lay awake, listening to her father's step as he walked slowly up and down his chamber, and thinking of all his love and care for her in the past. Most vividly she remembered a weary, painful illness of her childhood, when it was supposed that she was 'sick unto death' with a contagious and repulsive disease, and when her father, then a gallant young officer, never left her side, day nor night, till all danger was past; and now she wondered if the husband she had chosen would ever be so tender, so devoted and faithful. Then she thought of his love for her mother, and how unselfish and chivalrously constant it was; how it had finally led him to sacrifice his profession of arms, to meet her wishes for a quiet, domestic life. Then she shuddered again with the shock of that mother's death, and with the memory of the terrible tempest of grief which swept over and prostrated her poor father. Then she remembered her mother's fond and proud affection for *him,* and the peculiar tenderness of look and tone with which she always addressed him, and how her liquid utterance seemed to steep his bluff, honest name in sweetness indescribable. He was never 'Mr. Campbell,' or 'major,' or 'husband,' or 'papa,' to her, but always '*dear Harry,*' always the lover of her happy girlhood. Now Elinor wondered if she could ever, *ever* call Mr. Ellsworth '*dear Charles;*' and so, remembering and wondering, she fell asleep soon after the footsteps in the next room had ceased, and she had heard her father fling himself wearily upon his bed.

The next morning, when Elinor descended to the breakfast-room, she found her father already there. He was alone, and standing before a portrait of her mother, looking at it with a sort of sad questioning in his pleasant blue eyes, which were glistening with unshed tears. As Elinor stole to his side, he bestowed his good-morning kiss with unusual tenderness, but said nothing of the letter she had given him the night previous. As she was making tea, however, he invited her to accompany him, immediately after breakfast, on a ride among the hills. Elinor consented willingly, but with a conscious blush so vivid that Julia, her younger sister, noticed it, and, younger-sister-like, questioned her as to its cause, which, of course, made the poor girl feel vastly more comfortable.

For more than a mile Major Campbell rode beside his daughter in perfect silence; his frank, open face wearing an absent, perplexed expression, most unusual with him. At last, rousing himself by an evident effort, he exclaimed, with rather a rueful tone and look,

'I 'm sorry, Nell, that the man is a parson.'

'Why so, dear papa?' asked Elinor, with a pleasant smile.

'Why, because, with profound respect for the ministerial calling, I must own to having a sort of Tony-Wellerish distrust of preachers in general, because I have found so few of them really manly and whole-souled, and brave in thought and word. Because I see so few really faithful in example, counsel, and rebuke. For the miserable Jews of eighteen hundred years ago, or the Catholic persecutors of the sixteenth century, they uncork the vials of divine wrath with a free hand; but on the bold transgressors and sleek sinners of to-day, — men who have attained to wealth and high places through cruel and dishonest means, — real betrayers and deniers of Christ, and persecutors of his peculiar children, the poor, — on these they sprinkle a gentle rain of brotherly reproof and admonition, administering the needful brimstone prescribed by the doctors of the church, cleverly disguised in treacle. Because they are so often hypocritical and pretentious. I can tell a preacher of this sort as far as I can see him; not only by the badge of his white cravat, but by the pompous pose of his hat, and a certain sanctimonious swing to his coat-tails. And, then, to my eye, there is something affected and womanish in all varieties of clerical robes — the long, white surplice especially. By George! I'd put on petticoats and have done with it! There is another class of preachers, principally to be found among the Methodists, for whom I have far more respect. These are, like the apostles of old, wanderers from place to place; they are often illiterate, and always poor, but honest and earnest men, — terribly earnest, indeed; speaking what they believe to be the truth, and the whole truth; thundering into ears polite the names of a place and a personage which should be unmentionable, and making the sleek hair of well-to-do sinners to stand on end with fear of the wrath to come. But I cannot suppose that the rector of the aristocratic Church of St. James is one of these.'

'No, father,' answered Elinor, with a confident smile; 'he is neither a Tartufe, a Stiggins, nor a Whitefield. There is no pretension, no pomposity, and no cant, about Mr. Ellsworth; he is neither bigoted nor fanatical; he is not even so much of an enthusiast as I wish he were,' she added, with a sigh.

'Ellsworth,' said Major Campbell; 'it is a New England name, I think. I have never heard much of him; he cannot be very famous, even in his own line.'

'No, he has not distinguished himself greatly as yet, though his talent is unquestionable.'

'And he frankly owns in his letter to me — I like that in him — that he has no fortune, and his salary is not large. Poor, undistinguished, a preacher — a Yankee! — what could have been the attraction for a gay, sensible, high-spirited girl, like you, Nell? Is the man handsome?'

'He is accounted so; and, indeed,' she added, with a blush, 'I think that he has the most classically beautiful face and form I have ever seen.'

'Aha! I see; you are all alike, you women, always hooked in the eye. And so he's a sort of clerical Antinous, this future son-in-law of mine. I distrust your handsome men!'

'It is well for me that my mother did not share your prejudice,' answered Elinor, with an arch smile.

The major feigned not to take this sly compliment to a personal beauty still remarkable, though somewhat on the wane, but continued, in a mollified tone,

'I suppose I *am* captious and unreasonable in my objections; but, the truth is, there is but one man I have ever known that I could right heartily welcome into my family as your husband, and that is Malcolm Bruce. He is a fine, frank, manly, and gentlemanly fellow, with brave, honest, Highland blood in his veins; in short, he is a laddie after my own heart.'

'Yes, papa, but not *after mine*,' replied Elinor, with a faint attempt at a pleasantry. 'I am sure he cares nothing for me, except as an ordinary friend;

and perhaps it is best so, for I do not think we are very well suited to one another.'

'Yet it might have been otherwise, if you had played your cards differently,' the major replied, rather brusquely.

'But, papa, I played no game — essayed no management; why should I have done so?' said Elinor, proudly. 'If Malcolm Bruce was inclined to love me, he was surely free to do so.'

'Well, well; you certainly worked against yourself, consciously or unconsciously, by your coldness, your caprices, and your absurd, duchess-like airs. I never meddle nor make with such matters; but, now that it is all past, I must tell you frankly that I think your behavior toward that poor boy, most of the time for the last two years, has been unbearable. I have seen Bruce, on horseback, clear a gulley eighteen feet broad and thirty feet deep, and perform all sorts of daring and dashing exploits in our mountain hunts, but I must confess that, had I seen him wooing you in one of your savage moods, my opinion of his courage would have been vastly heightened.'

Tears of vexation and wounded feeling sprung to Elinor's eyes at these hard, though playfully-spoken remarks; she bit her lip and forced them back, but there was a little tremor in her voice as she replied,

'If he had ever *wooed*, father, there might have been no savageness, no haughtiness even, in my words or manner; but he was always so assured, so indifferent, I was annoyed, stung, angered, by it. If he cared nothing for me, he surely need not have taken such pains to convince me of it. His manner might have had more friendly warmth and chivalric deference without my presuming upon it. I could not endure his smiling ease, his imperturbable coolness.'

'All put on, I believe in my heart, Nell; indeed, to tell the truth, I *know* so, for on that shooting party, the day before Bruce left, while we were alone for a half-hour or so, he took occasion to sound me in regard to your feelings toward him.—Take care there, Elinor! you'll infuriate that horse, if you bear so savagely on the curb.—After all I had observed and heard you say, I really could not, in conscience, give the poor fellow any encouragement, though I told him, as I have told you, that there was no man in the world I would rather receive as a son. Ah, well! it may yet come about; who knows? Our Julia is growing up into a pretty, high-spirited girl; rather too thoughtless and giddy,—poor motherless child!—but a fine, generous creature at heart.'

'O, Julia is not at all suited to him!' exclaimed Elinor, quickly, with a strange, undefined thrill of alarm and jealousy.

'Well, daughter, we'll not discuss that question, but return to your minister. When is the strange shepherd to take my pet lamb into his dull fold? In other words, when is the wedding to come off?'

'Not until the first of October,' answered Elinor, in a low tone.

'I am glad of that; it gives us time to prepare our minds for the dread, inevitable event. But here we are at the gate. Why, my child,' he added, as he assisted her to dismount, 'you look sad and perplexed. Have I troubled you with my rough jesting? Believe me, it never was further from my heart to give you pain.'

Elinor smiled and pressed her father's hand tenderly for answer, and then ran hastily up stairs. When she reached her chamber, she flung her plumed hat aside, and, sinking into a chair, wept in a slow, desponding, weary way, she scarcely knew why.

She was roused by a pert little tap at the door. It was Julia. The post had come in, 'and brought a letter for *somebody*.' The missive was not visible, as Julia held it behind her, expecting her sister to question, entreat, or struggle for it. But Elinor stood still, quietly waiting, till Julia, somewhat taken aback by her calmness, reluctantly resigned the letter into her hands, and left her alone.

Then Elinor sat down to the reading of the first real *love-letter* she had ever received — of the first letter from her betrothed husband. Slowly and quietly she read from the opening to the close, and then, with a sigh, let it fall into her lap. O, how unlike all she had dreamed of such a moment, in her early romantic days! Where was the quick flash of the eager eyes along the lines, —the proud heave of the heart under its new weight of love's exhaustless riches? where that delicious, childlike joy in the sudden flowering of the most marvellous and perfect bloom of the heart? where were those strange, sweet thrills, half fear, half rapture, responding to the power and mystery of passion, as, wave after wave, it swept over the soul?

She was shocked at her own statue-like quiet. She caught the letter to her bosom, she pressed it close against her heart, that it might impart to it a magnetic life and warmth. Alas! the letter, though breathing very 'noble sentiments,' and sparkling with graceful fancies, was wanting in the soul of faith and truth, and in the heart-heat of a genuine passion.

Our heroine's return home, the reässerted power of old scenes and associations, the morning's conversation with her father, — above all, separation from her lover, — had strangely chilled the current of her feelings; but she had hoped that the love-words of that letter would beat down upon her heart with the gentle violence of a warm spring rain, melt away the last ice of doubt and fear, and call forth the fervid blooms of hope and joy. They came rather like snow-flakes, falling lightly and softly, but folding that heart in a heavier chill and a more wintry gloom than before.

But, with much reproving and schooling of herself for her romantic, girlish ideas, and her exacting and misgiving spirit, by resolute putting down of doubt and discontent, she finally regained her native, hopeful cheerfulness, and with a calm, strong heart, thrilled alone by noble resolves and a pure and tender devotion, tranquilly awaited the time when the quiet and shaded rivulet of her woman's life should mingle with a stronger, deeper tide of being, and, lost in its bosom, sweep on through the wide, unshadowed fields of the world, toward the eternal sea.

CHAPTER IV.

Sigh no more, ladies, sigh no more!
Men were deceivers ever;
One foot in sea, and one on shore,
To one thing constant never;
Then sigh not so,
But let them go,
And be you blithe and bonny,
Converting all your sounds of woe
Into Hey nonny nonny!

SHAKSPEARE.

Better be off with the old love,
Before you are on with the new.

OLD SONG.

THE summer had passed, the autumn come, and it was the close of the last day of September, — the eve of Elinor's wedding day.

There was a long avenue of noble elms leading from Major Campbell's house to the highway, and here it was Elinor's custom to walk alone at sunset, often till late into the twilight. This evening she surprised her merry sister Julia by an invitation to accompany her. She was expecting Mr. Ellsworth, and might meet him here.

As the sisters were returning from a protracted but somewhat dull walk, in which the burden of the conversation had certainly not been borne by the bride elect, a travelling carriage came up the avenue, and overtook them. It contained Mr. Ellsworth, who, recognizing Elinor, alighted and walked by her side. This was the first time they had met since their betrothal, as Elinor had been absent during the entire summer, making the north-west tour and travelling in the Canadas with her father and brother, while Mr. Ellsworth had been visiting in New England. The meeting was affectionate, but by no means rapturous. Julia opened her pretty brown eyes in artless astonishment that there were no kisses exchanged,—that there was not even an interlocking of arms.

'You tremble, dear Miss Campbell,' said Mr. Ellsworth, in a gentle, kindly tone; 'the air is somewhat damp,—had you not better wrap your shawl a little closer about you?'

Elinor quietly drew up the shawl, but she knew that all the wraps in the world could not drive away that chill which, starting from her heart, ran through every vein, and shook her usually calm voice into a broken, bashful utterance, which her lover might, and doubtless did, misinterpret. It was the tremble and the trouble of a nameless foreboding that thus agitated her. It seemed that her *angel* was silent as he approached—did not whisper to her heart,

'*This* is the man!'

But after a few moments the old charm stole over her willing senses like the magic of exquisite music, and subjugated her like the power of perfect art. She felt a thrill of womanly exultation in the graceful yet eminently manly beauty of her lover, in the refined modulations of his voice, in the pride of his bearing,—and she wished that he would offer her his arm, that she might lean upon it, and feel that his strength was for her help and repose,—that she had in him a wise guide and a sure defence for all life.

Major Campbell was a country gentleman of the old school, and, as such, a sturdy stickler for all the good old country customs; so it was scarcely to be wondered at that he resolved and declared that Elinor should have a good, old-fashioned, country wedding, with a grand universal gathering of friends and neighbors, plenty of generous viands and luscious fruits, of good wine and hot punches, fiddling and dancing, to make merry withal.

It was in vain that Elinor, in behalf of her clerical lover, remonstrated against the indecorum of such a proceeding; the major's will was up, and he would not listen to a word of objection, even from her. So invitations were sent out far and near, and preparations for entertainment made on the most prodigal scale.

The wedding night had come. The weather was fair, and the air balmy, the heavens clear and bright, and all went well and merrily on. The rambling old country-house of the Campbells was alive in every wing and angle with cheerful bustle, — astir with hurrying feet, the rustle of silk, and the soft flutter of white muslin, and radiant with gorgeous flowers, bright-eyed, blooming girls, and innumerable lights. Out through the unblinded windows streamed the festive brightness — far out into the dark, tangled shrubbery of the garden, where the leaves and flowers seemed dancing because of it, and the zephyrs to have wakened to frolic in its beams; naughty inconstants, those zephyrs, coquetting with all the marriageable roses till their wings were perfumed with the sighs of their victims, snatching kisses from the shy violets, — even whispering their light flatteries into the cold ear of the nun-like lily, standing apart in saintly contemplation, gazing at the star of her worship.

Even the humming-bird, disturbed in her domestic repose, amid the lilacs, by the strange light, chirped cheerfully to her mate, remembering her own wedding in the pleasant spring-time, and the happy honey-moon which followed.

The guests were fast arriving. Up the long avenue they came, in carriages and on horseback, rattling and galloping, chatting and laughing more and more merrily as they neared the fine old mansion, every open window of which seemed sparkling and blinking with a jovial hospitality.

Major Campbell stood at the great hall door, shaking every guest heartily by the hand, now and then saluting the youngest and prettiest ladies in a manner somewhat more tender and paternal, — a proceeding which on such an occasion could not but be taken in good part, and which, to tell the truth, was more than once responded to with an innocent readiness and apparent relish.

The bride was in her chamber, being arrayed by her maids and her kind friend Mrs. Morris for the altar. Her dress was a soft, creamy-hued white satin, with a light cloud of delicate blond floating over it. On her head was the appointed wreath of orange-blossoms — that pure, sweet coronal which should ever crown a womanhood nurtured into perfect bloom by the tropic warmth of a fervid love. In her bosom she wore a little bouquet of natural flowers, — simple violets, and daisies, and sprays of white jasmine. Fanny Morris looked very much astonished when Julia told her, in an awe-struck whisper, that her sister had gathered them that evening 'from mamma's grave.'

As Elinor was arranging these flowers, a pin or small brooch was wanting, and her second bridesmaid, Helen Bruce, suggested that she should use a little pearl cross which lay in her jewel-box, — a pretty trinket which Malcolm had given her as a birth-day present, long ago.

'No, no — not that!' exclaimed Elinor, quickly motioning it away.

'I think poor Malcolm would be pleased to know that you wore his gift on your wedding-night,' said Helen, timidly.

'Do you really think so? Then I will wear it, certainly,' said Elinor, fitting it in her bosom with a pleasant smile.

Elinor was to wear her mother's bridal veil. She kissed it as she took it out of the box where it had lain ever since that mother's hands had placed it there. It was of costly antique lace, and, when fastened upon her head, fell about her in rich, royal folds, peculiarly suited to her tall, stately figure.

Elinor was very beautiful that night; pale and calm, with a brave yet sweet serenity of face, and with a dewy tenderness in her eyes, not bright enough for smiles, and not sad enough for tears.

The bridegroom was in his chamber, putting the

last artistic touches to his elegant toilet before a large swinging mirror, with the aid of his sable valet Tony.

At length all was finished; the bridegroom stood resplendent in a new black suit of exquisite fineness, in white satin neckcloth, white brocade waistcoat, white coat-facings, and white kids. No — one thing more. A superfine white cambric handkerchief is taken from a box on the toilet-table, perfumed with '*Extraite de rose*,' and thrust into the coat-pocket.

'Now you may go, Tony.'

But Tony did not move. A thought seemed suddenly to strike him; he plunged his hand into the depths of the pocket of his own 'long-tailed blue,' and brought up a crumpled letter, which he extended to his master, stammering out,

'O, Massa Charles, I begs pardon, 'deed I does; I 'se mighty sorry, 'deed I is, — for I teetotally forgit to deliver dis letter dat I took out ob de office de day we leff de city. I 'spect it am from one ob de fair sec', de paper and de writing being so mighty nice; which moreober explains why I hab been smelling muskrats, ebery now and den, since I hab de honor to carry it in my pocket.'

Ellsworth saw the garrulous Tony out of the room, and locked the door before he opened the letter, which he did with a blanched cheek and an unsteady hand, for he had noted instantly the post-mark, '*New Orleans*.'

It was from Estelle Le Grange, written in haste, in agitation, and more than commonly broken English; but, as it revealed some heart, such as it was, it is perhaps worth our giving here. It ran thus, without any address prefixed:

'*Mon Dieu!* what do I hear? You will marry another, — you have all forgotten Estelle! But, no; you cannot love *her* as you loved me, — *c'est impossible.* I have read in your eyes a passion immortal — it can perish never. It is true I have rejected you, driven you far away; but I have no happiness of life after that time any more. Your beautiful eyes have looked too deep down in my heart — they make so great a trouble there I cannot laugh it and I cannot dance it away, — ah! they haunt me, those beautiful eyes! *J'ai beaucoup pleuré,* — I have weeped much, and my eyes — *les yeux noirs* — you have so much praised, shine not brightly any longer. Ah, *mon ami,* my poor heart, it is breaking every day!

'*Mon père est mort* — my papa is dead — I am free — I am rich, and — *je vous aime!* — I cannot write it in English, for my blushes — I cannot say more for my tears — *je vous aime.* ESTELLE.'

For several minutes after the reading of this letter Ellsworth sat like one thunder-struck, — silent, immovable, almost breathless. Then he sprang suddenly to his feet, and began walking his chamber with a hurried, unsteady step, striking his forehead, muttering and exclaiming to himself, in a pitiable state of agitation and bewilderment, as his brain caught again the swift whirl, and his heart again struggled vainly with the rapids of the mad passion which had once swept away his manhood.

At last he seemed to have taken an important resolution; for he suddenly left his chamber, crossed the hall, and knocked at Elinor's door. It was opened by one of the smiling bridesmaids, whose smiles quickly fled at sight of the paleness of his face, and the weak tremor of his lips, as, in a tone of ill-assumed calmness, he asked,

'Can I see Miss Campbell for a few minutes, *alone?*'

Permission was immediately accorded; the bridesmaids and Fanny Morris flitted, half-frightened, from the room, and stole wondering and whispering down the hall, and Ellsworth stood alone with his betrothed.

Elinor turned to greet him, with a little look of wonderment and questioning in her thoughtful eyes, and some unwonted and unconscious pride of mien—a subdued womanly exultation in her own beauty, for she knew that her lover had never seen her to such advantage as he would see her at that moment.

As she advanced a step or two to meet him, in her pure bridal array, with a soft glow upon her cheek, a smile half proud, half shy, upon her lips, with that dewy light of tender thought in her welcoming eyes, and, for the first time, called him 'Charles!' she seemed to him such an angelic vision of sweetness and purity that he could scarcely forbear falling at her feet, grasping her robe, and crying, 'Save, or I perish!'

For a moment he remained mute and irresolute, more than half inclined to invent some excuse for his intrusion, retreat to his chamber, and let matters take their course. Then there floated up before him the beautiful, bewildering vision of Estelle, and again his soul sank down powerless, entangled in the strong, unholy spell with which she had glamoured him.

With quivering lips and averted eyes he stammered,

'Elinor — Miss Campbell — there is something about which I should have spoken to you before our engagement, had I not believed in my soul it was all over — forever. I was mistaken — I — I fear I have not quite known my own heart. This evening, within this very hour, I have received a letter from — one who — but perhaps I had best relate from the beginning a story which, I confess, should have been told to you long ago.'

He then gave Elinor a hurried and somewhat confused history of his acquaintance with Estelle, — his love, his offer, and the unlooked-for rejection which he had received. Elinor listened calmly, speaking only twice during the narrative, then merely saying, 'Go on!' when he paused in agitation or embarrassment. The only signs of emotion which she betrayed were alternate flushings and palings of the cheek, and a slightly-quickened breathing.

Ellsworth, who was looking to witness a passionate outburst of grief, or a storm of outraged pride, was astonished, almost frightened, at this strange calm; and, for a moment after he had finished the unhappy history of his infatuation, stood looking at her in mute amazement. Then, standing still and upright before him, with eyes that searched his inmost soul, she asked, in clear, icy tones,

'Do you love that woman still?'

He bowed his face in his hands, and, for the moment, bent before her, as he answered,

'God only knows! I *did* love her, deeply, madly; but I have long struggled against my unworthy and unhappy passion, and, since I have known you, I have believed that it had perished, and a nobler sentiment sprung up in its place. But, ah! the roots of a first passion strike deep in the heart! I am bewildered, distracted, by that passionate, incoherent letter, from a woman who has rejected me, — who flung my proud, true love aside, as carelessly, it seemed, as she could have flung away a flower that had withered in her hands! I am humiliated inexpressibly that her words of tardy tenderness have power to shake me thus. I feel that this is a baleful spell, an evil temptation, to which I should not yield.'

'What, then, do you propose to do?' asked Elinor, still in a cold, measured tone.

'To fulfil my engagement with you. My honor is pledged, nor can I be so heartless as to forsake you now. I feel that it is best for *me*, also, that I should cling to this love, and tear myself from the other. I only ask that our wedding may be postponed for a short time — a few weeks — until my strength, my calmness, my *reason*, come back to me. Will you grant this, in pity to me, Elinor?'

'Yes, it shall be postponed for weeks, for months, for years, *forever!*'

'Nay, nay, I do not ask that! I would not have it so,' exclaimed Ellsworth, starting forward, and attempting to take Elinor's hand. But she waved him back, as she said,

'Not for my life, not for the lives of us both, would I marry you *now!* You should have told me this before,' she continued, after a momentary pause; 'yet, God knows, *I* am not the one to reproach you. Let us both thank Him that the disclosure has come in time to save us both from utter wretchedness. I do not say marry Miss Le Grange, — you may not have loved wisely. May the All-wise One instruct you how to act; but we two must part — at once — and for always. Do not think of me — do not delay a moment, but *go!*'

But Ellsworth stood still. A strange revulsion had come over him. He had been roused by Elinor's noble dignity, and stung by her coldness into something more like passion than he had ever before known for her. If she had flung herself weeping at his feet, or burst upon him with a torrent of reproaches, he would have felt more like flying from her. Now, he only realized the pricelessness of the pearl he had flung away; and an eager desire sprung up in his heart to regain it.

'Elinor, *dear* Elinor!' he began, clasping his hands and bending toward her in tender entreaty, when there came a quick, impatient rap at the door.

Elinor opened to her sister Julia, who whispered, quite audibly,

'Are you not ready, Elinor? It is half an hour after the time set for the ceremony, and papa is getting very impatient. He has just been to Mr. Ellsworth's room, and I have been obliged to tell him that he is here. And papa frowned, as though he thought it rather strange.'

'Well, never mind, I will explain all to him; and,

dear, please go away, and keep others away, for a few minutes longer, and all will be well,' replied Elinor, in a tone so tranquil as to calm the vague fears of the pretty maid, who tripped lightly back to her chamber.

Then Elinor, closing the door, hastily crossed the room and opened another, exclaiming to Ellsworth, as she did so,

'You must fly instantly! Here is a private stairway, leading down to the garden; from there you can easily make your way to the stable; take the first horse you find, and ride to the next village, where you can take the coach for R—— in the morning. Your servant and baggage shall be sent after you. There,—that is my father's step! If you stay to confront him, it is at the peril of your life—go!'

And he went. One moment he paused on the landing, for some word or action of farewell. But she stood quite still, with her head held proudly up, her lips firmly compressed, and her steady, unfathomable eyes fixed upon him, yet looking as though they saw him not. With one hand she held a lamp to light him down the steps, with the other she held back her long bridal veil. Murmuring some hurried words of regret and adieu, he passed her, pulled his hat over his eyes, ran quickly but softly down stairs into the garden, and was gone!

Elinor closed the door and staggered to her dressing-table, where, setting down the lamp, she began to unfasten the bridal veil from her head. As she did so, tears of wounded pride and wasted affection sprang to her eyes. But she sternly dashed them away, knowing that the time for weeping had not yet come.

Major Campbell's knock and voice, imperiously demanding admittance, were at the door; but Elinor stood silent and immovable, listening intently till she heard the fast galloping of a horse going down the avenue. Then she opened the door, and, drawing her father in, closed, locked it, and stood before it.

'Bless my soul!' exclaimed the major, struck by the marble-like whiteness and rigidity of her face, 'what does all this mean? Where 's Ellsworth?'

'Gone!'

'Good God! — gone where?'

'Back to R——. We are to have no wedding, father. Mr. Ellsworth found, at the last moment, that he did not love me as he had thought he did, — and that he loved another better, at least more *passionately*; — and I let him — I *bade* him go. Surely *your* child could not have done otherwise. But where are you going?'

'After the infernal villain! That must have been he I heard galloping down the avenue, not ten minutes ago, — a coward, as well as a knave, — I 'll have him yet! I 'll rouse our friends, — we 'll mount and chase him down, — *shoot* him down, — like the miserable thief that he is! Stand aside, Elinor, and let me pass, to revenge the vile insult put upon you, upon me, upon all of us!'

'No, father,' said Elinor, firmly, still standing against the locked door; 'you must not do it.'

'Do you know what you are saying?' he replied, drawing himself up, angrily. '*Must not — to me!*'

'Yes, father, I know, and I repeat, *you must not do it!* Unless,' she added, in a voice of appealing sadness, 'you would quite break my heart — crush me utterly. Listen: the fault is not wholly his; I, too, have erred — I see it plainly now. I did not love him, at the first, as I should have loved my betrothed husband; and though of late he has grown more dear to me, yet, in my soul, I think it is best, every way best, that we part. And now, father, help me to meet the consequences of my mistake and his, without humiliation and without dismay. Believe me, I know what is best to be done to vindicate my own womanly dignity. Put away your vengeful thoughts, — yield to me this once, I entreat you! No, no, dear father, do not thrust me away! do not turn your face from me! be guided by me this night; *I ask it for dear, dead mother's sake.*'

That appeal acted on the incensed man like a holy spell. He turned, bowed his head on his daughter's shoulder, and burst into tears of mingled grief and anger, while his strong frame shook with the storm of contending passions which convulsed his heart. Elinor laid back the locks from her father's forehead, — thick and glossy they still were, but gray ever since her mother's death,— and kissed him tenderly; she, the comforter, instead of the comforted.

At length he raised his head, dashed the tears almost fiercely from his eyes, and said, half sadly, half querulously,

'You knew, Elinor, that I could not resist *that* appeal, and it was hardly fair in you to make it. Well, I will do as you direct *now;* but, mind, I make no promises for the future. Let that black-coated villain cross my path again at his peril! And, now, what is it that I must do, commander?'

'Simply hand me down to the drawing-room. I will myself make the necessary explanation to our friends. But first call brother Fred, and tell him, as briefly as possible, what has happened. I must have a promise from you both not to use violent language before our guests, nor to encourage idle questioning or animadversions upon Mr. Ellsworth's conduct from them. The party must go on as nearly as possible as though nothing unusual or painful had occurred.'

Fred Campbell was summoned, and came at once. As he entered the room, in a hurried and flurried way, and with a face expressive of much wonderment and some alarm, Elinor retreated to a little boudoir, and closed the door, leaving her father to break the strange tidings to the proud and somewhat hot-blooded youth. As it was, a quick volley of sharp-toned expletives, and a booming oath or two, reached her ears.

As soon as she supposed that the first fury of the storm was past, she reëntered her chamber, and added her loving entreaties to her father's dogged commands, that he should be directed by her what course to pursue under the present circumstances of humiliation and embarrassment.

A wondering, impatient company had been waiting in the large drawing-room for more than an hour, when Elinor entered, leaning on the arm of her father, and accompanied only by her bridesmaids. She had taken off her bridal-veil; she had laid aside her wreath of orange-blossoms; but one rich, royal rose, which she had hastily snatched from a vase on her table, blushed amid the dark waves of her hair, and imparted a little glow of festal brightness to her white, statue-like figure.

She was very pale at first, but as she felt concentrated upon her the gaze of hundreds of questioning, astonished eyes, a vivid color kindled in her cheeks and lips. With her head borne proudly, but not defiantly, and with grave, untroubled eyes, she faced them all bravely, saying, in a voice but slightly shaken by the wild throbbing of her heart,

'Dear friends and neighbors, I have to announce to you that there is to be no wedding to-night. Mr. Ellsworth, who was to have been the bridegroom, received, at almost the last moment, a letter which was the means of convincing him that his heart was not truly in this marriage. You will not censure me, I am sure, that I dismissed him at once; and, not knowing all the circumstances, you should not censure him that he has gone. Rather thank God, with us both, that the conviction did not come too late to save us from that misery of miseries, an unhappy marriage!

'And now,' she added, after a slight pause, 'if you indeed love us, kind friends, you will not break up this party in dissatisfaction and dismay. You came for an evening of innocent enjoyment, in social intercourse, in feasting, music, and dancing. Let all these things go on as they were planned. Father, if you please, we two will open the ball.'

Through a lane of guests speechless with astonishment, the bewildered but obedient host led his daughter to the ball-room, she calmly smiling, and bowing now and then slightly to friends on the right and left, as they passed on.

They took their places for a quadrille, and a set was soon formed, containing the bridesmaids and groomsmen that were to have been. Then other sets were quickly formed, and the dancing commenced to the inspiring strains of an admirable little band of self-taught Ethiopian musicians.

Elinor swam through the dance with a stately grace peculiar to herself, and with a noble dignity and sweetness of demeanor that at once impressed and touched every heart. No supercilious smiles, no whispered impertinence, followed her steps; but looks of wondering pleasure, and murmured tributes of admiration and respect.

She danced with many of her friends, and sang several light songs, in complaisance, not for distraction; for the secret burden of sadness and humiliation was not to be whirled from her heart in the swift dance, nor was the sudden chill and shadow which had fallen on her glowing and sunny spirit to be charmed away by mirthful music.

None of her guests presumed to make any allusion to what had happened, except her friend and confidant Fanny Morris, who stole to her side, soon after the close of the first dance, and whispered,

'I am glad of it, Nell; I am heartily glad of it. I have had my doubts, all along. He was too handsome a man to have made a good husband. His face always seemed to me too calm and classic, and at the same time too irresolute in expression. Now, I admire a thousand times more such a face as my

Frank's, with the impress of an honest soul stamped roughly upon it, striking all the beauty *in*.'

Elinor smiled at her friend's earnestness and wifely complacency, but bitterly she felt in her heart that her words were true; and, as she glanced across the ball-room to where Frank stood, his plain, cordial, *reliable* face was, for the first time, actually handsome in her eyes.

Major Campbell and his son followed Elinor's lead to admiration; but, to a close observer, gave evidence of a much less gentle and Christian spirit. There was in each an affectation of carelessness and hilarity, yet an incoherence of speech, a stern compression of the lips, and a dull fire in the eyes, — a manner half defiant, half defensive, which said plainly enough to even the best of their friends, 'Let any man dare to speak to me about this affair, and I 'll knock him down!'

At supper the party became really unconstrained and merry, in spite of the strange and unpleasant *contre-temps* with which the evening began. As the wine circulated, and jokes and jests and hearty toasts went round, Elinor, who sat opposite her father, thought that she saw symptoms of an outburst of the long-pent-up passion.

'Health and long life to *Miss Campbell*,' with decided emphasis on the name, was proposed by some bold friend of the family, and drunk with the honors; when Major Campbell sprang to his feet, and, instead of responding to the toast in Elinor's behalf, as was expected, exclaimed, with a look of intense excitement,

'Now, *gentlemen*, fill your glasses with good

brandy-punch, stiff and piping hot! I am going to give you *my* sentiments: Here 's confusion and distraction to all false-hearted, sneaking par—' Here he caught his daughter Elinor's reproachful, entreating eyes, paused, stammered, and then, with a brightened look, continued, 'to all sneaking party hacks and political flunkies!'

This sentiment was received with enthusiasm, though its point and relevancy were not very apparent.

For the remainder of the evening the gallant major constrained himself, and nobly redeemed the pledge he had given. He felt immeasurably relieved, however, when the last guest departed; and not a little proud that his demeanor had been such that no word of idle inquiry, or what he would have considered more unpardonable, *sympathy*, had been addressed to him.

Elinor was deeply grateful for his consideration of her. Tender and lingering was her good-night kiss, and cheerful were her good-night words, as she parted from him at the door of her chamber.

But when that door was closed, and she was alone in that bright festive room, with all its bridal decorations of flowers and ribbons and snowy drapery, its white desolation so smote upon her heart, that she sank helplessly upon a couch, and gave way to a fit of passionate, convulsive weeping. Lower and lower she crouched, shrinking shudderingly from her bitter and stinging recollections, while her regal, heroic womanhood seemed melting away in the abundant flow of those weak, girlish tears.

At last she roused herself, and began to move

wearily about the room. On her table lay the wedding wreath and veil which she had taken from her head. The wreath she flung hastily, almost fiercely, aside ; but she folded the veil with reverent care, and laid it away, with the sacred flowers which had withered on her bosom. Then she extinguished the lamps, which were flaring into the dawn, and, in the waning light of the stars, knelt at her bedside and repeated a simple prayer which her mother had taught her in her childhood, and which she had never failed to repeat before sleeping; for, she said, prayer with her was always the timid, childlike asking of the heart, not the wrestling of the spirit with God's strong angel.

Then she took off her bridal dress without a sigh, and laid herself quietly down, not to steep her ringlets in tears, but to sleep tranquilly till far into the morning.

CHAPTER V.

He that loves a rosy cheek,
  Or a coral lip admires,
Or from star-like eyes doth seek
  Fuel to maintain love's fires ;
As old Time makes these decay,
So his flames must waste away.

But a smooth and steadfast mind,
  Gentle thoughts, and calm desires,
Hearts with equal love combined,
  Kindle never-dying fires ;
Where these are not, I despise
Lovely cheeks, or lips, or eyes.

THOMAS CAREW.

ON the day succeeding the wedding party which was *not* a wedding party, Major Campbell proposed to his daughter Elinor, in as delicate a manner as possible, to accompany him on a visit of a month or two to some relatives at the north. But Elinor, who only saw in the proposal a cowardly plan of flying from the observation and gossip she had bravely resolved to face and live down, firmly replied,

'Pardon me, sir, but I cannot go.'

'Why, what then do you mean to do?'

'To stay *here;* to live as I have always lived; to visit and receive my friends, and *try* to be useful and happy. Why should I not, father?'

And she *did* keep on the even tenor of her way, with a pride and reserve so natural, and withal gentle, and a dignity so quiet and cheerful, that she was never called upon to bear the sore infliction of friendly advice or censure, or the polite impertinence of pity.

In her family no direct reference was ever made to the strange and mortifying event which had occurred, and the most delicate and affectionate consideration was shown towards Elinor in all things and at all times.

The only manner in which Major Campbell manifested the still embittered state of his feeling toward Mr. Ellsworth was by bearing even more hardly than formerly upon 'the cloth.' He positively refused to attend church, and began to patronize a certain old Methodist preacher, a respectable and evangelical stone-mason, who held forth three times every Sunday, principally to an audience of negroes assembled in a large barn on the Campbell plantation. Though an illiterate, simple-hearted man, he was, in his small way, a faithful and effective minister of Christ's Gospel; and, as such, the honest major had a genuine respect for him, and strove hard to be insensible to his want of respect for the king's English.

One morning in November of that same year, Major Campbell sat in the breakfast-room, reading the papers and letters which had just been brought from the village post-office. While glancing over a southern journal, he suddenly started, cast a look of apprehension at his daughter Elinor, who sat near him, then hastily folded the paper, and thrust it into his pocket. It contained an announcement of the marriage of Mr. Ellsworth to M'lle Le Grange, and of the reverend gentleman's resignation of the charge of the parish of St. James, in R——.

Little did the kind and careful father imagine that the letter which Elinor was so calmly reading at that very moment was from Mr. Ellsworth himself, announcing that marriage and resignation, and his intended departure for Europe.

He could not, he wrote, resist the strong desire which he felt to write to her before going abroad. 'For I cannot feel,' he added, 'that in parting from you, even as I did, I have wholly lost a friend, much less gained an enemy. I must believe that your nature is too magnanimous — and, pardon me for adding, your regard for me too deep and tender — for your heart to have been utterly turned against me by the unexpected and painful declaration which I found myself obliged to make to you, under such unfortunate and embarrassing circumstances.

'I am sure that I do not overrate your goodness when I say that I believe that you will feel a generous pleasure in my present happiness, — a happiness for which I am indebted to your unselfish devotion, — and take a sister's kindly interest in my hopes and plans for the future.

'Estelle, my three days' wife, is a marvellously lovely creature, about your own age, yet seemingly much younger. She is a very child; indeed, a *spoiled* child, I fear, — but so beautiful and charming in all her wilful, whimsical ways, and odd girlish caprices, — so *naïve*, piquant, and peculiar, — that I cannot wish her other than she is, *just yet*.

'Still, though charmed, *spell-bound*, if you will, by her thousand nameless graces and enchantments, I am not, believe me, without an earnest desire to influence to noble purposes, and lead upward to a higher life than she has yet led, this thoughtless child-wife of mine. She loves me, — in the passionate, exacting, jealous way of a true southern woman, it is true, but she *loves me*, and I hope much from that. I love her with an absorbing devotion, an utter idolatry, perilous, I have sometimes feared, to my manhood, — to my very soul; but I trust yet to gain such an ascendency over my own heart, and over her wayward but loving nature, as to be able to realize that noble plan of a true life which you have so often marked out for a truly wedded pair, — a life in which the beautiful shall be sanctified by the useful, and the useful glorified by the beautiful.

'I have resigned the charge of the parish of St. James, but by no means my "high profession spiritual." We go abroad to spend a year or two only. Then it is my design to return home, and, with an enlarged experience, and, I trust, with views and aims in no way narrowed or lowered, to resume my sacred calling.

'You, who know so well my love for art, architecture, and music, can understand the eager, almost boyish enthusiasm with which I set forth on this visit to the Old World, — this pilgrimage to the grandest shrines of the poet and the artist. I should be deeply, utterly happy now, could I cease to reproach myself for *your* unhappiness. Though Heaven knows I meant you no wrong, I acknowledge that I committed a grave error, and I humbly entreat your forgiveness.

'I can do no more, but pray that God's blessing,

and the ineffable comfort and sustaining strength of his Spirit, may be yours.

'Always your friend, C. E.'

Elinor replied to this letter briefly, but kindly and cheerfully. She assured the writer of her friendly sympathy in his happiness, and begged that he would allow no vain self-reproach, and, above all, no memory of her, to cloud or mar it henceforth. But she had too much knowledge, both intuitive and acquired, of the heart of man, to believe that it would really add to Mr. Ellsworth's happiness to know that she was less unhappy than he had supposed, *because her love had been less*. So she did not tell him that she had not suffered, was not suffering still, because of their separation — sorrowing over those beautiful vanished dreams, sweet visions of love and home, which shone before her so bright and near for a time, and then faded away forever. She had not that poor pride which shrank from allowing her once betrothed husband to believe that he had been dearest of all the world to her heart, — that she had given him the deepest faith and the most glad and perfect devotion of her nature. She rather felt a noble shame that she had not *better* loved him to whom she had been plighted in the most solemn and endearing of compacts.

That same month brought Elinor another letter, — one which she did not read in the breakfast-room, in the presence of her family, but in her own chamber, alone. It came on a balmy, gold-misted morning of the Indian summer, — a season of all others most fitting, for that letter seemed to bring back to Elinor's weary heart and shadowed spirit much of the glow and joy-light of the vanished summer of her early girlhood. It was from Malcolm Bruce. He wrote from Florence, darling city of art, lapped in loveliness, and breathed upon by the very airs of Paradise, floating over purple hills and singing waters, vineyards and orange-groves, and wilds of entangled blooms, incensing all heaven with thick clouds of ascending sweets. But, without the inward glow of a hopeful, happy spirit, one finds even Italian sunshine dim, and all the bloom of the gardens of the south cannot make glad a lonely and saddened heart; and oftentimes the memory of some beloved human form will cause one to turn away weary and dissatisfied from the highest creations of the sculptor and the painter. So Malcolm Bruce wrote sadly, even from Florence; not but that his words were cheerful and manly, but a tone of loneliness and renunciation sighed through them. He had heard of Elinor's engagement and approaching marriage, and for the first time he flung aside his pride to acknowledge his hopeless love.

'Ever since you came from school, dear Elinor,' he wrote, in a simple, straight-forward way, 'I have known that you did not love me, or care for my love. Up to that time, our childish betrothal had been to me something as real and sacred and certain as your present engagement can now be to your own pure and loyal heart. But with you I soon saw that it was different — ah, how sadly different! You scorned and repudiated that romantic compact. I met your pride and coldness with assumed carelessness, indifference, and airs of boyish trifling, which I only regret now, because they *were* assumed. I blush at the recollection that I so long acted a falsehood; I, who felt every proud, or cold, or careless word from your lips, in every quivering fibre of my own proud heart,—for indeed I loved you, Elinor,—I have loved you always, deeply, tenderly, and solely; and I tell you so now, when the avowal costs my manly pride a pang more bitter than you may ever know. I think I take a sort of fierce pleasure in crucifying that false pride which for a long time so belied the dear love which had sprung up in my true, boyish heart, which had been nourished by the very springs of my life, which had expanded with the growth of thought, and flowered with the season of romance, and at last colored and kept pure the wild years of early manhood with the fervor and sweetness of its secret bloom.

'It was but a miserable jealousy which led me to guard ever from your eyes "that perfectest flower of the heart." I should have been content to have laid it at your feet. You would not, I am sure, have trampled upon it, and it might have brightened your way for a moment.

'I do not doubt that you have chosen wisely—for you are wise above most women; and while I cannot believe that your betrothed husband can love you better than I have done, I acknowledge that it may be better for you to love him. I know that you have outgrown me in intellectual and spiritual life, during the last few years. I have not, like you, cultivated diligently that wise lôve of the beautiful, those enthusiasms, and high unselfish aims, which give a sacred dignity to life. I have either been absorbed, brain and soul, in science, or letting my physical energies run riot in manly sports and feats of strength and daring, content, like a young Greek, with the fulness of the outward and physical life. All I know of poetry I have learned of love; and, as for religious faith, I sometimes fear that the swift round of even what are called the *innocent* pleasures of youth have whirled me away from God.

'From the shame and sorrow of actual sin I have been thus far preserved by two angelic influences; one radiant helper has been the memory of my mother, — one dim, sweet presence, the hope of you.

'And they shall save me still! I will never kneel under a burden of shame at my mother's grave; and, though I can never call you mine, I can keep myself worthy to have loved you. God bless you — God love you forever! MALCOLM BRUCE.'

A clear, startling, almost blinding light, burst upon Elinor's mind in the reading of this letter. It flashed down into the innermost recesses of her heart, and revealed the silent secret passion lurking there. It was like a sudden gleam of friendly lightning, showing her the gulf on whose edge she had been standing, led on by false lights, in the restless wandering of a dissatisfied spirit. Before letting the long-imprisoned and unsuspected waters of affection have way, bearing a light of joy and a murmur of deep content in every wave, and steeping her soul in life's divinest sweetness, she bowed her head in meek, awe-struck gratitude to Him who had saved her from the penalty of falsifying the holiest instincts of womanhood — from a life-long perjury.

She was humble then — O, very humble! — and, in the beautiful purity of her nature, felt that a mistake like hers was a stain upon her womanliness, upon the chaste constancy of the soul, which, perhaps, even Malcolm's generous love could not and should not forgive.

She wrote to him a frank, brave letter, confessing, first of all, her love; then the errors into which she had been led by an overweening pride, and the false ideas which she had caught from poets and romancers of the formal, chivalric deference, the exalted homage, the almost divine honors, which should be paid by the lover to the mistress of his heart; telling *naïvely* how she had donned her beautiful womanhood as a crown, and felt every inch a princess, and would have no homely wooing; and how, with a great heart glowing in her breast, and a prodigal sense of life thrilling in every vein, she would fain have played statue, and been warmed by the woful sighs animated and drawn from her pedestal by the wild prayers of a passionate and poetical love.

Then she gave him a faithful history of her engagement with Mr. Ellsworth, and of its termination; disguising nothing, glozing over nothing, in her account of that painful and humiliating separation, at the very steps of the altar. From him she did not hold back the truth, that she was deeply grateful to God that the severest, sole punishment of her error had been the martyrdom of her pride, in that scene of trial and bitter mortification.

Malcolm Bruce replied to this letter from Rome —

the city of desolation and eternal sadness; but a tone of jubilant life rang through his letter, and his thoughts came bathed in the golden light and freighted with the immortal sweetness of love's own 'morning land.'

And thus they were betrothed. A wild wintry sea stretched between them, but over its dark waves met their two hearts, undismayed by its tempestuous surging, unsaddened by its foreboding moan.

Again the autumn had come round; again Elinor Campbell was looking for the coming of her lover; her heart heaped with the abundant gifts of ripened love, as earth with the fruits of that bounteous season. The joy of welcome already fluttered in her breast; her impatient thoughts far outran the slow hours, and would have urged on grave old Father Time with childish chidings.

At length the long-hoped-for, long-prayed-for day arrived, and again at twilight she walked down the avenue to meet her betrothed — but this time she went alone.

Under the deep shadows of an old elm, near the gate, she waited till she had watched out the last gleams of sunshine, had seen the dull face of heaven kindle with the faint smile of the first stars, and then the kindly moon come up to comfort the bereaved earth. The most restless birds had ceased their twittering, and slept, rocked by the night-winds that swayed the long branches of the elm, and shook down the first leaves that had 'suffered a *fall* change, into something rich and strange.' The dew lay heavy on the grass, the katydid took up her shrill song, and — at last, at last, it came! — the quick galloping of a horse, far down the road. With heart that beat time to every bound, with hands tightly clasped, and eyes straining to pierce through the waving shadows of the elms, Elinor stood waiting. There was a little pause at the gate, and then up the avenue dashed a swift, strong steed — Malcolm Bruce's own 'gallant gray.' The moonlight fell full on the face of the rider. It was he! Elinor's first impulse was to shrink further back into the shade and let him pass; but, the next instant, she sprang forward, almost into his path, calling his name in a glad, tender, childlike tone. With a cry of joyful surprise, he leaped from the saddle, and flung his arms about her. Ah, if she 'trembled' then, as at that other meeting, it was against his heart; and if any words were spoken by either, they were too sacred to be repeated here.

Before the winter was past there was a real wedding at Major Campbell's. There was the same gay party assembled; but this time, need I say, no ominous putting off of the marriage ceremony, no retraction and escape of the bridegroom, no startling *entrée* of a wreathless and veilless bride, announcing her own desertion. Precisely at the moment appointed, the bridal party entered. The bride came with a solemn joy swimming in the tearful light of her deep eyes, and a smile of ineffable contentment on her lips, glowing with maiden modesty and moving with a chastened pride, which was no longer of or for herself. Again she wore her mother's veil; but, instead of orange-flowers, a natural wreath of the buds of the blush-rose. None understood the change; but her thought was that the orange-flowers had been for her the symbols of a merely intellectual love, if love it could at all be named; while these rose-buds were the types of a yet purer sentiment, touched by the warmth of human passion.

The bridegroom's slender yet powerful figure, Greek-like in its rare grace and symmetry, seemed that night endowed with the exultant lightness of a young Mercury; his frank, manly face was so illuminated with happiness, his lips so overflowed with smiles, his eyes so danced in light, that he really seemed to move with his head in the heaven of the immortals, if not to feel the quivering of wings at his heels.

But, if the bride was happy, and the bridegroom transported and half translated, what shall we say of the bride's father? The darling but long-despaired-of plan of his life was at last triumphantly accomplished, and his great heart could not contain the abundant measure of its pride and gratulation. There was that night a rich, jolly gurgle in his laugh, a sparkle and effervescence of wit in his talk, and a continual bubbling over of his fine, mellow-flavored, old-fashioned humor, altogether delightful and inspiring. He offered no highly-spiced *political* sentiments at the supper-table, and during the entire evening he was observed to be particularly courteous to the clergyman who had officiated at the marriage, and who was *not* the Reverend Simeon Hawkins, of the Methodist persuasion.

As the wife of a country physician, a man whom she deeply loves and honors, and as the mother of a noble boy, the child of perfect love, Elinor has found that a life of generous aims, and deep, ennobling sympathies, is possible; and that, however narrow and lowly the sphere of her daily duties, there are above it, and above the widest and grandest fields of human action, the same heavenly heights to climb.

Charles Ellsworth has never returned to America. Madame Ellsworth has become too much wedded to the delights of Paris, especially since the establishment of a gay imperial court, to forego them for comfort, quiet, and respectability, at home. And who can wonder? There she finds the very atmosphere on which to unfurl her frail, butterfly wings. Beautiful, rich, gay, *piquante, spirituelle,* she is one of the divinities of society—irresponsible, despotic, absolute. Her whimsical caprices are made authorities, and her freaks become fashions. She never appears but with an almost royal train of courtly followers, young French counts, Italian marquises, German barons, English 'Mi-lors;' and she sparkles and flutters, and scatters smiles, and soft, bewitching words, and makes herself generally adorable; while her husband, from far in the background, scowls his helpless discontent upon the brilliant group, but most of all upon her. Or he wearily waits her coming, pacing moodily up and down a comfortless chamber, at home. *Home*—she has become so thoroughly a French woman, as to ignore the word.

Poor, little, soulless Estelle!—we must not be too hard upon her. Love built his fairy structure upon the sands, and the rising flood of the world swept it away forever! She is proud of her husband's beauty still; but no longer in love with it.

She shrugs her pretty shoulders at what she calls his puritan ideas, while his depressed spirits, and listless, disappointed air, fill her, she says, with *ennui.* As for his occasional gentle reproaches, and remonstrances, and mild marital lectures, they — I know it is an ugly word — infuriate her.

His love for art yet remains — or rather the pale ghost of that kindling enthusiasm which haunted his youth, and peopled the chambers of his classic mind with fair shapes of ideal beauty. He frequents much the noble galleries of the Louvre; but finds that the most gorgeous pictures strike no sweet human glow into a heart chilled by bitter disappointment, and that the contemplation of the grandest statuary in the world is but 'cold comfort' for a cheerless home.

He has now a far better consoler. He is sometimes seen walking in the gardens of the Tuileries, leading by the hand a lovely child, a sweet, gentle little girl, whose heart clings to her father with a peculiar passionate affection, which sometimes rouses her mother's jealousy — almost the sole sign of interest which the capricious Estelle ever deigns to manifest for the child.

Mr. Ellsworth would have called this daughter 'Elinor,' and respectfully offered the name, or rather made a mild suggestion of it, to the mother. But Estelle overruled him, and had her christened 'Adrienne,' after a character in which M'lle Rachel was just then drowning all Paris in tears. The father yielded, without argument, and without remonstrance, — but in his heart he always calls the child *'Elinor.'*

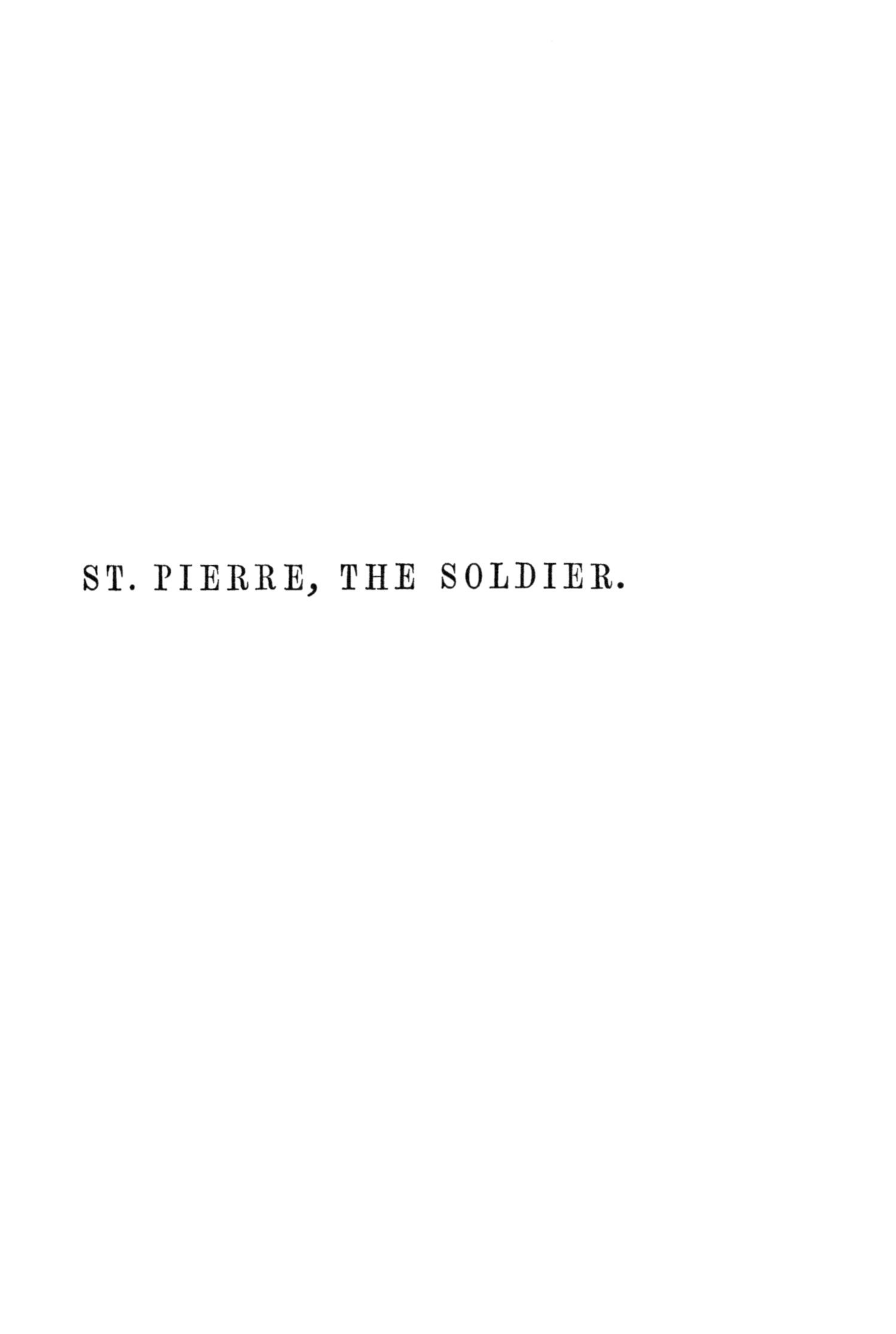

ST. PIERRE, THE SOLDIER.

ST. PIERRE, THE SOLDIER;

A STORY OF

THE AMERICAN REVOLUTION.

FOUNDED ON FACT.

CHAPTER I.

THE PRIVATE AND HIS FRIENDS.

I have not loved the world, nor the world me,
But let us part fair foes ; I do believe,
Though I have found them not, that there may be
Words which are things, hopes which will not deceive,
And virtues which are merciful, nor weave
Snares for the failing. I would also deem
O'er others' griefs that some sincerely grieve ;
That two, or one, are almost what they seem;
That goodness is no name, and happiness no dream.

BYRON.

In the spring of 1781, a detachment of the French troops, under the command of Count de Rochambeau, was stationed for a time at a quiet little town in New England.

Though deeply grateful to their generous allies for countenance and help in their time of bitter need, the simple and puritanical people of W—— shrank from associating familiarly with the foreign soldiers quartered in their town.

They had little or nothing in common, except a love for liberty; and there was such an essential difference in the quality of that sentiment that perfect sympathy, even here, was impossible. With the sturdy Yankee it was a vital principle, strengthened by long and profound thought, sanctified by religion, and made invincible by the force of a dogged yet fiery will, a sort of sullen fanaticism.

With the Frenchmen it was a sudden and novel enthusiasm, an intense and uncomprehended passion, a generous frenzy, that, a few years later, degenerated into the blind rage of brutal ferocity, which glutted itself with carnage, and slaked its fiery thirst in blood.

Few of these soldiers spoke English, and fewer of the villagers French; so, had not the will been wanting, a great degree of social intercourse would have been out of the question. There was scarcely a healthful, able-bodied young or middle-aged man left in the town; all were away with the army, and the old people, the youths and maidens and little children, were very shy of the '*fureign sojers,*' or '*monseers,*' as they called them. But they treated them with kindly hospitality, and a simple native courtesy, which was better than their own formal and often artificial politeness.

The officer in command of this detachment was a Colonel la Motte, a stern, passionate man, overbearing to insolence, and a strict disciplinarian when his men were concerned, but for himself frequently given to gross indulgence. It was whispered that he had royal blood in his veins, though it certainly did not come to him through direct and honorable channels ; which may account for both his pride and his profligacy.

Among the privates there was one handsome and gentlemanly young soldier, apparently not more than twenty or twenty-one years of age, whose dark, dejected face touched all hearts, especially the tender hearts of mothers and young girls. This soldier, whose name was St. Pierre, was either very haughty or strangely reserved in disposition, for he was never seen with his comrades, except when on duty. At all other times he evidently sought to be alone, sitting hour after hour in the little vine-sheltered porch of the cottage wherein he was quartered, with his head bowed on the railing before him, or, as often as he could obtain leave from a kind and somewhat indulgent captain, wandering off in the lonely woods, apparently giving way to fits of sadness and despondency, or absorbed in mournful recollections.

Sometimes he would smile a faint, transient smile, as though a drop of sweetness had been infused into the bitter cup of his memories ; and then a deeper shadow of weary hopelessness and recklessness would fall upon his face

St. Pierre was master of the English language, but seldom spoke it voluntarily, except to children, of whom he seemed fond. He lodged at the house of a widow, with two children — a noble boy of eleven, and a sweet little girl of eight or nine. The husband and father had been killed at Bunker Hill.

Mrs. Huntington was a brave and patriotic woman. Her ardent enthusiasm for liberty had not grown cold on the dead heart of her husband; not even *his* blood had quenched the generous flame, but rather baptized it into a more sacred fervor. She felt toward the humblest of our French allies, even, a glowing gratitude, almost amounting to reverence; so she received young St. Pierre, though a soldier of the ranks, as an honored guest, as a noble knight, a heroic defender.

Her enthusiasm was not a little dampened when she finally ascertained from him, in a moment of unusual confidence, that he really understood and cared very little about the merits of our quarrel with the mother-country. He was wretched, he said, and indifferent, more than indifferent, to life; he had enlisted under Count Rochambeau for the double purpose of leaving France and seeking a speedy death, without the sin of direct self-destruction, which, for the sake of one who loved him, he was unwilling to take upon his soul.

Good Mrs. Huntington was greatly shocked, but she kindly and solemnly expostulated with 'the poor boy,' as she called him, on the wrong he was doing himself and the world, by indulging in his morbid melancholy and selfish indifference to the great interests of freedom.

To little George and Fanny, however, all this made slight difference. Children are rarely politicians, or even patriots. These saw that the stranger was lonely and sad, and gave him, in their shy little ways, the instinctive sympathy of childhood. They felt, too, that the poor private was a *gentleman*, and yielded him respect and admiration, as well as affection. And he responded to their interest, in a languid, melancholy way, that saddened while it deepened their own tender regard. The boy he sometimes allowed to accompany him in his aimless wanderings through the woods. He usually walked very fast, plunging into the wildest and most shadowed paths, with little George, a quiet, unobtrusive companion, running at his side. But at evening, when he sat on the rustic porch in the moonlight, he often took little Fanny on his knee, and held her head against his breast, and wound his fingers in her soft, curly hair, which was of a peculiar golden brown. For hours the child would sit thus, nestled up against his breast; and sometimes she would fall asleep there, and the young soldier would rise up very quietly, and carry her gently in to her mother, who hardly knew what to make of this strange intimacy.

One morning Fanny went to the chamber of St. Pierre, to give him some message. She found the door ajar, and entered so softly that he did not hear her. He was sitting in his usual dejected attitude by the window. As Fanny stole noiselessly to his side, she saw that he held in his hand a miniature, on which he was gazing earnestly, while tears were dropping fast upon it from his dark, sad eyes. Fanny stood very still a moment, then burst into a fit of sympathetic weeping. St. Pierre kindly took her in his arms, and, to soothe her, showed her the miniature at which he had been looking. It was that of a beautiful young girl; a sweet, glowing, southern face, with the expression of noble womanliness and exalted thought we oftener see in colder northern faces. As Fanny gazed at this, with eager delight, she exclaimed,

'O, *monsieur*, that pretty lady's hair is just like mine! Is n't it?'

'Yes, *ma mie*,' replied St. Pierre, thrusting the picture into his bosom, and laying his hand on the child's head more tenderly than ever before. Alas! it was the last time little Fanny ever felt the touch of those fingers amid her curls!

That morning, on parade, St. Pierre had the ill-luck to offend his colonel by some maladroitness, growing out of his melancholy abstraction. La Motte burst upon him in a most violent manner, and St. Pierre was observed to flush, and then to grow more deathly pale than before, while his eyes flashed hate and defiance, and he clenched his musket convulsively, almost threateningly. But he controlled himself, and the storm passed by for the time. Unfortunately, he was that night placed on guard before the officers' quarters. Colonel la Motte had given a dinner; a drunken revel it proved to be, on his part at least. About midnight he came out, to see some favorite guest off, and caught sight of poor St. Pierre, standing lost in one of his profound fits of abstraction, leaning on his musket, and forgetting his duty in gazing at the stars, his thoughts far away in a lovely valley in sunny France, from which he had often looked up at those stars with one beloved and lost. The enraged and intoxicated officer reeled up to him, and, before he had time to recover himself, struck him with the flat of his sword, hissing through his teeth at the same moment some insulting reprimand for this neglect of duty. With a fierce cry, an absolute yell of rage, the private turned and drove his bayonet through the body of his colonel!

The alarm was raised at once, and St. Pierre was arrested. He had not stirred from the spot. The next day Colonel la Motte's wound was declared mortal (though he ultimately recovered); St. Pierre was tried by a court-martial, and sentenced to be shot early on the following morning.

Of all this the children, George and Fanny, knew nothing; for, though the shocking account of the stabbing, the trial, and the sentence, had been carried through the town, Mrs. Huntington carefully kept it from them, and put them off with the most unconcerned manner she could assume when they missed their friend and questioned her about him. On the morning of the execution, she gladly permitted them to go out into the woods to gather flowers, thinking that they would thus escape all knowledge of the dread event till it was passed. But she unfortunately did not know the place of execution.

The children rambled on through their familiar woodland haunts, gathering wild-flowers and chatting merrily together. At length George said, rather impatiently,

'I wonder what has become of that St. Pierre? It's too bad in him to stay away so long; though, to be sure, he is n't very good company.'

'No,' said Fanny, 'he don't talk much, and he looks very low-spirited; but he sometimes smiles *such* a sweet smile, it is better than any talk, than even fairy-story-telling. Come, George, let's gather some of those blue violets that grow in that sunny place we know of, and put in the little vase in his room. He likes them, for he says they are just like the violets that grow away off in France, only not so sweet.'

Thus they talked till they came to a small open space, where the thick green grass was profusely enamelled with pale blue violets. As they were gathering them, the boy suddenly exclaimed, 'See, sister! somebody has been digging a great hole here; I wonder what it's for?'

'It looks like a grave,' said Fanny, shrinking back with a shudder.

'No,' replied George, with a wise shake of the head, 'it isn't deep enough for that. Maybe somebody has been digging for treasure.'

Just at that moment the sound of a muffled drum, and the slow, measured tramp of feet, came to them faintly down the shadowed forest path.

'The soldiers are coming!' cried Fanny, running to hide behind a thick screen of sweet-brier and blackberry bushes that grew near.

George was not a timid boy, but even he did not like the idea of facing those black-bearded foreign soldiers in that lonely spot. So he hid with his sister, meaning to lie quiet till they should go by.

Nearer and nearer came the sound of the drum, beating a slow, mournful march, and at length there appeared in the little glade two soldiers, bearing a black coffin, followed by the prisoner, St. Pierre, with an officer on one side and a priest on the other. After them came a file of soldiers.

St. Pierre walked with a firm tread, and his handsome face expressed even less melancholy and despondency than usual. He was dressed in his uniform, and his arms were free. He had been so quiet, and evidently indifferent, since his arrest, that the officer in command had spared him the humiliation of being bound, or even very closely guarded. In fact, it was suspected that, had he chosen to escape, no very eager or strict search would have been made for him, so thoroughly was Colonel la Motte detested by his regiment.

As all entered the glade, they halted. The coffin was set down beside the grave, and the prisoner stood before it. As the soldiers were taking their places opposite him, he stooped and plucked one of the violets that grew in the grass at his feet. He looked into its dewy cup a moment, kissed it, and then let it slowly drop from his fingers.

'O, George!' whispered little Fanny, who had been peeping through the briers. 'It's our St. Pierre! What are they going to do with him?'

'I don't know,' answered George, beginning to tremble violently, 'but I'm afraid they are going to shoot him!'

'O, no, no! They can't be so cruel! Let us run out to them, brother, and beg them not to! Let us tell them how good and kind he is, and how much we love him!'

'Hush, Fanny!' said George; 'we can't do any good that way; they don't understand English, and so would n't mind us; and you must keep still, for if they hear us, maybe they'll take us for Indians, and shoot into the bushes, and kill us, too.'

The poor little girl submitted, and nestled down

against her brother, trembling and sobbing below her breath.

The priest read some prayers, and the prisoner, taking a gold-clasped prayer-book from his pocket, read also, in a low but firm and fervent voice. This done, he took from between the leaves of the book a letter, or a small package of letters, which he handed to his captain, with the request that he would forward it to its destination in France.

The officer read the address aloud, with an expression of much surprise, — '*A Monsieur le Marquis de Villiers,*' — and then added,

'Pray, *Monsieur,* what is *he* to you?'

'*Il est mon père,*' replied St. Pierre, simply.

Captain Gardette involuntarily touched his hat, but his tone betrayed some incredulity, as he asked,

'And why did not Monsieur reveal his rank, or the rank of his family, before the court-martial? It might possibly have saved his life.'

'Ah, *mon capitaine!*' replied St. Pierre, 'it was because I did not wish for *life,* but for *death.* As well meet it here as in battle,' he added, with a slight shrug of the shoulders; 'only, instead of English muskets, I shall fall by those of my comrades, who, I am sure, will not mangle me.

'Of you, captain, I but ask that you will promise me, on a soldier's honor, to faithfully carry out my wishes in regard to this packet; that you will allow me to look death in the eye, — that is, will not compel me to be blindfolded; and that you will see that I am buried just as I fall, — that nothing about my person be removed or disturbed.'

The officer solemnly promised, and the private merely added,

'Adieu, my captain! adieu, comrades, — till the great muster-roll calls us all together!'

He then took a kind leave of the priest, gave one long look at the sky above and the earth around him, then knelt upon his coffin, and calmly awaited the swift messengers of death. The soldiers reluctantly levelled their muskets at the command of their officer; he visibly shook as he gave the fatal word; then came the fearful volley, and St. Pierre fell forward upon his face, dead!

The two children hid in the briers shrieked at this appalling sight, but in the report and reverberation of the muskets their cry was lost. The next moment George saw that little Fanny had fainted. She was a sensitive, nervous child; he had seen her swoon before, and was not so much alarmed by her present state as to lose the calmness, judgment, and courage, which distinguished him above most lads of his age. He laid his sister down softly on the grass, and stole away to a rivulet which ran past the glade, a few rods distant. Here he dipped his little felt hat in the cool water, and, hastening back, bathed the poor child's face and throat, weeping bitterly the while for his dead friend, whom he heard the soldiers hastily burying but a few yards away.

By the time that Fanny had revived and opened her bewildered eyes, all was over, and the soldiers were leaving the glade. It was not until the last sound of the drum had died away in the distance, that the two frightened children crept out of their covert, with faces deathly white, and eyes wild with horror.

Little Fanny trembled most, and clung to her brother, who tenderly supported her. Timidly they approached the grave. There was nothing to mark the spot, save a very low mound; all the sods had been carefully replaced. There was not much blood upon the ground, though the children remarked with a shudder that several tufts of violets were hung with dark red drops, instead of the bright dews of the morning. As they stood near the grave, George noticed something shining through the trampled grass at his feet. It was the gold clasp of the little prayer-book of St. Pierre, which had dropped from his hand when he fell, and had been overlooked by his executioners. The boy took it up and reverently preserved it, though it too was sprinkled with blood.

'I mean to pile up some stones here,' said George, softly.

'I will plant a rose-bush,' whispered little Fanny; 'and I know the violets will always grow thick upon his grave, because he loved them so, — poor, poor St. Pierre!'

Here the child burst forth into violent sobbing, and her brother, frightened at her excessive grief, though weeping with her, drew her away, and almost carried her home.

The result of this terrible experience was for Fanny a dangerous illness, from which she was very long in recovering. George rallied from the shock after a few days of grieving and nervous prostration; but the effect upon the characters of both children was deep and lasting. They had looked upon death in one of his most awful forms, and the sight had prematurely chilled and saddened their warm young hearts. They became serious and thoughtful beyond their years, but in no way hard or unlovely; and though the tone of that widowed and fatherless household was quiet almost to sadness, it was never gloomy, or harshly puritanical.

In the fall following the execution of St. Pierre, Fanny planted a rose-bush on his grave, and literally watered it with her tears. George had some time before piled up his rude memorial of mossy stones. The rose-tree took root, and in the early summer put forth many blossoms. Little Fanny said, with childish awe in her look and tone, that they were richer and redder roses than the bush had ever borne before, and that perhaps it was his blood that made them so. Wild violets also grew in profusion upon that grave in the lovely forest glade.

CHAPTER II.

THE MARQUIS DE VILLIERS.

> Then grave and hoary-headed hypocrites,
> Without a hope, a passion, or a love,
> Who through a life of luxury and lies
> Have crept by flattery to the seats of power,
> Support the system whence their honors flow.
> They have three words: well tyrants know their use,
> Well pay them for loan with usury
> Torn from a bleeding world: — God, Hell
> And Heaven.
>
> SHELLEY.

SEVEN years had passed. The war was long ago ended, and our French allies had all returned to their native land, now on the eve of that fearful political convulsion that shook the world.

In the quiet country town of W—— there was little apparent change. The French troops had been gone all these years, and were nearly forgotten, with the exception of poor St. Pierre, whose sad story was told and wept over around some humble hearths in the long winter evenings. To some happy homes husbands and fathers and sons returned from the wars; but many were the widows and the fatherless, many the sad mothers who still mourned for their brave sons lying in far-off soldier graves.

Into the golden-brown hair folded about the noble head of the widow Huntington a few threads of silver had stolen; but her face was yet placid and gentle, and even less sad than of old.

George, now a fine, manly youth of eighteen, was managing his mother's farm, with no higher ambition than to be what his father had been before him, — a sturdy New England farmer.

Fanny, at sixteen, had all the grace and beauty which her lovely childhood promised. She was a delicate, poetical, ethereal creature, — just one of those young girls of whom wise old ladies are often heard to declare, with a doleful shake of the head, that they are 'not long for this world.' Nevertheless, I am happy to say that gentle Fanny *did* live to comfort her beloved mother throughout her earthly pilgrimage, — did live to be a mother, ay, a *grandmother*, herself. I throw this little piece of information in for the gratification of my readers, my story having nothing to do with Fanny after she reached the blooming age I have mentioned — sweet sixteen.

One afternoon, during the summer of that year, a foreign-looking gentleman, accompanied by a servant in quiet livery, drove into the village of W—— in a handsome but plain travelling-carriage. The stranger stopped at the modest little inn, engaged apartments for the night, and then inquired the way to the cottage of Mrs. Huntington. It was pointed out to him, and he proceeded thither alone.

Fanny answered his knock, and, as she showed him into the little parlor where her mother and brother sat, they noticed that she was very pale, and seemed agitated. The visitor was tall and dark, and there was something strangely familiar in his face. With a tone and manner courteous and singularly elegant, but in somewhat imperfect English, he addressed Mrs. Huntington:

'Is it that I have de honor to see Madame Huntington?'

'Yes, sir,' replied the widow, simply, but with a courtesy of manner equal to his own.

'Ah! den you once have in your hospitable *maison*, in de time of de war of America wid Angleterre, *un soldat Français,*—*pardon,* one French soldier, who named himself St. Pierre—*n'est-ce-pas?*'

'O yes, sir!' answered Mrs. Huntington, with much earnestness; 'he lodged with us for some weeks. Do you know anything about the poor young gentleman?'

'*Ah oui*—yes, madame—he was my brother!' rejoined the stranger, mournfully; 'and I am de Marquis de Villiers.'

Thus was the familiar look in the face of the stranger explained to all in the cottage.

Having accepted a seat by a door which opened upon the little rustic porch, where his unfortunate brother had so often sat, the marquis related to the widow and her children the story of a life of which they knew too well the sad and tragic sequel; a story which satisfactorily explained, to the young girl, at least, the mysterious gloom and dejection of their friend.

Auguste and Eugene St. Pierre Duchatel were the only sons of the Marquis de Villiers, the head of an ancient but somewhat decayed family in Brittany,—a proud, cold, haughty man, with an inflexible will, and very primitive ideas of parental authority and filial obedience. Between his two sons there happily existed a peculiar and affectionate sympathy; and though their prospective fortunes were very dissimilar and unequal, there was neither condescension on the one part, nor jealousy on the other. Auguste was the heir to the title and estates of his father, while Eugene was destined for the church. The brothers received their early education together, but as soon as they reached manhood they were separated. Auguste entered the service of the king, at court; and Eugene commenced his theological studies under a Jesuit priest who was established as chaplain in his father's chateau.

Eugene had no natural inclination for the profession chosen for him; his tastes rather led him to the lighter pursuits of literature and art. But his character was not strong or decisive, and in this matter he yielded, as he had done in all others, to the powerful will and positive judgment of his father. But the nearer drew the season when he must take the first public steps toward entering upon his priestly office, the more decided and intense became his secret dissatisfaction. Especially was he revolted, through a singularly clear sense of truth and honor, by the cruel craft and unscrupulous expediency of Jesuitism, as revealed to him by his tutor. While in this peculiar mental and moral condition, an event occurred which was the means of deciding him firmly and finally against the church. There came to reside at the chateau, to cheer and brighten its dull and formal life, a lovely young girl, the only child of a hapless younger sister of the marquis, who, having made a *mésalliance* with an artist, had been cast off by her proud family, and disowned by them even after her husband's death. On her own death, however, the stern marquis had so far relented as to consent to receive her daughter into his household.

But though Marguerite Valence was poor and untitled, she possessed a dower of beauty for which many a duchess would barter coronet and diamonds. Every one felt its spell, streaming like sunshine through the chill and gloomy chateau.

Even the old marquis, whose snowy hair and cold gray eye seemed typical of a no less wintry and cheerless spirit, found some unacknowledged comfort in its genial light and warmth.

Marguerite's nature was gentle and tender, yet exalted and devotional. She was already an inspired enthusiast, and only needed the martyrdom of her loving womanhood to become a saintly *devote*. Alas! the martyrdom came all too soon!

Marguerite found herself very lonely in the grand old chateau, till she met her cousin Eugene; he had always been lonely since his brother left him, till he met her. Love, between two such beings, so situated, was almost inevitable. A strong and ardent attachment, no less deep rooted for its sudden growth, sprung up in each heart, to be fed by the pure dews of poetry, and to open its perfect bloom to the summer air of youth. The life which to the eyes of each had seemed, even in its spring-time, so shadowy and chill, flashed into noontide light, and flushed into tropical warmth and beauty.

The impetuous strength of a first passion gave a degree of energy and will to Eugene's character which it had not before possessed. He bravely faced his stern father, and acknowledged, or rather *proclaimed* his love, and his determination not to enter the church, but to marry his cousin Marguerite, depending for support upon his talents, and a small property which he inherited from his mother.

The marquis was alarmed at this sudden exhibition of spirit and courage, and for once had recourse to management, instead of violence. He did not forbid the marriage, but only asked that his son should defer it for a year, during which time he should travel, and thus fit himself for the artist or literary career he seemed bent upon leading, while Marguerite, his betrothed, should remain at the chateau. Greatly softened by this unexpected kindness, Eugene willingly assented, and the lovers parted, with many fond hopes and tender protestations.

For the first six months, while Eugene was in Italy and Greece, there was a frequent interchange of letters; then Marguerite's came somewhat less frequently, and Eugene fancied that their tone was changed. It had not grown cold, but it was certainly less light and cheerful, and now lofty and gravely religious. At last they ceased altogether; but, as he was then travelling in Palestine, he comforted himself with the somewhat melancholy supposition that many letters had doubtless been written and failed to reach him. But, on returning to Europe, he found only one awaiting him, and that a brief, wild letter of renunciation and farewell. Marguerite had entered a convent, and was about to take the veil.

During her lover's absence, a cruel and systematic effort had been made to convince her that in plighting her troth to Eugene she had done him an infinite injury; that she was barring him from a life of sanctity and good works; thrusting herself and her sinful human passion between him and heaven itself. The wily Jesuit slid his subtle poison into her bewildered and impressible mind, making her believe that human engagements, however dear and solemn, were not binding, where the good of the soul and the interests of the holy mother church were concerned. At last she grew to believe that love itself commanded her to forswear love, and that only by the sacrifice of all that was dearest and most beautiful to her on earth could she secure to her beloved the immortal blessedness of heaven. Then came the struggle, the agony, the death-in-life, and the deed was done!

The lover returned in much haste to Brittany, but arrived too late. In vain he sought to obtain even an interview with his Marguerite. He was refused admittance to the convent — driven away from the gate. He then disappeared from the neighborhood and the country, and no word was heard from him until his family received the packet of letters written the night before his execution in America.

To the haughty marquis, the news of a death so shameful, inflicted on a member of his proud and noble house, on a son whom in his stern way he loved, was a crushing blow. It literally struck him to the earth. But when he recovered from the deep syncope in which he had fallen, he solemnly and almost fiercely forbade the name of his lost son to be ever again mentioned in his presence. *He* never spoke it till he was on his death-bed, when, starting suddenly from a slumber, or stupor, of several hours, he called it aloud twice — and died.

As soon as possible after this event, the young marquis had left France for America, for the pious purpose of obtaining and taking home the remains of his brother, to give them Christian burial in the chapel of the family chateau. With this object he had visited W——, and was now at the house of Mrs. Huntington.

Fanny timidly asked to hear more of Marguerite Valence.

She was still living, he said, at the convent, under the name of '*la sœur Cécile*' (Sister Cecilia), that had been given to her for her singing, which was 'divine.' Many went to the chapel of the convent at vespers, to listen to her voice, soaring exultingly toward heaven in the chant. But when the last letter of her dead lover came to her, breathing through all its devotion and tenderness a tone of gentle, unconscious reproach, the fanatical enthusiasm of her vain self-sacrifice forsook her forever, and with it, strange to say, her glorious voice. She never sang again.

That evening, at sunset, George and Fanny accompanied the Marquis de Villiers to his brother's grave, in the little forest glade. When they reached the low, violet-covered mound, the marquis flung himself upon it, with a passionate burst of tears, crying,

'*Ah, Eugène, Eugène, mon frère!*'

With instinctive delicacy George and Fanny walked away, and left him alone for some time. When they returned, he was calmly seated on the little pile of stones at the foot of the grave ; and Fanny noticed that he held in his hands a bunch of violets, which were glistening with tears.

Then the marquis questioned them of the circumstances of his brother's execution, as witnessed by them. He would know every slightest particular, however painful; and they faithfully told him all. When Fanny related how Eugene had plucked one of the violets that grew at his feet, and kissed it, the marquis pressed those he held to his lips, and then hid them away in his breast. Then the three walked slowly back to the cottage through the deepening twilight.

On the following morning the exhumation took place, in as private a manner as possible. The body was placed in a metallic coffin, and taken to New York, to be shipped for France; the marquis, of course, accompanying it.

The rose-bush that grew upon the grave was of necessity taken up; but George, in his delicate thoughtfulness, preserved it carefully, and brought it home, to be replanted in his sister's little garden. Fanny took from it an opening rose, which she pressed in Eugene's prayer-book, and gave to the marquis, 'for Sister Cecilia.' He promised to place the sad and sacred mementos himself in the hands of the nun.

The courtly marquis parted from his simple republican friends with much apparent feeling, after pressing upon each a noble remembrancer of his visit.

Little of my story now remains to be told. By a

strange political and social revulsion, the distinction of rank, the timely revelation of which might have saved Eugene St. Pierre Duchatel from an ignominious death, was, ten years later, the cause of a yet more ignominious death to his brother. The Marquis de Villiers perished by the guillotine, for no greater crime than the accident of noble birth.

Mrs. Huntington, George, Fanny, are all gone, now, having lived pure and blameless lives, and 'done good in their day and generation.'

Long, long ago, that withered rose from the grave of poor Eugene, and the withered heart of his Marguerite, on which it lay, mingled their dust together. For the dead bloom of that rose there is no resurrection; but the love which once glowed in that heart has arisen to life and beauty immortal, in the paradise of our God, '*who is love.*'

ALICE'S TRYST.

ALICE'S TRYST.

I have seen her rise from her bed, throw her night-gown upon her, unlock her closet, take forth paper, fold it, write upon it, read it, and afterwards seal it, and again return to bed; yet all this while in a most fast sleep.

A great perturbation in nature! to receive at once the benefit of sleep, and do the effects of watching. SHAKSPEARE.

ALICE AUSTIN stood at the window while the sun was setting — an open, French window, whose flowing white curtains half hid the slender form of the young girl. She was not looking towards the west, though the sunset pageant was beautiful to behold; she was looking toward the east — not at the shadowy sky, not at the dark, forest-crowned hills, but far away down the dusty road, with her lovely, smiling, expectant eyes. The gold and crimson of sunset passed away, the dews and shades of twilight came on, and still Alice stood at the window. A servant entered and lit the lamps, and, as he went out, looked back at the fair girl with a pleasant, knowing smile; then Alice's mother came in, quietly arranged a slightly disordered table, looked at her abstracted daughter silently, but with a fond, proud, most motherly expression, and passed from the room.

The twilight deepened, and the stars of a glorious June evening came out in heaven.

Alice steps through the open window into the piazza, and bends forward, as listening intently. Surely she hears the distant gallop of a horse! Yes, now it comes across the bridge, down in the ravine; now it ascends the hill, now comes the gleam of a white horse dashing up the road, urged by an eager rider; and Alice Austin turns quickly, and reënters the parlor, where she demurely seats herself at a table, and takes up a book.

Through how many twilights during the past year had Alice waited and watched for the coming of that milk-white steed! She had grown to know his gallop across the bridge as well as she knew the voice of his master. Alice's lover lived in the city, three miles away; and in all seasons and all weathers came to visit his liege lady on this favorite horse, a beautiful and powerful animal. But this was the last time that Alice would watch with loving anxiousness at that eastern window for the coming of the bold, impetuous rider — for to-morrow they were to be married.

A sweet ideal of early womanhood was Alice at that moment, with her love-radiating face bent over her book, of whose contents she saw not a word; with the forward fall of her light, wavy hair, half shading her shy, tender, soft blue eyes; with the tremulous play of her parted lips, and the vivid flushings of her fair, rounded cheek. She was dressed with childlike simplicity, in a lawn of that most delicate blue we see in the far sky, with flowing sleeves, half revealing arms of faultless symmetry. Her white neck was uncovered, and, in place of a brooch, she wore at her bosom a bunch of pale blush-roses.

How her high-beating heart rocked them, and shook out their perfumes! — how eloquently, how fitly, her love spoke in the rise and fall of those rose-buds, and breathed in the fragrance they exhaled!

There is a quick step in the hall without; the door is flung open. Let us look up with Alice at him who stands on the threshold.

A figure of medium height, manly, yet more delicate than robust; a face intellectually handsome, though exceedingly fresh and youthful, the full, red lips all smiles, the large brown eyes all tenderness, a deep flush on the slightly-bronzed cheek, the dark, curly hair somewhat disordered and blown about the broad brow by the fresh night-wind; so stood Henry Lester, — but only for an instant stood, a little blinded by the light, then stepped joyfully forward. Alice rose, half-fond, half fearful, the passion of the woman at strife with the shyness of the child, to meet his glad embrace.

'You are late, to-night, dearest?' she said, in an inquiring tone.

'Yes; my groomsman, Charles Mason, came to-night. I had not seen him for nearly a year, and so we had many things to talk about. I never liked the fellow so well. Indeed, I believe I love all my friends the better for loving you so truly, Alice. Like Juliet, "the more I give, the more I have."'

'Is not such, dear Henry, the infinite, divine nature of love? — Did you find the evening pleasant?'

'Glorious! The air was both soft and invigorating; the starlight is very pure, and there is a trifle of a moon, you know, just enough to swear by. O, Alice, I never was so happy as to-night! My heart was as the heart of a child, brimming and bubbling over with happiness. I sung, in riding through the dark pine woods, some wild tune, and I know not what words — little beside your name, I believe. I took off my cap, and let the winds frolic as they would with my hair; feel, now, Alice, and see how damp it is with dew.'

Alice laid her hand caressingly among the shining curls, then drew it away with a blush, while her lover continued,

'I remained so unspeakably happy — sometimes urging on Selim at a furious rate, the sooner to quench the eager thirst of my heart in your presence; sometimes checking him up and sitting quite still, to let the great waves of joy dash over me — till I came to the burial-ground on the hill beyond the ravine. I had passed this a hundred times with only a momentary shadowing of my heart, as a swift stream is shadowed by flowing under a willow; but to-night, at the first sight of the gleaming, ghastly tombstones, I reeled in my saddle and groaned aloud!'

'Why so, dear Henry?'

'Because, love, I remembered that *you* were mortal, and not one of God's own imperishable angels, as I had dreamed you were; that you might leave my love, my bosom, for one of those low, cold, lonely beds of sleep and dark forgetfulness. O, great heaven, the agony of the thought!' he cried, hiding his face against Alice's breast, while tears, that were no reproach to his manhood, dropped fast upon those pale blush-roses.

Alice bowed her head over him, and said, with tender solemnity:

'"I am persuaded that neither death, nor life, nor angels, nor principalities, nor powers, nor things present, nor things to come," can divide us now, or destroy our love, which is of God. Though I perish to all the universe beside, I can never die to you.'

'But, ah, Alice,' he replied, with something of the fond waywardness of a loving child, 'if *I* should go first, would you grieve for me any? Would you ever come to my grave to weep, and remember how dearly I loved you?'

'For a little while,' she added; 'not long, I think.'

Henry looked up bewildered, and she continued, with a quivering lip: 'Because, dearest, I should so soon be lying by your side. And now,' she added, smilingly, 'let us talk of brighter things. I never saw you in a mood so melancholy and foreboding. Clouds of all kinds are so foreign to your sunshiny nature.

'I rode over to our house with mamma, to-day. Everything is in perfect order there, now. The last thing I did was to arrange your books in the little library. Your dear mother says that she will have the parlors lit up and tea all ready for us, the evening we get back from the Falls.'

'Say the evening we reach *home*, Alice. I want to hear you speak that word, so I may be sure I am not *dreaming* of a pleasant, quiet home, and a blessed little wife of my own.'

'Well, then, *home,* — your home, our home, — to be presided over by an ignorant little "child-wife," a thousand removes from an angel, but in your love indeed "blessed among women." Now are you satisfied?'

After receiving her lover's unspoken yet eloquent response, Alice laughingly resumed: 'I fancy we shall have an odd sort of a *ménage* — both so young, so totally inexperienced, and with, to say the least, such exceedingly modest means. I wish we could live like the fairies, on dew and honey; or rather, as the angels live, on pure love. O then, Harry, we could "fare sumptuously every day." But, alas! we are only a poor pair of mortals, and so we must be industrious and prudent, and rub along as we can.'

'Why, Alice, dear, I am not so very young; I was twenty last March. I shall be admitted to the bar in about two years. In the mean time, my father will do all he can for us, though he don't esteem early marriages very prudent things. I mean to prove to him that I can be as steady, studious, diligent, and economical, as any plodding, money-making old bachelor in town. I shan't hear of your giving up any of your accustomed luxuries, Alice, or making your dainty hands hard and unkissable with any sort of work; but I have already given up play-going and cigars, and I think some of selling Selim.'

'Never!' cried Alice. 'What! sell the faithful creature which has borne you so surely and so swiftly to me every blessed Saturday evening in the year? It would make us too much like the reduced and disenchanted couple I have somewhere read of, who killed and cooked the very carrier-dove which had flown back and forth with their love-letters.'

At this moment a bright little lad of ten years opened the door, saying, 'Sister Alice, a big band-box has come for you from the city.'

'O, then bring it in here,' she replied. The lad vanished, but reäppeared in a moment with the box, which Alice eagerly opened, and took out a dress of plain white silk, and a long white veil of delicate lace.

'This is dear papa's gift,' she said. 'Is n't it a beautiful veil, Harry?'

'Yes,' he answered, 'very beautiful. What is it made of—book-muslin?'

Alice smiled at his ignorance, assuring him that it was of lace, and that of a superior quality.

'Don't you admire the dress?' she asked, after a moment's silence.

'O, yes, greatly; but it is not so pretty as the one you have on. By the way, I think—I am sure I remember that dress. Is n't it the very one you had on at Commencement, the first time I saw you?'

'Yes,' answered Alice, with a bright blush; 'it is rather old-fashioned now, but I thought, if you should happen to recollect it, you might be pleased to have me wear it to-night.'

'Dearest Alice, how good—how just like you that was. I have always thought this just the loveliest dress in the world; the color belongs to you by the right of your eyes; and, now I think of it, Alice, can't you be married in *blue?*'

Alice laughed outright at this, saying that the idea was quite absurd and impossible.

'My milliner meant to have my bridal array quite complete,' she said, 'for here is the wreath of orange-blossoms. What think you of this, Harry?'

'Away with it!' he replied; 'there is something stiff, stately, and exotic, in those flowers. Do wear, instead, a few just such rose-buds as those in your bosom. They are almost white, they are simple and sweet, and they breathe of home. You will wear them, won't you, dearest?'

'O, gladly! for these, too, have their associations. The tree that bore them was your first gift to me, Henry. I would like to humor you about the blue dress, also, but that is altogether out of the question.'

As the lovers finally turned away from the table whereon stood the bandbox, their eyes fell upon Willie, Alice's young brother, who was fast asleep in his chair. Henry laid a hand upon his head. He started up, and, rubbing his eyes, said, 'I am sitting up so late because I want to fetch Selim for you; but you need n't be in a hurry.'

The young man laughed, looked at his watch, and told the lad he might go for the horse at once. Willie darted off to the stable, brought out Selim, but had the pleasure of exercising the beautiful animal for several minutes in the yard, before its master came forth to claim it. All that time was Henry Lester taking leave of his affianced, — always going, but never gone. He felt in his heart a strange, sad yearning; some wild, inexpressible foreboding; a fearful shrinking from the night without, beautiful and peaceful as it was; a something that caused him to snatch Alice again and again to his heart, as though some dread power, unseen, but darkly felt, were striving to glide between them, and part them forever.

At last Alice gently unwound his arm from her waist, and took a step backward. He yielded her up with a sad smile, but kissed her once again, and said 'Good-night!' Alice raised her finger with a gesture playfully forbidding, and said, 'Remember, now, you have kissed Alice *Austin* for the last time!'

Henry laughed, and Alice followed him to the door to see him off. She patted the impatient Selim on the neck, and whispered to him to bear his master safely, very safely.

As Henry gathered up the reins, and was about starting, he said, suddenly, with a glance at Willie, 'O, Alice, a word in your ear!' She drew nearer, and put up her face; her lover bent, not to her ear, but her lips, and so kissed Alice *Austin* once more. Then, with a merry laugh and another good-night, he dashed through the gate, and down the road.

Alice soon ascended to her chamber, but she did not retire to rest. Flinging a shawl about her shoulders, she sat down by the window, and looked out upon the night. Then she spoke low to herself, in all the unconscious poetry of love: 'How far the stars can see, with their clear, unveiled eyes, so high in heaven! but I cannot believe that in all the vast universe they behold a happier child of the All-Father than I.' She looked downward. She could not see the roses, but she drank in their fragrance, and said, 'As the roses sweeten all the night air, so love sweetens life for me. O gracious God, I bless thee alike for those far-rolling worlds whose light is yet on our homes, and for the earth-brightness of flowers; for life, and, more than all, for *love!*'

As Alice gave utterance to this solemn ecstasy of a religious and loving heart, she bowed her head upon the window-sill before her. Suddenly she started, leaned forward, and listened eagerly. She was sure she heard her own name called, in an imploring voice. It seemed to sound from the ravine beyond the hill. Once more it came, — a wild, sorrowful, piercing cry. It *was* Henry's voice! She stole down stairs, passed noiselessly through that eastern window, and ran down the road. She was not mistaken, for a little way beyond the bridge Selim was standing, with his head drooped sadly over his master, who was lying on the grass of the roadside.

As Alice passed over the bridge, she saw that a plank had been broken through.

She flung herself down by her lover, crying, 'Henry, dearest Henry! are you much hurt?'

He seemed to have fainted; but he soon revived, and, looking up, murmured, brokenly, 'O Alice, have you come! Now it will not be so hard to die!'

'Dear Henry, don't talk so! I hope you are not badly hurt.'

'Alice,' he whispered, 'I am *mortally* hurt. Selim broke through the bridge, and threw me, cutting my head here in the temple; then, in extricating himself, he fell on me with all his weight. I afterwards got strength to crawl out of the dust on to this grass, and to call you twice; but Alice, Alice, I *know* I am dying; my breast seems all crushed in, and my lungs seem filling with blood.'

'O, then let me run or shout aloud for help!'

'No, dearest; only take me in your arms, and let me lie on your bosom, under the stars; alone with you, I have strength even to die.'

Then Alice — bewildered, broken-hearted, but strangely calm — raised Henry's head, and pillowed it on her breast. Those thick curls she had seen so little while ago all bright with dew, were now dark and heavy with blood trickling from a severe wound in the temple. O, then Alice was no longer shy or chary of her tenderness. She passionately kissed the lips, the eyes, the brow, the already cold hands, of her lover. She lavished on him all the endearing names, the fond protestations, her diffident, girlish heart had been storing up for the use of the wife through years of trial, sorrow, and ever-deepening affection. Then she wept and prayed, and folded that poor wounded head against her breast, as though to stanch the blood, which only flowed the faster for the warmth; it stained all her bosom, and turned those pale blush-roses to deepest crimson. Henry, who seemed to have been again insensible, suddenly opened his eyes, and whispered,

'My blood will spoil that beautiful blue dress!'

'O, my love! my soul!' cried Alice; 'would to God it flowed from my own heart! Would to God I could die for you, or with you; for I cannot, will not, stay in this dark world when you are gone, Henry, for my life is in your love!'

'My dearest, do not grieve so bitterly; something tells me, even now, that we shall not be long parted; only be patient, love, for a little while.'

After lying quite silent for some moments, looking upward, he exclaimed, almost in his usual voice,

'My spirit is passing, Alice. Heaven is ready now; all the stars seem to have rushed together and formed one great central brightness — a world of light, to which I rise!' Then, reaching up his arms, and winding them about her neck, he murmured, 'Kiss me once more, my Alice, my dear, only love, — my wife,— once more, good-night!'

As he breathed these words, a stream of blood, looking so fearfully black in the dim star-light, poured from his lips, his arms dropped, and Henry Lester was dead!

Then Alice fell forward upon his breast, and sent forth shriek after shriek, so fearful and piercing that every slumberer in her home was roused, and, guided by the voice of her long-pent-up agony, came to look upon the piteous sight of her sudden bereavement.

In that pleasant parlor where but an hour before had sat the betrothed lovers in life and love, — in love's most blessed hope and most unutterable joy, — was now extended the form of one, ghastly, bleeding, dead; while over it hung the pale, distracted face of her who kept all night her watch of speechless, tearless, unimaginable sorrow.

Alice Austin could not follow her lover to the grave. After her last lingering look upon his face as he lay in his coffin, she for the first time fainted. She was borne to her room, where she remained insensible for some hours. That night she said to her mother, who watched at her side,

'Where have they laid Henry?'

'In the south-west corner of the grave-yard, under the large elm-tree,' was the reply. All the succeeding day, Alice's grief was bitter and despairing; but at night she was calmer, and earnestly desired to be left quite alone. Early the next morning her mother went to her chamber, and was surprised to find her looking much like her former self, and speaking almost cheerfully; but towards night she relapsed into fits of passionate weeping, — a most desolate and hopeless grieving. Again with sleep seemed to come peace, even an exaltation of spirit, which endured only for the morning hours; and so it continued throughout the week. The poor child gave her mother a beautiful explanation of this mystery. 'Every night,' she said, 'my Henry comes to me in a vision. He folds me in his arms, and lays his hand on my hot forehead, and looks so pitifully into my eyes; he wipes away my tears, and comforts me, O, so divinely! He looks as he always did on earth, only yet more beautiful. I was so proud of his beauty, mother, that I did not think it possible he could grow more beautiful, even in heaven; but he seems so in my dream. He gives me strength and joy to sustain me till we meet again; but I am so weak, that before the long day is through it leaves me. Yet he never fails to come to me, or draw me to him, I scarce know which. I seem in a state like that of the Apostle, when he knew not whether he was in the body or out; I only know I am with *him*, and content.'

A strange rumor spread through the neighborhood, and finally reached the family of Alice, that some belated travellers had seen, in the midst of the night, a shape of shining white gliding about the grave of Henry Lester. But no one among his friends was so superstitious as to heed the story.

On Saturday night, just one week from the time of the heart-breaking tragedy, Alice's father, who was a physician, was riding homeward some time after twelve, and, as he was passing the grave-yard, in sight of his house, he was startled to observe some white object at the grave of young Lester. Dr. Austin was a truly brave man, and, after a moment of indecision, he dismounted, and entered the lonely burial-place. The appearance at the grave grew more and more distinct as he drew softly near. It was a human form prone upon the earth! One moment more, he had reached the spot, and found his own daughter Alice, in her bridal dress, lying beside the grave of her lover, with her face upon the mound, and one arm flung over it. Shocked and alarmed beyond measure, he called her name, laying his hand on her arm; but she did not rise, or move. Then, looking more closely in her face, he saw that she was sleeping the strange, wonderful sleep of the somnambulist. He raised her gently in his arms, and was about to bear her homeward, when she awoke to complete consciousness.

'My God! where am I?' she exclaimed, looking wildly around.

As tenderly as possible her father told her what had happened, as he half-carried her home. She wept, and seemed much agitated, but begged that she might go quietly to her chamber, without disturbing her mother.

From that night Mrs. Austin always remained with

her daughter, watching and wakening her whenever she rose in her sleep, put on her bridal dress, and prepared to steal out to her grave-yard tryst. It was needful, but it was cruel; for, from that time, Alice sunk in body and spirit. She seemed to utterly lack the miraculous sustainment she had known at first; the vision and the comfort it brought were gone together.

One day, seeing her mother weeping, she said, 'Is it not written that a man shall forsake father and mother, and cleave unto his wife? Can a wife do less for her husband? Mother, God has wedded me to Henry; my soul so cleaves to his that they cannot be separated, and when he calls I must go to him, even from you.'

At a later period she said, 'Mother, dear, I want you to see that no ghostly shroud is put on me, but a soft, white muslin dress; and fold my bridal veil about me, and put white roses in my hair, that all may know that I am *his* bride, and not Death's. And O, mother, keep very sacredly the blue lawn I wore on that last night, and never let them wash Henry's blood out of it. Most of all, I want you to promise me to plant, with your own hand, that blush-rose tree that Henry gave me, between him and me, so that the roses will fall upon us both.'

Before the leaves of the elm-tree over Henry Lester's grave were goldened by the autumn frosts, his Alice was lying at his side. When June came round again, the grass was long and green, and the rose-tree grew more beautiful than ever there; and when the evening winds shook the branches, they scattered a sweet largess of leaves upon the mounds, and swung out a fragrance on the air sweeter than aught else, save the memory of the lovers sleeping below.

Often has my mind dwelt long and deeply on those dreams, which were yet no dreams; those sweet, exalted visions, those trances of love and sorrow, which drew that tender and delicate girl, arrayed in her bridal dress, night after night, to the lonely grave of her betrothed. O beautiful, adorable mystery of love! O grave, where was here thy victory! O mortality, where the might of thy prison walls! As of old, an angel came in the night-time, and led forth the prisoner.

There is, there is, a wondrous hidden life within us all, deeper and truer than that of which we have an every-day understanding and consciousness; a life triumphant over death and pain and sorrow, — all the mournful conditions of our mortal being. When they who loved the maiden would have feared her suffering from the night-darkness and cold, with the grosser physical senses sealed, she walked in light ineffable, and breathed the soft airs, the balm of celestial day. When the chill dews descended on her delicate frame, she was shielded, folded about by arms of immortal tenderness; when her soft cheek lay against the hard grave-mound, she was hiding her rapt, contented face in the bosom of her love!

THE CHILD-SEER.

THE CHILD-SEER.

Our life is two-fold : * * *
* * * * * *
* * * with the stars
And the quick spirit of the universe
He held his dialogues ; and they did teach
To him the magic of their mysteries ;
To him the book of night was opened wide,
And voices from the deep abyss revealed
A marvel and a secret. BYRON.

THE little story I am going to tell is a true story of pioneer life in America. It is known to many descendants of the early settlers among whom it happened.

One of the darkest pages in American history is that relating to the sufferings of the inhabitants of Tryon County, New York, during the war of the Revolution, from the attacks of the Indians and royalists, under the Mohawk chief Brant, and the more savage Captain Walter Butler. Early in the war, Cherry Valley was selected as a place of refuge and defence for the inhabitants of the smaller and more exposed settlements. Block-houses were built, fortifications were thrown up, and finally a fort was erected, under the direction of General Lafayette. The inhabitants of the surrounding settlements came in and lived for several months as in garrison, submitting to strict military regulations.

Among the families which took temporary refuge in this fort was that of Captain Robert Lindsay, formerly a British officer, brave and adventurous, who only at the entreaty of his wife had left his farm, which stood in a lonely, unprotected situation, several miles from any settlement. This Captain Lindsay was a reserved, melancholy man, about whom the simple and honest pioneers wondered and speculated not a little. His language and manner bespoke at once the man of education and breeding. His wife, though a quiet, heroic woman, was evidently a lady by nature and association.

Captain Lindsay had a native love of solitude and adventure, the first requisite for a pioneer; and for several years no other reason was known for his seeking the wilds, and exposing his tender family to all the perils and privations of a frontier life. But at length an emigrant coming from his native place, in the Highlands of Scotland, brought the story of his exile, which was briefly this: Captain Lindsay, when a somewhat dissipated young man, proud and passionate, had quarrelled with a brother officer, an old friend, at a mess-dinner. Both officers had drunk freely, and their difference was aggravated by hot-brained, half-drunken partisans. Insulting words were exchanged, and a duel on the spot was the consequence. Lindsay escaped with a slight wound, but his sword pierced the heart of his friend. He was hurried away to a secure hiding-place, but not before he had learned that in the first matter of dispute he had been in the wrong.

Lindsay made all the reparation in his power, by transferring his paternal estate, for the term of his own lifetime, to the homeless widow and young daughter of his friend. Then, with his wife's small property, and the price of his commission, he secretly emigrated to America. He left his family in New York, while he went up the Hudson, purchased a small farm, and built a house for their reception. He was accompanied in this expedition by an old family servitor, who, with true Highland fidelity, clung to his unfortunate master with exemplary devotion.

Mrs. Lindsay's heart sank within her when she found that her new home was so far from any settlement, literally in the wilderness; but she understood her husband's misanthropic gloom, almost amounting to melancholy madness, and did not murmur. Yet her forest home was very beautiful, — a small valley-farm, surrounded by densely-wooded hills, dark gorges and mossy dells. The house was a rough, primitive-looking structure, containing but three small apartments, and a low chamber, or rather loft. But it was comfortably and securely built; and, overhung by noble trees, and overrun by wild vines, was not unpicturesque. Under the tasteful care of Mrs. Lindsay, a little garden soon sprang up around it, where, among many strange plants, bloomed a few familiar flowers, whose fragrance seemed to breathe of home, like the sighs of an exile's heart.

The family, at the period of their taking refuge in the fort at Cherry Valley, consisted of three sons and an infant daughter (the last born in America), the man Davie, and a maid-servant. Douglas, the elder son, a lad of twelve or thirteen, was a brave, high-spirited, somewhat self-willed boy, tall and handsome, and the especial pride of his mother; not alone because he was her first-born, but because he most vividly recalled to her heart her husband in his happy days. Angus, the second son, was a slight, delicate, fair-haired boy, possessing a highly sensitive and poetic nature. Unconsciously displaying at times singular and startling intuitions, — dreaming uncomprehended dreams, which were sometimes strangely verified, and uttering involuntary prophecies, which time often fulfilled, — he was always spoken of as 'a strange child,' and, for all his tender years and sweet pensive face, was regarded with a secret, shrinking awe, even by those nearest to him. In truth, the child seemed to be gifted with that weird, mysterious faculty, known as second sight.

Archie, the youngest son, his father's own darling, was a sturdy, rosy-cheeked, curly-headed boy of five. Effie was yet at the mother's breast, a little rosy bud of beauty — a fair promise of infinite joy and comfort to her mother's saddened heart.

As I have stated, this family took refuge in the fort in the spring of 1778, somewhat against the will of Captain Lindsay, — who, as he remained neutral, had little fear of the Indians, — and also of his eldest son, who fancied there was something cowardly in flying from their forest-home before it had been attacked. The latter, however, was soon reconciled by the opportunity afforded him, for the first time for several years, of associating with lads of his own age, of whom there were a goodly number at the fort and settlement. The sports and exercises of the men and youth were entirely of a military character; and Douglas, who had inherited martial tastes from a long line of warlike ancestors, and who had been instructed by his father in military rules and evolutions, soon became the captain of a company of boys, armed with formidable wooden guns, and fully equipped as mimic soldiers. Angus was made his lieutenant; but this was a piece of favoritism, the child having little taste or talent for the profession of arms.

One bright May morning, as these young amateur fighters were parading on the green before the fort, they had spectators whom they little suspected. Upon a hill, about a mile away, Joseph Brant had posted a large party of his braves, where, concealed by the thick wood, they were looking down on the settlement. It had been his intention to attack the fort that night; but this grand parade of light infantry deceived him. At that distance he mistook the boys for men, and decided to defer the attack till he could ascertain by his scouts the exact strength of the place. In the mean time, he moved his party northward a few miles, to a point on the road leading from Cherry Valley to the Mohawk river, where he concealed them behind rocks and trees. At this spot the road passed through a thick growth of evergreens, forming a perpetual twilight, and wound along a precipice a hundred and fifty feet high, over which plunged a small stream in a cascade, called by the Indians Tekaharawa.

Brant had, doubtless, received information that an American officer had ridden down from Fort Plain, on the Mohawk river, in the morning, to visit the fort, and might be expected to return before night.

This officer had come to inform the garrison that a regiment of militia would arrive the next day, and take up their quarters at Cherry Valley. His name was Lieutenant Woodville; he was a young man of fortune, gay, gallant, handsome, and daring. He was dressed in a rich suit of velvet, wore a plumed hat and a jewel-hilted sword, and let his dark, waving hair grow to a cavalierish length. He rode a full-blooded English horse, which he managed with ease. This Lieutenant Woodville lingered so long at the settlement that his friends tried to persuade him to remain all night; but he laughed, and, as he mounted, flung down his portmanteau to one of them, saying, 'I will call for that to-morrow.' When it was nearly sunset, the little garrison came out into the court-yard to watch his departure. Among the spectators were the boy-soldiers whose parade of the morning had daunted even the terrible Brant. Foremost stood the doughty Douglas, and by his side the timid Angus, gazing with childish curiosity on the dashing young officer, and marking with wondering delight his smiling mastery over his steed.

Suddenly the boy passed his hand over his eyes, grew marble-white and rigid for an instant, then shuddered, and burst into tears. Before he could be questioned, he had quitted his brother, rushed forward, and was clinging to the lieutenant's knee, crying, in a tone of the most passionate entreaty,

'O, sir, you maun stay here to-night,—here, where a' is safe! Dinna gang; they 'll kill ye! O, dinna gang!'

'Who, my little lad—who 'll kill me?' gently

asked the officer, looking down into the delicate face of the boy, struck by its agonized expression.

'The Indians. They 're waiting for you in yon dark, awfu' place by the falls,' replied Angus, in a tone of solemnity.

'And how do you know all this, my little man?' asked the officer, smiling.

'I hae seen them,' said Angus, in a low, hoarse tone, casting down his eyes, and trembling visibly.

'Seen them! When?'

'Just noo. I saw them a' as weel as I see you and the lave. It 's the guid God, may be, that sends the vision to save you frae death. So ye maun heed the warning, and not put your life in peril by riding up there, where they 're waitin' for ye in the gloaming.'

'What is the matter with this child?' exclaimed Lieutenant Woodville, turning to a friend in the little crowd. The man, for answer, merely touched his forehead significantly. 'Indeed! So young!' replied the officer. Then, laying his hand gently on the head of the boy, and smiling pityingly into his wild, beseeching eyes, he said, 'But, indeed, I must go, prophet of evil. Indians or no Indians, a soldier must obey orders, you know. Come, dry your tears, and I will bring you a pretty plume for your soldier-cap when I return. Adieu, friends, until to-morrow?'

Saying this, he bent to loosen Angus' hands from the stirrup; but the child clung convulsively, shrieking out his warnings and entreaties, until his father broke through the crowd and bore him forcibly away.

Lieutenant Woodville galloped off, with gay words

of farewell; but, as some noticed, with an unusual shadow on his handsome face.

Mrs. Lindsay took Angus in her arms, and strove to soothe him in her quiet, loving way. Yet the child would not be comforted. He hid his face in her bosom, sobbing and shuddering, but saying nothing for several minutes. Then he shrieked out, 'There! There! O, mither, they hae killed him! I hae seen him fa' frae his horse. I see him noo, laying amang the briers, wi' the red bluid rinning frae his head, down on to his braw soldier-coat. O, mither, I could na help it; he would na believe the vision!'

After this, the repose of a sad certainty seemed to come upon the child, and, sobbing more and more softly, he fell asleep; but not until the return of Lieutenant Woodville's horse, with an empty saddle stained with blood, had brought terrible confirmation of the vision. Next morning the body of the unfortunate young officer was found in the dark pass, near the falls of Tekaharawa. He had been shot and scalped by Brant himself.

As may be supposed, this tragic verification of Angus Lindsay's prophecy excited surprise and speculation, and caused the child to be regarded with a strange interest, which, though not unfriendly, had in it too much of superstitious dread to be altogether kindly.

The boy instinctively shrank from it, and grew more and more reserved day by day. Some regarded the prediction as naturally resulting from the omnipresent fear of savages, common to settlers' children, taking more vivid form in the imagination of a nervous and sickly boy, and the fate of Woodville as merely a remarkable coincidence. But more shook their heads with solemn meaning, declaring the lad a young wizard; and went so far as to intimate that the real wizard was the lad's father, whose haughty and melancholy reserve was little understood by the honest settlers, and that poor little Angus was his victim, — the one possessed.

The expression of this feeling — not in words, but in a sort of distrustful avoidance — made Mrs. Lindsay consent to the proposition of her husband to return to their home for the harvest. Several families were venturing on this hazardous step, encouraged by the temporary tranquillity of the country, and thinking that their savage enemies had quenched their bloodthirst at Wyoming, — thus rather taking courage than warning by that fearful massacre.

The Lindsays found their home as they had left it three months before; nothing had been molested. They all speedily fell into their old in-door and outdoor duties and amusements. And so passed a few weeks of quiet happiness. Captain Lindsay and his man always took their arms with them to the harvest-fields, which were in sight of the house. The two elder sons usually worked with their father. On the last day of the harvest, when little remained to be done, the boys asked permission to go to a stream, about two miles away, to angle for trout.

In his moody abstraction of fearlessness, Captain Lindsay consented, and the boys set out in high glee. Little Archie, who was also with his father for that day, begged to be taken with them; but the lads did not wish to be so encumbered, and hurried away. Just as they were passing from the clearing into the little cow-path leading through the woods to the creek, Angus looked back and saw the child standing by his father, in tears, gazing wistfully after his elder brothers.

'Ah, Douglas,' exclaimed he, 'let us tak' Archie wi' us. See how the puir bairn is greeting.'

'No, no; he 'll only fright the trout, and we canna wait. Come awa.'

The lads reached the creek in safety, crept stealthily along its shaded bank, selected their places in silence, and flung their bait upon the water. Douglas seemed to enjoy the sport keenly; but Angus was remorseful for having said nay to his little brother's entreaty.

'O, Douglas!' he exclaimed, at last, 'I canna forget Archie's tearfu', wistfu' face. I 'm sae sorry we left him!'

'Dinna fash yer head about Archie, but mind yer fish!' replied Douglas, impatiently.

Angus was silent for another half-hour. Then he suddenly gave a short, quick cry, made a start forward, and peered anxiously down into the water.

'What noo?' said Douglas, petulantly; for the cry and movement had scared a fine trout that seemed just about to take his hook.

'O, brother,' answered Angus, trembling, 'I ha' seen Archie's bonnie face in the burn, and it had sic a pale, frightened look! I doubt something awfu' has happened! Let us gang hame.'

Douglas laughed, as he replied, 'It 's yer own face ye saw in the burn, and no Archie's. How could it be his, when he 's maist twa mile awa?'

'I dinna ken, Douglas,' replied Angus, humbly; 'but I maun believe it was Archie's face. There it comes again! And father's, and Davie's! O, brother, the Indians!'

Shrieking out these words, the poor boy staggered backward, and fainted. Douglas, though a good deal alarmed, had sufficient presence of mind to apply nature's remedy, fortunately near at hand; and, under a copious sprinkling of cold water, Angus speedily revived. Douglas no longer resisted his entreaties; but, silently gathering up their fishing-tackle, and taking their string of trout, set out for home, walking slowly, and supporting the trembling steps of his brother. As they neared the borders of the clearing, where they were to come in sight of the harvest-fields and their home, Angus absolutely shook, and even the cheek of the bold Douglas grew white.

The first sight which met their eyes, on their emerging from the wood, was their house in flames, with a party of fiendish savages dancing and howling around it. The boys shrank back into the wood, and, crouching down together beneath a thick growth of underbrush, lay sobbing and shuddering in their grief and terror.

At length, Angus gave a start, and whispered joyfully, 'O, brother, I've seen mither, and wee Effie, and Jenny — an' they're a' safe — hid away in the bushes, like us.'

'But do you see father, and Archie, and auld Davie?' asked Douglas, believing, at last, in the second sight of his younger brother.

'No, no,' replied Angus, mournfully, 'I canna see them ony mair. They maun be a' dead, Douglas.'

'I'll no believe that,' said the elder brother, proudly; 'father and Davie baith had their arms wi' them. Davie is no' a bad fighter, and ye ken a braver soldier could na be found in a' the world than father.'

They lay thus, talking in fearful whispers, and weeping silently, until the shouts of the savages died away, and silence fell with the twilight over the little valley. Then slowly and cautiously they crept from their hiding-place, and stole through the harvest-fields to the spot where they had left their father, and little brother, and Davie.

And they were all there — dead. They appeared to have fallen together. Faithful old Davie lay across his master's knees, which he seemed embracing in death. Little Archie had evidently lingered longest alive; his flesh was yet soft and slightly warm, and he had crept to his father's arms, and lay partly across his breast.

All, even to the sinless baby, had been tomahawked. Yet, bathed in blood as they were, the poor boys could not believe them dead; but clasped their stiffened hands, and kissed their lips, felt for their heart-beats, and called them by their names, in every accent of love and sorrow. At last, finding all their frenzied efforts vain, they abandoned themselves to grief.

The moon rose upon them thus weeping wildly over their murdered father and brother, stained with their blood, and shuddering with their death-chill. Never did the moon look on a more desolate group.

Captain Lindsay's brow seemed more awfully stern in its light, and his unclosed eyes shone with an icy gleam. Archie's still tearful face showed most piteously sad; while the agonized faces of the two young mourners, now bent over their dead, now lifted despairingly toward heaven, seemed to have grown strangely old in that time of terror, and horror, and bitter grieving. Thus the hours wore on; and, at last, from utter exhaustion, they slept — the living with the dead.

They were awakened by the warm sunlight, and the birds which sang — how strange it seemed! — as gayly as ever, in the neighboring wood. The boys raised their heads and looked each into the other's sad face, and then on the dead, in the blank, speechless anguish of their renewed grief. Douglas was the first to speak. 'Come, brother,' he said, in a calm tone, 'we maun be men noo. Let us gang back to the fort; may be we shall find mither there, wi' Jenny and the bairnie, 'gin you're sure ye saw them a' in yer vision.'

'But we canna leave these here to their lane,' said Angus.

'We maun leave them; we are no' big enough to bury them; but we 'll cover them ower wi' leaves and the branches o' the pines; and when we get to the fort, we 'll ask the soldiers to come and make graves for them. Come wi' me, Angus, dear.'

Angus took Douglas' hand, and rose; but soon staggered and fell, murmuring, 'O, brother! I 'm sair faint and ill. I think I am dying. Stay wi' me a little while, and then ye may cover us a' up togither and gang awa'.'

'Dinna say sic sorrowfu' things, Angus; yer no dying, puir laddie; yer but fainting wi' hunger, and I the same,' said Douglas, in a tone of hopeless despondency. Just at the moment his eye fell on a small hand-basket, in which the laborers were accustomed to take their luncheon to the harvest-field. It was now lying where the dead had left it, against a pile of wheat-sheaves, and was found to contain some fragments of bread and meat, of which they partook.

Somewhat refreshed, the boys set about their melancholy duty. They did not attempt to move the bodies from the positions in which they had found them; they left little Archie on his father's breast, and faithful old Davie with his face hid against his master's knees.

Douglas took out his pocket-knife to sever a lock of hair from his father's and his little brother's heads, for mementos. 'O, dinna tak' that lock, Douglas!' said Angus, with a shudder; 'did ye na see the bluid on it?'

Alas! it was difficult to find a lock on the head of either father or child not darkened and stiffened with gore.

When they had taken the last look, the last kiss, and had completed their mound of boughs and leaves, the two children knelt beside it, and prayed. Surely the God of the fatherless was near them. Better, in his sight, their pious care of the dead, than the most pompous funeral obsequies; sweeter to him the simple prayer they sobbed into his ear, than the grandest requiem.

It was nearly noon when the boys left the little

valley, and took their way toward the fort. They had first visited the ruins of their house, and searched around them and the garden diligently, but vainly, for any trace of their mother, and nurse, and sister. From a tree in the little orchard they filled their basket with apples, and set forth.

They had advanced but a mile or two on the dark, winding forest-path, when they heard before them the sound of footsteps and voices. In their sudden terror, thinking only of savages, they fled into the thickest recesses of the wood. When their alarm had passed, and they sought to regain the path, they found, to their grief and dismay, that they had lost it. Still they kept on, apparently at random, but angel-guided, it seemed, in the direction of the fort. Yet night came upon them in the dense, gloomy wood; and, at last, very weary and sorrowful, they sank down, murmured their broken prayers, and, clasped in each other's arms, fell into a chill and troubled sleep.

Douglas was awakened in the early morning by a touch on his shoulder. He sprang to his feet, and confronted — Brant! Behind the chief stood a small band of savage attendants, eagerly eying the young 'pale-faces,' as though their fingers itched to be among their curls.

'Who are you?' asked the warrior, sternly.

'I am Douglas Lindsay; and this is my brother, Angus Lindsay.'

'Is Captain Lindsay your father?'

'He *was* our father,' replied Douglas, with a passionate burst of tears; 'but ye ken weel enough we hae no father noo, sin' ye 've murdered him. Ay, and puir auld Davie, and the wee bairn Archie — ye divils!'

'No, boy,' replied Brant, in a not ungentle tone, 'we did not murder your father. I am sorry to hear he has been killed. He was a brave man, and never took part with the rebels. I promised him my protection. It must have been some of Captain Butler's men; they are about now. I would have risked my life to have saved his. I will protect his children. Where were you going?'

'To the fort,' put in little Angus, eagerly; 'may be we shall find mither and Effie and Jenny a' there. O, Mister Thayendenagea, tak' us to the fort, if it's no' too far, for we hae lost our way.'

Brant, who was an educated man, and had little of the Indian in his appearance or speech, smiled to hear himself addressed by his pompous Indian name (a stroke of policy on the lad's part), and replied: 'That is easy to do. Cherry Valley is just over the hill, only a little way off. Let us go.'

Saying this, and briefly commanding his warriors to remain where they were until he should return, — an order received in sullen silence by the savages, who glared ferociously upon their lost prey, — the chief strode forward through the forest, followed by the two boys. When they reached the brow of the hill overlooking the settlement, he paused, and said, 'I had better not go any further. I will wait here till I see you safe. Good-by! Tell your mother that Brant did not kill her brave husband. Say he's sorry about it — go.'

The children sought to express their thanks, but he waved them away, and stood with folded arms under the shade of a gigantic oak, watching them as they descended the hill.

Mrs. Lindsay's part in the sad story is soon told. On the day of the massacre she heard the firing in the harvest-field, and from the windows of the house witnessed the brief struggle of her husband and Davie with their foes. The fearful sight at first benumbed every faculty; but one cry from her baby aroused her from her stupor of grief and terror. She snatched the infant from the cradle, and rushed with it into the woods, followed by Jenny, the maid. The two women concealed themselves so effectually in the thick under-brush that they remained undiscovered, though the shouts of the savages came to their ears with horrible distinctness, and even the blaze of their burning home reddened the sunlight that struggled through the thick foliage above them.

When, at length, the party left the little valley, it passed within a few yards of the fugitives. O! how fervently the mother thanked God that her baby slept tranquilly on her bosom, and by no cry betrayed their hiding-place! They did not venture to leave their leafy sanctuary until evening. They were on the side of the clearing opposite the harvest-fields, and near the road leading to Cherry Valley. This they found, and set out at once for the settlement, which they reached in safety about midnight, and were kindly received at one of the fortified houses. The next day a party of brave men, moved by the passionate entreaties of the two women, set out on what was thought a hopeless search for Captain Lindsay, his sons, and servant. They reached the harvest-field safely, found there the bodies as they had been left, hastily buried them; and, after vainly seeking for the missing boys, returned to Cherry Valley, taking a dread certainty and a faint hope to the afflicted wife and mother.

Prostrated by her fearful bereavement, yet not wholly despairing, worn-out with cruel anxieties and fatigues, Mrs. Lindsay at last slept, watched over by her faithful nurse. She awoke early in the morning, raised herself eagerly from her pillow, looked around, and then sank back in tears.

'O, Jenny,' said she, 'I hae had sic a blessed dream! I dreamed I saw my twa boys — only twa noo, Jenny — my brave Douglas, and bonnie Angus, coming over the hill wi' the sunrise. But they'll no' come ony mair — they are a' taken frae me — a' but this wee bit bairnie,' she murmured, pressing her babe to her bosom, and sprinkling its brow with the bitter baptism of her tears. For some minutes she lay thus, weeping with all that fresh realization of sorrow and desolation which comes with the first awakening from sleep after a great bereavement. Then she arose and tottered away from the bed, saying, 'Lift the window, Jenny; I maun look on the hill o' my dream.'

Jenny obeyed, and supported her mistress as she looked out on the lovely landscape, kindling in the light of an August morning. 'Ah, Jenny,' she said, 'it is a' as I dreamed; the yellow corn on the hill-side, and the dark pines aboon, the soft blue of the sky, the clouds a' rosy and golden, and the glory o' the sunlight spread a' abroad, like the smile o' the Lord on this wicked and waefu' world. And — look! — look! O, mercifu' God — there are the bairns!'

This history, fortunately, has nothing to do with the terrible massacres and burnings which, a few months later, desolated Cherry Valley, and the neighboring settlements. Mrs. Lindsay and her children were then safe in the city of New York. Immediately on the close of the war they returned to their friends in Scotland.

Among the Highlands, Angus Lindsay lost his extreme delicacy of health, and, gradually, his mysterious faculty; yet he was ever singularly sensitive, thoughtful, and imaginative; and when he grew into manhood, though not recognized as a seer or a prophet, he was accorded a title which comprehended the greatest attributes of both — Poet.

Mrs. Lindsay returned to the family estate with her children; but the widow of her husband's friend was not deprived of her sad sanctuary, to which she had finally a dearer, if not a more sacred right, as the home of her daughter, the wife of Douglas Lindsay.

THOMAS DE QUINCEY—*continued.*

ESSAYS ON THE POETS AND OTHER ENGLISH WRITERS. CONTENTS: The Poetry of Wordsworth — Percy Bysshe Shelley — John Keats — Oliver Goldsmith — Alexander Pope — William Godwin — John Foster — William Hazlitt — Walter Savage Landor. 1 vol. 16mo. 75 cents.

HISTORICAL AND CRITICAL ESSAYS. CONTENTS: Philosophy of Roman History — The Essenes — Philosophy of Herodotus — Plato's Republic — Homer and the Homeridæ — Cicero — Style — Rhetoric — Secret Societies. 2 vols. 16mo. $1.50.

AUTOBIOGRAPHIC SKETCHES. CONTENTS: The Affliction of Childhood — Dream Echoes on these Infant Experiences — Dream Echoes Fifty Years Later — Introduction to the World of Strife — Infant Literature — The Female Infidel — I am Introduced to the Warfare of a Public School — I Enter the World — The Nation of London — Dublin — First Rebellion in Ireland — French Invasion of Ireland, and Second Rebellion — Travelling — My Brother — Premature Manhood. 1 vol. 16mo. 75 cents.

ESSAYS ON PHILOSOPHICAL WRITERS AND OTHER MEN OF LETTERS. CONTENTS: Hamilton — Mackintosh — Kant — Richter — Lessing — Herder — Bentley — Parr. 2 vols. 16mo. $1.50.

LETTERS TO A YOUNG MAN, AND OTHER PAPERS. CONTENTS: Letters — Greek Tragedy — Conversation — Language — French and English Manners — California and the Gold Mania — Presence of Mind. 1 vol. 16mo. 75 cents.

THEOLOGICAL ESSAYS AND OTHER PAPERS. CONTENTS: On Christianity as an Organ of Political Movement — Protestantism — On the Supposed Scriptural Expression for Eternity — Judas Iscariot — On Hume's Argument against Miracles — Casuistry — Greece under the Romans — Secession from the Church of Scotland — Toilette of the Hebrew Lady — Milton — Charlemagne — Modern Greece — Lord Carlisle on Pope. 2 vols. 16mo. $1.50.

THE NOTE BOOK OF AN ENGLISH OPIUM EATER. CONTENTS. Three Memorable Murders — The True Relations of the Bible to merely Human Science — Literary History of the 18th Century — The Antigone of Sophocles — The Marquess of Wellesley — Milton *vs.* Southey and Landor — Falsification of English History — A Peripatetic Philosopher, &c. 1 vol. 16mo. 75 cents.

THOMAS DE QUINCEY.—*continued.*

'Who that knows anything of recent literature, does not appreciate De Quincey as a man that stands alone and unapproachable in his sphere, a sphere that is, in itself, a magician's island, filled with strange and beautiful visions, and beaten all around by the waves of a deep, shadowy, and lonely ocean of power, that sound forever against the shore, in a strong, sweet, and melancholy music? The wild and the simple, the marvellous and the familiar, the nearest impulses with most remote associations, fresh spontaneity with elegant and various learning, are mingled in the matter of De Quincey's writings, as the mind of no living man could mingle them, and the spirit of them finds expression in a style of such weird-like pathos, of such manly, yet mournful eloquence, as comes from the depth of a genius, in which the fountains of the heart have been terribly opened, in which *thought* has been purgatory on the margin of despair, escaped, and to which authorship has been at once penance, consolation, and confession.'—*Henry Giles.*

'The great and crowning glory of De Quincey is that mastery over the English language which made us to call him the greatest of prose writers. Since the English language has been written, we know of nothing comparable to his style, in splendor, variety, ease, idiomatic richness, and grace—in all the qualities of style considered purely as form, and without reference to composition. If any one desires to see what our language is capable of, let him study De Quincey.—*London Leader.*

CHARLES MACKAY.

POEMS. Voices from the Mountains and from the Crowd. A new edition, revised and enlarged. 1 vol. 16mo. Cloth, $1.00 ; gilt 1.50; full gilt, 1.75 ; calf and half calf binding.

'Charles Mackay is one of the most soul-stirring lyrists of our day. His poems must always be popular.'—*London Critic.*

'Mackay is a poet through and through. This new edition of his pieces will gladden the heart of all English readers.'—*London News.*

'The author of "A Good Time Coming" is always a welcome bard every where.'—*New York Tribune.*

HENRY W. LONGFELLOW.

POEMS.

COMPLETE POETICAL WORKS. 2 vols. 16mo. Boards, $2.00; cloth, 2.25; cloth, gilt edge, 3.00; cloth, full gilt, 3.50; calf, gilt; half calf gilt; 3 vols., including The Golden Legend, calf gilt; do. half calf, gilt.

THE GOLDEN LEGEND. 1 vol. 16mo. Cloth, $1.00; do. gilt edge, 1.50; do. full gilt, 1.75.

IN SEPARATE VOLUMES.

EVANGELINE; A Tale of Acadie. 1 vol. 16mo. Cloth, 75 cents.

THE SEASIDE AND THE FIRESIDE. 1 vol. 16mo. Cloth, 75 cents.

VOICES OF THE NIGHT. 1 vol. 16mo. Boards, 75 cents.

BALLADS AND OTHER POEMS. 1 vol. 16mo. Boards, 75 cents.

SPANISH STUDENT; A Play in three Acts. 1 vol. 16mo. Boards, 75 cents.

BELFRY OF BRUGES, AND OTHER POEMS. 1 vol. 16mo. Boards, 75 cents.

THE WAIF. A collection of Poems. Edited by Longfellow. 1 vol. 16mo. Boards, 75 cents.

THE ESTRAY. A collection of Poems. Edited by Longfellow. vol. 16mo. Boards, 75 cents.

Each of the above may also be had in the following styles of binding, viz.: plain cloth; cloth extra, gilt side and edge; cloth, extra gilt.

HENRY W. LONGFELLOW.—*continued.*

PROSE WORKS.

OUTRE-MER; A Pilgrimage beyond the Sea. A new edition. 1 vol. 16mo. Cloth, $1.00; do. cloth, gilt edge, 1.50.

HYPERION; A Romance. A new edition. 1 vol. 16mo. Cloth, $1.00; do. cloth, gilt edge, 1.50.

KAVANAGH; A TALE. 1 vol. 16mo. Cloth, 75 cents; do. cloth, gilt edge, $1.25.

POETICAL AND PROSE WRITINGS. 6 vols. Cloth, $6.00; do. fancy cloth, red and blue, 6.50; do. cloth, gilt edge, 8.75; do. calf, gilt; do. half calf, gilt.

ILLUSTRATED EDITIONS OF LONGFELLOW'S WORKS.

EVANGELINE. Beautifully Illustrated and bound in Morocco antique, assorted styles, $5.00.

VOICES OF THE NIGHT. Beautifully Illustrated and bound in Morocco antique, assorted styles, $6.00; do. cloth antique, assorted styles, 4.00.

POEMS. Beautifully illustrated and bound in cloth antique, assorted styles, $6.00; do. morocco antique, assorted colors, 8.00.

HYPERION. Beautifully Illustrated and bound in morocco antique, assorted colors, $8.00; do. cloth antique, 6.00.

THE GOLDEN LEGEND. Beautifully Illustrated and bound in cloth antique, $4.00; do. morocco antique, 6.00

'One of the most pleasing characteristics of Longfellow's works is their intense humanity. A man's heart beats in every line. He loves, pities, and feels with, as well as for, his fellow "human mortals." He is a brother, speaking to men as brothers, and as brothers they are responding to his voice.'— *Gilfillan.*

GRACE GREENWOOD.

GREENWOOD LEAVES. A Collection of Stories and Letters. First and Second Series. Each in 1 vol. 12mo. Cloth. For sale separate or together. In cloth, gilt, $1.25 each; gilt edge, 1.75; full gilt, 2.00.

HAPS AND MISHAPS OF A TOUR IN EUROPE. A brilliant and admirably drawn Narration of the Author's residence abroad, containing sparkling pictures of men and things as she saw them. A most captivating volume, which has gone rapidly through numerous editions. 1 vol. 12mo. Cloth, $1.25; gilt edge, 1.75; full gilt, 2.00.

POETICAL WORKS. A new and enlarged edition. With fine Portrait. Cloth, gilt, 75 cents; gilt edge, 1.25; full gilt, 1.50.

GRACE GREENWOOD'S JUVENILE BOOKS.

MERRIE ENGLAND. Travels, Descriptions, Tales and Historical Sketches. With 12 Illustrations by Devereux. 1 vol. 16mo. Cloth, 75 cents; gilt, $1.00.

HISTORY OF MY PETS. With 6 beautiful Illustrations. Price 50 cents; gilt edge, 63 cents.

RECOLLECTIONS OF MY CHILDHOOD, and other Stories, with 6 beautiful Engravings. 50 cents; gilt edge, 63 cents.

'The name of Grace Greenwood has now become a household word in the popular literature of our country and our day. Of the intellectual woman we are not called to say much, as her writings speak for themselves, and they have spoken widely. They are eminently characteristic; they are strictly national; they are likewise decisively individual. All true individuality is honestly social, and also, in Miss Clarke's writings, nothing is sectional, and nothing sectarian. She is one of the spiritual products of the soil, which has of late given evidence of spiritual fertility, and she promises not to be the least healthy, as she is not the least choice among them.' — *Henry Giles.*

'Grace Greenwood is well known as one of the most interesting story writers in this or any other country. As a poet, also, we are disposed, if but for a single effort, to place her in the very highest rank of American poets, both male and female. We allude to her "Ariadne" — a poem as rich in passionate expression and classic grace, as any thing to be found in all Griswold's collection of American poetry.' — *Tribune.*

CHARLES KINGSLEY.

THE VOYAGES AND ADVENTURES OF SIR AMYAS LEIGH, of Burrough, County of Devon, in the reign of Queen Elizabeth of Glorious Memory. By the Author of 'Hypatia,' 'Alton Locke,' 'Yeast,' &c., &c. 1 vol. 12mo. Just published. Price, $1.25.

'Its whole tone is grand and stirring, and the portraits of some of the heroes of the time are truly magnificent.' — *Boston Post.*

'Of all the writers of fiction of the present time, Charles Kingsley is the most brilliant, the most in earnest, the most imaginative, the most free in thought and pen, and, in his special field, the most useful.' — *Springfield Republican.*

'One of the most powerfully written novels of the present day, and one whichwillmake a powerful sensation in the literary world. It is founded upon the adventurous history of one of the sea captains of Queen Elizabeth's reign, and his explorations in America and hostility to the Spaniards.' — *Hartford Courant.*

GLAUCUS; OR, THE WONDERS OF THE SHORE. 1 vol. 16mo. (Just ready).

'A middle-aged friend with a family, starting on his annual excursion to the sea-side, may be called the text. The author paints his friend's listless, do-nothing days, with the same or mischief on the part of his children. And then he shows how this ennui might be got rid of by a taste for natural history. The sea-shore and its wonders is not, however, the only, though it is a prominent, theme. Geology, living animals, the history and literature of natural history, are rapidly handled. With these topics are mingled others that relate to manners or morals. Mr. Kingsley dwells upon the necessity that now exists for urban youth being incited by some pursuit to force themselves into the country, as well for mere health as for manliness of character; he shows how a business that leads a man into the remoter places in the country, or even a pursuit — as that of the angler or the sportsman — may give advantages over the regular scientific man. This is not done in a dry or dead-lively littérateur manner, but with the spirit arising from the convictions of a man who has looked on life with reference to its actual wants of more than bread. The general remarks show the wide sympathy, the deep thought, and the rich eloquence that characterize Mr. Kingsley.' — *London Spectator.*

THE POETICAL WORKS of Mr. Kingsley. In press.

NATHANIEL HAWTHORNE.

THE SCARLET LETTER. A Romance. 1 vol 16mo. Cloth, 75 cents.

HOUSE OF THE SEVEN GABLES. A Romance. 1 vol. 16mo Cloth, $1.00.

TWICE TOLD TALES. A new edition, with fine Portrait. 2 vols. 16mo. $1.50 ; do. cloth, gilt edge, 2.50.

THE SNOW IMAGE, AND OTHER TWICE TOLD TALES. 1 vol. 16mo. 75 cents.

THE BLITHEDALE ROMANCE. 1 vol. 16mo. 75 cents.

MOSSES FROM AN OLD MANSE. A new and enlarged edition 2 vols. 16mo. $1.50.

HAWTHORNE'S WORKS. The above 8 vols. cloth, gilt edge, $10.25 ; do. calf, gilt ; do. half calf.

HAWTHORNE'S JUVENILE WORKS.

TRUE STORIES FROM HISTORY AND BIOGRAPHY. 1 vol 16mo. With Engravings, 75 cents ; do. cloth, gilt edge, $1.00.

THE WONDER BOOK, FOR GIRLS AND BOYS. With Engrav ings. 1 vol. 16mo. 75 cents ; do. cloth, gilt edge, $1.00.

TANGLEWOOD TALES. Another Wonder Book. With Engravings, 88 cents ; do. cloth, gilt edge, $1.13.

Following immediately a careful perusal of his works, we have no hesitation in saying that in imagination, power, pathos, beauty, and all the other essential qualifications requisite to the completeness of a first-rate romance, Mr. Hawthorne has equalled if not surpassed any other writer who has appeared in our country during the last half century.—*Transcript.*

www.ingramcontent.com/pod-product-compliance
Lightning Source LLC
LaVergne TN
LVHW010145110826
845151LV00002B/427
* 9 7 8 1 4 2 5 5 3 7 3 6 4 *